SEVENTEEN
LAST MAN STANDING
JOHN BROWNLOW

HODDER &
STOUGHTON

First published in Great Britain in 2022 by Hodder & Stoughton
An Hachette UK company

1

Copyright © Deep Fried Films, Inc. 2022

The right of John Brownlow to be identified as the Author of the Work has been
asserted by him in accordance with the Copyright, Designs and Patents Act 1988.

Scripture taken from the New King James Version®. Copyright © 1982
by Thomas Nelson. Used by permission. All rights reserved.

A CIP catalogue record for this title is available from the British Library

Hardback ISBN 978 1 529 38253 2
Trade Paperback ISBN 978 1 529 38254 9
eBook ISBN 978 1 529 38255 6

Typeset in Plantin Light by Hewer Text UK Ltd, Edinburgh
Printed and bound in Great Britain by Clays Ltd, Elcograf S.p.A.

Hodder & Stoughton policy is to use papers that are natural, renewable
and recyclable products and made from wood grown in sustainable
forests. The logging and manufacturing processes are expected to
conform to the environmental regulations of the country of origin.

Hodder & Stoughton Ltd
Carmelite House
50 Victoria Embankment
London EC4Y 0DZ

www.hodder.co.uk

For my mother, who taught me
the importance of having enemies

PART ONE

I

Being a spy, it's not what you think.

It's boring.

I don't mean boring as in dull.

I mean boring as in mind-crushingly, ass-clenchingly, teeth-grindingly tedious.

Sitting in a cubicle, one of a hundred identical little beige cages, wearing your office shirt and your office shoes and your office tie, listening to the hum of the AC as you wonder what the special will be today in the commissary, fantasising about allowing yourself a non-decaf after 11.30 a.m., as you pore over six-month-old Azerbaijani newspapers in the hope of scraping some pointless little tidbit of information about exploitable tensions in the lower levels of the Baku political hierarchy.

Baku is insane, by the way. Off the hook. Like Dubai on steroids, but with more arm wrestling. They like jam in their tea and the national sport is played to a musical accompaniment. But you don't know that because you haven't been there.

That's because you're a spy – or, as your job title reminds you at each increasingly negative performance review, an analyst – stuck four feet from your co-worker who has yet to be introduced to the marvels of modern deodorant technology, wearing shitty government-issue headphones that make your ears hurt because the padding wore away six months ago and there's a freeze on spending on account of Congress can't get its head out of its ass for long enough to pass a budget.

And so your life ticks away heartbeat by heartbeat as you listen to interminable, poorly recorded conversations between Omar the Taxi Driver and Hussein the Fruit Vendor discussing the relative merits of the offside trap in the diminishing hope that at some point they will reveal why Omar's brother-in-law, who now lives in Toronto and has introduced them to the exciting world of NHL hockey, suddenly has more money in his bank account than you earn in a year, or are ever likely to.

It's not all bad. Sometimes they let you scan satellite pictures of the Eritrean or Mongolian desert until your eyeballs bleed. The most exciting moment in your career so far came when you thought you'd spotted a missile silo under construction on the North Korean peninsular but when you took it to your supervisor she pointed out it was a sewage treatment plant.

But, you know, points for trying.

What I'm saying is, all that stuff you see on TV and in the movies? Travelling to exotic locations where you burn rubber in brightly coloured exotic sports cars, sprint across rooftops under fire from automatic weapons while performing parkour, fuck glamorous personalities of diverse ethnicities and suspect allegiances, and blow interesting people's heads off using silenced weapons for reasons that remain opaque until the third act, at which point they come roaring back to bite you in the ass?

There's none of that.

Literally, none.

Not even a little bit.

Unless you're me.

2

The Bugatti Veyron is overkill, but the expenses for this job were particularly generous and if I have one motto it is this: ride the horse in the direction it is going.

Today the horse is lemon yellow and purring along at 204 km/h in the outside lane of Bundesautobahn 9 en route from Munich to Berlin, just outside Nuremberg. Half of me wants to make a detour east to the Nürburgring and do a couple of loops around the circuit, but you have to leave some fruit on the tree. It isn't even halfway to its top speed but I'm trying not to appear any more of an asshole than is absolutely necessary.

Because today it is absolutely necessary.

There are two schools of thought about visibility.

You can either be visible, or invisible.

There is no in-between.

Invisible means: you're the harried middle-aged woman juggling her handbag and the Starbucks cup as she fumbles for her ID on the way through the security checkpoint. You're the janitor with poor English and thinning hair sluicing the floor with a mop around the tables where a brace of Harvard legacies are discussing whether it's better to rent a floatplane or a yacht to get to the island and can't even be bothered to move their feet. You're the grey man on the subway with greasy hair and patches on his elbows who looks like an out-of-work antique dealer down on his luck, toting a plastic shopping bag full of old books back to a safe house, where you will steam open the flap of one of them to reveal new identity documents.

You have no digital footprint. You do not use credit cards. You use burner cellphones which you change every week, or more often, or preferably not at all. Wherever possible, you communicate using physical means, from dead drops to the postal service. You remain analogue in a world of ones and zeroes.

Security by obscurity.

The problem with that?

It doesn't work. Not any more.

Biometrics will fuck you up. And not just automated facial recognition, which is everywhere. You could put a paper bag over your head and the AI will pick you out by your gait, by the way you favour one leg over the other, by the way you over-pronate, by your flat feet, by the cock of your hips or the way you wiggle your ass. And good luck crossing an international border unless you're carrying a passport from a country that doesn't use biometrics yet, like Russia, which will draw all the attention you need and more.

The other school of thought?

Security by being totally-fucking-out-there.

Hence the Veyron.

When people see a supercar, all they see is the car.

Nobody gives a shit who's driving it. At best they see some loathsome private equity lizard, a dotcom bro, some minor Saudi princeling, or the Botoxed trophy wife of a Central Asian mobster-turned-oligarch. Nobody wants to meet their eye. They look away.

I'm none of those things, but the blazer and the Rolex and the open shirt and the sunglasses and the slicked-back hair let them make up their own stories and judge me accordingly.

6

You're judging me now, I can feel it. You want to look away. Good.

It's working.

In Berlin, I pass up the opportunity to gawp at the remnants of the Wall. Those Cold War days seem almost quaint now, desperate people floating over the wall in balloons or splashing knee-deep in shit through sewers or lying bleeding to death in the kill zone between the inner wall and the outer one, victims of the snipers in the East German sentry towers, harried Stasi officers hurrying out in unmarked cars to snaffle up the bodies before the bad news could leak out.

The irony was that East Germany didn't stop at the outer wall. That wasn't the border. The East Germans built a buffer zone of a few yards to allow them to maintain the western side of the wall if they needed to, but which was also open to the West. The West German authorities had no jurisdiction over it, and it became a party zone, a true no-man's land, a place where no law could reach you. There are stories from back in the day of bodies being dumped there with bullets in the backs of their heads. The CIA would dump their victims in the French zone, the French in the British zone, and the Brits in the American zone, which tells you more about the state of Western diplomatic relations between nuclear powers at the height of the Cold War than a four-year political science degree.

I head past the tourist trap that is Checkpoint Charlie, and turn down into the underground parking of one of the soaring glass-and-steel banking monoliths just off Potsdamer Platz. The moment he sees the Bugatti, the valet shoots out of his little cabin. He barely even clocks me, so intent is he on the car. He's sixty if he's a day and from his expression he just got the first natural hard-on he's had in a decade as he slid into the gloriously supple leather of the bucket seat.

'Don't scratch it,' I tell him. I don't give a shit, actually, but I want to make him sweat so his fingerprints are easy for the forensics to lift. Underneath, they won't find mine, thanks to the calfskin driving gloves, but you can't be too careful.

I take the ticket and head to the parking elevator.

He doesn't see me put it in the trash.

I give the Bugatti a last look as he drives it away.

And think to myself: I fucking hate that car.

3

I haven't told you my name. That's because it isn't mine any more. It belongs to somebody else, somebody who used to be me, somebody I stopped being a long time ago. There probably aren't ten people alive who have a memory of that person, not because I did anything to them, but because that person was a nothing, a nobody, a cipher, a sentence that had no meaning.

I left them behind. I don't miss them and they don't miss me.

To people I meet every day, I'm whoever it's useful for them to think I am. It's not a question of acting, any more than acting is a question of acting. It's about being. The great thing about having no actual identity, no fixed personality, is that you can slither from one persona to another like one of those naked hermit crabs sliding into a new shell every time the dishes pile up too high in the sink of the old one.

To people in the business, I'm one word.

Madonna, Cher, Pelé, Beyoncé, Michelangelo, Plato, Seinfeld, all rolled into one.

I'm Seventeen.

Younger than you expect.

Well groomed, flashy, sometimes a bit too loud.

One of those American accents that's hard to place.

A little obnoxious.

Well, no. *Fucking* obnoxious.

If you don't like me, that's okay. It's not a business where being liked is a big deal.

Seventeen, because there were sixteen before me.

To wear a number is a badge of honour. It's like being the forty-fifth president of the United States, or the twelfth Miss Universe, or the reigning heavyweight boxing champion of the world. It means, simply: you're the best. The most power-ful, the most beautiful, the strongest or, in my case and the cases of the sixteen before me, the most deadly, and for that reason the most feared.

No-one's sure who was first. My money is on Zigmund Markovich Rosenblum, who you might want to Google if you have someone handy to chase your eyeballs after they pop out and roll down the street.

He's the only one you'll find on Wikipedia. The second was a child whose parents were murdered by the Tsar, ended up homeless, was kidnapped by German intelligence at the outbreak of the Great War, trained in espionage and sabotage, then returned to the streets of St Petersburg where he reported on troop movements, but secretly turned against his German masters and became a double agent. All before the age of twelve.

Three through fifteen are all confirmed dead. It won't surprise you that none of them expired from natural causes, unless you count falling out of a window or a 737 (Seven, Thirteen respectively).

Sixteen, my predecessor, is an unknown. He simply disap-peared. Retired, for reasons completely opaque to everyone, at the top of his game. Stone quit, never to be seen again.

Me? I slid into his shell.

4

The elevator takes me up. It's on the outside of the building, Berlin sliding away from me as I rise, the Reichstag building, the Tiergarten, the Schloss Charlottenburg all parallaxing into view. At the seventh floor, the elevator stops and a girl in a blue pencil skirt and white blouse gets on, holding a bundle of files. She looks Italian, with dark hair pinned back behind her ears. She smiles at me and for a second I feel sorry for her, working here among these concupiscent jerks, one of whom will probably propose to her, marry her, then insist she give up her job and bring up a brood of replicants in one of the giant stone McMansions that now circle the city like a bear trap waiting to snap shut.

I glance at her hand. He's already proposed, a chunky engagement ring glinting.

Maybe you think I'm being an ass assuming all this. Probably you're right. But this is the way the world rolls. Banks, private finance, venture capital, it's not what you might call an equal-opportunity playground.

I wonder if her fiancé, whoever he is, is one of the people I'm about to kill.

The elevator bings. Her floor. She gets off.

I watch her go.

I hope for her sake he is.

There's another girl on the reception desk, wearing a ton of make-up and imitation pearls. These are the ones you have to watch, because they're smart. They live in the real world. They deal with everyone from mailmen to heads of state. The younger associates, the ones still working eighty-hour weeks and working up proposals every night until 3 a.m., predate them with no intention of ever taking them home to Mummy and Daddy.

She sees me coming and I can tell before I've taken off my sunglasses that she's got my number. She smiles but the smile says she hates everything about me, from the hand-tooled leather of my shoes to the crease in my pants to the pattern on my tie to the too-white of my expensively straightened teeth.

I love her already.

She is glassily polite to me, which I am sure takes all her strength. I tell her I have a 3 p.m. with Gerhard Meyer, which is true. He's sell-side, which means that he has oleaginous vermin like me in and out of his den all day long. He thinks I represent a teacher's pension fund based in Toronto, hoping to unload some rickety private placement, the commission on which will pay for his third divorce, since he's now boinking his executive assistant.

I've never met the man, and never will, but I know these people.

The waiting area is tessellated by knots of suits, supplicants at the court of Mammon with attaché cases on knees, heads together, and armpits damp with nerves, all hopeful that this meeting, unlike the nine previous, will unlock the line of credit and prevent the unstoppable force of their failing venture's burn rate colliding with the immovable object of No Money Left. But Meyer's selling, not buying, and he's not going to keep me waiting.

His assistant appears, and it's a young black man – Somali, maybe? – impossibly slim, with high cheekbones and narrow-waisted grey pants that fit him perfectly. He seems nice. Is

Meyer boinking him? If so he has better taste than I gave him credit for.

The assistant's name is Bashir. I have no desire to kill him so I alter my plan slightly, passing the conference room that contains my target and following him instead to Meyer's office where Meyer rises to greet me, palm outstretched. He has a moustache that won't stop, and I'll leave it at that. Bashir offers to get me coffee and I ask for a double espresso macchiato, knowing that will take him a while, then apologise to Meyer and ask where the washroom is.

He tells me. I leave my attaché case, which the police will discover later contains only a copy of Derrida's *Of Grammatology*, partly to give it a believable heft, but mostly because if you're going to leave a clue, you might as well make it as confusing and meaningless as possible.

I head out.

In the washroom, I catch sight of my reflection.

Men of my trade – not the women, women are different – I can spot a mile off. Sometimes it's the breadth to their shoulders that tightens the back of their jacket. Their soldier's walk. Sometimes it's as subtle as a webbing belt or as obvious as a broken nose. Sometimes it's the carefully grown-out regulation haircut, or the stubble and dead eyes of the SOF who took a little too much pleasure slitting the throats of teenagers in the dusty backstreets of Central Asia. Some, the most dangerous, have a stillness to them that can be unsettling. If you glance at their hands you will notice they are largely free of rings. Google 'de-gloving' if you have a strong stomach and want to know the reason.

I have none of those tells.

I look less built than I am, my clothes expensively tailored to conceal the wire of my musculature. Hair you'd swear has

13

never felt the tang of a boot-camp razor. Tall enough to look you in the eye but not tall enough to intimidate you unless I mean to. A nose that's been broken three times, but you'd never know because I pay a man in Beverly Hills to have it reset perfectly each time. I moisturise, not out of vanity, although there's that, but to hide the effects of desert sun or arctic wind on my skin.

On the third finger of my right hand there's a plain silver ring with an inscription inside.

When we know each other a little better, I may tell you what it says.

I reach under my jacket and from the concealed holster I remove the pistol I'm carrying.

5

Amateur photographers love to talk about cameras. Professionals couldn't give a shit generally. I mean, they have preferences, but a professional photographer can get the shot with a pinhole camera made out of a baked-bean tin, and it will be better than anything you, an amateur, could achieve with the most expensive camera in the world.

But you dig a little deeper, and you'll discover there's always one camera that still holds magic for them. Maybe it's a Leica M2 with a 35/1.4 pre-aspherical Summilux for that Cartier-Bresson glow. Maybe it's a beaten-up old Rolleiflex TLR, like the one Hitler used. It could be a Widelux, clockwork driving the lens through 150 degrees to make a panorama. Or . . . well, you get the idea.

The one thing they all have in common?

They are mechanical. Nothing automatic about them. They do what you tell them, nothing more and nothing less. They are the stick-shifts of the camera world.

Which brings us to the B&T VP9 Welrod 9mm.

Swiss made, manually operated, bolt-action with a built-in suppressor, it's one of the only silenced pistols that's actually quiet. *Hollywood* quiet. The VP stands for 'veterinary pistol', as it was originally designed for vets to put down animals without frightening the neighbours. My God, the feel of the thing. There is no show to it, no flash.

It just sits there, black and perfectly smooth, and whispers to you: I know what you have to do, and I will do it, and I will not judge you.

If it took pictures, I'd be a hell of a photographer.

6

I exit the washroom. I know where the conference room is, not just because Bashir took me past it, but because I've had access to the building plans for six weeks now and I know every inch of every floor. As I head there I take deep diaphragm breaths: in, hold, out through the mouth. I want my heart-rate to be as low as possible.

On a good day, I can get it down to fifty beats per minute or so without any trouble.

I check my pulse, fingers on my wrist. Ten seconds. Eight beats. Forty-eight.

I push open the frosted-glass door.

I already know who will be inside, and I know their seniority from the org chart, which tells me roughly who will be sitting where. The org chart on the website helpfully only includes photographs of executives. Someone once told me you should always be nice to assistants, and that includes not killing them unless you absolutely have to.

I also know there won't be security. Why not? Because this is home turf.

You know how money – real money, fuck-you money, the kind of money that swills around in private Swiss bank accounts, the proceeds of arms deals and state-backed coups, the kind of money that never needs to be laundered because, courtesy of matryoshka-like corporate entities it never appears

17

on the radar of anyone remotely connected to taxation or law enforcement – moves around the world?

It's not through Bitcoin.

Here's what happens. You, a billionaire with blood on your hands, wish to move money from A to B. You meet with one of your people in a SCIF – a Secure Compartmented Intelligence Facility, a room enclosed in a Faraday Cage, impermeable to electromagnetic radiation, acoustically and electrically and atmospherically isolated. Trust me. You're a billionaire. You have one.

You give them instructions. They call a number in Zurich, a gnome in a suit gets on a private jet, and twelve hours later your private banker is standing in the SCIF with you. You tell him you would like to move money from A to B, and how much. He gets back on his private jet, flies back to Zurich, and executes the transaction on the extravagantly hardened computer system that runs your accounts.

It's the kind of cryptography that no hacker will ever crack, because there is nothing to crack.

Except there's a weak point.

The gnome. He's on his way back to the office from Flughafen Zürich when his limo is T-boned. Masked men drag him off to a warehouse somewhere where they apply what is known in the business as 'rubber-hose cryptography' because it involves, in its crudest form, beating the target with a rubber hose until they tell you the password.

It is quick, violent, and extremely effective.

Like me.

Point being, if you're the billionaire, you're not the one who takes risks. Your workplace, your glass-and-steel tower, is your safe space.

Your house, your supposed home, is full of squabbling fail-sons and -daughters whose main preoccupation is who will inherit what and how soon, and a spouse who loathes you with good reason, but is bound by the terms of the prenup, and is currently obsessed with what kind of slate you should import from Italy for the roof on the south wing.

It's a warzone, frankly.

You begin to relax when you slide into the plush black leather of the armour-plated limo, but you don't feel truly safe until you duck into the maw of the parking garage, and – ah! – up the private elevator to the Shangri-La of your cavernous penthouse office with its tasteless cocobolo desk or ironic faux-*Jetsons* mid-century tat or gold-plated dictator-chic, or whatever the fuck it is you think makes you look important, or younger.

It's your castle, your court, your realm, the place where you are King, where your word is law.

Once in a while you emerge for a board meeting or a pitch and the peasants tug their forelocks as you pass. It makes you feel wanted. Loved.

And because of that, your guard is down.

Just the way I like it.

7

Turns out there *is* security. He must have been inside when I passed before.

No big deal. I like to be proved wrong.

The guy is huge, a mountain of muscle and testosterone bulging out of a suit a size too small, with cropped hair and, perched on pink piggy ears, those terrible tactical sunglasses all security guys think are obligatory but scream *erectile dysfunction*, and restrict their vision indoors when confronted by people like me.

There are six targets inside and the VP9 magazine only holds five shots, so I was going to have to reload anyway. I walk straight past him, then stop, turn and say 'Hey!' to someone behind me in the corridor. He checks to see who it is, only there's no-one there and I put a bullet in his temple. A Rorschach-blot of blood spatters against the smoked privacy glass of the conference room. Part of me feels bad for him, but if you're in the game, you're in the game.

I have to step over his body to push my way into the conference room, where people are already rising in panic.

Four shots left.

There are three male VPs in their thirties who are the main physical threat, the kinds of guys who mountain-bike and do CrossFit in an effort to make up for the endless dinners and cocktails they are forced to endure trying to separate clients from their money or women to whom they are not married from their underwear, or both simultaneously.

Thock, thock, thock. Done and done and done.

In my peripheral vision, a twenty-something Associate begins crawling along the wall, trying to leave. He's shaking, terrified. I put a round in the wall just by his head to let him know that he's being a fucking idiot and because I need to reload anyway. He concedes the point by curling into a foetal ball.

Good lad.

I reload, the movements so instinctive I could do them in my sleep, which I'm told by people in a position to know I sometimes do.

I'm working my way up the org chart now. The Comptroller is a woman in her fifties with a mumsy air. I would feel worse about killing her if I didn't know that the numbers she juggles and fakes represent tanks and helicopters and automatic weapons shipped via third parties and fake export certificates to regimes who do not, as a rule, have the best interests and welfare of their citizens at heart.

I'm not saying what I do is a public service exactly, but actions have consequences.

The Chief Executive is early sixties. He looks like he's having a heart attack already, which would make it his fifth or sixth. I know from my research a mine he helped finance in Brazil collapsed, killing something in the region of a hundred indigenous miners. Euthanising him with a veterinary pistol seems oddly appropriate.

Which leaves the Old Man.

This guy, I mean. I almost admire him.

You remember Adnan Khashoggi. The arms dealer who was worth $4 billion in the 1980s, back when $4 billion was real money? Helped broker Iran–Contra, thick with Imelda Marcos? He died penniless. Where did the money go? you ask.

The answer is standing in front of me.

He's eighty-something now, and he's not even scared. He's known this moment was coming for years, decades probably.

He smiles, and his teeth are crooked and yellow. You see this in rich men when they come from nothing. They wear bad teeth as a sign of pride, as a reminder of where they came from, as a fuck-you to anyone who would judge them.

I get it, I really do.

'Young man,' he says in German. 'Whatever they're paying you—'

I put two shots in his chest before he can finish.

For some crazy reason, it isn't enough.

He's still moving, blood coming out of his mouth.

I put my last bullet in his head.

8

It all takes less than ten seconds. I pull out my phone and photograph the dead, becoming aware as I do of the crying and whimpering of the ones I left alive. Then I walk out.

People are coming out of offices. From behind me a scream as someone realises what's happened. I keep the gun visible, but low. Nobody is going to try to stop a man with a gun who has just killed six people — no, wait, seven. I head back through the office, where Gerhard stares at me uncomprehendingly as I pass. Bashir is emerging from the kitchen in front of me with the espresso macchiato and, bless him, I could use it, but it's not the time. I'm heading for the service elevator, not because I want to take it but because there are service stairs by the side of it and those are by far the best way down.

So far, with the exception of the extra security, it has all gone exactly according to plan.

This inevitably makes me nervous.

And then it happens. I hear something – a woman's voice yelling *du Bastard.* I turn, and see she's running towards me, spattered with other people's blood, a Wagnerian Fury in a business suit. She's holding something – for a moment I can't tell what it is, then I recognise it as a speakerphone from the conference room that she has literally ripped out of the table. In my head I replay the scene from the room. She was sitting to the left of one of the CrossFit guys. When I came in she was smiling at him. Her left hand wasn't visible. Fuck.

She had it on his thigh.

I have killed her lover in front of her.

Pro tip: you almost never want to do this.

She's almost on me now. I instinctively raise the gun, but she's a civilian and there isn't time to find a reason to hate her, to absolve myself, and self-preservation doesn't count since all she's armed with is a speakerphone and the righteous anger of a wronged woman.

Besides, I shot my entire magazine. I planned to have three spare shells, more than enough in ordinary circumstances, but one went on the guard, one in the wall, and I used an extra on the old man.

I do the only thing I can think of. As I pass the kitchen I grab the coffee pot and hurl it at her. At exactly the same moment she hurls the speakerphone at me. The two objects pass in mid-air. The coffee pot hits her squarely in the chest, spilling all over her. I figure it's office coffee so the burns aren't going to be too severe.

The speakerphone, on the other hand. I don't know who the fuck this woman is but grief and fury have given her an arm that could pitch in the majors. It whirls towards me like some kind of oversized plastic shuriken, flailing cables, and hits me dead centre of the forehead.

I'm only out for a second, but it's long enough to be on the floor, and now people are running towards me from every direction, no longer seeing me as a vicious gunman but as some kind of weakling reduced to throwing lukewarm coffee pots at professional women.

I scramble to my feet. The stairs are out of the question now so I do the only thing I can: step into the service elevator, press the button, raise the VP9, and pray that nobody's (a) been counting (b) knows what a VP9 is or how many shots it has in the magazine.

My pursuers stop at the door, seeing the gun. It's a stand-off. No-one's sure what to do.

Why aren't the fucking doors closing? I hit the button again.

Then there's a voice from the back of the terrified, angry mob. It's some dickweed of a mailroom assistant with acne.

'That's a VP9,' he says in German. 'Only five shots in the magazine. I counted ten.'

They lunge for me.

Their bodies slam against the doors as they close.

9

I exit the building in a janitor's stolen coveralls, wadding blood from the cut in my forehead with blue paper towel. German police and anti-terrorist units are already screaming through Potsdamer Platz.

Sometimes security by obscurity is called for.

This has not been my finest hour. But the target is dead, no civilians were harmed – unless you count the security guard, which I don't, and the three CrossFit bros who, frankly, I put out of their misery. I check my pulse. Ninety and slowing.

It's all going to be okay.

I am already fantasising about the hotel room, the shower, the fresh set of clothes I will buy on the way, the dinner, the bar, and whatever other pleasures and adventures the evening may bring, when my phone rings. I don't need to check the caller ID, because there is precisely one person on earth who has this number. Problem is, they really, really, really shouldn't be calling me.

I answer.

'What the fuck? You know you can't just—'

'Shut up and listen,' says Handler. And I do, because when Handler says shut up, he means it. 'Where are you?'

'Berlin.'

I'm deliberately vague. It's a burner phone, a day old. I had cell service off the whole time until I left the building. There's no way I can be tracked. But you can't be too careful.

'I know you're in fucking Berlin. Where in Berlin?'

'Mitte Central.'

'Good,' says Handler. 'We have a new commission. Just came in.'

'Who?'

'Like it matters.'

'No, I mean—'

'We don't have a full description. Male, bearded, five nine. Not sure of the ethnicity.'

'That definitely narrows it down,' I say. 'I'll get right on it.'

'He's scheduled for a brush pass in the Tiergarten, between 1800 and 1900 local.'

'Pitching or receiving?'

'The latter.'

'Payload?'

'Unknown. At least, the client won't tell me.'

'Any information about the counterparty?'

'A woman. She'll be pushing a stroller with twins. Starbucks cup in the holder, showing a name beginning with N.'

I stop for a moment, checking around. There's no sign of anyone following. As far as I can tell, I'm completely clear. But alarm bells are ringing in my head.

'Come on, Handler,' I tell him. 'This is bullshit.' Because it is. 'It's not 1985 any more. A brush pass in Berlin, all this cloak and dagger stuff? Maybe we should do it at Checkpoint Charlie in the fog with Visage playing and go the whole hog.'

There's a silence at the other end. I have pissed him off. Oh, well.

'You want this job or not?'

'Not particularly.'

'What if I told you how much it paid?'

He does and I experience a moment of what I can only describe as intense emotion.

'Are you still there?' he asks.
'What are the parameters?'
'Client needs the payload. The end.'
He hangs up. I check the time. It's 1730 already.

10

The Tiergarten is massive, one of those sprawling imperial theme parks like Madrid's Buen Retiro where royals could work off their neuroses by hunting stags instead of the hoi polloi. Telling someone you'll meet them there is about as helpful as saying you'll meet in Ohio.

But a brush pass needs physical contact. Two people bumping into each other as they pass, a note or an object slipped into a pocket, an attaché case transferred. It only works where there are other people, lots of them, heading in different directions, where a moment of physical contact will draw no attention.

There are two obvious locations in the park. The first is the zoo. Midday it teems with schoolkids and tour groups and lovers and elderly Berliners with season tickets, full of little alcoves and dark places, vivariums and snake houses where you'd have privacy to make an exchange. But the more I think about it, the less appealing it seems. It's open until 9 p.m., but 6 p.m. is the dead hour, the time everyone's leaving, or at home having a bite to eat, or in a bar waiting to meet their date. If you're under suspicion – the entire point of a brush pass – then going to the zoo at a time when everyone else is leaving raises all sort of red flags.

'Well, Sergei, we followed you all day. And guess what? You went to the zoo. You, who have no interest whatever in the natural world, suddenly decide, instead of taking your normal route home, to make a visit to the Berlin Zoo at 6 p.m. We also checked your

internet search history and the only thing you checked was the opening times. Please explain.'

You'd have a cover story, but this is not the kind of conversation you want to be having with well-built men from Department 5.

The other location is the Victory Column, the totemic colonial phallus standing erect in the centre of the Tiergarten. A statue of Victoria, the Roman goddess of victory, emerges from the tip in shimmering gold like gilded metaphorical Prussian spooge.

There is no guarantee that's where the drop will happen, but I decide to play the odds.

As I cross over the Tiergartenstrasse I have time to think. Why a physical pass? There are a thousand ways to communicate securely using digital means: ProtonMail, Tor, Signal . . . Christ, even Zoom offers end-to-end industrial-grade encryption now. But there are still solid reasons for an old-fashioned meatspace transfer.

For your garden-variety drug trafficker, money launderer, arms dealer, or paedophile, commercial encryption is probably good enough. But if you're doing something really bad, something that genuinely threatens somebody's national security, if you make the mistake of putting yourself on those guys' radar – all bets are off. The hard truth is you, an individual, cannot prevail against the might of a national intelligence agency with billions of dollars to spend, the brightest minds of a generation at its disposal, and technology to hand which is ten years ahead of anything available commercially.

The easiest way is to put a rootkit on your device – your phone, your computer, your Apple Watch – that silently gives them complete control and access to everything. Or use complex side-channel exploits which eavesdrop vestiges of information the code your device is running leaves in memory. Or fully functioning networked computers hidden in the cord that attaches your keyboard. Or . . . let's just say I'm not even scratching the surface.

A simple brush pass of a handwritten note circumvents all of these. Genius, really.

Halfway there now. The Tiergarten is also starting to make more sense. Berlin, like every Western capital, is blanketed with CCTV, much of it networked to a central system that automatically tracks things like licence plates and biometrics. For civilian use, there are strict controls, but intelligence agencies follow no such rules. Maybe you don't think the NSA, who have a tap on all the world's major internet superhighways, have access to every camera you pass and your biometrics on file, but are you willing to bet your life on it?

There is almost no CCTV in the Tiergarten.

So it all makes a certain kind of sense. But it means these people are extremely serious, that what they're doing potentially threatens lives, possibly hundreds or thousands of lives.

Which raises another, even more troubling, question.

Why me?

Yes, I'm good. And I'm here. But I'm a beast of no nation, and Berlin is one of the great spy capitals of the world. This place was the sharp end of the Cold War spear. All of the great intelligence agencies of the world still maintain stations here. There are at least eight organisations who could have a full team here within ten minutes, three with airborne surveillance, and keep the whole thing in-house.

Given the amount they're paying me, it would probably be cheaper, too.

I'm almost there now. I consider calling Handler, but I know it's pointless.

The job is the job is the job.

II

The Victory Column stands in the centre of a massive traffic circle where five of Berlin's avenues intersect. Pedestrian pathways feed into four tunnels under the roads, with two exits to the central island, to the east and west respectively.

With a brush pass you can't specify an exact time. Both parties have to make sure they're not followed, which takes who knows how long. Somebody always gets there first, and they need a place to wait without attracting attention.

There is only one place here, and that's the column itself, where teenagers and couples are lounging around on the concrete base, kids running round playing tag as weary tourists check TripAdvisor to figure out where to have dinner.

So that's where I go. I pull out a pack of cigarettes I bought on the way, not because I smoke, but because smoking gives you an excuse to just sit there and look around. I'm still in my janitor's coveralls, just another skidmark on the underwear of the city.

I wait for twenty-five minutes. There are men with beards, but they pass through quickly without looking around. A woman with twins appears, but they're not in a stroller, five or six years old. There's no Starbucks cup, and her husband's with her.

I'm starting to second-guess myself when he appears. Greying, fifties, with a neat beard and hair trimmed forward into bangs, an odd look, like a kid's, or Moe in the Three Stooges.

He heads up to the column and sits right next to me. Clever, the kind of thing I'd do, simultaneously allowing him to check me out and making it impossible for me to watch him closely without being obvious. I offer him a cigarette. He declines with a wave, but I get a good look at him. He's nervous, his forefinger and thumb rubbing together constantly. He takes off his steel-rimmed glasses and cleans them on his tie, then puts them back on, scanning around.

Whoever he's waiting for, he doesn't know them.

We sit there for ten minutes. I smoke two more cigarettes. He checks his watch three times.

He sees her first. I can tell, because his fingers stop rubbing.

I follow his gaze, and there she is, where the underpass ramp emerges into the light. Late twenties, black hair pulled back in a ponytail, Middle Eastern or maybe Southern European, a pink top with BEBE in sequins, jeans, a hijab and white sneakers. She's pushing a double stroller with twins. She stops in the light, takes a coffee cup from the holder, drinks, making sure the Starbucks logo and the name written on it – *Nasrin* – are both visible.

Moe stands. He heads down the steps towards the woman with the twins. I let him go. It's well done. She's standing in the middle of the subway exit, almost blocking it, so it's natural for him to pass close. And as he does, so fast that the eye can barely follow it, he takes the Starbucks cup, and heads into the darkness of the underpass.

I don't want to give the game away, so I wait. After a few seconds, she pushes the stroller away, and I hurry down the steps into the tunnel. It takes a moment for my eyes to adjust, and for a moment I think I've lost him, but then I see him, now heading towards the Englischer Garten.

The janitor's coveralls, once camouflage, are now a liability. Given a few minutes to prepare, by now I'd have a baseball cap, a jacket, *something*, stowed in a backpack or a messenger bag to pull out and change my appearance on the fly. But I don't and right now, short of mugging a passer-by for their clothes or stripping down to my boxers, I'm stuck.

Moe passes the teahouse still heading north. I tail him, keeping my distance. He's good, never looking back, showing no further signs of nerves. It's far too public to do anything here, but he's most likely heading for the Bellevue S-Bahn, which will present limitless opportunities.

Then, as he passes the squat brutalist cube of the Art Academy, he does something unexpected. He stops to watch kids swinging from monkey bars in the children's playground. But really it's to give him the opportunity to check for a tail. I'm 200 yards back, but the coveralls, the ones he sat next to, are a stone tell. His eyes meet mine, and I know instantly that he's made me.

Fuck.

He doesn't look away. Instead, his eyes locked on mine, he very deliberately removes the lid from the Starbucks cup, drains the contents, and dumps the cup into a trash bin.

12

The real problem?

Wannabees.

Assholes who think they have what it takes to be Eighteen.

I contemplate this in the dark hole that is the bar of the boutique hotel I have checked into, outfitted entirely from Gap – I will correct this at the earliest opportunity – freshly bathed, a half-decent meal inside me, and allowing the warm glow of a third dirty gin martini to envelop me. Funny how ten 9mm shells seemed like an elegant sufficiency when the day began.

The foyer has turned into a nightclub, music from a DJ pounding away, the floor crammed with soccer players and their camp followers, including a large number of impossibly thin women with East European cheekbones, six-inch heels and handbags. Through the door I can see a train of champagne bottles held aloft, illuminated by sparklers, as some gullible douchebag in the VIP area drops a couple of grand on bottle service to impress his equally douchebag friends.

I'm not judging, I've done it myself.

The bar's so dark I can barely see my hands. They're clean now, illuminated by black light, the thunk of the 808 kick drum from outside vibrating the floor. Normally I face the exit, just in case, but today has worn me down and I'm at the bar.

If some aspirant to the throne wants to come after me, fuck it.

Let the cards fall where they may.

Today has been a hard day. My head still aches from the speakerphone, and for some reason the grief and hatred etched into that woman's face as she hurled it won't leave me, however hard I try to shake it off. Which is odd because that was not the worst thing that happened.

In the safe in my room there is a small sealed padded envelope. Inside that is a Ziploc bag. Inside that is a sixty-four-gig memory card, the size of a fingernail. It is still covered in blood. And somewhere towards the end of the U9 line, German police are scratching their heads over a body they just found on the tracks, a man in his fifties with a beard and a Three Stooges haircut. He's been decapitated by a train, and they might have dismissed it as just another suicide if he hadn't previously been strangled, and his stomach ripped open to expose the contents.

I could pretend it wasn't me who did it, but I figure I owe you the truth, more or less.

Everything about the operation bothers me. The fact that it was a physical drop. The way the call came in at the last minute, giving me no time to think about it. The coincidence of just happening to be in Berlin at the moment I was needed. The crazy determination of the man swallowing the memory card, knowing that if I caught him he had signed his own death warrant. The stink of blood and gas mixing with the sharp ozone of the electrified rails as I ripped his stomach open with my knife and plunged my hand in, the contents still warm. But most of all what bothers me is what he said as he backed away from me down the U-Bahn track, his face illuminated by the sodium lights of the platform a hundred yards behind me.

36

He said it over and over again, with increasing desperation as I moved towards him, as if he expected me to know what it meant.

Parachute. Parachute. Parachute.

When I didn't react, he turned and ran. I chased him down the tracks and tackled him around the legs. I couldn't risk a shot, even with the VP, because what I had to do could take a while and I couldn't risk drawing attention. So I strangled him.

And even as I strangled him he kept trying to say it.

Parachute. Parachute. Parachute.

Until the life went out of his eyes.

13

The music's so loud, the bar so dark, that the first I know of her is when she sits next to me.

She's wearing a business suit, late twenties or early thirties, all put together, hair in one of those cuts that's so simple and precise you know it cost mid three figures. She's wearing make-up, though you can barely tell. Her hands are slim. One nail is cracked. She orders a gin martini, very dry, dirty, straight up, with an olive.

'Jinx,' I say in English, indicating mine.

'Whatever.' Her accent is middle European. Czech, maybe? But she really doesn't want to talk, especially to an asshole like me who clearly has only one thing on his mind. It's all the encouragement I need.

'Hard day?'

No answer. She lifts her glass and I notice her hand is shaking slightly.

'Me too,' I say.

I go back to my drink.

There's a TV above the bar, sound off. But it's showing a news clip, the outside of the building near Potsdamer Platz, now surrounded by ambulances, police vehicles, media trucks, even an anti-terrorism command centre.

She watches it for a second, then she says: 'I was supposed to be in that room.'

'What's that?'

'The room where those people were killed. I was supposed to be there.'

I stare at her. Her face is unfamiliar, definitely not on any org chart I saw. And she's not an assistant: age is all wrong, her clothes are too expensive and she's got executive written all over her.

'How come? Why weren't you?'

'I just got transferred. They wanted me to shadow one of the senior executives. But some asshole rear-ended me on the way in. I was stuck there for forty-five minutes dealing with the police and insurance. By the time I got an Uber in . . .'

She tails off.

'Shit,' I say. No wonder her hands are shaking. 'Did you know any of them? The people who were killed?'

She shakes her head. 'I only came in from Strasbourg a couple of weeks ago. We didn't have much dealing with the principals.'

They're showing pictures on TV now, photos of the dead with their families.

'You know why anyone would want them dead?' I ask.

She gives me a stare.

'The old man, the sons . . . they had blood on their hands. Of course, they didn't kill anyone themselves, not personally. But they got what was coming to them.'

'Yet you work there.'

'Worked. I figured . . .'

'It was God's way of telling you to find another career.'

'I don't believe in God,' she says.

'Neither do I,' I say, and we both order more drinks.

14

Her name is Adela and she is indeed Czech. Her surname – Nepovim – means 'I'm not going to tell'. Apparently Czech surnames are like that. She had a boyfriend once whose surname was Driving With Manure. She's curious about what I do so I spin her a line about government service, leaving as much to the imagination as possible.

At the end of the evening she tells me she doesn't feel like being alone so we go back to my room and drink some more and go to bed. Afterwards, we lie side by side for a while in a comfortable silence, and I consider the significance of the small scar I felt in the small of her back.

It's an hour later that it happens. I feel a slight movement on the other side of the bed, and with one hand I catch her wrist, the one holding the six-inch ceramic blade she took out of her bag when I went to the bathroom. With the other I pull the pistol from under the pillow where I placed it when she took her turn in the bathroom, and put it against her temple.

'Drop the knife,' I say, but she doesn't. I press the pistol against her head harder, and she does. I sit upright and force her to the side of the bed. She pulls the sheet around her, as if it could protect her.

'Name?'

'Kovacs.'

'Trained in?'

'Belarus.'

'So, what, you're one of Osterman's?'

She nods. A weird silence, as we both sit there, me butt-naked, her half wrapped in a sheet, considering our lives.

'How did you know?' she asks finally.

'I know what an exit-wound scar feels like,' I say.

And it's true. She had me fooled. The whole act was perfectly done, leveraging her own fear of me into a cover story full of genuine emotion. If I hadn't felt the scar, I'd be dead now.

'How long have you been in the field?'

'Almost ten years.'

'What did Osterman tell you?'

'That I was getting old. Soon I wouldn't be able to pull this kind of thing off.' She gestures at the bed, meaning sex. 'At least, not as easily as I did. But I had what it took to be Eighteen. If I wanted it badly enough.'

I notice that her hands are shaking again.

'Aren't you going to kill me?'

'I should,' I say. But there is something about her, some vulnerability, something that is making me hesitate. It isn't that we just shared a bed – at least, not just that. It's her fear, I think.

'You would if I was a man,' she says, and she's probably right.

'If you were a man we wouldn't be sitting here in the first place,' I point out, although, to be honest, you never know.

By now she's shivering, her whole body, arms wrapped protectively around herself.

'You have money put away?' I ask.

She nods.

'Emergency passport, unused identity, all that shit?'

Another nod.

'How accessible?'

41

'I can get it,' she says.

'Then for Christ's sake,' I say, 'put your clothes on, walk out of here, and go somewhere nobody will ever find you. As far as Osterman is concerned, you simply bailed on the job and disappeared. I never even knew you were in the game.'

She nods. Then, quietly: 'Thank you.'

I watch her as she dresses, defeat in every movement.

At the door she hesitates, turns.

'Look,' she says. 'If you ever need anything . . . if you ever need to contact me . . .'

She fumbles in her bag for something.

'Let me just give you—'

She only gets the little snub-nose .38 a few inches out of the bag before I shoot.

15

I put her body in the tub and call Handler for a clean-up team. By the time I leave the room at 3 a.m., they are already in the corridor, for all intents and purposes a standard housekeeping crew, except they're male and a little more burly than you'd expect. Another followed behind with a laundry cart. It was an odd feeling lifting her with my arms under her armpits, feeling all of her hundred pounds and change, when only an hour or so before we'd been just as close, and she'd been alive.

16

Handler is smooth, I'll give him that.

That's not his real name, any more than mine is whatever I choose to sign it – 'Jones', currently. Unlike me, his real name still signifies something, because it's on the title of the thousand-acre organic vineyard he runs up in Sonoma, which means more to him than any being on earth, living or dead.

We are in Paris, a cliché of a sidewalk cafe on the Rive Gauche, all wrought-iron bistro tables and checked table-cloths. Handler has already made himself unpopular with the wait staff by asking for oatmeal milk in his decaf latte. From their expressions he might as well have asked them to put ketchup in it, but he exudes the wealth and power before which even a Parisian waiter quakes.

Handler is in his early fifties, wearing an exquisite grey Italian suit, with the kind of polished pink skin that speaks of moisturisers and exfoliation. He wears just enough cologne to make you wonder what it must have cost. Most men his age opt for a businesslike crop that shows off the grey at their temples but Handler sports an odd pageboy cut that swishes around his immaculate collar, as if to remind you that although his business is death and betrayal, he retains an artistic side.

Handler has a Hollywood agent's habit of looking just over your shoulder as he's talking to you, in case somebody more important walks by. The point of it is not to see if anyone more important is walking by, but to let you know, even as he is blowing smoke up your ass, that somebody more important could walk past at any moment.

He is one of exactly two people on earth who make me nervous just to think about them. There used to be three, but that was a long time ago.

Handler lives in what he likes to describe as a palazzo. I've never been there – people like me don't get invited to the houses of people like him – but I can mentally picture it in every detail. It's in the Coachella Valley, probably somewhere between Palm Desert and La Quinta, tennis capital of the world. He thinks of it as an Italian-style art deco estate but in fact it resembles nothing more than a nineties-era Miami shopping mall, all palm trees wrapped in fairy lights, and pink marble, with twice as many bathrooms as bedrooms, a twenty-car garage, indoor and outdoor wet bars, a fake waterfall, and not a single bookcase to be found anywhere on the property. Plus twelve-foot walls and twenty-four-hour armed private security, but, you know, tastefully done. Apparently the uniforms were done by someone who used to work for Versace.

I couldn't even begin to guess at Handler's sexuality. I'm not sure he even has one. If I close my eyes and imagine his boudoir, it has mirrors on the ceiling, but only so he can look at himself.

Handler's domestic security is mostly for show, or maybe he just likes having well-built men with double-digit IQs, tribal tattoos, Ray-Bans, and good muscle tone around the house. He exists in a weird bubble of untouchability, courtesy of his profession. This is why we are sitting outside drinking coffee in the Paris sunshine and not huddled in a SCIF feeling each other up for recording equipment. Handler is the gatekeeper to a very particular kind of expertise – mine – that is useful enough to all the people who might be a threat to him that they treat him with kid gloves. If Handler got the sense that he was being monitored, much less threatened, by a potential client, his services would no longer be available. This would place them at a competitive disadvantage, so by a kind of gentleman's agreement which is uncommon in the world of assassination and treachery, they leave him alone.

I am Handler's main priority, but I am not stupid enough to think that he doesn't have other fish to fry, and he makes a point of reminding me at every opportunity. The relationship between handler and client is always murky. Officially the handler works for the client, and takes a cut, but it's never that simple. Without the handler, the talent – me – simply doesn't work, or is reduced to bullshit organised crime gigs which inevitably draw the long-term attention of law enforcement, a complication from which my current activities are thankfully free.

There are four stages to a hitman's career:

1. Who is Jones?
2. Get me Jones!
3. Get me someone like Jones!
4. Who is Jones?

Right now my sense is we are somewhere between two and three, but these things can change quickly.

Handler finally gets his decaf oat-milk latte.

'So?'

I hand him the phone. He flicks through the photographs. Ends on the old fucker. Pinches to zoom in and make sure.

'Any trouble?'

'Nothing worth talking about.'

The face of the woman hurling the speakerphone at me flashes into view, and I have to stop myself rubbing my forehead, where there is still a tender spot.

46

'And the other job?'

I reach into my pocket and pull out the mailer containing the Ziploc and memory card. I slide it across the table. He picks it up with distaste, sensing what's congealed inside around the contents.

'No photos?'

'There wasn't time. Berlin transport police were all over me like a rash. But your client can pull DNA off the contents. Should be easy to match if they need to confirm the provenance.'

He smiles, a thin one. 'You're a cold-blooded motherfucker, aren't you?'

'That's why they pay me the big bucks. You and me both.'

'I wasn't complaining.'

'What's on the card, anyway?' I ask.

Handler gives me an odd look. 'Why do you care?'

'Just curious. I mean, when a guy would rather have you rip his stomach open than give up the goods, and that very evening someone comes along to kill you, it makes a body suspect that it's something more than family photos.'

'I have no idea,' says Handler.

Handler is ex-Agency and those guys know every possible tell and how to hide them. But Handler himself is so used to lying to everyone about everything that telling the truth stresses him out. Consequently, unlike most people, he has a tell for the truth, which is tapping the side of his coffee cup with his fingernail.

His fingernail does not tap the side of his coffee cup. He's in his comfort zone. Which means he may not be lying exactly, but for goddamn sure he isn't telling the truth.

So I press on. 'You think Kovacs was because of this?'

Handler stares at me. 'Why would she be?'

'Because I don't believe in coincidences any more than you do. She knew I was in Berlin. She knew about the hit

47

earlier that day. If she knew about this too, it means she had total visibility into my operations. Which means she probably had total visibility into *your* operations. Doesn't that scare you?'

Handler shrugs. 'My understanding is she was based in Prague. The hit in Berlin had your fingerprints all over it. It hit the wires an hour later. It's an hour by chopper. She could have been there by early evening. If she's any good, she knows the kinds of places you like. So she hits the bars of the hotels in descending order of how expensive the hookers are in the lobby. She hits you on, what, the third try?'

There's a sudden sour taste in my mouth. Handler knows my history. I don't give him the satisfaction of a reply.

'Besides,' says Handler, 'if she knew about the memory card, she knew about the dead drop. The mook you hit for the memory card was a far softer target than you. Why wouldn't she just take him? Why risk everything by going one on one with Seventeen?'

He's right. It makes no sense. But his fingers still aren't tapping. And now he's looking over my shoulder, that Hollywood glance, as if he's hoping to see someone, anyone, to find an excuse for this part of the conversation to be over. Only I'm not ready for it to be over.

'What does "Parachute" mean?'

He looks back to me in what seems like genuine surprise. 'What?'

'The catcher. He kept saying it before I killed him. *Parachute. Parachute. Parachute.* Like it should mean something to me. Should it?'

'No.'

His finger taps his cup. The truth.

'But it does to you,' I say.

His finger stops tapping.

'Look,' says Handler, finally. 'You're getting all wound up about this fucking job. It was a throwaway. You happened to be in the right place at the right time. That's all. It was nothing to do with Kovacs. Nobody has visibility into your operations, or mine. "Parachute", it doesn't mean anything. He probably wasn't even saying "Parachute". That's just what you heard. Probably "fuck you" in Farsi. Or "please don't kill me". Or, how the fuck do I know what it means? But "Parachute"? It makes no sense. And who cares? It's over. Done. The cheque cleared. It's all good. Forget about it.'

His irritated look says it's all I'm going to get. Maybe it's all I deserve. In Handler's world, I'm just the hired help. Yes, maybe I'm Seventeen, but we both know, somewhere out there, there's an Eighteen. Sweethearts like me, we're fungible assets, to be liquidated as soon as we begin to depreciate, as soon as the carrying cost gets too high.

17

Handler watches me for a second, and I realise why he's so good at his job. It's because to him it's a people business. Sure, he takes care of the operational details – clean-up crews, documents, payments, travel – but that's just housekeeping. His real abilities are psychological, to know how far someone can be pushed, to sense when they're starting to wobble, to reassure, to cajole, and when necessary, to cut bait.

'Something bothering you?' he says eventually. 'Beyond all this bullshit about memory cards?'

'Why would there be?'

'Okay.'

'What does that mean?'

'It means we go a long way back,' says Handler, 'and I would appreciate you being honest with me if something is bothering you. Because that way we can fix it. And if it can't be fixed, I need to know.'

He's right. There is something bothering me. And not just whatever the fuck is on that card.

'I let her live,' I say, eventually.

'Osterman's girl? I paid for a clean-up crew.'

'I mean, I didn't kill her right away. I should have, but I didn't. I knew who she was. But I could tell she was frightened. Osterman must have put the thumbscrews on her, told her that her career was over if she didn't do this. I don't know what the hell she was thinking ... she wasn't ready for it. I tried to tell her. I thought she'd listen. But she didn't. I tried to do the right thing and she interpreted it as weakness.'

Handler digests this.

'You made a mistake,' he says finally. 'It happens.'

'Not to me,' I say.

'Look,' he says. 'The important thing is not to let it get to you.'

He shifts in his seat as he says it, and I sense a tiny chip in our relationship, like a fragment of glass chiselled out of a windshield by a stone, tucked away down there in the corner, just sitting there, for weeks or months or years, waiting to turn into a hairline crack, then a splinter, until finally it travels all the way across the windshield, ruining it completely.

'I'm not even sure it was a mistake.'

'Doing the right thing is always a mistake,' he says.

He senses the chip too, and is trying to apply the clear plastic resin that will make it invisible, that will stop the rot, take it back to perfect. 'You let them live, they come back. You know this. Harder, better, faster. If you'd let her walk out the door, she'd have come back. And brought friends. And if not her, somebody else. Christ's sake, I don't have to tell you this shit.'

'You want the truth? I felt sorry for her.'

'I do not want to hear this.'

'This is not about you.'

'Of course it's fucking about me.' He leans forward, agitated, his mop haircut falling out of place. 'I'm the one who goes to bat for you. I'm the one who says Seventeen's still got it. Seventeen's still hungry for it. Seventeen's the one who'll get the job done. I'm the one who sells you. It's a performance, for fuck's sake, and I have to mean it, every word of it. My reputation is at stake here. My *brand*. If you fuck up, it's on me. The consequences are mine. Of course it's about me.'

51

He sits back, tries to put the errant strand back in place. As he does, I glimpse his roots, pulled back further than they should be, and realise without any surprise that he's had a facelift.

'Look,' he says finally. 'If you're saying, I don't know, that you're not sure if you still have it . . .'

This is exactly where I do not want the conversation to go. Like one of those spousal exchanges that spirals unexpectedly out of control. You start out trying to agree on what to eat for dinner and before you know it you've both dredged up two decades of grievances and are filing for divorce.

'I'm not saying that.'

'. . . then we can handle it.'

'I am not saying that. Fuck's sake, I'm just . . . talking. You asked me what's bothering me, and I told you. Who the hell else am I supposed to talk to about this stuff?'

'Don't go soft on me.'

Soft. For Christ's sake. The man lives in a palazzo and makes organic wine.

'I am not going soft. I'm sorry I said anything.'

'Me too.'

The two of us, we're like an old married couple. The image of it comes unbidden. Me in a polo shirt, golf pants hoiked up to my waist, a flat white cap, and those weird wraparound sunglasses that go over your prescription ones. Him as wrinkled as a raisin, with white hair coiffed into a helmet and claw-like purple fingernails.

'So what's next?' I say. I need to get the image out of my mind. 'You have a job? Give me something. Anything.' I rap the metal table so hard his cup jiggles in the saucer.

I have the sudden sense that he's rearranging Scrabble letters in his head to make a new word. Maybe not the word he would like to make, but a word nevertheless.

'Yes,' he says finally. 'I have a job.'

18

Handler reaches into his jacket's side pocket and pulls out a small manilla envelope and slides it across the table. The flap is open. Inside, there's a photograph, as there always is.

It's a man in his late forties, maybe older. A little weather-beaten. Short grey hair thinning into male pattern baldness. The kind of guy you see in the hardware store buying pressure-treated 2x6s and chatting easily to the woman with the orange apron about the advantages of various types of deck screws. You just know he owns a compressor and a torque wrench.

I put it back in the envelope, and slide it back across the table.

'Absolutely not.'

'You don't get to pick and choose,' says Handler.

'Read my lips.'

'He's an old man, for fuck's sake. He's been retired for years.'

'Maybe I should look into it.'

It drops on to the table like a conversational turd. But it's true. I have enough money put away in hidden bank accounts to live comfortably for the rest of my life, and Handler knows it. He stares at me.

'What's wrong with you?'

I take the envelope again, rip out the photograph, hold it up for him.

'You know who this is?'

'Of course I fucking know.'

'You know the name of this man?' I jam it into his face.

'Of course I know his name.'

'Tell me. Come on, tell me.'

Waiters and *bon chic, bon genre* matrons at other tables are starting to look round. If there's one thing Handler doesn't like, it's a Scene, at least one he isn't in full control of.

'You know as well as I do what his name is,' he hisses, leaning forward.

'Tell me!'

Handler sighs. 'His name is—'

I cut him off.

'Death. The name of this man is death.'

19

That's not his name. I could reel off a dozen aliases he's used over the years. Whatever he's going by now is anybody's guess, but it doesn't matter, because the picture is undeniably, obviously, unquestionably that of my predecessor, Sixteen.

Twenty years at the top of his game, longer than anybody else. Never missed a hit, never fucked up, never betrayed a moment of conscience or weakness, and then one day disappeared, severing every known link. It's as if he stepped off the planet, leaving no trace, a stone plopping into the black water of a midnight lake without creating as much as a ripple.

I am who I am because of him. I studied him. I studied the others, too, all the way back through history, but Sixteen to me was Hendrix, the Beatles, Public Enemy, Sleater-Kinney, Tupac, Bacharach, Marvin Gaye and Kendrick Lamar rolled into one. You wear your influences, you outgrow them, you repudiate them, you grow to love them or hate them, but you never escape them. They remain with you, as much part of you as your skin and your bones.

Handler takes the photograph out of my hands and puts it back in the envelope.

'I thought you were the best.'

'I am the best,' I say. 'Currently working.'

'You're afraid of him,' says Handler. His fingers are tapping the cup again. 'Is that it?'

I don't answer, because of course I am afraid of him. I would be a fool not to be afraid of him. When I think about Sixteen, I am Osterman's girl with her chipped fingernail, standing in the doorway of the bar trying to summon the guts to sit next to me, knowing in her heart she should just walk away instead, off into the night, and take her chances with whatever lay there instead.

'You know,' says Handler. 'The truth is, you had it lucky. You never had to earn your stripes.'

'I fought my way up.'

'Sure. From the little leagues to the big leagues. All the way to the final bracket. But you never faced him, did you? He pulled his disappearing act, and you stepped into his shoes like you were the rightful owner. But they're still his shoes.'

I shift uncomfortably, a hermit crab in a borrowed shell.

'Seven years—'

'Eight.'

'Eight, then. Whatever. Eight years, you've had it easy. Eight years you've stood tall in another man's shoes. But it's time to buy your own. You take this job, or—'

'Or what?'

'Or I'll find somebody who will.'

'Like who?'

'Dykstra. He's good. A rising star.'

He's deliberately provoking me.

'Dykstra's a butcher. An amateur. He wouldn't stand a chance.'

'At least he's not a coward.'

And there it is. It's all out in the open now. Handler has never spoken to me this way before. I've heard stories of his vindictiveness, of the way he turns on those he considers have failed him. But this is my first taste of it. It tastes like metal, or blood, and I don't like it at all.

'What do you think happens when word gets out that you have the fear? Right now, you think you're untouchable. And you are, because you're in their heads, Dykstra and all the others. But you turn down this job and they start to talk. *Seventeen's lost his edge.* The work dries up, but that's not the worst part. The worst part is people start to come for you, out of the woodwork, only they're not afraid of you any more.'

That taste in my mouth. I want to spit it out.

'The Osterman girl. Do you know how good she was? World class. As good as you? Maybe, maybe not. It doesn't matter, because her fear was her undoing. She was afraid, not because you were better than her, but because of your reputation. But if she heard the whispers? That you turned down this job? That Seventeen was human after all? Maybe the whole thing would have played differently.'

I think of Kovacs sitting next to me. Her jangling nerves, the chipped fingernail.

'And that's the least of it,' he says. He's a hammer now, piling on blow after blow. 'You show weakness, people start to worry. They start to worry about all the things you know, all the stuff you have locked up here.' He taps his head. 'You know what happens then? They transfer you from the column marked "assets" to the one marked "liabilities". They begin to consider you a risk. An unmitigated risk. And you know what happens to unmitigated risks? They get mitigated. You've made a good living out of that. So have I. But the wheel of fortune turns.'

I realise my hands are playing with my espresso spoon, but it's too late. Handler knows he's got me on the run.

'You look forward to that? Looking over your shoulder every time you unzip to take a piss in case Dykstra is there behind you?'

'I'm not afraid of Dykstra.'

'Andersen. Kurzweil. Bernier. Talman. Harkonnen. Any one of LeBrun's team. There are others. You think you can take them all? Because you'll have to. And one day you'll get tired of it. You'll drop your guard. Not for long. Maybe just a tenth of a second, like you did with the Osterman girl. But it'll be enough.'

He stops, knowing he's made his point.

I take the envelope back.

'So where is he?'

20

We stroll south into the Latin Quarter, to a street lined with bookstores, some with cardboard boxes of remainders out front. Each one has a speciality – the classics, geography and maps, technical subjects. One deals entirely with chess. Finally we arrive at a decrepit little hole with the sign of a revolver hanging over the door, and a window full of pulp fiction.

Handler takes me inside. The elderly man at the desk knows him, because he simply nods in acknowledgement as Handler takes me to a section at the rear marked *Espionnage*.

'So,' he says, sandwiched between bookshelves that look like they could topple if you breathed on them, the musty smell something between a wet dog and an old man's suitcase. 'Eight years, and nothing. Vanished without trace. I checked every contact I could think of and then some. Every bank account he was ever associated with cleaned out and closed. Not a single hit on biometrics the whole time. I'm figuring the guy is already dead, but—'

'No way,' I say. 'Nobody takes that much trouble to disappear unless they plan on living a long time afterwards.'

'Right,' says Handler.

'So you come up snake eyes. Then what?'

'I put the word out among a certain class of people that I'm looking for him. And one day a package arrives up at the vineyard. Hand delivered, no return address. Got a certain weight to it. And inside?'

He reaches up and pulls a book off a shelf.

It's tacky, with gilt letters on an embossed cover, fake bullet holes and an obligatory dribble of blood. You've seen a thousand of them.

He hands it to me. The title is *Breach of Protocol*, and the author's name is Sam Kondracky.

'Spy fiction,' I say, 'is not really my thing.'

'Trust me,' says Handler.

21

Kondracky can write.

His prose is as blunt and unsentimental as a crowbar.

It takes me four days to devour the six novels the old guy at the desk packaged up for me, but I'm only halfway through when it hits me: I know all his stories.

He's clever. He changes dates, locations, genders. He plays Islamabad for Karachi, Prague for Vienna. The female cipher clerk with a coke habit in CIA's Beirut Station becomes a drunken male translator in Phnom Penh a decade later. And he overlays the whole thing with a thick gloss of pulpy bullshit and macho make-believe, a gooey confection of Hollywood schtick to make it go down easy on the eight-hour plane ride. But underneath the clown make-up you always sense the presence of the grinning skull.

Somewhere in a box in a shipping container in Rhode Island which has remained locked for most of a decade, there's a stack of binders, each stuffed with press cuttings, intelligence reports, everything I could ever lay my hands on. I don't have to go fetch them because they're all in my head, memorised. I could recite them by heart. And here they are, transmuted, transmogrified, excavated, manufactured into literary heroin for insurance executives on a layover.

So, like I say, he can write. You'd never mistake him for Margaret Atwood. But he can write.

I call Handler.

'It's him,' I say. 'Kondracky, he's Sixteen.'

'Congratulations,' says Handler. 'Now go kill him.'

PART TWO

22

My mother's name was June. People called her Junebug. She was ash-blonde and willowy and she never had a chance. Her father was a religious nut who beat her and, I imagine, did other stuff to her that she never cared to mention to me. She was alcoholic from the age of thirteen, and soon found respite in other substances. She was a year younger than I am now when she died, and had managed to hang on to most of her looks, but I've come to realise that her death was just the final act in a tragedy which had been playing out since long before I was born.

Junebug never told me who my father was. Maybe she didn't know, or maybe she wasn't sure, or maybe she just thought it was better I didn't know. Somehow she clung on to me through a vicious and escalating series of battles with the San Joaquin CPS as they attempted to wrest me from her on the grounds of child endangerment. But she prevailed, thanks to tearful promises about addiction clinics and twelve-step programmes and not to consort with criminal types and so on. She meant every word of it, I have no doubt, but the life she found herself in was like quicksand: the harder she struggled to free herself, the deeper it sucked her in.

Towards the end she talked about moving away, Oregon or somewhere she'd never been but could dream about. She would start to save the money she made, which came from an endless stream of male visitors to whatever firetrap of a motel or rooming house we were shacked up in at the time. She'd manage to stay off the junk for a week or two, and tell big stories about how our life would be once we got the fuck out of Stockton in particular and California in general. I'm sure she believed them at the time, but inevitably a day would come where she could no longer face her existence. Whatever she'd saved would be blown on some epic binge that would last for three or four days while I put endless bags of popcorn in the microwave with the cracked yellow handle, which followed us from room to room, to sustain myself. And that would be that, for another few months.

I can't hate her. I can't even blame her. Junebug was broken, and she loved me desperately in her broken way. Even back then I guess I understood she was trying to fix herself the only way she knew how.

23

The offices of Friedman & Franklin are just shy of Central Park, in one of those generic, square Manhattan office towers Spider-Man swings from, with the name in brass above the door in Bank Gothic. There's a bookshop by the entrance where, let me assure you, they do not sell remainders of anything published by Friedman & Franklin.

I sit waiting patiently, my courier bag on my lap, wearing a slim pair of khakis, checked shirt, and shoes with no socks, before an assistant takes me through to meet Henry Chu, who is Kondracky's editor. I reiterate what I told him in my email: that I'm pursuing a Masters in Editing and Publishing at NYU, and I'm particularly interested in the process by which the raw material of an author's first draft gets massaged and shaped by the brilliance of an editor into the perfectly shaped charge of an airport novel.

Henry asks for my student ID, apologising. It's just that these days we have to be so careful. I show it to him. He checks it carefully and returns it. He's in his mid-thirties, with a picture on his desk of what I assume is his husband and their kid, either adopted or surrogate, it's hard to tell. I like him, and I want him to like me, so I let him witter on for thirty-five minutes about the business of publishing, demographics, quadrants, imprints, branding, advances, copy-editing and publicity. He's genuinely proud of what he does, and frankly who am I to judge?

I keep an eye on the clock. I'm going to need fifteen minutes to get what I need, and he kept me waiting five minutes while he sorted out some mix-up with who was supposed to be doing the pick-up from preschool, so at the forty-minute mark I casually drop into the conversation that I've decided to take as my case study spy writer Sam Kondracky.

It stops Henry in his tracks.

'Sam?'

'Kondracky, yes. I was hoping to interview him, get his side of the process,' I say brightly.

'Mr Kondracky doesn't give interviews.'

'Just by phone would be fine.' I'm so goddamn perky you could bottle me. 'Or email. Even if you were just able to forward a list of questions for my dissertation.' I pull a typed list from my bag. They are good questions, even if I say so myself. 'And obviously I'm happy to—'

'No, I mean, he doesn't give interviews of any kind.'

I arrange my face into a disappointed shape, but I know all this because the internet exists, and I have read, as far as I can tell, every single article ever written about him. The word 'recluse' doesn't capture the totality of it. He's a cipher, a complete unknown, a zero.

'I'll be honest,' says Henry. 'I really think, just from personal experience, that you'd be better off choosing someone else.'

'Personal experience? So you've met him.'

'No. That's my point.'

I deploy the secret weapon of all TV interviewers every-where. I say nothing, just let the silence hang. They call it uncomfortable for a reason: the human inclination to fill it is almost irresistible. And Henry, after about ten seconds, obliges. He gets up and closes the door.

'We get a manuscript. Mail, UPS, Fedex, never the same thing twice. Always hard copy, always typed out on manual typewriter. There's no address, no phone number, no email.'

I frown. 'There must be a chain of title.'

'Of course,' says Henry. 'I can't go into detail, but off the record there's a Delaware corporation, an assignment of rights and liabilities, and an NDA. There's no advance, and all potential royalties go to a cancer charity. Once we receive the manuscript, we have the right to make whatever revisions we deem necessary, up to five percent of the overall length. Sometimes we hire ghost writers to punch it up. If we have problems, our lawyers talk to the lawyers for the loan-out. If they had any doubts we wouldn't publish. But they don't, and we do. The truth is I have no more idea who Sam Kondracky is than you do.'

'Come on,' I say. 'You must speculate. The postmarks on the packages, the tracking on the UPS package. There has to be a clue there. Don't tell me you haven't tried to figure it out.'

Henry smiles. 'Of course we have. But they're always different. Wisconsin, North Dakota, Nebraska, Minnesota . . .'

'I guess there's no chance you keep the mailers, the envelopes?'

'Sorry,' says Henry, but he shouldn't be, because if they did I would need to leave with them, and that would involve the firearm concealed in my courier bag, and the associated unpleasantness. I doubt Henry would give me much trouble, what with the husband and the kid, but there's always a chance it could go to shit and make the papers, which would alert Sixteen, and remove what is literally my only advantage at the moment: surprise.

I sit there for a second trying to decide if Henry is telling me the truth. If Kondracky is truly paranoid he'll have built in some kind of tripwire to the process, some way of Henry alerting him that some geeky kid with no socks had been around asking questions. But it's hard to see how he'd do that without laying a trail to his own door.

Henry mistakes my silence for disappointment. He leans forward, all fatherly though he can't be more than four or five years older than me, and says:

'Look. I'd love to help. But when someone goes to such great lengths not to be found, even if you do manage to find them, what are the chances that it's likely to end well?'

Henry is right, and I would do well to listen to him, but he has already given me everything I need.

24

There's no sign to mark the transition from Minnesota, just a subtle change of road surface. South Dakota's slogan used to be 'The Land of Infinite Variety' which at least showed they had a sense of humour, since 'The Land of Infinite Fucking Horizons' would seem like a more appropriate tagline, because from what I can see ahead of me it's the very Platonic ideal of flat.

South Dakota's main claim to fame is America's regrettable tattoo, Mount Rushmore, so I figure things must get more exciting, geologically speaking, to the west. It takes guts to carve the head of a man who owned six hundred slaves, fathered six children with one of them, and emancipated exactly two during his lifetime into the granite of sacred mountain pledged to the Lakota Sioux in a treaty which the United States government immediately broke, then call it the 'Shrine of Democracy', but America is weird like that.

You'd think the film office would be in Sioux Falls, which is at least a proper city, but no, it's in the state capital, Pierre – congratulations, now you know – another four hours and change west, population somewhat south of fuck all.

The building is strange, a modern brick cube with the air of a medieval castle due to the curious drawbridge which leads from the parking lot over a kind of ravine to the foyer, which unaccountably sits on the third floor. My appointment is with Mary Petty, a friendly black woman in her thirties whose

Subaru Outback radio is, I suspect, permanently tuned to NPR.

It used to be that all you needed to be a producer was a phone and a Rolodex, but now it doesn't even take that. Competition between states to land productions is intense, the state film commissions are well funded, and due diligence almost entirely absent. All it took was a single email from a throwaway Gmail address announcing we were scouting possible locations for an indie movie, and an hour later I had the appointment.

Mary ushers me into her office, which has posters of notable films shot in South Dakota, such as *The NeverEnding Story III*, and (I kid you not) *Starship Troopers*. I ask her about Terrence Malick's *Badlands*, which until now have been the only part of the entire state that held interest for me, but it's a sore point because they shot the entire damn thing in Colorado.

We chit and we chat, swapping movie gossip I have gleaned from script tracking boards and the industry insider site *Deadline*, while I sip vile lukewarm coffee out of a plastic cup. I tell her the movie is being funded by a conglomerate of bored dentists looking for a high-risk, high-return investment which *The Indie Filmmaker's Handbook* tells me is how these things are done. Apparently she buys it, because eventually she smiles and asks in a slightly surprised tone of voice, 'So, why South Dakota?'

Which is a better question than she knows, since South Dakota was the one state Sam Kondracky never sent a manuscript from. But the others formed a donut around it, and it seemed to me Kondracky would instinctively not want to shit on his own doorstep. Moreover, if you were fixing to disappear off the map entirely, the Land of Infinite Variety – about large parts of which Google Maps is entirely ignorant – would be the ideal place to do it.

'We're just exploring options,' I tell her. 'We're talking to Nebraska and Wyoming too. We may look at Montana. But my sense is that we're going to find what we're looking for here.'

'And what's that?' she asks.

'Buttfuck,' I say.

Her smiles freezes. Evidently 'buttfuck' is not an NPR word.

'I'm sorry?'

'Buttfuck.'

'You're going to have to be more specific.'

And so I am. Because I have figured it out. I know Kondracky – I'm gonna call him that – I've studied him, and I know how he thinks. I know his preferences, his habits, his comfort zones. I know how he plans, how he works. And because of that I know the kind of place he lives. Not so much the house itself – though it has its own list of requirements – but how it's situated, the community, the topography, its distance from major routes and centres of population.

If I had six months I could find it myself, but I don't.

The only things I don't know yet are the map co-ordinates.

I describe the above to Mary, who listens and takes notes.

'You have some pretty specific requirements,' she says doubtfully.

'If you don't think you can help—'

'No, I mean, I'm sure we can help you,' she says quickly. Apparently mentioning the other states has fuelled her competitive instincts. 'We've a huge number of locations on file if you'd like to—'

'I'm sorry,' I say. 'I'm not sure you understand. This place, wherever it is, it's not going to be on file. It's not going to be some place that's ever been in a film or a TV show before. It's not going to be any place that anybody's ever heard of. We're

73

not interested in that. We need something fresh. A real sense of isolation. The end of the world. The last place anyone would think of. Buttfuck.'

'I see,' says Mary. 'And the house itself. You'll build it, or . . . ?'

'No, it needs to be real. I'll know it when I see it.'

'Well,' she says finally. 'We have a couple of tame location managers . . .'

Bingo.

Location managers are the unsung heroes and heroines of the film production world. They know every inch of their territory and if they don't have what you're looking for filed away in their heads or on disk, they'll get in their car and find it for you. You get two or three of them working for you and you can save six months of your own shoe leather, and never risk blowing your cover.

'I just need a couple of details, then I'll put the word out,' says Mary. 'Movie, right?'

'Correct.'

'Genre?'

'I guess you'd say, thriller.'

'And this is where the action takes place?'

'Some of it, at least.'

'Is there a script?'

'Not as such,' I say. 'The way it plays out will depend on the location. A lot of it will be improvised.'

'Oh, how interesting!' says Mary, brightening. Evidently she was a drama major. 'And the title of the production?'

I smile.

'Of course,' she says, and writes it down.

I see her pen moving.

Buttfuck.

25

Junebug never caused much trouble and, for reasons which weren't clear to me at the time, the cops left her pretty much alone, even when the motel we were staying in was closed down on account of it being a house of prostitution.

Cops were never the problem. The problem was me. We never had more than a single room, and the last thing she needed was a nine-year-old audience. During the day, if I wasn't at school, which was most of the time, she'd send me out to wander the streets with a couple of bucks to buy whatever I wanted at the 7-Eleven until an hour had passed. I knew to listen at the door and, if I heard voices or other sounds, wait round by the ice machine until the client had left.

I became an expert on ice machines.

But at night a nine-year-old kid wandering the meaner streets of Stockton was likely to attract attention of one kind or another, and none of it good, so she kept me home. For a while I'd just hang out by the ice machine, but that ended with another guest calling the cops on me. I knew better than to let them catch me – they might cut Junebug slack over the hooking, but a second strike of child endangerment would likely prove decisive with CPS. So I ran and hid in a gas station washroom until I was sure the coast was clear, which wasn't until the early hours of the following morning.

Junebug was incandescent, when I finally made it back around 3 a.m. She thought someone had taken me to do to me what her father, I am guessing, had done to her. The thought of losing me seemed to cause something to snap inside her. That's the only time I remember her hitting me, her hands flailing around my ears as I held up my arms to protect myself, but her heart wasn't in it and we ended up in a hug, both crying.

After that, when a man came she'd simply put me in the closet with sliding doors that sat by the side of the bed and I'd wait there until the business was completed. She made me swear not to look, and I didn't, but I heard everything.

Afterwards, after she'd showered, or not, no matter what the time, she'd take me out to some twenty-four-hour place where we'd get ice cream or a slushy or a hot dog and Coke or some other such junk.

Sitting at a stained Formica table under flickering neon, watching the traffic ebb and flow on Walker Way, a pimply teenager mopping the floor around our feet, chairs stacked on tables for the witching hour, some homeless dude outside panhandling quarters while the older hookers worked the graveyard shift, with Junebug pushing her lank blonde hair back over her ears as she chatted away about Oregon or Winnipeg or Poughkeepsie, places she knew nothing about apart from they had pretty names, while I sucked sweet goop through a red plastic straw . . . to this day, those are the happiest hours I have ever known.

26

Pierre has one of every chain motel and chain restaurant known to man. Accommodation choices range from Days Inn by Wyndham to Baymont by Wyndham, Super 8 by Wyndham, and AmericInn by Wyndham. Dining options comprise McDonald's, Subway, China Buffet, DQ, Arby's, Burger King, Taco Bell and Pizza Hut. There's a place called Bob's Lounge but, no.

I hole up in the Days Inn where I bounce off the walls for two days watching CNN. The US is trying to gin up international support to either nuke or invade Iran on the basis of what they claim is an intercepted comms stream between Iranian-backed terror groups plotting some kind of radiological attack on the US – a dirty bomb, maybe?

Colour me sceptical.

The dirtiest of all dirty secrets about the business of intelligence is that it's political. The way it's *supposed* to work is that intelligence community work product is non-partisan, factual information which the political leaders of the day use to make well-informed and sensible decisions about foreign policy.

The way it *actually* works is that, at best, intelligence is cherry-picked by political appointees to support whatever military adventures the executive has a hard-on for. At worst, career intelligence officers produce assessments tailored to legitimise the actions of their political masters, because if you don't, they will very quickly find a rival of yours who will.

Maybe there is some Iranian plot. I wouldn't put it past them. But that's not why the US wants to invade. The US wants to invade because it wants to invade. The new intelligence, if it even exists, is just a rhetorical device to get the rest of the world in the mood to party.

The last time they tried this, in Iraq, it cost a couple of hundred thousand to a million civilian lives, depending on whose estimate you accept. Afghanistan didn't go a whole lot better, and look how that ended.

It's not that I'm squeamish. It's just the Kabuki that offends me. If you feel the need to fuck some shit up for the sake of it, why not just say so?

Vote Seventeen! Let's fuck some shit up! Mostly brown people!

I'm just considering a career move into politics when a thought tickles the back of my brain. *Nukes, Iran, a woman in a headscarf.* Could the brush pass in Berlin have something to do with the intercepted messages? I rack my brain for the name that was written on the cup. *Nasrin.* It's a Persian name and when I Google it, the first page of results is all Iranian women.

Is that why Handler was so reluctant to discuss the operation?

The connection borders on vestigial. But what went down in Berlin still troubles me – I don't know how Kovacs knew I would be in the bar that night, or why Handler was so keen to reassure me it was a coincidence – so I've made a habit of checking the German papers. Moe's death was reported the day his body was found. There was never any coverage of Kovacs – Handler's clean-up crew were professionals. And then on my second evening in Pierre, scrolling through the *Berliner Morgenpost* on my phone, I see it: a report of a woman's body found in a wooded area outside the city. It's been decapitated and the hands removed, presumably to delay identification. But I know instantly who it is, because the torso is wearing a sequinned pink T-shirt with BEBE written on it.

The pitcher and the catcher are dead. Kovacs is dead. Whatever was on that card has cost the lives of two, possibly three people. And I'm beginning to wonder if it's the reason I'm sitting in a shitty hotel in Pierre trying to find the one man on earth who is most assuredly capable of killing me.

You're probably thinking the smart thing would have been to check the contents of the card before giving it to Handler, right?

Right.

27

I was walking away from the hotel with Kovacs' body cooling in the bathtub when it hit me maybe killing me was just a means to an end, the end being the memory card.

I needed to know what was on it. But for all I knew it was stuffed full of industrial-strength malware. So I bought a laptop from a Berlin pawn shop with cash and rented a room by the hour in a sex hotel on the Kurfürstenstrasse, the kind of place no questions are asked. There, I disconnected the camera and the speakers, did a low-level format on the hard drive, installed a hardened Linux which I downloaded with a throwaway VPN. I physically disconnected the internal wifi. Only then did I insert the memory card.

I'm not sure what I expected to find. Intelligence reports. Blueprints. Diplomatic cables. Zero-day exploits. Satellite imagery. Some other James Bond shit. Or just a bunch of inscrutable encrypted files with names like SJ627E.R07 that would mean nothing to me at all.

Wrong.

Porn.

It was absolutely full of porn.

And not even good porn. Soft-core commercial nineties vanilla schtick, all hormonal pizza delivery boys and busty housewives in the same over-lit set with a dusty rubber plant and a room divider. Nothing to give you a hard-on, nothing you could remotely use to blackmail someone, and more to the point, nothing that Moe or Kovacs would have been willing to give their lives for.

That meant whatever juice the memory card held, it wasn't the porn itself. It was hidden *in* the porn, just as you can hide a message in a Bible by making tiny pinpricks above the letters that make up the words.

I didn't have the tools or the time to crack weapons-grade steganography, which was likely what I was dealing with. So I created a bit-perfect image of the card, encrypted it, reattached the wifi, uploaded it via an anonymiser to a free storage site and sent the link to Vilmos.

Vilmos is gay, 200 pounds overweight, and on the spectrum. His main claim, apart from being one of the world's leading authorities on the *Star Wars* canon, comes from exposing a backdoor in an NSA-authored crypto library which has become an industry standard. NSA claimed the vulnerability was accidental, but it gave them the ability to backdoor the routers and switches that power the internet, enabling them to siphon traffic from network hubs around the world.

Maybe you believe in coincidences. I don't.

NSA tried to silence Vilmos with the offer of a job, but Vilmos told them to go fuck themselves. So the Feds did the next best thing, which was to arrest him for his proof-of-concept, which involved gaining access to a backbone node in Long Island and inserting the entire text of Lenin's *Left Wing Communism: An Infantile Disorder* into the syslog.

He got two years in a Supermax for that. When he got out, he relocated to a country without an extradition agreement with the US, and went straight back to what he was doing before.

Vilmos's mix of bloody-mindedness and Aspie focus means he can crack problems nobody else would even attempt. He does it for entertainment and refuses to accept payment: his income comes from a massive multi-GPU Bitcoin rig which allows him to throw comical amounts of computing power at problems that have no potential pay-off, and heats a small town into the bargain. The only downside is you can't bug him. Doing so breaks his concentration, and once it's gone, it's gone, and he'll move on to something else. All you can do is send him the problem and wait. Eventually, after a day, or a week, or a year, you'll get your answer.

I still don't know what was concealed in those acres of oscillating pink flesh.

Not yet. But I will.

28

On my third day in Pierre I finally get a reassuringly heavy couriered package from the film office, courtesy of Mary's flock of location managers. But as I rip it open on the rickety round dining table in the privacy of my efficiency unit, my heart sinks. Whatever South Dakota lacks in swagger, it makes up in Buttfucks. Page after page of them. Buttfuck upon Buttfuck. A fuckload of Buttfucks. Fortifying myself with the contents of the minibar, I take the pile of documents and hit Google Earth, with the topography layer switched on. It takes until 3 a.m. – and by the end of it my eyeballs feel like they're pinballs – but I narrow it down to seven candidates.

I drain the last alcohol from the minibar, and plot a route.

The following morning I leave at dawn. The first three are busts. One is a ghost town, the doors of the abandoned gas station flapping in the wind, the sign hanging off one hinge, the gas prices dating back four years to the last spike. One is small, but bustling, the centre of a thriving agricultural community, with a subdivision under construction on the edge of town. Too big, too busy. The third is all kinds of wrong, some kind of religious community with women in old-fashioned dresses and bearded dudes in blue coveralls sitting on porches, watching me pass with a creepy inbred glaze to their eyes that makes me feel like I'm about to re-enact *Deliverance*.

The fourth is a possibility, but what the map doesn't show is that it's on tribal land and something tells me Kondracky doesn't have the requisite bloodline.

Five and six are close, but no cigar. The towns themselves, if you can call them that, are fine. But the topography of the first is all wrong, and though the topography of the second is perfect, the cherry on the cake, the house itself, is an un-renovated gothic ruin that doesn't have the lines of sight I know Kondracky will require.

Which leaves the seventh.

By the time I get there I've driven close to a thousand miles, a complete loop around the heart of South Dakota, and the sun is dipping below the horizon. There's nothing to announce the place, not so much as a broken-down sign, but the moment I see Milton, South Dakota's single flickering streetlight I am filled with an absolute and unshakeable conviction that I've found both it, and him.

29

My childhood ended one sweltering Friday evening in midsummer.

Junebug had settled on Portland as a destination. The whole hippy vibe appealed to her on some level – she loved to doodle daisies and other flowers, and she wore a scent I later learned was called patchouli and that I can't smell without being teleported back to our motel room. She showed me the money she'd saved – a couple hundred bucks, I guess. It seemed like a fortune at the time to both of us.

That evening she was nervous. I wasn't sure why and didn't know how to ask. Around ten thirty she put me in the closet with a dim flashlight and a Spider-Man comic I hadn't read. The closet door didn't fit too well but if she kept the light on, which she mostly did, nobody noticed the glow.

I turned my back to the door and lost myself in Spider-Man. It was the one where Fusion breaks Spidey's neck, and I was so gripped that I lost track not just of time, but of what was happening in the room, though I was dimly aware of a man's voice, more talk, and less moaning and bed creaking than I was used to.

The voices got louder, which they sometimes did, but it wasn't until I heard Junebug cry out in pain that I lifted my head from the comic. When she cried out again, I clicked off my flashlight and pushed the closet door open a slit. At the time I didn't know the word for what he was doing, but I know

now that he was raping her, simultaneously beating her in the face with his fists. She tried to fight back, but he was too strong. He pulled out, pushed her back on the bed and said something like, 'You're not going anywhere, bitch.'

Then he strangled her to death in front of me.

As he pulled on his pants, I caught sight of something. It was a tattoo on his calf, a grinning skeleton holding a rifle, wearing something that looked like an old German infantry helmet from WWII. Of the entire horrific scene, it was the skeleton that frightened me most.

Why didn't I do something? Why didn't I scream, or run out of the room for help, or grab a table lamp and brain him with it? Why did I let somebody murder my mother in front of me?

All I can tell you is this: I was nine years old, I was scared out of my wits, and I had no idea even when he was strangling her that he would end up killing her. Junebug used to tell me 'We're survivors, you and me', and I believed her because she had survived a thousand things already.

I guess I trusted her to survive this too.

And running out into the hallway, or into the street, and shouting for help? That would only bring the police, and they would be unable to ignore this, so there'd be another round with CPS which we'd lose, and I'd lose Junebug, and she'd lose me.

And so I did nothing.

The man with the tattoo buckled up his belt and left my mother there, half naked and still warm.

Years later I tracked down the police report. They got an anonymous tip that there'd been a disturbance in the motel. When they got there, there was a boy of nine or so who refused to let them into the room. They had to handcuff him to get past, which is where they found the body of a known prostitute who appeared to have been manually asphyxiated. They found drug paraphernalia in the room, along with a microwave, a couple hundred dollars in cash, and a quantity of microwave popcorn. The boy was placed in the custody of Child Protective Services.

No-one was ever arrested for my mother's murder. They never even had a suspect. She was just another dead junkie hooker. Occupational hazard. After the autopsy, they cremated her and buried her in a pauper's grave. I went there once. There was just a tiny concrete slab with her name and date. Except that wasn't her name. Her name was Junebug. I never went again.

If you think I forgot about it, you're wrong. But it took me another eight years to do something about it.

30

I cruise into town as night is falling, one of those perfectly clear evenings when the blue of the sky darkens to an inky indigo and the rim of the horizon burns orange. I say town, but Milton isn't a town. It's not even something approaching a town. You could pass through without even noticing it. One road in and one road out, but there are other, bigger roads heading in the same direction, twenty miles north and south, that will get you wherever you happen to be headed, faster.

It is not a place where you arrive by accident.

The flickering streetlight illuminates a mom-and-pop gas station, with convenience store attached, stocking exactly enough to keep a body alive and supplied with reading material, tobacco, alcohol, household necessaries and sanitary supplies, and nothing more.

On the way in I pass a run-down motel with a weather-beaten sign proclaiming COLOR TV IN EVERY ROOM. It looks abandoned, except there's a light on in the office, and a female figure with her back to me, looking for all the world like one of those shipwrecked souls in an Edward Hopper painting.

Across from the gas station there are a couple of other buildings, rusting sheet metal, places to get your car fixed or a hydraulic hose repaired, or a bag of feed, or a replacement pivot for your 3-pin hitch fabricated. And that, my friends, is it.

It, except for the road on the other side of town which snakes up a hill, nothing crazy, just a couple of hundred feet, to where I can make out a single-storey mid-century ranch house with panoramic windows looking out over a deck to the town below. The windows give an unrestricted view of the road to the house, which dead-ends in a turnout a hundred yards further up the hill. A couple of acres of neatly mowed yard surround it, the brush beyond cut back for a clear view. A wire fence that is higher than it looks rings the property, a deceit helped by the slope of the hillside. The only visible sign of security is an electric gate, but I'm guessing there are kennels tucked under the deck built for one of the larger breeds of canine. It's far enough out of town to be private, but not so far the occupant can't keep a close eye on everything that's going on.

This place, it's exactly where I knew he would be.

A place where everybody knows everybody else.

A place where there is nowhere, absolutely nowhere, to hide.

A place where a visitor is an event that gets talked about for weeks afterwards.

A place where, in short, the entire fucking town is an early warning system.

There's only one thing that confuses me, and that is the forest.

It sits to one side of the ranch house, off to the right of the highway, a wooded area rising up to a hill which crests in a bluff on the other side of the road, slightly higher than the house itself. If it were me, if it were my house, it would make me uncomfortable. It offers too much cover, too many places to hide. It's not bad, exactly, but it's not ideal either.

And that bothers me, because Kondracky doesn't make mistakes.

89

So it looks like a mistake, but it isn't a mistake.

It's deliberate.

Which means one of two things.

Either it's a trap.

Or there's some other imperative, some other factor at work here I'm not yet aware of.

And what you don't know can kill you.

I've deliberately run the Jeep almost to empty. There's spare gas in the trailer, but I pull into the gas station instead and step out as if to stretch my legs.

It's full-serve, and an old-timer heads out to help me.

'Fill with high test,' I tell him, and he nods, sets about his task. He's wearing pants hitched up too high, a plaid shirt missing buttons, and a red trucker hat advertising smoked meats.

'Come far?' he asks.

'A ways,' I say.

'Just passing through then?'

'I guess.'

He nods and goes back to the gas. I turn away and glance into the lighted window of the store. There's a woman in there, blonde, fifties maybe, but I can't tell anything else. The faint sound of a radio playing seventies country music. She's singing along.

The price ticks up on the gas pump. I scan around. A couple of trucks – a seventies-era Ford Ranger and a rusting Jimmy – are parked nearby. The old dude's and the blonde's, if I had to guess. I file this away.

I look back to the house, and that's when I see it.

A set of headlights, heading down the hill.

There's only one place they could have come from: the ranch house.

I feel my heart-rate spike.

If I'm right about this place, and right about Kondracky, and right about the house, there's only one person in the world it can be.

31

I keep the truck in my peripheral vision as it rumbles up, a battered old Ford with a pair of thick-chested, square-jawed mongrel hounds in the back who look like they came free with a junkyard. It rolls right into the gas station, other side of the pump, dinging the air-line bell.

I try not to react. *He can't know who I am. It's not possible. There's no way.*

Seeing the old-timer, the dogs go crazy, up on the side of the truck bed, baying away. He heads over, reaches into his pocket, and gives each of them a dog cookie, which they take greedily from the palm of his hand. He wipes slobber off on his pants as the driver gets out.

It's him. Sixteen.

He's tall, six two or three, still an inch taller than me. His face is older that the photograph, tanned and leathery from outdoor work. He's late fifties now, maybe even early sixties, with grizzled stubble. He pulls off his trucker hat to scratch his head and I see that his hair is thinning, a little greasy.

'Mack,' says the old-timer. Apparently that's what he goes by here.

'Vern,' says Kondracky.

'Usual?'

Kondracky nods. He's wearing a flannel shirt, work boots, work pants. He moves a little stiffly but there's not an ounce of fat on him. He's all muscle and sinew. If you didn't know better, you'd dismiss him as just another blue-collar asshole in a pick-up truck.

He pays no attention to me, but I've no doubt he's already taken in everything about me, including the fact I'm not carrying. Eventually he glances over, nods millimetrically, then ambles towards the convenience store, betraying nothing.

The pump is old, still clicking away, so I move round to get a better look in his truck. The bodywork is battered and rusted out in places but it's camouflage, pure theatre – the V8 burble as it rolled in was perfectly tuned, the tyres are as aggressive as the bullbars, and a couple of inches of lift reveal high-end aftermarket shocks. Racked up at the back of the cab there's a recently cleaned Savage hunting rifle. Like the truck, it's theatre – you can score it for under 500 bucks, but it's as accurate as an Olympic target rifle, especially when partnered with a Schmidt & Bender scope worth maybe ten times as much as the weapon itself.

I guess I get too close to the truck, because suddenly the dogs lunge for me, jaws snapping in the air inches from my face. I step back in shock, and Vern slams the side of the bed, yelling, 'Get back in there, ya bastards!'

The dogs back off.

'Sorry, friend,' says Vern. 'They get a little feisty around strangers.'

Kondracky's in the store now, talking to the blonde.

'Figure I need a few things.'

Vern nods. He holsters the pump on my side, fixes the gas cap back. 'You can pay inside.'

I grab my wallet out of the glove compartment. Vern heads off to see to Kondracky's truck, and I take the opportunity to swipe my pistol too, slipping it into my jeans at the back.

The door bings as I enter. Kondracky and the blonde are sharing a joke as she rings up milk, eggs, bread, a six of Coors and a couple of newspapers. In the small of his back too, under the flannel, I can make out the shape of another pistol.

I could kill him here, I think. Fate has handed me a target of opportunity. His back to me, he'd never know what hit him.

But then I see that he's watching me in the curved mirror above the counter.

I duck behind a display rack filled with magazines, snacks and trinkets, and pretend to browse. There's another curved mirror at the end of the aisle. Again, I see Kondracky glance up, still watching. I have to remind myself: he hasn't made me, it's just training, habit, that hard-wired situational awareness that manifests as the absolute need to know where everyone around you is at all times. I suffer from the same thing.

Kondracky pays and heads out to his truck, not giving me a second look.

I go to the counter with a family-size bag of Hot Doritos.

'Find what you were looking for, hon?' She smiles. Her voice is husky from cigarettes. She has an amateur tattoo half hidden under one short blouse sleeve that hints at a more interesting past than you might expect.

I smile back. 'Sure did.' She rings me up.

I head out towards the Jeep, but as I do I almost bump into Kondracky, heading back in.

He holds the door open for me, grins. 'Ladies first.'

The fucker. It's a perfect ambush. He's not sure about me so he came back for seconds. He's holding the door open so he can get a proper, close look, close enough to smell me.

'Thanks,' I say.

I can feel the gun in the small of my back, and he's going to be looking for it. But I'm wearing a down puffer jacket, thick enough to hide it, so I just sail past with the Doritos, heading for the Jeep. I can feel his eyes boring into me.

'Hey kid,' he says, as I pull open the door. 'What's your business up here?'

I freeze, play innocent. 'What do you mean?'

He nods at the Jeep. 'Arizona plates. Long way from home.'

'Rental,' I tell him. 'Picked it up in Milwaukee.'

'What you hauling back there?'

The U-Haul, still riding low.

'Piano,' I tell him.

'Yeah?' He closes the door again, heads over, all smiles and friendly interest. 'Long way to go for a piano. What kind?'

'Chickering Quarter Grand,' I tell him. 'Nineteen eleven, light mahogany. Got it from an estate sale. Five grand, probably worth five times that once it's cleaned up. Two or three of those and I made my year. You play?'

'Used to,' says Kondracky. 'But I quit.'

And with that he heads back into the store, bell dinging behind him. I climb into the Jeep and watch him for a second. He points to a box of ammo on the shelf and the blonde gets it for him. I fire up the Jeep and pull out. Through the window, he watches me go.

Did he make me? I don't think so. Some kid hauling a baby grand across South Dakota. It's just stupid enough to be true. If he checks the piano story he'll find a Chickering Quarter Grand in need of restoration sold for $4,800 at auction a week earlier in Milwaukee.

Just not to me.

32

I turn back on to the highway the same direction I was going. Two miles later, with no other vehicles in sight, I hang a left and follow dirt roads to loop back to the other side of town. There's nothing out here, just a farm every mile or two. Forty-five minutes, two wrong turns and a tricky U-turn later, I land back on the highway.

I missed it the first time, but a few hundred yards before the motel I see what I'm looking for – a logging road heading up into the forest that sits the other side of the road to Kondracky's place. For a second I consider the motel – my shoulders ache from driving, I could really use a stiff drink and something more than Hot Doritos for dinner, and my lizard brain is curious about the female figure I glimpsed in the lighted window – but the risks are too great.

So instead I turn up on to the muddy track, past the PRIVATE PROPERTY sign, the Jeep and trailer lurching in the ruts of the track, until I'm far enough off the highway that I'm confident I can't be seen. Then I kill the lights and engine, recline the seat, and let the desire to sleep overwhelm me.

33

The iPhone alarm shrills me awake just before first light. The inside of the Jeep is damp from condensation. I wipe the glass clear, to see mist rising from the floor of the forest, silver-blue in the dawn.

The U-Haul trailer is packed tight, but the things I need are all accessible. Amid the petrichor of damp earth and pine needles and the squawking of crows, I unload into the rear of the Jeep, then back the trailer into a clearing and cover it with camouflage netting and foliage. The tyre tracks are unavoidable, but you could drive past up the hill and never even see it.

I have topo maps of each of the locations, but I only need the one which includes Milton. You can see most of this shit on Google Earth, but in the field hard copy is everything. I mark the position of Kondracky's house, a second spot that looks likely, and figure out how close I can get before I need to start hiking.

I drive another mile and a half up the forest track before it peters out entirely. Nobody's been up here for months, maybe years. The only signs of human existence apart from the track itself are a few old shotgun shells from hunters. I pull out my backpack, throw another camouflage net over the truck, take a compass bearing, and head for the second spot I marked.

A half-hour later I crest a rise. Dawn is breaking, a choir of birds harmonising the dawn chorus, but it's still dark enough that I see the light of the house glimmering in the distance.

The spot I chose is perfect, high enough to overlook Kondracky's abode a half-mile or so away, but far enough back in the bush that unless I do something stupid I'm not going to give myself away.

I pull off my backpack. There's a high-powered spotting scope and tripod inside. I check through it, and there he is, Kondracky, moving around his house in a T-shirt and boxers, fixing coffee and filling the dogs' bowls with food.

I pull out the rest of the contents of the backpack. Bivouac bag, two camouflage sheets, some rope, MREs, waterproofs, a notebook and a pencil. I set up camp, using more branches and foliage to break up the shapes I'm making. And I settle down to watch.

34

I watch him for five days, each morning a little colder, a little more damp, and a little more uncomfortable.

The days are almost identical.

He makes coffee, he feeds the dogs, and then he takes a shit. Before breakfast, he works out, alternating cardio with body-weight exercises in a basement gym I can just glimpse through the walkout under the main deck. Then a half-hour with a punchbag. Then a shower.

After breakfast, he pecks away at a typewriter, letter by letter, agonisingly slowly. The words don't come easily. Sometimes he sits there for half an hour not writing a thing, or gets up to stare out the window. He gets through a couple of pots of coffee before lunch, which he makes with the oxymoronic approach to nutrition of his genera-tion, taking pills and juicing carrots, then slapping baloney and alfalfa between slices of wholewheat slathered with Miracle Whip.

He tries to write in the afternoon but he generally gives up after an hour, and occupies himself instead with housework or playing with the dogs. Then, as the light fades, he cracks open a beer, cooks dinner, and settles down to watch TV. His favourite is cable news – every night, in between the ads for reverse mortgages, there's another story about the situation in Iran, which seems to be heading for some kind of pointless military climax that will cost blood and gold and achieve nothing – but sometimes he gets bored. At one point he watches a British baking competition for two hours solid.

Around ten he pours himself a Jack. He's in bed by eleven thirty. The dogs sleep outside, roaming free in the grounds. He doesn't feed them at night. He likes them hungry while he sleeps.

Almost identical, because after he showers and before he starts writing he picks up a white egg cup he keeps on the kitchen table and rolls a single die.

It takes me three days before I get it: the die is how he keeps his routine unpredictable.

The first day, he spends an extra hour on the treadmill.

Day two, he cleans weapons, bringing them up one after another from what I can only presume is a well-stocked armoury in the basement, tucked out of sight at the back of the house, where it folds into the hillside.

Day three, treadmill again.

Day four, he sets off on foot out of the house, accompanied by the dogs, carrying a chainsaw. He follows the road as it dips out of view, and I lose sight of him, but after a couple of minutes I hear the buzz of the two-stroke. It comes a couple more times, increasingly distant, then an hour and change later he heads back, saw in hand, and into the house.

Day five, there's something odd. When he sees the die roll, he smiles. Then he loads the dogs into the truck, hooks the rifle up on the rack where I saw it the first day, opens the electric gate, and heads down the hill.

I need to know where he's going so I jump up and sprint after him. The road snakes down the hill but I half run, half skid down the fall line over logs, boulders and streams to keep him in sight. Then as I shoulder through a thicket, the ground abruptly disappears from beneath me. I flail into mid-air, weightless, then the hidden drop slams me into steep rock, tumbling me head over heels until I manage to grab on to a sapling. I hang there for a moment, trying to figure out if anything's broken. It isn't, so I let go and slide the rest of the way down to where the slope flattens out.

By the time I find my feet again Kondracky's truck has gotten away from me completely.

I'm sweating, bruised, and covered with mud.

Only it doesn't smell like mud. Because it's not mud. It's shit.

I have literally rolled in some animal's shit.

I try to wipe it off, discovering in the process it contains berries, moth wings and what appears to be fur. If I were more au fait with the natural world this would probably tell me something useful and important, but I am not and it doesn't.

With the remnants of the scat still clinging to me, I take the opportunity to scout the road. The windows of the house may or may not be bullet-proof, but I can't take the risk. He's momentarily available in the transition from the house to the truck, but the shot from my bivouac position is too long to attempt on anything but a static target, and again I can't take the risk of missing.

As I get closer, I immediately understand what Kondracky was doing with the chainsaw. Every possible vantage point, each place where the road bends, forcing a vehicle to slow, anywhere there's a pinch point, has been cleared, the brush cut back a hundred yards or more into the forest, every trunk under four inches removed, every vestige of understory cleared to make concealment impossible.

Which suggests that Kondracky regards the road as a weakness.

Which suggests it is.

35

There are three sharp bends in the road as it winds down into town, places where he's forced to slow, heading towards or away from me, to give me a straightforward shot. But they've all been clear-cut to deny them, so now I'm looking for something else. Something subtle, perhaps almost invisible. A potential vulnerability Kondracky, who never misses anything, might have missed.

It takes three hours pushing my way through thorns and brambles before I locate it.

It's a fourth bend in the road. It's subtle, barely there at all, just a jink really. The brush hasn't been cut back, presumably because Kondracky didn't consider it necessary. But as I push my way through the undergrowth, clambering over rocks and dodging between tree trunks, I unexpectedly find a position that could work. A foot to the left, a foot to the right, there's nothing. But here, in this exact spot, a little higher than the road, looking down on that final subtle bend, there is, just maybe, a shot.

Everything about the shot is insanely difficult.

The distance – 200 yards – is the easy part. In ordinary circumstances I can pick a fly off of his windshield at that distance. But these are not ordinary circumstances.

For a start, the vehicle is moving left to right, which means I have to follow him. The grade is downhill, so his truck will be moving fast, barely slowing for the corner, then accelerating downhill with a straight shot down to the highway. He drives slower uphill, but the angles don't work, his roof blocking the shot.

Second, at around 40 mph, he's exposed for less than a second. Less than a second to find the moving target, settle, and fire, with no chance whatsoever of a second shot.

Third, and this is the clincher, there's no visibility on the target until the very moment it appears between the trees. The road is completely masked at all points north. That means there's no way to predict the exact moment he appears. The only clue is the sound of the engine, but it's not nearly enough.

Then there's the bail route, or more precisely the lack of. If everything goes to shit and, God forbid, I miss or only wound him, I have a 400-yard uphill sprint followed by a twelve-minute drive down a muddy, deeply rutted forest track that only emerges on to the highway in one place.

Meanwhile, he has a straight shot into town then down the highway to cut me off.

I time my route and use Google Earth to figure out his travel time.

No matter what I do, he gets there first with a minute to spare.

No pressure, man.

It takes me twenty minutes to get back to the top, and I'm almost there when I hear the familiar engine note. It's Kondracky, heading back up. I drop to my elbows as the truck roars past, engine straining against the grade. As it passes, the two dogs leap up from the bed, barking frantically. I glimpse Kondracky peering up from the driver's seat, a bag from the convenience store and a couple of newspapers beside him, but he can't have seen anything, because the truck continues up, noise of the engine fading until it's just me and the forest and the sound of the rain.

Gentle at first, but then louder, great drops cascading down, ripping through leaves like bullets. By the time I make it back to the bivouac I'm already soaked.

36

It rains all day and all night, and then does it all over again.

I'm cold, I'm wet, I'm uncomfortable, but I've had far worse and my mind is on the shot. Kondracky has had years to prepare for this. I owe myself at least a couple of days to think.

I watch him make breakfast, lunch, dinner, feed the dogs, drink, scratch his balls, work out, clean weapons, and mainline cable news.

The primetime shows are all Iran, all of the time. The captions tell a story of their own.

Iran Denies Nuke Plot
UN Briefed in Closed Session
Russia Backs Iran, Warns NATO
Terror Messages Used Weapons-Grade Encryption
Navy Places Sixth Fleet on Alert

In between the news blasts, there are panels of talking heads yelling at each other amid library footage of tanks and helicopters and aircraft carriers and missiles and mullahs and oil wells burning in the desert, and the occasional mushroom cloud. It's obvious where this is headed.

My mind inexorably goes back to Berlin and my part – if that's what it is – in the debacle.

I still don't know what 'Parachute' meant.

I still don't know how Kovacs knew to find me in the bar, or who was paying her.

I still don't know what game Handler is playing.

I still don't know what was hidden on the memory card.

And I still don't know what Sixteen has to do with any of this, if anything.

I shake my head clear. My job here is Sixteen. I cannot allow myself to be distracted.

And yet, and yet, and yet.

I am just watching Kondracky turn off Fox when I hear the crack of a dead branch behind me.

I spin round, rolling on to my back, pulling the pistol I brought with me from the Jeep.

It takes a moment for my eyes to register the reality of what I see.

It's a bear.

A motherfucking bear.

Huge, brown, ugly, with shaggy wet fur and piggy eyes. Twenty yards away, and rearing up on its hind legs to get a better look at me.

Well, I think to myself, *at least I know what bear shit looks like now.*

It charges.

37

A .38 between the eyes will stop even the biggest and meanest of bears, but Kondracky surely knows the difference between the clap of a pistol and the crack of a hunting rifle. He'll come to investigate, the dogs will lead him to the dead bear, and the .38 in it will destroy any chance I have of taking him unawares.

So I do the only other thing I can think of, which is to run.

Now, you may have heard that you can't outrun a bear, but the bear is 600 pounds minimum, and I have run this route once already trying to keep up with Kondracky. With the bear thundering down the slope behind me and my feet slipping and skating on rock slicked by rain, I beeline for the outcrop where I fell before. Just before the edge, I hook on to a tree trunk to stop my fall and swing sideways. The bear thunders past, so close I can smell its breath, swiping at me with a claw that rips my jacket to shreds, and though it tries to stop, its enormous momentum sends it hurtling over the edge.

It's not a cliff, just a fifteen-foot drop to a steep slope, but it's enough to send it tumbling downhill like a hairy bowling ball. I flail back uphill, using every atom of parkour energy and knowledge I have. As I do, I pull my knife, using it to stab the ground for purchase and haul myself up. And I'll fight the fucker with it if I have to. Below me, the bear scrambles to a stop, and sets off again after me, massive claws ripping gouges in the forest floor as it gallops upwards. I use hands, feet, tree trunks, rocks, saplings, anything to speed me forward, dodging left and right, gasping for air, quads and thighs burning, heart pounding out of my chest. I look back to see the bear is gaining on me, eyes black with ursine fury.

I make the Jeep a second ahead of the bear. It makes a final lunge for me as I get the door open, but its massive jaws snap shut on air and it comes crashing down on the hood. It swipes again, taking out one of the headlights, and its claw catches in the camouflage netting, which rips off as I frantically gun the engine, slam the Jeep into reverse, and hurtle backwards away down the forest track.

The bear lopes after me, still half tangled in the netting, but its heart is no longer in it, and the last thing I see is its ugly backside sashaying back downhill to investigate what's left of the MREs.

38

I skid to a halt a couple of miles down the track. I sit there for a moment with my head on the wheel, still gasping for air and wondering if I'm going into cardiac arrest.

I am not. But I am cold. I am wet. I haven't slept or eaten properly for five days and I'm shaking from the bear attack, can still smell its omnivorous stink.

Rain hammers on the hood and streams down the windshield. There are supplies a mile back in the U-Haul, but I'm not going to risk a second round with the bear. I could sleep in the Jeep, but I've seen videos of what bears can do to a truck if they're hungry. This one has my spoor and definitely now regards me as food.

It's tempting to simply hit the highway, drive to a town an hour away, find a motel and straighten myself out. But it's late, the bear has taken out one of the headlights and I risk getting stopped by a cop who is liable to start asking questions I'm in no position to answer.

The truth is, I'm off-kilter in this place. Sometimes, the last few nights, when I close my eyes I see that stupid woman, her face twisted with loathing, hurling the speakerphone at me. Other times it's a man's staring eyes, his guts ripped open, my hands covered in blood, and the lights of an U-Bahn train bearing down on me. Or the crumpled body of a woman lying in a hotel tub, one hand hanging limp over the edge, showing a chipped fingernail.

There's a part of me that wants to do what Kondracky did: simply disappear. But Kondracky quit while he was ahead, and I'm behind. Quitting makes me a loser, and being a loser will put a target on my back for the rest of my life, which is likely to be measured in months, if not weeks.

So: I can't stay in the forest, and I can't regroup in another town, and I can't quit.

There is another possibility: the worst, apart from all of the others. After ten minutes of consideration, my heart-rate finally dipping under triple digits, I point the Jeep downhill and turn right on to the highway towards a crooked neon sign promising COLOR TV IN EVERY ROOM.

39

The parking lot is empty. I don't need the Jeep to be seen from the road, so I splash through the potholes to the rear, where the only vehicle is a decaying Isuzu Trooper parked near the garbage bins. I head back round to the front. A sign on the office door says CLOSED but there's a light on inside, so I rap on the door.

After a while a girl appears. I say girl, but she's mid-twenties with a bob of black hair and some kind of floral-print thrift shop number of a dress. But as she comes up to the door and stares at me – bedraggled, muddy and clearly in trouble – what really strikes me are her eyes, emerald green set against skin which seems somehow simultaneously dark and pale.

She points at the sign and mouths 'Closed'.

'Please,' I mouth back, showing her I'm soaked through, opening my jacket to show I'm not hiding anything. Which I am: everything.

She doesn't realise I can read lips – everyone should learn – because she says 'Fuck's sake' to herself, unlocks the door, and opens it about an inch.

'What?'

'I need a room.'

'So?'

'Sign says you have vacancies.' I point at the neon.

'We're closed.'

'Please. I really need a room.'

'Come back tomorrow, you can take your pick.'

She goes to close the door again, but I jam my muddy boot in.

'Tonight,' I say. 'I need a room tonight. Now.'

'Listen, friend,' she says. 'You don't want me to call the cops, you get your fucking foot out of my door now.'

'How much?'

'What?'

'I'll pay whatever you want,' I tell her. 'Name your price.'

'Cash?'

'Cash.'

She opens the door a crack wider to get a better look at me. 'What happened to you?'

'I got chased by a bear.'

She peers behind me at the empty parking lot. 'How'd you get here? I mean, you walked, what?'

'I parked out back. There's some stuff in my Jeep I wouldn't want to lose.'

'Nobody boosts shit in the rain,' she says, which is perfectly true.

'City boy. Old habits, I guess.' I smile what I hope is a city boy smile.

'200 bucks.'

'A night?' I say, incredulous, though I'd gladly spend ten times that much right now.

She goes to close the door.

'Okay, okay,' I say. 'Two hundred. Whatever.'

She opens the door to let me in.

The office is shabby, with crooked blinds that don't close and a water-stained drop ceiling with one tile out. She watches me sign in then takes the book and reads the name.

'"Jones"?' She looks up, blowing a strand of hair out of her eye.

I don't have a type. But if I did, it would be girls who blow strands of hair out of their eyes.

'You need ID?'

I have it, close enough to real it makes no difference.

'Cash deal.' She shrugs. 'Don't need it.'

I fork over twenties.

She counts them. 'Two days?'

'Maybe more, maybe less. Just so you don't kick me out after breakfast.'

She turns to the board of keys, each with a rustic wooden fob. Evidently there are no other guests, because all the keys are there. She takes one at random. 'Here.'

I stare at the fob. It has '17' burned into it with the tip of an iron.

'Last unit that way,' she says, pointing. 'Near where you parked.'

'Seventeen? I only counted eight units.'

'Used to be sixteen. But one side burned down, so we had it demolished. That left nine through sixteen. Nobody ever wanted to stay in thirteen, so thirteen turned to fourteen, fourteen to fifteen, fifteen to sixteen, and sixteen to seventeen. So seventeen is really sixteen, if you see what I mean.'

The universe has chosen today to fuck with me.

40

The room is pure 1980s motel chic. A tube TV, queen bed with a threadbare yellow counterpane, hokey art of a sad-eyed child on the wall, AC unit stuck in the window, a flimsy door that only closes with a shoulder push, and a carpet riddled with cigarette burns. In the drawer of the bedside cabinet there's a Gideon Bible someone has illustrated with dick pictures.

Motels and me, well, you know the story there. Suffice to say this place gives me flashbacks.

The bed sags when I sit on it, but at least the sheets are clean when I turn them back.

I flick on the TV, still curious about Iran. Not that I give a shit, I tell myself, but if the world's about to blow itself to pieces and you might have had a hand in it, it's nice to stay informed. However, there's snow on every channel. I pull out my phone but there's no signal, nor any sign of wifi.

I trudge back through the rain to the office, where the door is again locked. I hammer on the glass and the girl appears again. She grudgingly unlocks the door, opens it a crack.

'TV's out in my room,' I say, holding my hood over my head against the downpour.

'Sorry, got behind on the bill.'

'What about the internet? Do I need a password?' I pull out my phone.

'There's a socket next to the phone where you can plug in.'

'Plug what in?'

'The cable.'

'You have one?'

'Not any more,' she says. 'They kept getting stolen.'

'Jesus Christ.' I can feel myself starting to lose it.

'Listen, "Jones",' she says. 'I'm not the one who came pleading for a room because I got my ass chased by a bear. You're welcome to find alternative accommodation if we don't meet your standards.'

'Okay, look, I'm sorry,' I say. 'It's been a long day. I just really need to make a fucking phone call, and I can't get a signal and—'

She holds up her hand. 'Go back to your room. Dial 1 for an outside line, wait for the dial tone, then you can call whoever you want. Twelve bucks a minute long distance. Local's free.'

'One other thing. Any chance I could get something to eat?'

'Restaurant's closed,' she says. 'So's the bar.'

'Fifty bucks for a burger and a beer.'

'Sixty.'

41

The shower is weak but at least the water's hot. By the time I exit, my skin is pink and for the first time in days I am not shivering. Freshly scrubbed, I dial for an outside line.

Dial. There's literally a dial. An avocado-green phone with a handle, a curly lead and a rotary dial. It takes me a while to figure out how it works, but I finally get the hang of it, feeling like a character in some goddamn seventies movie. Finally I get a proper dial tone and laboriously enter Handler's digits. The first time I get it wrong and someone's *abuela* answers in Spanish. I apologise and try again. This time I get his voice.

'Handler.'

'It's me,' I say.

'Where are you? What the fuck's going on? Why is this line so bad? Are you done yet?'

'I'm in a place called – let me just check – oh yeah, Buttfuck.'

'There's actually a place called Buttfuck?'

Handler is from California. He does not have a highly developed antenna for sarcasm.

'No,' I say. 'It's not actually called Buttfuck. And no, I am not done yet.'

'What's the hold-up?'

'I got chased by a bear.'

'Are you being sarcastic?'

Like I told you.

'No,' I say. 'An actual, literal bear.'

'Wow. That's a new one.'

There's the sound of a voice on the other end of the line. Male or female, I can't tell, and I suspect it doesn't much matter to Handler as long as they're young. It's telling him to roll over, and I realise he's getting a massage.

'So what's the lay of the land?' he asks.

I'm on a landline, so I need to be even more circumspect than usual. I do my best to explain the situation, keeping it as vague as I can.

'Cut the shit,' says Handler. 'You can do it or you can't?'

'I'm just saying, it's not exactly a straightforward assignment,' I tell him.

'Huh,' says Handler, packing so much implication into the single syllable that I'm surprised it doesn't collapse into a black hole. It's followed by a silence, and I wish I could tell what Handler's thinking because the next thing out of his mouth is entirely unexpected.

'You want to call it off, just say the word.'

'What?'

'You're running out of time,' says Handler.

'You didn't tell me there was a deadline.'

'I mean you're running out of time before certain people take the view that you're not up to this,' he says. 'That you're stalling.'

'I am not fucking stalling.'

'I'm just saying, if the job isn't done promptly, my clients are going to start exploring other avenues. That's just how it is.'

'Wait, you've already had this conversation?'

'You do the job,' says Handler, 'and then there's nothing to worry about.'

'Fuck you.' I am yelling now.

'Listen to me, kid,' says Handler, and there's a tone in his voice I've never heard before. 'This is business. My business.

Thirty years of this shit and I'm still here. Why? Because I provide solutions, not problems. And right now you are showing every sign of becoming the latter. I like you, I count you as a friend. But in the end it's simply business. If you live or die, I don't give a shit, as long as the job is done and my clients go to bed happy. Now, are we clear?'

My mind is so full of the desire to stamp on his face I can barely speak. But I master myself.

'Look,' I say. 'It's all under control. Nobody needs to explore any other options. Your clients will go to bed happy, I guarantee it. You tell them the truth, that I've never let you down. Tomorrow I'll scope the route again. There's one spot that's a possibility. Okay?'

'Okay,' says Handler.

'We good?'

'Just fucking get it done,' he says, and hangs up.

I sit there for a while, the receiver in my hand. Handler has never spoken to me like this. It means something, but I don't know what. And as I sit there I become aware of something else. There's static on the line, no doubt a by-product of the mid-century piece-of-shit phone, the cheap-ass mouse-bitten telephone wire throughout the motel and whatever antique switchboard system there is at the front desk.

But there's something else too. It sounds like breathing. I listen for a moment, then there's a soft 'click' and it stops.

42

Hair still damp, I head back to the front office, partly because I am still hungry but also because I need to know if the girl was listening in.

The sign still says CLOSED but the door is open. The bell dings, and I follow the sound of canned music to a tiny wood-panelled restaurant tucked away at the back, complete with hunting prints, a deer head, a couple of tables and a fake-wood Formica bar with a bunch of dusty well drinks. There's Coors on tap and a few premiums in the fridge.

A table has been set for one. I take a seat, and the girl brings me out a cheeseburger and a Sam Adams, lays it down without comment, then takes up a position at the bar where she watches me eat, yacht rock oozing out of a ceiling speaker.

I pull out a book and read it with one hand, feeding myself with the other.

'How's the burger?' she says, eventually.

'I swear to you this is the best goddamned burger I have ever tasted in my entire life,' I lie. 'And this—' I take a swig of stale Sam Adams, 'this is the goddamn nectar of the gods.'

'Maybe I should raise my prices.'

I go back to my book, but she keeps watching me.

I don't know if she listened to the phone call. But she's curious about me, and she's smart. And because she's smart, her curiosity is an asset. This fumbled attempt at a town is Kondracky's intruder alarm, but the more curious she is about me the less likely she is to alert him. There's no trace of anyone else living here, or even working here, and her tough act is pure defence, the scar tissue of someone used to living on her own. If I intrigue her, so much the better. She'll want to keep me as a curiosity all for herself.

'The bear,' she says, out of the blue. 'Black or brown?'

'Brown.'

'So you were up on the ridge?'

'How'd you know?'

'That's where she lives. Her name's Martha. You were lucky. She had cubs last year, no way she'd have let you go if you'd gotten between her and them.'

'You know this because?'

She shrugs. 'Hunters. That's our main business, in the season at least. Rest of the year, pffft. Martha's kind of a mascot. The regular hunters leave her alone. So, what were you doing up there anyway?'

I lift up the book and show the cover: *Birds of the Dakotas Field Guide, Third Edition.*

'I got an alert about a Great Kiskadee up here.'

'A what?'

'Great Kiskadee. *Pitangus sulphuratus.* Lots of them down in south Texas and Mexico, but you hardly ever see them up here. Handsome bird, bright yellow chest, black stripe on a white head. Flycatcher family. They saw the first one up here back in 2016, made all the papers, but nothing since. Trying to get a shot of it, you know.'

I mime clicking a camera shutter.

'That's what's in the truck. Photo gear. The big fast lenses are four figures. I have insurance, but they don't insure not getting the shot. Got into a tussle with my agent earlier. That's why I needed the phone. He's afraid we're going to get scooped.'

'Your agent?'

'Client is *BirdLife* magazine. Editor is afraid *Bird Watcher's Digest* will get the scoop. He's so fucking paranoid he won't even let us mention the bird's name on the phone.'

She stares at me, unable to work out if I am shitting her or telling the truth. Which is just what I want. If she listened to the phone call, now she's running back through it in her mind. Is *that* what they were talking about? If she goes to check the Jeep, she'll see well-thumbed copies of both magazines on the passenger seat, and a blanket thrown over what might or might not be camera cases in the rear.

I finish the beer, wipe my mouth with a paper napkin and deposit it on the empty plate, snap the book closed and stand.

'Anyway, it's been a day. Thanks for the food. Okay if I settle up in the morning?'

She nods.

I head out into the parking lot and back to my room. I wait ten minutes, then I slip out again, head round the back of the motel to where a light is on. There, I find it's coming from a back office, with blinds open enough for me to see through, where the girl is tapping away on an ancient Dell desktop surrounded by piles of ancient comics. I glimpse a *Spider-Man*.

Well, I guess we have that in common.

Her browser pulls up a page of search results. She clicks through to the first, and the screen fills with the unmistakable plumage of a Great Kiskadee.

43

The shot isn't just difficult. It's impossible.

I'm in position, rifle on its tripod, scope adjusted, breech and magazine empty, tucked in behind a screen of foliage. I've been here four and a half hours, waiting for an opportunity to check out the hit in real time. Finally it happens: a bright yellow propane truck appears and grinds up the hill towards Kondracky's house to fill the tank. The driver evidently takes his time to shoot the shit with Kondracky, because it's two hours before I hear the sound of the propane truck heading towards me. I snug the weapon to my shoulder and slow my breathing.

The yellow of the truck appears in my sights a moment sooner than I expected. I adjust my aim as quickly as I can, trying to re-establish my cross-hairs on the driver's head, but by the time I pull the trigger and – *click* – dry fire, I'm targeting solid rock behind which the truck just disappeared.

The problem is reaction time. Humans react far quicker to touch and sound – an insect landing on you, or a rifle shot – than to visual stimuli. My reactions are fast – the psych student who measured them said they were the fastest they'd ever seen – but the lag is enough to deny the shot.

If I could practise for a week, learning the way the engine sound bounces off the rock wall before it becomes visible, I could improve my odds. But I don't have a week, and I'm not sure I could get them past fifty-fifty.

And fifty-fifty isn't close to good enough.

I dig around in the U-Haul for ten minutes before I find what I'm looking for: a set of wireless surveillance cameras, cute little things the size of a pack of cigarettes. Plus a USB-powered wifi router, a set of lithium polymer batteries, climbing gear, and a toolkit which includes a battery-powered soldering iron.

Sitting in the Jeep, I check the LiPos are charged and wire the cameras to use them instead of their internal batteries. That should keep them running for forty-eight hours or more. The last LiPo I solder to a USB cable to run the router. I get it all running and make sure I can log into the cameras from my iPhone, using the router as a repeater to boost the weak signal. The cameras are weatherproof but the router isn't so I wrap it in a black garbage bag and tape it closed.

I use the last light of day to head back towards the road and rig the cameras, using the climbing gear to mount one thirty to forty feet up in a tree at each of the first three bends where the brush has been cleared. I checked for Kondracky's own cameras yesterday on my way back up, but he's old school and I found nothing. I locate the router where it can see the signal from all of the cameras up in another tree, then hike down to my firing position to check my phone can see the signal from the router. I log into each camera in turn, using an app designed for home security to scroll from one to another. The first is labelled 'LIVING ROOM', the second 'HALLWAY', and the third 'BEDROOM'.

It works.

There's still one more thing I need to do.

I head back to the Jeep, out of the forest, back into town, flick my lights off and head up the winding road towards

Sixteen's eagle nest. I'm not going all the way, just a couple of hundred yards past the second camera. There I U-turn, and head back down past HALLWAY to BEDROOM, then count the seconds before I reach the slight final bend.

Exactly eleven seconds.

I hold my breath as I pass, half expecting him to be there, taking the shot instead.

When he isn't, I'm almost disappointed.

Maybe this fellow is human, after all.

44

The first rule of cover is *play your cover* so I head back to the motel to shit, shower, shave and get the stench of Deet off.

Hair still damp, clothes clean, the copy of *Birds of the Dakotas* in one hand and oversized wooden key fob in the other, I head back to the office. The door's unlocked. I follow the sound of soft rock to the snug back room, where I find her propped up behind the bar, reading, with an open beer beside her. She glances up as I enter and sends a second beer, already open, sliding down the counter towards me. My hands full, I barely catch it, but I do and it's ice-cold.

She nods at the table, where a burger sits on a plate.

'Saw you come in,' she says by way of explanation, 'after, you know, "bird-watching".' She doesn't actually air-quote it but her eyebrows take up the slack. 'Figured your dining options were limited. Plus, I could use the cash.'

'Thanks,' I say, and settle down to the burger.

'Any sign of the Greater Kiskadee?'

'The Great Kiskadee,' I correct her. Is she testing me? 'Caught a glimpse, just for a second. Bright yellow, but it was moving too fast to get a shot.'

I give up on the burger, which is borderline inedible, as was the last. 'What you reading?'

She lifts the book, and I'm surprised to see it's a dog-eared copy of Sun Tzu's *The Art of War*.

'You read it?'

I shake my head.

'Bullshit,' she says with a smile. 'Everybody's read it. It's such a cliché they put it on the reading list for MBAs so assholes in suits can pretend they're samurai when they're screwing someone on an equity split. I once saw it quoted in *Teen Vogue*.'

'Yangban,' I say.

'What?'

'Sun Tzu was Chinese. Samurai are Japanese. The Chinese warrior class were Shi.'

'Thought you hadn't read it.'

I hold up my hands in admission. 'Birding's a highly competitive field.'

'So's high school,' she says. 'This and Machiavelli were the only things that got me through. You want to know my favourite part?' The book falls open naturally to a page. '"If you wait by the river long enough, the bodies of your enemies come floating past." No kidding. Charlene Brady, homecoming queen and alpha bitch, got herself knocked up a month before graduation in the back of a Camaro by star quarterback Jimmy McIvor. Real prize. Flipped the Camaro while he was drunk and gave himself a traumatic brain injury. Subsequently got fifteen to life for a home invasion, left her living in a trailer with four kids, a bad perm and a meth addiction. Sometimes the bodies wash right up. You done with that?'

I nod. She clears away the half-eaten burger, then finds another couple of beers, plunks them down, and sits opposite me.

'These on the house, or . . . ?' I ask.

'Depends,' she says.

'On what?'

'The quality of your conversation.'

'I can't promise anything.'

'That's okay,' she says. 'I have low expectations.'

125

45

'You ever hear of Sarkis Soghanalian?' I ask her.

'Should I have?'

'Arms dealer in the eighties. They called him the Merchant of Death. The CIA hired him to sell arms to Saddam during the Iran–Iraq War. He sold guns to everyone, always with the backing of the CIA, who protected him. Made millions, lived large. Then when the Gulf War broke out he went public. Blew the whistle to *60 Minutes*. The Americans turned on him, just like that. He was arrested and convicted, then bartered his sentence down by informing on other arms dealers. But by the time he was let out, the world had changed. The Cold War was over, so most of his contacts were no longer of any use. But he carried on spending like a drunken sailor. Died broke.'

'Huh,' she says. 'Bird Boy knows this how?'

I shrug. 'Went down the Wikipedia rabbit hole one day.'

'Okay. And?'

'He used to say the secret of good conversation was talk with your ears and listen with your mouth.'

'Is that supposed to mean something?'

'I figure it means you tell a person who you really are by asking the right questions.'

She thinks about this for a moment, then looks me in the eye.

'Fine, Sarkis. Have at it.'

'Name?'

'Kat.'

It suits her, the monosyllable as sudden and inscrutable as a stubbed toe.

'Short for?'

'Not short for anything. Kat. That's my name.'

'Okay, here's what I really want to know. What the hell are you doing here?'

'Here, in this room? Here in this motel? Or here in glamorous Buttfuck?'

Buttfuck. Is she telling me she listened in?

'I'm guessing they all have the same answer.'

The look she gives me tells me I'm right. She hesitates for a moment, as if deciding whether I'm worthy, then flicks her eyes around the room. The wood panelling, the laminate counter, the prints, the trophy heads. 'This place . . . it was my mother's. She was a hippy chick, believe it or not, kind of a wild child, only she was fifteen years too late for Woodstock. Her grandparents had this place in the fifties, then after they died, nobody else in the family wanted it and it wasn't worth the trouble to sell. She was up in Marin County by then, some kind of commune, but life wasn't going so great . . . the last dregs of the hippy movement wasn't a whole cavalcade of fun, all acid casualties and balding guys who viewed chicks as common property and the word "no" as a bourgeois affectation. So she blew off the commune, packed what she had into a suitcase, took a Greyhound here, moved in, cleaned up, and started running it.'

'Your father?'

'Literally some guy who passed through one day.'

She tries to make it sound casual. It isn't.

'You never tried to track him down?'

'She never gave me anything to go on. Made it abundantly clear she had no interest in me knowing who he was. As far as

I can tell she regretted the whole thing. I mean, we got on okay, I never starved, but becoming a parent really wasn't part of her agenda. I think she'd have been just as happy without me. Happier, probably.'

'Christ, that's harsh.'

'No, just true. I always felt like an alien here. Skipped town as soon as I finished high school. I was big into comics back then, so I went to State for illustration, worked my ass off to pay my way, made enough bad choices to pave a driveway, then a couple of years into it, Mom got sick. Cancer, started in her breast, ended up in her brain, only it wasn't fast. She couldn't handle the place on her own, had no insurance, so I dropped out, came back to take up the slack. I ended up looking after her. Four years later, she died.'

'I'm sorry.'

'Yeah. Means a lot, thanks. Which left me, and this place. Couple of years now.'

'How's it going?'

She looks around. 'How does it look?'

'You never thought about selling it?'

'It's not mine. She never got the title. Besides, guy I knew from high school, his grandma died, left him a house round here. He sold it and bought a mattress.'

She looks around again, a little sadly.

'It's a shithole and all, but she spent her life here, half of it. It's all her, all of this. What am I supposed to do, leave it to rot?'

'You get lonely?'

She smiles. 'You think there's some other reason I'm talking to you?' Then the smile fades. 'After I left, I used to come back sometimes. Christmas, Thanksgiving, that kind of thing. And I'd see girls I knew, girls a couple of years older, and they were already becoming their mothers. Like it was obligatory, a kind of mission. And I used to swear to myself, make myself a promise that I'd never let that happen. And here we are.'

She lifts the yellowed book, detached pages off-kilter with the rest, others folded down to mark their place. '"To know your enemy, you must become your enemy." Yay, me.'

'Sometimes you just have to cut bait,' I say.

'Easier said than done.'

I shake my head. 'The hard thing is being who you've always been. Who your circumstances made you. Who you've been told you are for the whole of your life. You didn't choose that person, so why should you *be* them? You can choose to become someone else any time you like.'

'Are we talking about me or you?' she asks.

'I made my choice a long time ago.'

'Was it a good one?'

'It's a lot better than who I was before.'

She nods. She's quiet for a moment, thinking.

Then she looks me dead in the eye.

'You're here to kill him, right?'

46

A perfect sucker punch. And she's watching for my reaction.

Listen with your mouth.

'Excuse me?'

'The only reason you're pretending to be interested in my life story is because you want to know how much I know,' she says. 'Well, here goes. Yes, I listened to your phone call. No, you weren't talking to your little buddy about snapping some goddamn bird. Yes, there was a Great Kiskadee in South Dakota four years ago, but it was a unicorn, a once-in-a-lifetime thing. No reason to expect it back and no chatter on the birding forums. No photo credits to "Jones" in *BirdLife* or *Bird Watcher's Digest* or any other birding magazine. You lecture me about Chinese samurai and arms dealers. You camp out in the bush when there's a motel in town, and the only reason you turn up here at all is because you got your ass chased by a bear. You park out back so nobody knows you're staying here. The magazines are a nice touch, but there's no Audubon sticker, rookie error. You pay cash, and sneak out before dawn, clearing your room first so there's nothing for anyone to find. Did I miss anything?'

'Jeep's a rental,' I say. 'The Audubon sticker's on the VW wagon, but I needed 4x4.'

'And the rest?'

'I have literally no idea who or what you're talking about.'

She nods towards a beige phone on the wall behind the bar,

130

with a tangled curly cord like you see in old sitcoms. 'So it'd be okay for me to call him up now?'

'Who?'

I try to keep my voice relaxed but I can hear the tension in my throat.

'The guy you're here to kill. The same guy who offered me a thousand bucks to tell him if anyone turned up here whose story didn't check out. You want to know how badly I could use a thousand bucks?'

She takes in my silence. 'Okay, then, let's do it.'

She rises to get the phone, but I grab her wrist, hard.

She glares at me. 'Get the fuck off me.'

'Sit down,' I tell her.

'Let go of me.'

I do. The white mark where I held her slowly fades.

'So. Are we done pretending?'

'Look,' I say. 'If it's money you want—'

'If I wanted money I would have called him already.'

'So why didn't you?'

'How do you know I didn't?'

'Because I'm still alive,' I say.

'You see?' she says. 'Now we can have an actual conversation.'

47

She goes to get two more beers.

The sensible thing to do is simply bail. I'll be on the road by the time she calls Kondracky. There's no way he'll come after me, because that would be exposing himself. Maybe I'll get pulled over for the headlight, but fuck it. I'll regroup. I'll come back with a Plan B. Stronger, better, faster.

But this time he'll be ready for me, assuming he doesn't come for me first. And there's Handler's ticking clock to consider. At this point retreat looks a whole lot like defeat.

There is another option.

There are no other guests, and it doesn't look like there will be any time soon. Given the story she just told me, no-one would bat an eye if she simply left one day, and probably no-one would miss her. There probably wouldn't be a missing persons report filed for months.

But then I remember the weight of Kovacs slumped in my arms, the smell of her hair as I dumped her in the bathtub. And Kovacs was a professional, someone who'd been in the game for years, knew what she was doing, and had tried to kill me. This girl, she's a civilian. And besides.

Besides what?

I watch her for a moment opening the bottles, her back to me. And her slender figure suddenly takes me back to a Formica table under a flickering light in a 7-Eleven on Walker

Way, watching Junebug pay for slushies from money she earned an hour ago and that she should be saving for her escape.

And I know I'm not going to do it.

48

'So,' she says, dumping a beer in front of me. 'The truth. You're here to kill him, or . . . ?'

'There is no "or",' I say.

'Why?'

I don't answer. She flicks her eyes over to the phone. The implication is clear.

'Because certain people want him dead and they think I'm the only one who can do it.'

'Are you?'

I nod.

'Has he killed people? Mack?'

I nod.

'And you?'

I nod.

'So, that's what you do? For a living?'

I nod. She's quiet for a moment, taking this in.

'It bother you?' I ask.

It takes her a moment to answer. 'Should it?'

'It does most people.'

'Do I seem like most people?'

'No,' I say. 'I will give you that.'

'Well, then,' she says, shrugging. 'It's like the man says: "He who wishes to fight must first count the cost."'

I watch her drink her beer for a moment, sensing I'm missing something, something that explains her. But I have no idea what it might be. Maybe she doesn't either.

'Listen,' I say. 'Kondracky gets wind you know anything—'

'Kondracky? Who's that?'

'Guy you call Mack. Writes spy novels as Sam Kondracky. Right now, as far as he knows, you're not in the game. You know anything that puts you in the game, such as who he really is, you become a target. He's not known for leaving witnesses.'

She's silent for a while, stirring the O of condensation left by her beer with her finger.

'Mack's a killer, huh? Makes sense. I never liked him.'

'He do something to you?'

'What? No. He used to come by sometimes, at night, when Mom first got sick. He was new in town back then. They'd sit here, like you and me, only she couldn't drink because of the chemo.'

'They had a thing?'

'He never stayed the night, not that I knew of. I don't think she even liked him that much. She used to call him "that asshole" behind his back. But she got lonely sometimes, and she was scared, and I think it helped to talk to someone, even if it was only him.'

'But you have a problem with him because . . . ?'

'He was weird around me. Wouldn't look me in the eye. He'd come in the back way so he wouldn't have to talk to me at the front desk. When she died, he came to the funeral, but he didn't talk to me. Didn't say he was sorry. Didn't even acknowledge me. Then two weeks later, once he realises I'm not going anywhere, he offers me a thousand bucks to act as his snitch. And still won't look me in the eye. I truly can't tell if he's afraid of me, or he wants to nail me, or he just fucking hates the sight of me.'

'Or maybe you just remind him too much of her.'

She looks at me, amused. 'Well, aren't you the romantic?'

135

I probably don't have to tell you that nobody has ever accused me of that before.

'Anyway,' she says. 'In short, fuck that guy.'

We drink some more. For some reason the truth about what I do doesn't interest her that much. And as far as I can tell, for all her threats she has absolutely no intention of alerting Kondracky. But I need more than that. I need to be sure. So I make a decision to spill my guts, telling myself it's purely instrumental, a tactic to build an emotional connection. Nothing more.

I tell her about Junebug, the motel rooms, the nights under fluorescent lights in the 7-Eleven, my familiarity with corridor ice machines. Junebug's crazy, doomed plans, the closet, the Spider-Man comic, the tattoo, the cop with the moustache. CPS, juvie, David, the midnight prayer sessions, and what happened afterwards. Not everything, but enough.

She listens, quiet and intent, only interrupting me to clarify the odd detail. And like I say, it starts as a tactic, trying to manipulate her into some kind of misbegotten loyalty, a belief in some kind of phony emotional bond, but it turns into something entirely other. I suddenly find the words flooding out of me, unstoppable truths, things I'd buried or forgotten or placed on high shelves, far out of reach, in corners of my memory where I no longer choose to visit.

I tell her things I have never told a living soul before.

At the end of it, she just sits there quietly for a moment.

Then what she says is, 'Poor fucking kid. I can see why you chose to become somebody else.'

For an hour or two, I almost forget about Kondracky. But as the clock ratchets towards midnight I make some dumb joke about turning into a pumpkin. I need to sleep, to clear my head, to be ready for whatever the next couple of days will bring.

Kat clears the empty bottles off the table, wipes it down, then walks me to the front door. As she holds the door open, the cool night air blows in, and with it a sense of possibility that has me standing there a moment longer than I should.

'So,' she says. 'You're really going to do it?'

I nod. 'You going to tell him?'

'No,' she says, and I believe her.

I'm about to say something else, but she closes the door and locks it.

49

In the blurred state between wakefulness and sleep, I run over what I have to do in the coming days, trying to wear a groove in my subconscious like a point guard visualising a three-pointer, and in the process attempting to calm the waves of memory still lapping over me from what I told Kat in the bar.

I'm almost asleep when a noise at the door jolts me out of bed, pistol in hand, adrenaline pumping. I sprint to the door, keeping low and away from the window, bare feet silent on the carpet, just as a key turns in the lock and it opens.

I'm ready to put a bullet in Kondracky's head, but it's not him.

It's Kat, with a half-drunk beer in her hand.

She takes in my gun, where I'm standing, and without saying another word, puts the bottle on the table, pulls off her top and skirt, and climbs into bed.

My rule has always been no entanglements on mission. Kovacs was different: the job was done. But it's too late. I'm mid-mission and we're entangled. For reasons I can't properly explain we're entangled as *fuck*.

She already knows more about me than anybody else on earth.

She could kill me with a single phone call if she wanted to.

I slip into bed beside her. My hand locates the small of her back.

I'm searching for an exit wound. I don't find one.

50

I dress in layers, trying to ignore the knot in my stomach.

Handler was right: I never fully paid my dues. I fought my way to the top but I never defeated the champ. Today the bill finally comes due.

It's still dark, but I've been awake for an hour. There's no sign of Kat, her side of the bed neatly made. For a second I wonder if I imagined the whole thing but there's a half-empty bottle of Coors Extra Gold on the table, a dark hair on the pillow, and a vestige of her scent still clings to me.

I sit on the bed to monitor my pulse. I can't get it below fifty however slow and deep I breathe. I try to convince myself that this adrenaline is necessary, that it will give me the edge I need. But I can't help thinking about Kat, about the feel of her skin on top of me and underneath me.

I shake it off as best I can and pull on my coat, feeling in the pocket for the keys to the Jeep.

They're not there.

I experience a moment of mental freefall, like reaching the bottom of the stairs only to find there's another step. Then I see them on the bedside table. I pick them up and head out with my things.

I climb into the Jeep. The sky is beginning to lighten. I think about Kat again. I have no intention of ever coming back this way, nor of leaving her any way of finding me. But as I start the engine, I have that feeling again, that sense of freefall. I look over to the motel office. The placard is still turned to CLOSED, and there's not a light on anywhere, not a single sign of life. The highway sign is still lit, but it now proclaims NO VACANCY.

Something is happening to me. It's been happening ever since Berlin. The keys are a symptom, a clue. The woman hurling the speakerphone at me was a clue. Kovacs with her shaking hands and her chipped nail was a clue. Kat's scent lingering on me is a clue. My pulse is a clue.

Even the fucking bear was a clue.

Suddenly, and without any consciousness of making a decision, I find myself climbing out of the Jeep, heading to the motel door, and hammering on the glass. It's almost an out-of-body experience, watching myself. *What the fuck are you doing? How do you think this girl is going to save you? Why are you trying to drag her into this? What good can possibly come of it?*

There's no answer.

I hammer again. Still nothing.

One more time.

Nothing.

I climb back in the Jeep.

51

I turn left off the highway, up the forest track to the U-Haul, unload what I need, then drive the Jeep as close as I can to my position by the final corner. Day is already breaking and I have wasted crucial minutes in the motel parking lot staring into the void.

I choose the lighter of two ghillie suits in the trailer. It's not as effective, but the thick one is monstrously heavy and hard to get out of. The rifle I choose is a standard M107, the lighter version of the Barrett .50, not as accurate at long distances, but I'm not pushing the envelope here, at least not for the gun. I strap a pistol to my leg just in case. And that's it.

I leave the keys in the Jeep, and head down my bail route. I'd have cleared the brush to make escape easier, but it would give the game away. Brambles rip at my face and snag the ghillie suit as I make my way down to the corner.

I find my position. Nothing has been disturbed. Good.

I set up the rifle and tripod, make final adjustments to the focus, and ensure my shot is clear. I chamber a round. I turn on my iPhone, setting it against a rock, and log into the surveillance cameras. I check they're all working, and the battery levels.

I flip to LIVING ROOM, the camera that looks out on to Sixteen's house and gates.

There he is.

Kondracky's in the kitchen, frying eggs. The die lies on the table, next to the white egg cup. He must have already rolled. He's making odd movements and it eventually dawns on me that he's dancing, probably to some corny-ass country music radio station, the only kind they have out here apart from the Christian stations, soft rock oldies and the one on the nearby reserve, which would be my preference. He seems happy, which is something I haven't noticed before.

I check my pulse. It's hovering at fifty or so. The cloud of existential dread that enveloped me earlier is beginning to lift along with the threads of mist that snake between the trees. This is what you do, I remind myself. This is your comfort zone. This is who you are.

I snug the rifle a little tighter to my shoulder.

He does the dishes, wearing pink gloves and cleaning them with a white plastic scrubby brush, then dries them on a tea towel and puts them away. The dogs snake around him, hungry as always after a night without food, but for some reason he doesn't feed them. I see him bend down to one, scratch it between the ears and say something, but the picture is too fuzzy at this magnification to read his lips.

He finishes up, looks out the window for a moment, pulls on a coat, then picks up a set of keys. And it hits me: I'm not going to have to worry about the batteries lasting.

I slip the safety off.

Kondracky's electric gate opens and the truck curls out. The dogs are in the bed, jowls flapping in the wind. The truck slides off the first camera and I swipe to the next. Now I can hear the distant V8 tone filtering towards me as it bounces off trees and rocks. But there's something else too, something I can't quite make out until the truck enters the view of the second camera. The sound dopplers as Kondracky takes the

bend, window wound down two-thirds of the way, and I realise what the sound is.

It's the Eagles. 'Take It Easy'. He's singing along. Is he
mocking me? I square my eye back against the scope. My
heart thumps. I take a deep breath, hold it. Thump, thump,
thump.

Kondracky slides out of view and I swipe to the third
camera. The Eagles are getting louder.

I move my finger to the trigger.

The gap between the second and third cameras is the long-
est stretch. I try to concentrate on my breathing but unwanted
images flood into my mind: the contorted face of the woman
pitching the phone, the dead weight of Kovacs' body, her
cheek against mine, still warm. My hand inside the guts of the
bearded man, groping blindly in his entrails for the memory
card. Kat's body tightening around me. The weightless feeling
of not finding my keys.

My left hand is slippery with sweat. I wipe it against my
right sleeve as Kondracky's truck appears in the third camera.

I see him clearly now. The rifle behind him, the dogs grinning in the back, all muscle and tongues and teeth. Kondracky's
singing along. He looks like a man without a care in the world.

He turns the third corner, and slips out of view. The engine
note rises. He's headed towards me. I take my left eye off the
phone, close it, so that all I can see is the scope, take up first
pressure on my trigger finger, draw a final deep breath, and
begin the count I rehearsed in the Jeep.

Eleven.

52

I was seventeen the first time I killed someone.

Junebug's death flipped a switch in me. There was a diagnosis in the medical notes that followed me year after year from foster home to children's home to secure youth facility – *Antisocial Personality Disorder* – a not-so-subtle code for the forbidden word 'psychopath', but I've met enough to know that whatever I am, it's not that.

A series of overworked child psychs tried to get me to talk about my feelings, and I didn't have the language at the time or any interest in explaining myself, but the whole point was I didn't have any. Not any more. The only way to be rid of the pain of losing Junebug was not to feel anything. And if the world could be like that to me, then I could be like that to the world.

It was a child's reasoning, but I was still a child.

The axioms of my new logic were both simple and powerful.

If I saw weakness, I exploited it.

If I saw strength, I undermined it.

If I saw something I wanted, I took it.

If someone fought me, I fought back harder.

There was no place for emotion in my new existence, only sensation. From the age of ten onwards I chased it as if my life depended on it. In a way, it did. Adrenaline, drugs, alcohol, sex, every kind of risk. The docs and social workers wrote it up as self-destructive behaviour, but they were wrong. The sex, the drugs, the fights were what *saved* me, because the only viable alternative I could see was to head over to Walker Way, say a prayer to Junebug, and step in front of an RTD bus.

And so, eventually and inevitably, aged fifteen I ended up in juvie, full of rage, with a reputation and booking sheet to match. That's where I met David.

Ten.

53

David was a guard. He wasn't huge, but he worked out, lifting weights in his basement at night. He was a born-again Christian, an evangelical, and a lay preacher in the church he attended twice a week. It was one of those big, mostly white, evangelical places where they preach the gospel of prosperity, which is to say give you permission to do what the fuck you want to who the fuck you want, as long as they are smaller or less powerful than you, because Jesus has already given you an endless supply of hall passes.

David had short red hair and a shiny, smiling face that looked unthreatening. He was regarded by the management as a model employee, someone who bonded with the inmates. They didn't call us that, of course – officially we were 'residents' – but we were prisoners just the same. David was a good influence, they thought, a role model even.

What they didn't realise, or pretended not to notice, was that some of us were afraid of him, and with good reason. During the day there was nothing to fear, but when it was his two weeks to pull nights, he would wait until the other guards were asleep, or drunk, or fucking each other, or simply glued to the TV, and then he would stroll out of the guard office and down the hallways to whichever room he chose that night, and let himself in, carrying a Bible, a nightstick and Taser, for what he liked to refer to as a prayer session.

Prayer sessions began with the two of you sitting on the bed together, the Bible open on his lap, only partially concealing his hard-on, and ended in one of two ways. Either you sucked him off or let him rape you – dealer's choice – or he would beat and Taser you before hitting the panic button for backup. At which point half a dozen of his buddies would pile in and very, very methodically kick the shit out of you.

I had only been in the Sacramento facility for two weeks when David came into my room for the first time. It wasn't just that I was new: it was also that I was small for my age and slender – I was at the beginning of my final growth spurt – which turned out to be his type. I was on to him from the beginning: I knew exactly what his friendly manner and shiny face portended. When he took my hand in his, put it on the Bible and began to recite the Lord's Prayer, I snatched it back and told him to go fuck himself. He Tasered me so many times I shat myself, then he called his buddies, and I left the room on a gurney with a ruptured testicle, broken ribs, a detached retina and a concussion that had me seeing double for six months.

I was back in the facility a week later, and a week after that he returned to my room, and every week after that until I was finally released at the end of the following year, with six weeks tacked on to the end because of my 'attack' on David during our first prayer session.

Nine.

54

David didn't know it, but he had taught me something.

Sitting there each night, waiting for the sound of his foot-steps in the corridor outside my room, I had time to think. I realised I was letting my anger get the better of me. I realised that once an institution had power over you, you were lost. The institution, the system, the people in it, could hit back harder than you ever could, and with total impunity.

The only way to fight them was not to fight.

Instead, I learned a skill. I learned to dissociate, to with-stand torture by going somewhere else until it was over, until he had done. And instead of fighting back, I stored my anger up. I treated it as an asset, banked it, nurtured it, watched the balance grow until it could be used.

I celebrated my release from juvie, and from David, with a Slurpee on Walker Way. There under the fluorescent lights I drank a toast to Junebug, and swore to myself that I would never see the inside of a facility again. I would never ever place myself in the situation where another person had control of my body or my actions. People are always surprised I never served a day in uniform, but that was never an option for me. I would find another way.

My seventeenth birthday was a week later, that January, and I used the tiny amount of money I'd saved up to buy a gun from another kid I'd met in juvie. I didn't know anything about firearms, but it didn't matter. I practised on that gun: stripped it, cleaned it, dry-fired it a thousand times. Blockbuster was already dying by then, but I had a job in one of the last stores, and at night I would watch movies, endless movies, always about the same thing. Revenge. My favourite by far was *Point Blank*, Boorman's 1967 flick with Lee Marvin and Angie Dickinson, the one where he's shot at the beginning and you can't quite tell if he's alive or dead throughout the whole thing. It has a kind of brutal dream logic to it, which resonated, because my life up until then had had a similar trajectory.

There's a shot in that movie, the iconic shot that everyone knows, where Lee Marvin is walking down a corridor. He only wants one thing: what he's owed. He walks down the corridor. And walks, and walks, the steel toe taps on his shoes echoing. He's unstoppable, relentless, terrifying. And all he's doing is walking down a corridor.

I wanted to be Lee Marvin.

Eight.

55

The Blockbuster job paid for a room in a boarding house where I worked out. Thanks to my growth spurt, I put on six inches in a year. I was still slim, but I'd installed a bar to do chin-ups in the door of my bedroom. By the end of March my muscles were still the same size, but I could bounce quarters off them.

At the end of the last week of March, on the Friday, I bought some nice clothes. A pair of chinos, a checked shirt with short sleeves, some dress shoes. On the Saturday I got my hair cut short. And on Sunday morning I went to church, the same church I knew David went to. I sang all the hymns and said all the prayers. After the service I hung around, and asked the elder who approached me offering coffee in a paper cup if there was anything like a prayer group or Bible study. Why yes, he said, and pointed out David, who was standing at the front surrounded by a knot of young people, a mousy woman who could only be his wife standing next to him.

Seven.

56

David heard his name, turned, and saw me heading towards him.

He had no idea what to expect, but I simply smiled and shook his hand.

'You probably don't remember me,' I told him. 'But you were very kind to me when I was in the Sacramento facility.'

'Right, yes, of course,' he stammered. 'This is —' and he used my real name here, my dead name. It was one of the last times anyone ever used it in my presence. He introduced me to the others, including his wife. Told them what an excellent student I'd been, and invited me to their Wednesday evening study, which I learned took place in a side room of the building we were in.

I don't know if David was fooled, or he was just playing along. I've thought about it a lot, and I've concluded it was the former. He was cunning, but he wasn't smart, and he had a narcissist's ability to believe the best about himself. After my initial stomping, I'd gone along with whatever he'd wanted, because I knew there was no way I could beat him there and then, but I also knew that if I stored up all the hatred and anger I had in my heart for him, it would become a mighty and unstoppable force later on, the kind of monumental vector of revenge that I would later associate with Lee Marvin.

So what I think happened was, he thought somehow that I'd come round, that I'd become dependent on him, that he turned me, that I'd become his pet. Something like that.

Six.

57

The first two weeks, I barely spoke to him. He was nervous at first, but I smiled at him, and sometimes when we were supposed to be praying I would look up and catch him watching me, and smile again, a little shyly. I left the gun at home because I couldn't trust myself with it, and I needed him to trust me first.

The third week, at the end of the meeting when the other kids were standing around in knots chatting or putting on their coats and heading out, I went up to David, waiting until his wife Sandy who ran the session with him was out of earshot, put my hand on his, and asked him if it would be possible for us to have a one-on-one session. I told him there were some things that had come up in the prayer session – things I didn't feel comfortable discussing in the group – I needed help with.

He pulled his hand back quickly and looked me in the eye, as if he couldn't tell if I was serious or not. I just smiled blankly. He glanced over to his wife, licked his lips nervously, and said, yes, well, maybe it would be possible. He would need to check if the vestry was free, but – next Monday?

The week crawled by. At Blockbuster, I watched Lee Marvin over and over again. On Sunday, I went to church, but David and I didn't speak, just exchanged a glance. As I was leaving I felt a touch on my arm and turned to see him.

He was sweating. He told me the vestry was free, and he would meet me there at seven the following evening.

Five.

58

On Monday, I called in sick to Blockbuster. I packed every-thing I owned, which wasn't much, into a suitcase. I stripped, cleaned and reassembled the gun, loaded it and put spare ammunition in my pocket. Then I walked to the church, forty-five minutes, taking a circuitous route because I didn't want to make it easy for the cops to figure out where I'd come from, but also because in my head I'd become Lee Marvin, and I was walking down a corridor to take my revenge.

Clip, clop, clip, clop.

I got there five minutes early. I was going to wait out of sight, but David had gotten there earlier. I'm guessing he was more nervous than I was. I knocked on the door, which was locked, and he let me in, then locked it again afterwards. I followed him into the vestry, which was a comfortable kind of living room with a coffee table, posters and book-cases. There was a couch and two armchairs. I sat on the couch but he took an armchair, and started rubbing his hands together like there was something he needed to get off his chest.

'Look,' he said. 'Before we start . . . I just want to say . . . I'm sorry.'

David apologising was the last thing I was expecting. I could feel the weight of the gun in the small of my back under my checked shirt, but I could sense my inner Lee Marvin was ebbing away. No, I screamed internally, don't apologise. Don't say you're sorry. I don't want you to be sorry.

Four.

59

I needn't have worried. What is it they say, character is destiny? Whatever David meant to say when he set out, however genuine he was or wasn't, he just couldn't help himself.

'I mean,' he said, 'I'm sorry you took things the wrong way that first night. You have to understand ... I was scared. I didn't have a choice. I know the boys roughed you up pretty good when they came in, but they were just protecting their own. Anyway, I'm glad we were able to get past that. When you first walked into the church, I was surprised, I'll admit. But I'm glad you're here. I always thought we had ... a connection.'

'I wouldn't be here otherwise,' I heard myself say.

'So, was there something particular you wanted to talk about?'

'Like I said, it's personal,' I said, and moved over, making a space for him on the couch.

He got up, sat next to me, his right leg touching mine.

'It's okay,' he said. 'You can tell me anything.'

By now there was a familiar little tent forming in his dress pants.

'Maybe we should pray first,' I said.

He nodded and bowed his head, taking my left hand in his right.

Three.

60

'Our Father . . .' he said, then opened his eyes again in surprise. Because my hand was crushing his, bending the fingers back painfully. I guess that was the point he finally saw in my eyes what I intended. His hairy left fist came swinging at me, but he was too slow. The gun was already in my right hand, and I slammed it with all the force of my Lee Marvin rage, breaking his nose and teeth and maybe his jaw as well. He grabbed his face, wailing in pain. I stood up and pointed the gun at him.

Ever since that first time, with one exception, I have prided myself on killing people quickly. I take no pleasure in suffering. But David, he was different. I didn't waste words on him. The bullets were my language now. I killed him slowly. I put one in his left ankle to stop him running. Then one in his right. Then his knees. Then I pointed the gun at his head. He put up his hand in self-defence, so I grabbed it and shot him through the palm, his own personal stigmata. I did the same to the other hand, the hands that had touched me. Then I shot him in the balls. The last round, I put the gun in his mouth, pressed it against the roof of his mouth, and blew the top of his head off.

Two.

61

It never bothered me that he was gay, or whatever he was. I've been with both men and women. David was my first man, but I'd looked at boys before that. I think all men do at some point, though most won't admit it. Maybe he picked up on that too. Maybe that's why he came in that first night. No, it wasn't anything like that. It was the abuse of power, the sadistic knowledge that he could get away with it, his unshakeable belief that there would be no consequences, that he had been given the gift of impunity, the keys to the sexual kingdom. That was why I killed him.

I stared at his dead body. Like Junebug, years before, it was no longer a person, just a thing. And in that moment, I felt my anger evaporate. It was done, and all I felt was the emotional equivalent of a shrug. I thought about arranging him as if on a crucifix, mostly to confuse people, but it seemed like an amateur thing to do, and the one thing I knew, the one thing I knew with absolute certainty, was that I had no interest in being an amateur. I wanted to be a professional.

One.

62

No truck.

63

For a fraction of a second I think I've counted wrong, but then it appears, higher in the scope than I was expecting. I reacquire Kondracky's head, settling it into the reticule.

After I killed David, I changed my name and lit out for the territory, or in my case, Montreal, via upstate Vermont where the border is permeable. I had wasted years on anger and sensation, so before anything else, I had to educate myself. I spent months in the vastness of the Grande Bibliothèque, where one of the hundreds of books I read told me not to pull the trigger, but to squeeze it gently past the first point where the mechanism begins to bite, entering a kind of Zen void where you're no longer aiming, but part of an entangled system of weapon and target. If you're doing it right, the actual moment you fire is involuntary, almost a surprise, as if the gun had fired itself.

I'm past first pressure now, trigger finger squeezing, in that liminal zone where the gun could fire at any moment. In less than a second Kondracky will disappear behind a rock wall, my chance lost. But the gun isn't firing. It's as if my subconscious is deliberately intervening, running interference on my hand muscles, playing for time.

Maybe it knows something I don't.

Maybe I'm not going to fire. Maybe I'm just going to let him slide out of view. Maybe I'll unload the .50, pack my things back into the U-Haul, head down to the motel and see if Kat is back yet. The rest – well, we'll figure it out somehow.

And then I hear it. The soft click as the pawl, polished to reduce friction, releases. The springs – two coils removed to reduce the trigger pressure – driving the firing pin forward, striking the primer, igniting the main charge. The deafening crack, the shudder of the recoil against my shoulder, the bullet leaping away from me, autonomous, a free agent.

It's a perfect shot.

There's just one problem.

The motherfucker ducks.

PART THREE

64

The shell goes through the open window on the driver's side, past the back of Kondracky's head, and out through the passenger window, shattering the glass.

It takes me a moment to register what happened. I lift my head from the scope in shock. Kondracky is out of sight now, but I hear him slam the truck into a handbrake turn and floor the gas, tyres squalling in protest.

He's heading towards me.

How? Then I see what until now I hadn't seen. An old logging track running up the hill, so overgrown with understory it's almost invisible. You'd never see it unless you were looking for it, and I wasn't.

The adjoining forest, the uncleared corner. They weren't mistakes, liabilities, or oversights. They were assets. Intentional vulnerabilities directing anyone who came at Kondracky to a pinch point. A weakness in his defences to which we'd automatically be drawn. Believing we were making our own decisions when we were following a route he laid out for us. Imagining ourselves predators, when we were prey.

My guts knew this. I didn't, but they did.

His 4x4 comes crashing up the hill towards me. The oversized mud tyres and bullbars suddenly make sense. I raise the M107, but with the tripod it's far too heavy and there's no chance I can still make the shot with the truck lurching up and down, obscured by foliage. So I lower my aim and put two rounds in the engine block. Steam geysers out. I hit the radiator at least, but that's not going to stop him yet.

I turn and sprint up the bail route, dropping the rifle and pulling the .45 out of my leg holster as I go. The ground is still slick from the rain, and I lose my footing twice as the terrain steepens. Behind me his engine whines and the massive knobbed tyres throw up fountains of mud as they flail for purchase on the steep track.

I'm headed for the Jeep, but zigzag to keep Kondracky guessing.

I find traction again just as he loses his, the truck sashaying sideways as he hits a steep, rooted patch, ruts hidden by years of undergrowth. My quads still burn from the bear chase, but I'm gaining ground.

That's when I hear him yell at the dogs. 'Sic 'im, sic 'im!'

The two massive hounds leap out of the truck bed and gallop towards me. The ghillie suit catches on brambles, snaring me. I slough it off like a snake shedding skin, but it slows me long enough for Kondracky to find his aim. The crack of a pistol and a bullet rips through the leaves to my side. Then another, then another.

Ducking low under a screen of leaves, I scramble towards the nob of the hill. Behind me the baying of the dogs tells me they're closing, but the slope is too steep for them, so they divert round it, one to each side. Behind them the truck engine note drops as the wheels catch and Kondracky's truck leaps forward.

It's a frantic, flailing 200-yard dash to the Jeep. I fly through the forest, branches and thorns whipping at my face. The dogs reappear on my flanks, converging, teeth bared and ears back. Glancing back I see the nose of Kondracky's truck crest the rise. Once he's on flat ground there's nothing stopping him. I make the Jeep, yank the door open and slam it shut just in time for the two dogs to hurl themselves up against the windows, one right up on the hood, barking viciously, trying to bite me through the glass, slobber splattering.

The Jeep engine roars into life. Kondracky plunges through the bush towards me. I throw the Jeep into reverse, the mud from my tyres spraying up and splattering his windshield, and blast backwards, my head craned round to navigate the narrow track.

Which is when I see her.

It's Kat, sitting in the back seat.

65

'Hey,' says Kat, as if this were a completely normal encounter.

She's got Kondracky's book, *Breach of Protocol*, in her lap. We hurtle backwards, the rutted track threatening to tear the wheel out of my single hand, the other clinging to the top of the passenger seat.

'This Kondracky fellow, he's pretty good. Not much description, but lots of action.'

'What the fuck—?' Up ahead there's a gap in the trees where some logger must have cleared out a spot to stage raw lumber before it got loaded. If I can just—

'Did you really think I was the kind of chick you bang on a whim and that's it?'

I guess I could tell her how I hammered on the door of the motel in the half-light of dawn, but instead I yank hard on the handbrake, and slew the Jeep round through a ragged one-eighty, mud splattering up and against the windshield so thick I have to fire up the wipers. I slam the Jeep into second and floor the gas.

'Did you kill him?'

Kondracky's truck is no longer following, but his dogs are. I can't tell if this is good news or bad news.

'Does it look like I fucking killed him?' I yell.

Kondracky's truck bursts out of the bush at right angles in front of us.

We T-bone into him. My head smacks into the windshield. Kondracky's Ford pivots sideways with the impact, and ends up head on. Kondracky pulls something from the footwell. It's a Glock 18, with a massive 33-shot magazine.

He opens up from the driver seat, blasting out his own windshield.

'Stay down!' I yell. I jam the Jeep into reverse, and skid backwards as 9mm shells thunk into the engine block.

Another handbrake turn. I overshoot and two-seventy into the logging area, which has another overgrown track leading out of it. Saplings smack against the windows as the Jeep's tyres struggle to engage the ruts.

The engine temperature gauge crawls up. *Fuck.* T-boning Kondracky must have taken out my radiator. I glance back to see he's right behind me, but there's black smoke from his hood, which means I bonused an oil line earlier. The only question is whose engine seizes first.

'Where does this track go?' I yell back to Kat, now huddled in the rear footwell.

'Nowhere.'

'Listen to me. You need to get the fuck out the first chance you get. Straight into the bush, and lie flat until we're clear. And whatever happens, don't let Kondracky see you, or you're dead.'

She ignores me, pulls herself up enough to see out the side window.

'Go right.'

'What?'

'In a hundred yards, the track splits. Go right.'

The left fork dips down, to what I can't see, the other up.

'Left's downhill. Maybe we can get to a road.'

'There's a beaver dam. It's swamp, you'll get stuck. I told you, go right.'

I haul right. I can't even see what I'm supposed to be turning into, but it's another track, even more overgrown. Kondracky's further back now, black smoke billowing. Maybe we have a chance.

'I thought you said this doesn't go anywhere,' I yell back.

'It doesn't,' says Kat. 'But there's a logging yard.'

Up ahead, it appears, long abandoned, now used for storage. Piles of rotting logs, rusting machinery. An RV on blocks, windows broken. And in the centre, a sagging barn, a hundred years old, roof rusting but intact, weathered boards broken in places.

And absolutely no way out.

Kondracky's view is momentarily obscured by a bend in the track. I yell at Kat: 'Stay down, and brace,' and jam the Jeep into reverse again, just as Kondracky drifts round the bend. He stands on the brakes, but he's going way too fast to stop and augers hard into the back of the Jeep. I guess he disabled the airbags, because his face slams into the steering wheel. He looks up, nose bloody, just in time to see the H&K I pulled out from under the passenger seat. Shell casings ricochet around the Jeep's interior as I blow a hole in the Jeep's rear window, forcing him to duck under the dash.

Kat's curled into a ball, hands over her ears. I pull one hand away and tell her:

'Get ready to run.'

I roar forward thirty yards, and jink into a powerslide, blocking the entrance to the logging yard.

'NOW.'

I roll out into the mud, yank her door open and grab her. Keeping low, and using the Jeep as cover, we sprint for the barn. Kondracky rams the Jeep, trying to bulldozer it out of the way. But after a couple of tries his engine seizes.

170

We make the barn. Kat huddles behind the rusting shell of a Chevy flatbed. There's a big sliding door at the front. It doesn't budge. I duck back behind the Chevy as bullets rip into the rotting barnboard. Kondracky's behind the Jeep, using the hood as cover.

'I can't open the door,' I hiss at her. 'There may be another round the side. When I fire, run.'

I roll out from behind the Chevy and rake the Jeep. Kondracky drops down for safety and Kat runs, disappearing behind the corner of the barn. He still hasn't seen her. I loose another volley to keep him down and follow her around the corner.

There's a workshop door. Kat rattles it, but it's locked. I blow out the hasp and kick the door open. Kat runs in. I fire a final volley down the wall of the barn then follow her inside and pull the door closed.

The only light in the barn comes from missing boards and a window covered in green moss. I roll a giant industrial tractor tyre against the door, then throw myself to the ground as bullets rip through the boards. I crawl round a corner to where Kat is huddled against a central pole that soars up to the roof.

Behind me Kondracky rattles the man-door, but the tyre jams it shut, and he knows better than to make himself a target by trying to force his way in.

I sit next to Kat on the dirt floor, and pull one of the spare mags I grabbed from the Jeep to reload. We're still alive. But we're trapped, and I have no idea how we're going to get out.

66

The dogs circle the barn walls, panting, snarling, snuffling, giving the odd woof. They must be following Kondracky as he searches for a weakness.

Kat sits with her back up against the hewn wooden post, knees drawn up.

'Do you want to tell me what the hell you were thinking?'

'I don't have to explain myself to you,' she says, refusing to look at me.

She plays tough, but I can tell she's scared. Good. So am I.

'You thought this would be fun? What?'

'Fuck you.'

'We need to get out before he gets in. And he really, really needs to not see you.'

Finally she looks at me. 'You're the one who tried to kill him, not me.'

'Too late. You're in the game now. You know who he is and what he's done. If he kills me, you're a witness. And if he doesn't, you're leverage. If you can't attack someone directly, attack something they care about. Which, to be clear, I don't, but he doesn't know that.'

'Then why do you give a shit what happens to me?'

'I hate to see innocent people get fucked by their own stupidity.'

Outside it's gone quiet. Then there's a metallic clang – the tailgate of his truck dropping as he fetches something. I stand up and peer around with dark-adapted eyes. The barn is full of old machinery, rusting implements, rotting furniture, ancient hay bales, logging chains, circular saw blades. Some of it is covered with tarps. I start ripping them off, the cheap plastic so perished it falls to pieces in my hands.

The dogs start up again. Kondracky's back, working his way around the barn perimeter once more. Only this time there's a new sound – liquid glugging on to the base of the ancient boards.

'What's he doing?' She pulls a face as the smell hits her.

I nod. 'Gasoline. He's going to burn us out.'

'Why don't we run? If we go in opposite directions he can only chase one of us.'

'Two dogs. And his gun shoots both ways.'

'So what?'

'I don't know. There has to be— holy shit.'

I pull the tarp off a hulking piece of machinery, half hidden in a stall converted to a maintenance bay. It's a logging tractor, a Kubota. Eighties, maybe, orange paint flaked with rust. At the front there's a six-foot blade, like a bulldozer. To the rear there's a winch set into an inch-thick armoured-steel plate, to protect the driver in case the steel hawser snaps. The entire cab is encased in a metal cage to protect from falling lumber.

Kondracky is halfway round now, working steadily, in no hurry.

I climb into the tractor, the controls unfamiliar. The key's rusted into the lock. It takes some effort, but I get it to turn. Nothing happens.

'Battery's dead.'

'Maybe they keep one to jump-start,' says Kat, and I suddenly get the sense that she knows her way around a barn like this. Seconds later Kat's found an ancient battery, big enough to start a train, along with a set of filthy jump leads. She hauls the battery over – she can barely carry the damn thing.

173

'You know how to connect it up?'

She unfastens the battery panel and hooks it across the terminals. 'Basic country shit. Worked summers on a farm like everyone else. Glamorous, huh?'

Outside there's a sudden, low WHOOM as Kondracky lights the gasoline that now girdles the building. The boards are tinder-dry from years of sun and wind. This place, filled with old hay bales, oily tarps, and half-full cans of chainsaw fuel, is going to go up in seconds.

'Try it,' says Kate.

The dash lights up, but that's all. 'Battery's good, but it won't turn.'

From the bottom of the walls there's a glimmer of flame, waves of smoke rolling towards us.

'Make sure you're in neutral and drop the clutch.'

I'll give her this, she knows tractors. 'Nothing.'

The barn is properly aflame now. I can feel the heat on my skin, and a cloud of black smoke is forming above us. A stack of bales in the corner has caught, tongues of fire licking towards a horizontal fuel tank with a yellow nozzle attached. A minute, maybe less, before we burn.

'Check the PTO.'

I find the PTO switch, disengage it, drop the clutch. The starter turns, but there's just a grinding noise. Above us, the roof trusses are on fire. The roof beginning to sag, embers falling, starting more fires all around us.

'Starter's seized.'

Kate picks up a foot-long wrench and whacks the starter. I turn the key. Grinding. She whacks it again, harder. The engine turns, catches a couple of time, but doesn't start.

The heat is scorching now, almost unbearable, smoke stinging my eyes.

Kat climbs in beside me. The battery is tiring. The engine turns, slower and slower.

And then, just as part of the roof gives way, it starts, the diesel snarling into life. The metal tractor cab saves us, the heavy beam bouncing off, but it crashes down on the fuel tank, which splits. It's diesel, not gasoline, or we would be dead already, but a river of oil pours out, becoming a lake, then a wall of flame in front of us.

'You know how to drive this?'

Kat pushes me out of the way. I pull the H&K, and she drops the clutch. The tractor jerks forward. Kat ladders up through the gears and raises the blade to use as a battering ram. We roar through the wall of fire and crash into the curtain doors. Flaming planks spiral through the air as we burst out into the logging yard.

It takes Kondracky's brain a moment to register the Kubota exploding out of the building and barrelling towards him before he opens fire.

Kat lowers the blade like a shield and ploughs onward. The dogs scatter, yelping and howling. I open up through the cab's metal grid, forcing Kondracky behind a stack of decaying cedar rails. I keep him there as we pass, and now the heavy steel logging guard at the back forms a bulletproof shield. There's a peephole cut in it which I use as an archer's slit.

Up ahead are the Jeep and the truck. We crunch into them like a tank. I cling on to the cage as Kat brutally forces her way through, knocking the Jeep on to its side and Kondracky's Ford nose first into a drainage ditch.

Kondracky picks himself up and fires, but the shells ping off the rear guard. Kat cranks the Kubota into a road gear, the tractor lurches like a fairground ride, and it's all I can do to cling on. Kondracky runs after us, firing, then slows. He knows he's beaten. The dogs lope after us for a hundred yards, but he calls them back.

67

Two miles down the track, the Kubota runs out of gas.

Kat wants to go back to the motel, but Kondracky's seen her now. If he gets there first we're dead meat. If he outflanks us and ambushes us on the forest track the outcome is the same. The only option is to bushwack over to where the topo map showed open farmland.

Kat isn't happy with this tactic. She also isn't shy about saying so. I finally snap.

'Christ's sake. I didn't ask you to stalk me. You knew what you were getting into and you came along for the ride. You want me to leave you as bait for that psychopath? Fine. I don't have time to babysit you through every decision. We need a vehicle, we need gas, and we need to get the fuck out of here. Understand?'

She punches me in the face. An honest-to-God right hook to the jaw.

'The fuck?'

'I just saved your life, you ungrateful piece of shit,' she yells, shoving me in the chest. 'If it wasn't for me you'd be a charred piece of meat. It's not my fault you fucked up trying to kill him.'

'Okay, so you can drive a tractor. You know how to jump-start. You can free a starter. So what? If this man gets to you, you're fucked. Fucked in ways you cannot even begin to imagine. Right now, without me, you are dead. So factor that in next time you plan on taking a swing.'

She's silent for a moment, hands on hips. 'So, what's your plan?'

'Work our way cross-country to the edge of the forest.'

'Which direction?'

I point to what I calculate is east, working off the position of the sun.

'Okay.'

I swear, she does passive-aggressive better than anyone I've ever met.

'You have a better idea?'

She points fifteen degrees south of where I pointed. 'That way, mile and a half, there's an old farmhouse. Guy lived on his own. Set himself on fire burning garbage six weeks ago. Three sons, who all hate each other, and no will. They're still trying to figure out the estate. Meantime none of them are allowed to touch any of his shit. Ten to one, most of it's still there, including his car.'

'You know this how?'

'Basic country shit,' she says. 'Everyone knows everything about everyone.'

68

The farmhouse is turn of the century, at the end of a dirt road, with a bank barn and a couple of outbuildings. Kat finds a key in a plant pot by the back door ('basic country shit'). I check out the barn – an old sofa, a pair of rusting tractors, plough, sprayers and so on. Nothing of any use. Kat thought the guy had a truck, but it's gone – probably one of the brothers took it.

All that's left is a Dodge Charger.

I'm not talking the iconic blue and red muscle car that Richard Petty hustled to victory in the 1974 Daytona 500. I'm talking a rusting, late-seventies fourth-generation land yacht, eighteen feet of shit brown with a cream-coloured vinyl Landau top and shag carpet as standard.

One blessing: it's open. I slide into the cracked red leatherette of the driver's seat and find keys behind the sunshade. I try starting it, and to my amazement, after it coughs up a couple of hairballs, it sparks into life. Quarter tank of gas, not terrible.

Kat emerges with an armful of popsicles, which were the only things left in the fridge.

'There's a gun cabinet in the basement,' she tells me. 'Empty.'

I guess the brothers got to that too. I'm almost out of ammunition for the H&K, have a spare clip for the pistol, and that's it. The U-Haul is still half full, but Kondracky may have found it. If so, he'll either have cleaned it out or is currently staking it out and waiting for me to return.

Either way.

'Here's what I figure,' I tell Kat, sitting in the kitchen, a checked plastic tablecloth between us, both sucking on popsicles, cluster flies buzzing in the window. 'We stay here until nightfall. Then we head east. That way we don't have to go back through the town.'

'Then what?'

There's tension in her voice, but she's determined not to let it show.

'Then we figure the rest of it out.'

Once the sun's over the horizon, we pack blankets and cushions into the Charger in case we need to sleep in it, then climb in. Kat drives: I figure she's better with the wheel than she is with the H&K. What she doesn't notice is that I've dropped a claw hammer and a big screwdriver into the passenger footwell. If she asks, I'll tell her you never know when you might need to break into something. But that's not what they're for, not at all.

69

We bump down the dirt road from the farmhouse to where it connects to the highway and stop a couple of hundred yards shy of the intersection. Kondracky's truck is totalled so I have no idea what he might be driving. But the road is clear.

We roll out on to the highway. The imminent danger is past, so I take the wheel, head on a swivel. But the night is dark, and apart from the odd set of truck headlights flashing past, we're alone.

We ride in silence for a while, just the hum of rubber on blacktop to keep us company. I glance over at her a couple of times when she's not looking. She's sitting back, shoes up on the dash leaving muddy prints.

'So you gonna tell me what this is really about?' I say eventually.

'This?'

'You come to my room unasked—'

'I didn't hear you complain.'

'Then you take my keys, open the Jeep, bring them back and – what? Spend the rest of the night on the back seat? You don't think this is stalker behaviour?'

'Maybe I'm just cutting bait.'

'This is not how you do it.'

'Oh. Remind me how you did it.'

I think of David, lying there in the vestry, his brains spread over the back of the couch, blood soaking into the cushions and carpet and splattered all over the light fixture in the popcorn ceiling with one bulb out and a little heap of flies at the bottom of the glass bowl.

She hears my silence. 'I'm just saying, maybe you don't get to judge.'

Her turn to be quiet for a moment, then she says:

'So, "Jones". Guessing that's not your real name?'

'Nope.'

'What is your real name?'

'Don't have one. Not any more.'

'Bullshit.'

'The first time you kill someone,' I tell her, 'you don't just kill one person. You also kill the version of yourself that never killed someone. The life they were going to live, it's gone. *They're* gone. As dead as the person you killed. The name . . . it was theirs, not yours. You don't have any right to it. It's not yours. Not any more.'

She looks unconvinced. 'And why are you trying to kill Mack?'

'Because someone's paying me.'

'Enough?'

'No.'

'So why do it?'

I hesitate. But fuck it, she's far enough into this thing now I owe her some kind of explanation. So I lay out the bones of it. And at the end she says:

'Did it ever occur to you that you are completely full of shit?'

'You think those were blanks we were firing back there?'

'No.' She settles back in the passenger seat. 'I just think there are a shitload of questions you should be asking yourself.'

'Like what?'

'Kondracky, whatever you want to call him. One day, he just quits, right? Disappears off the map, leaving a void which you fill.'

A hermit crab sliding into a shell. 'Right.'

'Why?'

'Look,' I say. 'We do a lot of bad shit. Things people don't want to do for themselves. Perfect deniability, that's the goal. Now picture this: it's an election year. New guy-stroke-gal at the White House, Downing Street. Day one, someone takes them into a room in a basement, and leaves them alone with a box. Guess what's in the box?'

'You are.'

'Me and people like me. Sixteen, others. An army of buried bodies waiting to come marching out of unmarked graves. And now they're implicated, because they know about them. And they have to choose. Do they leave the bodies buried and risk them reanimating? Or do they start cleaning house?'

'Was it an election year? When Mack disappeared?'

'It's always an election year somewhere.'

'So he disappeared because he knew he'd become a liability, and it was only a matter of time before someone like you came against him.'

'That's my guess,' I say.

'So he was afraid.'

I stare at her. 'Did he look afraid to you?'

'If he wasn't afraid, then why did he quit?'

I don't have an answer.

'You see?' she says. 'Something must have happened. Something that made him feel vulnerable.'

'Vulnerable? He's as strong as a bull. Now imagine him back then.'

'Who says it's physical?'

The thought thuds into me.

'I mean,' she continues, 'you guys, you're fucked up. All of you. You said it yourself . . . the first time you kill someone, you kill your old self. That's fucked up, right there. All those dudes who came back from Vietnam, Iraq, Afghanistan, fucked up. They killed people, they saw people die, they lived on their nerves, they were afraid every moment someone was going to blow them to pieces, and it fucked them up. So of course he's fucked up. So are you. Let's not even mention all that shit you told me in the bar.'

This is what you get for spilling your guts to someone.

'I'm not that person any more,' I tell her.

'Keep telling yourself that,' she says, and plants her feet back up on the dash.

I watch her for a moment. Her fearlessness is an act, but so is mine.

Maybe Kondracky's is too.

70

Couple of miles later she breaks the silence again.

'So, do we have a plan?'

'Unlock your phone,' I say.

'Why?'

'Because that's the plan.'

She does. I take it. One-handed, I plug in a number and give it back.

'That's my cell. There are literally two other people in the world who have it. You do not call under any circumstances unless it's an emergency. Once I'm sure we're clear, Wisconsin, say, I'll drop you with enough cash for six months. You find a big city, somewhere the other side of the country. Somewhere you've never even thought about going. Check into the most generic motel you can find. Don't use your real name. And stay there.'

'For how long?'

'Until Kondracky's dead. Or I am.'

She stares at me.

'You're how he gets to me. You bought in, and now this is the only way out.'

She bristles. 'I can take care of myself.'

'No, you can handle yourself in a dive bar when some redneck is hitting on you. This is not the same thing.'

'Are you happy?'

Wham. Out of nowhere. Another perfect sucker punch.

'What?'

'Are you happy?'

'The fuck does being happy have to do with anything?'

'If you're not happy, what's the point of anything?'

'Right now the point is to survive.'

'And then what?'

It's a good question.

'Look,' I say. 'It was a one-night stand. We hooked up. The end.'

'I get it. You're scared.'

'I'm not scared.'

'You're fucking terrified.'

'For you.'

'Yes. But not just for me,' she says. 'Slow down.'

'What?'

She nods at the road ahead, an intersection with a couple of houses, a sodium streetlight, smaller even than Milton.

'Speed trap up ahead. Cops hide in the second driveway at the end of the month when they have to make quota on tickets. Don't want to get stopped driving a stolen car, do you?'

I slow, a speed sign half hidden in shadows. Seconds later we pass the bullbars of a prowler, tucked back into a driveway, a barracuda waiting for prey. I check the rear-view. It doesn't move.

'Don't mention it,' says Kat. She settles back in her seat for a moment, then changes her mind and reaches for the radio, twirling through crackling sports talk and soporific oldies. I snap it off.

'Do you still not understand what's happening here?'

'We're trying to get away from him.'

'There is no we. *You* are trying to get away from him. *I* am trying to kill him. Kondracky can't walk away from this any more than I can. The longer it goes on, the more likely it is we

185

attract third parties, wannabes who throw their hats into the ring. At that point . . . I don't even want to think about it. But whatever happens, you're the underbelly. The place where the armour's weakest. I may or may not make it through this. But there's not a chance in hell you will.'

'What if that's a chance I'm willing to take?' she says.

I stare at her. Is she serious? She meets my eye. Evidently, she is.

'Okay,' I say.

'Really?'

'It's your funeral. Just don't blame me.'

I go back to scanning for Kondracky.

She gives me a couple of looks. I guess she was expecting me to put up a bigger fight, but whatever.

Fifteen minutes later, the red light on the gas gauge flickers on. Another ten and the lights of a gas station appear, a mini truck stop with a tiny diner and a couple of rigs in the lot.

'You fill up,' I tell her. 'I don't need to be on CCTV right now. I've got cash.'

I hand her a traveller's waistband, the kind grandads wear to the airport.

Kat looks at me with all the suspicion a body can muster, then pointedly takes the keys.

I wait until she's filled up and is inside, then retrieve the hammer and screwdriver from the footwell. The good thing about these old Dodges: they are ridiculously easy to boost. Screwdriver in the lock, three blows with the hammer, and she's yours. The engine's already running by the time Kat appears from the store, arms full of road snacks, and sees what I'm doing. She sprints towards me but she's too late: I burn rubber as I peel out on to the highway, back in the direction we came.

★　　★　　★

Kat chases me out of the gas station on foot for a hundred yards or so, then gives up. Then, as she stands there in the dark on the verge of the highway, half silhouetted in the glow of the neon signs, the lights of another vehicle illuminate her momentarily like a theatre spotlight. The full beams are so bright they blind her, and she has to raise her arm to protect her eyes until it passes.

She feels defeat wash over her for a moment, then swears to herself and heads back to the gas station to look for a ride. And as a result she doesn't notice the battered Jimmy that just passed her pull into a wide U-turn, bald tyres singing on blacktop, and accelerate back towards the diminishing tail-lights of the Charger.

I learn this, along with a great many other things, later.

71

I reach for my phone. For once there's service. I pull up a contact, dial.

It rings three times. Four.

This is the opposite of a good sign.

Finally, the other end picks up.

'What happened?' says Handler.

'What do you mean, what happened?'

'Just tell me what fucking happened!' He's yelling.

This, too, is the opposite of a good sign.

'He ducked.'

'You missed?'

'I didn't miss. He ducked. He knew I was there.'

'How?'

'How the fuck should I know? He's Sixteen.'

'And then?'

'Everything went to shit. He came after me. But I lost him. I'm going back in before he has time to regroup. But I may need some backup.'

'No backup,' says Handler.

'Materiel,' I tell him. 'He may have located my cache.'

'I said no fucking backup.' He's yelling again.

A pair of headlights flash past. I catch a glimpse. The vehicle looks vaguely familiar but I can't place it. I check the rearview, just in case. The tail-lights recede.

Everything about the way Handler is reacting is sitting wrong.

'What aren't you telling me?' I ask him.

'Kondracky,' says Handler. 'He called me.'

'What? How the fuck did he—?'

'An old number. He must have had it. The point is – the point is you fucked up. You fucked up, and you need to put it right. And you get nothing more from me until you do.'

'Look—' I say, but Handler interrupts.

'No, you look. I'm not your fucking babysitter. No things. No backup. No nothing. Come back to me when Kondracky's dead. Until then—'

Call ended.

I stare at the phone for a moment, because none of this makes sense.

Maybe Kondracky threatened him, but Handler, for all his pretensions, isn't the kind to scare easily, or renege on a contract and risk pissing off a buyer.

But he's cutting bait.

He's setting me adrift.

And there are only two reasons he would do this.

The first is because he no longer believes I can do this.

And the second—

The second I don't even want to think about.

I consider calling him back. He won't answer but that's fine. I'll leave a voicemail.

Don't worry, I'll tell him. I'm coming back for you all right. Once Kondracky's dead, I'm coming back for you with a gun in my hand, and then we'll find out who's really working for who in this arrangement.

But I don't, because I glance in the rear-view.

There should still be a pair of tail-lights from the car that passed me.

But instead a pair of headlights is gaining on me.

72

Kat drops down from the tractor-trailer. The driver, Ben, is Canadian, and she now knows the entire run-on sentence of his life, how he used to work as a stylist in music videos before setting up his own hair salon which he ran for twenty years with the woman he married until he was T-boned fair and square by a mid-life crisis, discovered CrossFit, divorced his wife, disappeared to the Amazon where he paid a substantial sum of money for some variety of drug-enhanced spiritual awakening, then reappeared with a burning desire to fulfil his childhood ambition, which was to be an ice-road trucker, which is what he now does, only – there being no ice roads during the summer – he hauls back and forth across the Great Divide from California to the Great Lakes with his mountain bike and his kayak strapped to the rear of the cab and sleeps in a tent in national parks whenever he can.

He's carrying a mixed load of patio furniture and dish-washers, destined for a Costco hub in Salt Lake City.

Ben seems nice, but a little too intense in his conviction that we are all joined spiritually by some kind of indigenous Amazonian blabla, and Kat is equal parts thankful for the ride back to Milton, and grateful it is over.

She watches Ben's rig grind away into the night, then turns back to the motel. She knew the moment she saw Jones at the wheel of the Charger what he was doing. Well, fuck him. It's not the first time a man has run away from her, and probably won't be the last.

She'll follow his advice, at least for a few weeks, but there are things she will need on the road. She unlocks the door, then locks it behind her. The office is dark and cold, and she suddenly feels oddly vulnerable. But she has no intention of being a victim, even to a supposed psychopath like Kondracky. So instead of turning on any lights, she rummages in a cupboard, locates a yellow plastic flashlight and batteries, and pulls a rusty set of keys off a hook.

She closes the blinds in the office, and heads down into the basement. It takes all her courage because the basement is nicknamed the Snakepit on account of the fact that at certain times of the year it's where snakes go to reproduce. Three years ago she went down there to check a breaker and flicked on a light to find hundreds of them knotted into a writhing mass of venomous serpentry.

Kat is not afraid of many things, but she hasn't been down there since.

Fortunately it is not one of those times of the year, so she takes a deep breath and heads down the rickety wooden stairs. Past the boiler and the crates of unused Christmas decorations, old neon signs, gilt dining chairs, stacks of laminated menus, electrical panels and boxes of dusty crockery, she finds it. A gun cabinet, filthy with dust. It takes her a few tries to find the right key, but eventually the cabinet swings open to reveal a 12-gauge single-shot shotgun. She only knows about it because her mother told her if she ever needed it, it was on the premises, left behind mid-nineties by an out-of-state hunter who never came back for it. On a shelf beside it she finds a box of shells.

She takes the shotgun. She knows how to load and shoot because *basic country shit*. She cracks it open to check the breech. It's empty, so she loads in a shell, then closes it up. She shoulders the weapon, sights down the barrel, and imagines what it must be like to kill people for a living.

73

I floor the Charger. The big block V8 responds, and for a second the lights recede, but then the Charger coughs and misfires, so I ease off to lean out the mixture. I check the odometer. This thing's been to the moon and is halfway back. I'm going to hold a grudge.

I feather the gas, keeping the V8 smooth. The speedometer crawls upwards, but the headlights are gaining. A stern chase is a long chase, but I'm almost out of ordnance, and if that's Kondracky behind me he's loaded for bear.

Just a hundred yards back now. He pulls into the other lane to come broadside. As he closes the gap, I slam on the brakes. The old guy must have been a stickler for brake jobs, because they grab hard. Kondracky rakes the Charger with fire out of the open passenger window as he sails past. Bullets tear into the sheet metal, but the Dodge was built in the heyday of Detroit from American plate steel. It's practically armour-plated.

An oncoming big rig forces Kondracky back into my lane. It flashes brights as it roars past, horn blaring. He brake-checks me, but I let the Charger slam into his rear. His back end shimmies, which tells me his tyres are bald and he's light on the rear end.

Good. My turn to pull into the opposite lane. His brake light flares as he tries to pull broadside again. But instead I steer right, clipping his rear fender. He almost loses it, floors the gas to fishtail the Jimmy back on track, but he's fighting the wheel now. I say a prayer to the Chrysler gods and aim the massive deadweight of the Dodge at his tail end again. A crunch like bone splintering, and his truck ricochets across my path, spins out of control, and catapults into a barrel roll. In the rear-view, I watch it come to rest in a field. I can't tell from the headlights which way it ended up, but a moment later they bounce back towards the road.

Christ. Maybe he's not a man at all, just some kind of semi-sentient plant life, an unkillable species of poisonous weed in human form.

His headlights pull close again. It should only be a mile or two now. He closes a couple of times, but I fire backwards, out of the window, forcing him back. Ahead all I can see is the ruler of the road fading into darkness. Did I turn the right way out of the gas station? Did I miss a turn? Did I misjudge the distance?

No, there it is. The sooty light of a lone sodium street lamp. *Here goes.*

I pin the gas. The Charger's carbs must have cleaned themselves out, because all four hundred cubic inches roar into life. The needle creeps up and up – 100, 110, 115. The Charger shakes like a washing machine on spin – the front end was janky to begin with and I've done it no favours – but I hold it there. Kondracky's lights recede, then grow again as he throttles up.

I ease off just enough to fool Kondracky that he's caught me. He pulls out to pass, redlining the Jimmy. I can picture him lining up his shot, Glock balanced on the forearm of his steering hand.

Sucker.

I lay down the anchors and kill the headlights.

Kondracky flies past me, past the streetlight, and right past the bullbars of the prowler that's still waiting there in the shadows. I pull over, invisible in the darkness, and watch the cop scream out after him, light bar blazing and siren whooping.

Kondracky holds out for a second or two, but there's no way he can outrun a cruiser and the last thing he needs is a four-county police chase that ends in a spree kill and puts him first item on the evening news. He pulls over.

I give the cop time to exit the prowler, then flick the lights back on, and pull back on to the highway at a law-abiding pace. A quarter mile down the road, I pass them. The cop's a woman, a little heavy, a mom if I had to guess. Her back's to me. Kondracky's just sitting there, his hands visible on the wheel. He watches me pass, his eyes black with hatred.

I resist waving. Not because I'm not a cocky motherfucker, but because it looks like he's decided not to kill the cop, and I don't want to provoke him.

As an orphan myself, I hate to create more than are strictly necessary.

74

Kat empties the till, keeping the office light off. As she does, headlights rake into the parking lot from the highway. Edging to the blinds, she sees a wiry figure get out of a battered Jimmy, holding something in one hand. He looks around, then strides towards the office.

Kat ducks down into the space under the counter, next to an old rusty heater.

There's the sound of hammering on the door. She holds her breath.

Then the smash of glass. The butt of his pistol, probably.

She closes her eyes. The door being unlatched and opened. Footsteps. A man's breathing. He's looking around. She can hear the pulse of blood in her ears.

He comes closer. He's at the desk now. Rustle of pages turning – he's checking the register, turning it round to read the entries.

Crunch of glass as he exits, leaving the door open.

She waits until his footsteps are halfway across the parking lot before she allows herself to breathe again. She looks at her knuckles, white in the darkness, then remembers what her hands are wrapped around. The shotgun. Her finger on the trigger.

She could have killed him there and then.

She still could.

From across the parking lot, through the open door, there

comes the sound of splintering wood as the door to one of the units is kicked open.

The noise does something to her. This place might be shit, but it was her mother's and now it's hers. An armed man breaking into a motel run by a young single woman? Justifiable homicide. And then she doesn't have to run. Doesn't have to disappear.

Doesn't have to do anything but fix a couple of doors.

She gets up, edges towards the door. The light's on in Room 17, door open, spilling out on to the ground. A shadow moving around.

She exits, stepping around the broken glass. Taking deep breaths to quiet the hammering of her heart, she works her way along the covered walkway, pressed hard against the wall to keep in the dark. Finger on the trigger.

He could come out at any moment, but she tells herself the last thing he'll be expecting is a chick with a shotgun.

Closer now. She can hear him moving around. Pulling open drawers, moving furniture.

She stops at the window. The curtains are drawn, but there's a gap. She peers through.

Mack is standing by the bed. He's got the sheets off. He's, wait—

—he's fucking *smelling* them?

75

The Charger struggles up the forest track to where I left the U-Haul. I've bought myself a little time with the cop, but I don't know how much. For a second I don't see it and think Kondracky must have found and towed it, but then my remaining headlight glints on a panel hidden behind foliage and camouflage netting. It's still there.

Everything's as I left it. The Charger's trunk is a cavern, and I load in more than I think I'll need. Not just weapons, ammunition and explosives, but housebreaking tools, med kit and a tranq. I'm just about to climb back into the Charger when my phone thrums in my pocket. I pull it out, half expecting to send Kat to voicemail but instead the caller ID says:

BINKS, J.J.

I answer immediately.

'Fuck you,' says Vilmos.

'Vilmos, this isn't the greatest time—'

'Forty-seven hours of poor-quality straight vanilla porn? Really?'

'Vilmos—'

'You want to know what I learned or not?'

I scan the forest track leading back down to the road. No sign of Kondracky.

'Okay. What did you learn?'

'I learned I'm 100% homo.'

'What else? What was in the files?'

'Nothing.'

'What? You mean you couldn't find anything, or—'

'There's nothing in the video files. They haven't been altered. Those ancient skin flicks are all over the internet, the exact same ones. Half of them are on Pornhub, the rest you can torrent. I set up a bot to scrape them, then compared. Bit for bit identical. Most of them have been floating about for years. They've not been manipulated. Not a single one of them.'

'So maybe it's someplace else.'

'I looked for hidden filesystems, scanned the unpartitioned space, went through the Master Boot Record sector by sector. Nothing.'

I sag. 'Come on, Vilmos. There has to be something. It's not like you to give up.'

'Who says I gave up?' says Vilmos.

I sit up straighter on the hood of the Charger.

'Wait, you found it? Where?'

'You open up a folder on your computer, what do you see?'

'A list of files.'

'Right,' says Vilmos, 'because you're a nerd and you use list view. What do they look like to ordinary people?'

'Icons. Thumbnails.'

'You know what a thumbnail is, deep down? It's a plain old JPEG. Which means you can encode a message in the DCT coefficients.'

'You managed to extract it?'

'Of course.'

'And?'

'It's a string of hex. 154 characters. A2100FE2FD2 . . .'

'Vilmos, I love you, but could you cut to the fucking chase, please?'

'154 characters. Four bits each. That's 616 bits. You know what else is 616 bits?'

'Vilmos!'

'A 512-bit encryption key with a format header.'

It takes a moment for it to sink in. 'Christ,' I say, involuntarily.

'You know what it's for?' he asks.

'Tell me something. You looked at the metadata on the files, right?'

'Obviously.'

'Did any of them have subtitle tracks?'

'One or two.'

'What language were they in?'

76

'I fucked him, if you're wondering,' says Kat.

Kondracky whirls round, sheets in his hands, to see her standing in the doorway with the ancient shotgun, barrel still floured with dust, trained on him. It's heavy for her, and she can already feel her arms tiring, but adrenaline is giving her strength.

'Do not do this,' he says.

'I pull the trigger, I'm a hero,' says Kat. 'He told me who you are. Sixteen, right? Or would you rather I called you Kondracky? My mom had all your books. Now I know why.'

Kondracky takes his pistol off the vanity.

'Give me the gun, okay? That way you walk away from this.'

She shoulders the shotgun a little tighter. 'If you're imagining that I'm one of those chicks in the movies that won't pull the trigger, I have to warn you right now, you've got me all wrong.'

'You loaded it, right?'

'How dumb do you think I am?'

'Well, you screwed that little jerk, so who knows? Safety off?'

'No safety.'

'Huh,' says Kondracky. 'Competition trigger. Which means it's not yours. Which means you haven't fired one since, guessing, high school? Some dumb party getting stoned with the farmers' boys? Second base if they let you fire it?'

The shotgun is getting heavier by the second, which she knows is his intent. Her finger's on the trigger. She should just pull it, but she can't help thinking about what Jones said, about how when you kill a man you kill your old self.

Thing is, she doesn't owe her old self anything.

'Self-defence, Mack. One more step.'

Kondracky hesitates. She's full of bravado, this one, and he can think of at least one good reason not to underestimate her. But he can see a muscle tremor in the arm she's using to support the barrel. It could be fatigue, or fear, or a combination of the two.

Either way.

'Give me the gun,' he says, and takes a step towards her.

She pulls the trigger.

Kondracky was right about one thing. It's been a decade since she fired a shotgun. And she's forgotten how much they kick. Her grip's tight, the stock snug against her shoulder and her stance is wide, but her hands are slick with sweat, and the weapon leaps out of her grasp and slams into her forehead.

She stumbles backwards, dropping the gun, but as she does she sees Kondracky clutch his head. She didn't miss him. Not completely. The shotgun has blasted a hole in the drywall above and to the right of his head, but the penumbra of the pellet spread has taken off a significant chunk of Kondracky's ear, from which blood now pours through his fingers.

'Mother*fucker*!' he yells, and strides over to Kat. He kicks the shotgun out of reach and grabs her with bloody hands. 'Listen to me. The only reason I didn't kill you the moment I saw you is because you're useful. The moment you stop being useful—' He jams the pistol into her face. 'Understand?'

'Fuck you,' says Kat, and punches him as hard as she can on what remains of his ear.

Kondracky yells in pain, then grabs her by her hair and physically hauls her into the bathroom. She thinks he's going to kill her, but in fact he just grabs a towel to staunch the blood from his ear, then drags her out of the room and across the parking lot to the Jimmy. She rains blows on him with her fists and boots but she might as well be pounding a block of wood. He zip-ties her, hand and foot, and duct-tapes her mouth shut.

He's about to throw her in the back of the Jimmy when he hesitates. Kat sees him looking at her mother's Trooper, which she now uses. The Trooper's a piece of shit but the Jimmy's half wrecked: it's obvious what he's thinking. He rips the duct tape off her mouth and jams the gun hard in her cheek.

'Your truck. Where are the keys?'

She spits in his face.

Kondracky tapes her mouth shut again. He dumps her on the ground, and heads back into the building.

She's hogtied, more or less. But she knows from TV that going to a second location with an abductor is likely a death sentence. The keys to the Trooper are hanging on a nail in the office by the inner door. Maybe it'll take him a minute to find them. The moment he disappears inside, she starts worming her way across the potholes and mud of the parking lot, a human caterpillar, gravel digging into her elbows and knees and shoulders.

Only a few more yards from the treeline. Once she's out of sight—

Hands grip her ankles. Kondracky drags her by her feet all the way to the Trooper.

77

The subtitles were in Farsi.

Farsi, the language of Iran.

I was right. Berlin was all about Iran. And now I know how.

There are two kinds of encryption keys: public and private.

A public key is used to encode information. You don't care if it's stolen, because it can only encode, not decode. You give it to assets who then use it to encrypt stolen information and send it to you, knowing you'll be the only one who can read it.

A private key is what you use to decode. You care very much if it's stolen. It's what you give to an agent in the field to decrypt instructions from Centre so that they, and only they, can read them.

The memory card I intercepted didn't contain the terror messages, the encrypted comms stream describing a nuclear plot which the US is using to justify starting a war with Iran.

That never made any sense.

It contained the key which allowed them to read it.

No wonder Moe was willing to die to protect it.

No wonder Kovacs was willing to pit herself against me to obtain it.

If the US goes ahead with a ground war in Iran on the basis of the decrypts, I didn't just kill Moe and Kovacs that day in Berlin. I will unknowingly have had a hand in the death of a hundred thousand civilians, and possibly vastly more if things get out of hand.

Sure, I kill people. But most of them at least arguably deserve it. If they're not actually in the game, they're game-adjacent. But civilians, people who have no desire for anything but an ordinary life, people on another continent, people I've never even met, never even looked in the eye, who have not even a vestigial concept that there *is* a game?

That's another proposition entirely.

I try to push away the thought. This is not the time to be developing a conscience, however vestigial. I'm just a cog in a big fucked-up machine. If it hadn't been me, it would have been somebody else. And besides, if the Iranians really are cooking up some kind of nuclear plot, who's to say the Americans aren't right to do whatever it takes to stop them? All of this, and the dangling loose ends – Handler cutting bait, Kovacs knowing where I would be, Moe's desperate chant of *Parachute. Parachute. Parachute* – they're all distractions from the single task at hand: to kill Sixteen, and to avoid being killed by him in the process.

And yet, and yet, and yet.

78

I shimmy the Charger back down the forest track to the high-way, and head past the gas station to the intersection, where the road curls up to Sixteen's house.

I pull up at the electric gates. The dogs hurtle down from the house, snarling and throwing themselves up against the fence, which is helpful since it tells me it isn't electrified. The nylon pack with the tranq pistol has Beggin' Strips in it but I don't need it for these two. They have my spoor from their earlier adventure and they know I'm the enemy – or prey, depending on your point of view.

I put a dart into each of them. It takes two for the second, who's bigger. It would be easier to kill them, and I'm not senti-mental about animals who have tried to kill me, human or canine, but if there's one thing I've learned from watching Hollywood action movies, it's this: never kill another man's dog.

When I'm sure the dogs are insensible, I cut through the fence and duck through the wire, then drag their snoring asses up to the house, where there are chains attached to the porch supports.

All the exterior doors are hardened with steel surrounds and concealed hinges. The locks are high quality and would take far too long to pick, so I simply blow them with a shaped lump of C4. The noise of the explosion echoes down into the town below but this can no longer be considered a covert operation.

79

I'm inside Kondracky's house, but it feels like I am inside his head, my flashlight illuminating recesses of his cranium, lighting up his amygdala and medulla oblongata. I pull open drawers and cupboards. There are bank statements, piles of mail, knick-knacks, vegetable peelers, old family photographs from the forties. An uncle fishing, a wedding, someone playing with a dog in a back garden. All entirely humdrum, innocent. Not a single thing that would betray who he really is.

Say what you like, the guy knows how to compartmentalise.

On the kitchen table, there's the egg cup and single die, showing six. I resist the temptation to roll.

In the lounge there's, of all things, a lime-green conversation pit. This guy is peak mid-century sans the irony. The TV is high-end but old, a monumental Sony widescreen tube TV that must weigh 600 pounds and probably cost as much as a car new. There's a sound system attached to it – a full-on vintage British Quad 33/303 amp, big old veneered Klipsch speakers, and a turntable. There are, I kid you not, Johnny Cash records everywhere. I flip through his record collection. The closest he gets to modernity is Cheap Trick, and some Nilsson.

Hipster heaven except this guy wouldn't know a hipster if it ran over him on a fixie.

What there is not, anywhere in the house, is any sign of the internet, or even so much as a computer. The closest things to digital devices are a microwave and a VCR. You read that right. He's got a fucking VCR. The logo tells me it's VHS. I'm actually impressed that it's not Betamax.

True to form, the clock is flashing 12:00.

This guy is all analogue, all the time. *Security through obscurity.*

Upwind of the conversation pit there's a rickety old desk on which is perched a manual typewriter, a big-ass Remington, all black and curves. Within reach is a library of reference books. There are manuals on novel-writing, dictionaries, two different thesauruses, weapons catalogues, reference works on con men, volumes on history, textbooks on emergency medicine, along with neatly stacked copies of Kondracky's novels. I guess if you don't have the internet you need all this shit. He takes his work as a writer seriously, that much is clear.

In the desk drawer I find a manuscript, neatly typed. The title doesn't match anything on the shelf. I flip through it. Here and there are notes, emendations, crossings out, corrections. It doesn't have a title yet, just *Untitled, by Sam Kondracky,* but underneath it there's a spidery scrawl in biro that I eventually make out says *The Sixteenth Man.* Which, honestly, is not that great a title. The handwriting and a few editorial scribbles here and there suggest this may be the only copy, so I slip it into one of the bubble-wrap envelopes I find in the next drawer and hang on to it as a small but potentially significant piece of leverage.

I am headed down into the basement where his armoury is located, planning to blow the door with what is left of my C4, when my cellphone buzzes once more in my pocket.

I pull it out. O'CONNOR, KATHERINE.

So that's her name.

I speculate about letting it go to voicemail. But she knows the number is for emergencies and for all her eccentricity she doesn't seem like one to overdramatise. So I answer.

'Kat?'

'Guess again,' says Kondracky.

80

Adrenaline floods my limbic system, like one of those warm injections they give you before an MRI. If he has her phone, does he have her?

Fake cool. 'Cop let you go, huh?'

'I prefer to think I let her go,' says Kondracky.

'And yet you're the one with the ticket.'

'Fuck you,' he says.

I rattled him. Good. I'm on edge, but it sounds like he is too.

'I guess you think you're pretty smart,' he says, peak boomer.

'Smart enough to know why you're calling,' I say. 'You want to make me an offer. We nix the whole thing. Reboot, reset. Like none of this shit ever happened. You go back to your house on the hill. I fuck off to wherever I choose to fuck off to. You never hear from me again. I never hear from you again. Nobody else ever hears from either of us again.'

'Huh,' he says, all innocent. 'You think that could really work?'

'Nope.'

'Me neither,' he says. 'We both know what happens if you don't finish this. And if I don't finish you, next thing I know I got more fools like you on my doorstep, more shit I have to scrape off my shoe. Besides,' he adds, 'you tried to kill me. Call me thin-skinned, but I take that personally.'

'So what, then? What's the offer?'

'Come on,' he says. 'You're the smartass. You tell me.'

'All I know right now is you have her phone. Maybe that's all you have.'

His voice comes muffled, mouth away from the phone. 'Tell him, honey.'

'Go fuck yourselves, both of you,' she spits.

Well, at least she's breathing.

'Come on, Mack,' I say. 'You know the deal. No civilians.'

'She stopped being a civilian the moment she took up with you. Besides—' and here he pauses for a moment, his voice dropping a register, a darkness coming over it that I haven't heard before, 'we stopped playing by the rules the moment you decided to come for me.'

'What makes you think I give a shit about her?'

'You left her behind. If it was anyone else, you'd have used her. As bait, as a human shield, to buy shit for you, to pass as Mr and Mrs Smith. But you didn't. You cut her adrift. Only one reason you do that, Jones, and we both know what it is. Three hours, then I kill her.'

'You want the truth, Mack?' I tell him. 'You're showing your age. Maybe back in the day swinging your dick like a caveman got results. But the world's moved on, and we see threats for what they are: a sign of weakness. Nobody with actual power makes threats, because they don't have to. But you're not sure you can defeat me in a straight fight, so you're rolling the dice on me caring whether the girl lives or dies. But you don't actually know, and if you're wrong you either have to kill her to show me how big your dick is, or let her go and admit you're short in that department. Neither option is helpful to you in any way.'

There is a silence at the end of the phone. Maybe I'm getting traction. 'On the other hand, let's say you're right. Let's say there's a real, you know, connection, there. Only not enough to actually die for. Maybe if we let the romance blossom we'd get there. But two days? That's a stretch. So you end up killing her, what then?'

Still nothing, just that breathing.

'I'll tell you what then. There's a lot of ways for a person to die, and I have a lot of bullets. The one that kills you can be the first or the last. You let her go now, it's the first. You touch one hair on her head, it's the last. But, just so we're clear, that's not a threat. It's a promise.'

A long pause. Then there's a guffaw on the other end of the line.

'You talk a good game, Jones, I'll give you that,' he says. 'You got three hours.'

81

I have missed something, but I don't know what.

I blow the door on the basement but it yields nothing I don't already have stacked in the U-Haul. There's a safe, but I'm out of C4 and I don't have the time or patience to crack it. Besides, I know what I'll find inside – small denomination cash in multiple currencies, hard assets such as uncut diamonds that can be swallowed or concealed elsewhere on the person. Passports, driver's licences and other forms of ID under various names and nationalities. Probably some documents that act as insurance, maybe a few onetime pads.

The exact same shit that I have in safes around the world.

None of it is of any use or interest to me right now.

I need something else.

I don't know what it is, but I will know when I find it.

I head back upstairs.

What I need is not the kind of thing you find in the kitchen or the living room. So I head into the bathroom. I go through his cabinets, his medication, his trash, his underwear, his wardrobe. I find old suitcases and inspect them. I look under beds. I go through pockets of coats that haven't been worn for years. I check the soles of his shoes.

Nothing. I'm exhausted, sweating. I check my watch. I have wasted seventy-five minutes searching the house and I have nothing to show for it.

Worse, despite the sweat, I am starting to get a clammy feeling. The same feeling I would get in juvie, waiting in my room after midnight, knowing David was in the building. A feeling I haven't had since I was seventeen, since the day I decided to remake myself, to fight back. Not since the day I took the first step on the journey which led to this room.

Fuck this man. Fuck Handler. Fuck the girl. Fuck everything.

The anxiety hits me where it always did, in the gut. I am tempted to empty my churning bowels on to the lime-green shag carpet of the conversation pit, to demonstrate my disdain for this man in the most visceral way I can imagine. *How's that for a conversation piece, motherfucker?*

But I'm not an animal, so I use the bathroom instead.

I'm sitting there when I see it. A fragment of blue foil, a triangle torn off from a corner, hiding behind the trash can. There's something familiar about it. I clean off, bend down and pick it up, and I know instantly both what it is and what it means.

I go back to the cabinet and open it again. There among the orange bottles of pills is one whose significance I missed. *Sildenafil Citrate 25mg.*

I now know what I'm looking for, and where to find it.

I step into the shower, pull out my knife, and unscrew the floor drain. I lift it up and scoop around with my finger. Nothing. I jam my hand into the drain, making it small, feeling like the bones are being crushed. And then I feel it.

I tease it out with my finger, and hold it up to the light.

It's a hair. A single hair.

What's left of Kondracky's is short, but this is twelve inches long.

His is grey, but this is bottle-blonde, fading at the root.

And I know who it belongs to.

82

The piece-of-shit Jimmy that Kondracky chased me in. I remember now where I saw it. Parked beside the gas station. After we wrecked his car he must have taken hers.

The only question is what she means to him. But the care he took in extinguishing her existence from his house tells me she's more than a casual piece on the side. If I had to guess, I'd say they've been doing this for years. She's probably the one who posts his manuscripts.

Whatever she is to him, she's the closest I have to leverage in this situation. I can only pray it's enough.

I leave the dogs chained up in case I need to return, and head back down the hill in the Charger. I park kitty-corner from the gas station in the lot with the other old cars and tractors. In the darkness, the beat-up old Dodge disappears, a junker among junkers.

I watch the gas station for an hour.

Kondracky took her truck, so Barb – that's what he called her the first day – gets a ride with Vern in his old Ranger.

I follow at a discreet distance, lights off.

Vern drops her at the drive of a seventies split-level on a dirt road a mile out of town. I sail past as she heads up the driveway to the door and Vern turns round to head back to the old farmhouse by the gas station. I turn back at the next intersection, leave the Charger by the side of the road, and head up to Barb's house on foot. The nearest neighbour is a good half-mile away. Good.

I head up the driveway. More luck: no dogs, no kids. There's a pan of potatoes on the stove in the kitchen, boiling hard. The TV's on in the living room, and I learn there are people who still watch network news. No sign of Barb. I head up to the side split, where I can hear country music. It's Dolly, or Patsy, or Tammy – the distinctions are lost on me but I'm assured by others they are significant.

I head through the bedroom, as neat and tidy as everywhere else.

She's in the shower, singing along.

I let her sing, taking up position in the doorway with my gun drawn.

She steps out of the shower, hair plastered in her eyes, and fumbles for a towel, then turns to see me. She pulls the towel up to cover herself, but to my surprise she doesn't scream or do any of that stuff. She just looks at me, eyes calculating, and I realise this may not go as smoothly as I'd hoped.

'This yours?' I say, holding up the hair.

'Need my glasses.' She reaches for them.

'*Slowly*,' I say. She picks them off the vanity in slow motion.

I can already see it matches her roots perfectly.

'Guess so.'

'You don't seem surprised to see me.'

'He told me someone might come,' she says, adjusting the towel.

Apparently Barb is not someone who spooks easily.

'And if they did?'

She shrugs. 'Do whatever they say.'

I let her dry off and get dressed, a T-shirt and jeans, which she does quickly and quietly. I pull a roll of Gorilla tape from my pocket – way stronger than duct tape – and try to get her hands behind her back, but she tells me she has limited mobility because of arthritis in her shoulders so I tape them in

215

front instead, six loops that even I couldn't get out of in a hurry.

I follow her downstairs, gun in her back. We're about to head out the front door when I notice a dish on the telephone table. There's a set of car keys with a Pontiac logo. I pick them up. I've grown fond of it, but bullet holes and a smashed head-light make the Charger a liability.

'You've another vehicle?'

She nods. 'Grand Am. In the garage.'

'It run?'

She nods.

'Show me.'

We head through the kitchen. Barb wants to turn off the potatoes but I do it for her, because even with her hands taped I don't trust her with a pan of near-boiling water.

A door leads into the garage. It's dark.

'Where's the light?'

'Over here.' Barb clicks a switch on the wall, revealing an early nineties red Grand Am convertible.

'You'll probably need this,' says Barb. I turn to see what she's holding.

'Why? What is it?'

'Bear spray,' says Barb, and hits me full in the face with it.

83

Killer bees swarm into my eyes and nose, into my mouth and down my throat into my lungs. Barb kicks me in the balls, and as I drop to my knees, kicks me in the face.

I am a supernova of pain.

I scramble for my gun, but I've dropped it somewhere.

Honestly, I've had prouder moments.

I hear Barb run past me, back into the kitchen, and stumble after her. I open my eyes for a fraction of a second, just in time to see her hurl the pan of potatoes at me. I throw up my hands to protect myself from the scalding water, and a second supernova of pain explodes.

Barb runs out the front door, heading for the road.

I blunder after her, knocking over furniture and plant pots. I chase the sound of her footsteps down the driveway. I might be blind but Barb probably hasn't run in a decade, and with her smoker's lungs, I catch up with her twenty yards down the dirt road, where she just stops, bent over and gasping for air, coughing up her lungs, then drops to her knees.

I really, really don't need her to die on me now.

'Breathe,' I tell her, still gasping for air myself, snot streaming out of my eyes and nose, my eyes almost swollen shut. 'Control your breathing. Big one in. Now hold it in. Count to four. Then out slowly, like a tyre deflating. Again.'

Her breathing gradually returns to normal.

Back in the garage, my vision returning, I add another layer of Gorilla tape to fix her hands to her waist and add a loop around her ankles. She insists I lock up the house and leave food for the cat. At the road, I transfer the Charger's loadout into the Grand Am, and we cruise into the night.

I'll say this for Barb, she's cool. No hysterics, nothing. I get the sense she's had a tough life so maybe this isn't the worst thing that's happened to her. I'm not even going to hold the bear spray against her, as long as she doesn't go spreading rumours.

I'm about ready to call Kondracky on Kat's phone when she turns to me.

'The hair? That's really how you knew?'

'A torn-off piece of foil from a pack of Trojans. Purple pills. Then the hair. It didn't take Einstein. But he was careful. He did his best to protect you.'

'If he'd done his best I wouldn't be sitting here,' says Barb. If Kondracky gets through this he's going to have to do some weapons-grade apologising.

'What do you know about him?' I ask.

'What's in the books.'

'You figured they weren't just fiction.'

'He always acted like there was someone sneaking up behind him. Always looking over his shoulder, you know?'

'What did he tell you when he took the Jimmy?'

'That someone might come, and I should do what they said, but it would be better if I went somewhere. But you can't just leave a life behind.'

She's quiet for a moment, then she turns to me.

'He said you might have the girl with you. Kat, from the motel.'

'I left her behind. He took her,' I tell her.

'So, I'm what? Bait?'

'Not bait. Leverage.'

To my surprise, she laughs. 'Oh, sugar,' she says. 'Bless your heart.'

'What?'

She looks off to one side, smiling to herself.

'What?'

'You were in his house, right? That's where you found my hair.'

I nod.

'What else did you find?' she asks.

'Like what?'

'Like something he was working on?'

'You mean the book?'

I gesture backwards to the rear seat, where the manuscript sits in a thick brown envelope.

'Did you read it?' she asks.

'Been kind of busy staying alive.'

'You might want to.'

'Why?'

'Because you got everything backwards. Number one, him and me . . . it's nothing much. I like him well enough. But I don't love him any more than he loves me. So if you were counting on that, well, I wouldn't, is all.'

'And number two?'

She nods at the manuscript. 'Number two is in there.'

84

The rest stop is a loop that used to be the highway before they straightened it out. It's dark now, and we're tucked away behind a wall of trees, by a low brick restroom. Barb sits on the hood, illuminated by the interior light. I freed her hands but her ankles are still bound. She's tuned the radio to the old-time country station and is singing along quietly to Dolly-Patsy-Tammy. She knows every word.

Barb has more sangfroid in her little finger than most men I have known, including me. I don't frighten her even a little bit, or if I do she doesn't show it. You wouldn't know it from the statues, but America was built on the backs of women like her. Women of all colours and creeds who endured snow and heat, ploughed fields, milked cows, sawed wood, bore children, fed them, raised them and lost them, suffered at the fists of faithless, drunken husbands, and yet never let the flame of kindness be completely extinguished, no matter how low the wick of their fortunes burned.

I am camped in the rear passenger seat, door open, reading the raw tome I took from Kondracky's desk, insects spiralling in my Petzl as I flip page after page.

The book is entirely unlike the others, the ones he chose to publish. A different tone of voice. Sad, elegiac even, full of regret and sadness and missed opportunities, moments of redemption or grace that passed by him unseen. I can see why he didn't ever send it off: because it rings true, every word of it. Part confession, part love story, part justification. The auto-biography of a reluctant serial killer.

I get to the part that Barb told me about and look up.

'Holy shit.'

'I told you, hon.'

I have to put the manuscript down to recalculate, but I'm not sure I can even do the math. How do you integrate love? How do you calculate the square root of loneliness?

'So you knew her?'

'Sure. From kids. We pretty near grew up together.'

'And her eyes?'

Barb tilts her head. 'What do you think?'

85

I leave Barb at the car and walk out into the darkness, far enough away she can't hear me. Nobody needs to hear their life being bartered.

I dial Kat's phone. It picks up to silence, though I imagine I can hear a fire crackling in the background, someplace lonely where I would never find them.

'Kondracky, it's Jones,' I tell him. 'We need to talk.'

'Done talking,' says Kondracky. 'Time's up.'

'You kill the girl yet?'

'Maybe. Maybe not,' he says. His schtick is straight-up Clint Eastwood, which would be funnier if he wasn't capable of delivering on it.

'She's not Schrödinger's cat,' I tell him. 'Either you killed her, in which case your leverage is gone, or you didn't, in which case you were never going to. You get why threats are dumb now?'

'Fuck this shit, Jones,' he says, and I can hear the anger in his voice. Good. 'Maybe I'll pull the trigger right now.'

'Maybe I will too.'

'What do you mean?'

'I was in your place earlier. Your dogs weren't too friendly but they'll be fine in the morning. Anyway, it took me a while, but I found what I was looking for eventually.'

'And what would that be?'

'Let's just say you could do a better job on the shower drain.'

He's quiet for a moment.

'What makes you think I give a shit about her?'

'Yeah, she tried to sell me that line too,' I say. 'I'd buy it, if you hadn't tried so hard to hide her. I mean, you literally scrub your place every time she leaves. Change the sheets, vacuum, empty the garbage. Make sure there's no trace of lipstick on a cup or a glass. You don't do that for a goddamn booty call.'

'She's not part of this.'

'No rules. That's what you told me.'

Impasse.

'Here's the thing,' I tell him. 'I like Barb. I can see why you like her. I don't want to have to kill her. But even if I do, you're never going to pull the trigger on the girl.'

'And why would that be?'

'Because I found your book. The one you never sent off. I know who she is.'

'You don't know shit.'

'So prove me wrong. Kill her.'

Silence. Breathing. On the Grand Am's radio, something has just been thrown off the Tallahatchie Bridge, but Barb isn't singing along. She's looking at me.

I turn my back to her. 'You hear what I'm saying? We take them both off the board. No winners, no losers. We exchange prisoners, and they walk away. From here on in, just you and me.'

A long silence. Finally he grunts, 'Okay.'

'One more thing,' I tell him.

'What's that?' he asks warily.

'Want to grab a coffee?'

223

86

After the Berlin Wall went up in 1961, the only checkpoint controlled by the Soviets, as opposed to the GDR, was the bridge over the Havel River between the Jungfernsee and the Glienicker Lake. A year later, Rudolf Abel, convicted of spying in a bizarre case involving a newspaper boy, a hollow nickel, and a Finnish bigamist, was swapped for pilot Gary Powers, whose U-2 spy plane had been shot down at 70,000 feet over Sverdlovsk Oblast.

It became known as the Bridge of Spies. Spielberg made a movie.

Kondracky and I have settled on our own Bridge of Spies, but it's less glamorous: an ersatz diner in a dilapidated low-rise mall in Rapid City, decorated with old licence plates, posters of Marilyn and Elvis, and a fibreglass replica of the front of a vintage Chevy. The rules have been set beforehand. We meet at 1400, carry no weapons, and parley until the hostages are clear. Beyond that, all bets are off.

Kondracky and Kat are already there, laminated menus and scratched plastic water glasses in front of them, when Barb and I arrive. Kondracky is facing the door, which would worry me if he was likely to have any backup, but if anyone's going to kill me it's him, so I take my place opposite, Barb next to me.

Kondracky has some kind of an improvised dressing over his left ear which gives him the air of a redneck Van Gogh. I'm pretty sure I didn't hit him, so it suggests taking Kat prisoner was less than straightforward. This doesn't surprise me in the least.

A chirpy waitress with a retainer brings us coffee and tells us to order when we're ready.

Kat's paler than I remember and I realise despite her bravado she's scared, her green eyes darting left and right, continually trying to read how the situation is likely to develop. Does she know who Kondracky is to her yet? Does she even suspect? I can't tell.

Barb, on the other hand, is quietly furious, shooting Kondracky daggers over the table. He's avoiding eye contact and I realise in an odd way he's scared of her. I would be too in his shoes.

'You okay?' I ask Kat. She nods, rubbing her wrists, where I can still see marks from the zip ties.

'You?' asks Kondracky.

'Fuck you, Mack,' says Barb. 'Like you care.'

'You knew who I was,' says Kondracky, annoyed. 'You could have walked away at any time.'

'Okay, okay,' I say, not wanting this to descend into a marital argument. 'Let's draw a line under it, shall we?'

Kondracky nods. He reaches for his pocket, making a big show of it not being for a weapon, and produces a pair of Greyhound tickets, a folded timetable, and cash.

'These are for you two. There's a cab outside that'll take you to the bus station. You're home free. From here on in it's just him and me.'

He puts them on the table. Neither of the women move.

'So that's it,' says Kat. 'We get on a bus and leave you two to—'

Kondracky silences her, his hand clamping on hers.

Barb's fingers drum the table. They're yellow from nicotine and it suddenly hits me she hasn't had a smoke in eighteen

225

hours. 'Look,' she says. 'I don't pretend to know the full story here. But couldn't you two just settle your differences?'

'What the fuck do you think we're doing?' hisses Kondracky.

If he gets through this alive, Barb is going to make him regret it.

'So what happens if we call the cops?' says Kat.

'You get to live the rest of your life wondering how much of their blood was on your hands,' I tell her. From the way she looks away, she is not likely to pursue the idea.

Barb checks the timetable. It looks like she's done with Kondracky. 'There's one now if we hurry.'

Kat gives Barb a combative look, not ready to give up yet.

'Hon,' says Barb, 'I know what you're thinking. But you're not the asshole whisperer. Let these fools do what they want to each other. The world's a better place without either of them.'

I can't argue with a word of it, and neither can Kondracky.

But Barb isn't done. She turns to us. 'I swear to God, if I had my druthers I'd put you both out of your misery right now.' Then she grabs up the tickets and the money, and marches out.

Kat sits there for a second, staring at me.

'Well?'

I just shrug. I need her to hate me, and evidently it's working.

'You fucking abandoned me.'

'You told me you could handle yourself.'

By way of an answer, she picks up Kondracky's coffee cup and throws the now lukewarm contents in my face.

She turns to Kondracky, and holds her hand out.

'Phone,' she says. 'I want my phone.'

Kondracky holds it out. She takes it and heads out after Barb into the belly of the mall. By craning my head, I watch them head out the main doors and disappear into the parking lot, where a beaten-up silver minivan with a sign that says ACE TAXI is waiting.

I find myself wondering if it's the last time I will ever see her.

87

Kondracky watches me wipe coffee off myself with a paper napkin, amused.

'So,' he says. 'You realise I was on to you from the start, right?'

I do not feel like giving him the satisfaction of a reply. He takes this as encouragement.

'Jeep and a U-Haul, some bullshit about a piano. Vern tells me you drove off headed west. But then my buddy who farms the back hollow sees you headed back east down a dirt road like you didn't want to be seen.'

'I figure I'll give you a day or so to settle in. Check the forest, dogs find your bivouac in ten seconds flat, plus all the junk you used to cover the truck, plus tyre tracks. Looks like you left in a hurry. Bear scat tells the story, bet old Martha scared the shit out of you. Mean old girl, had a couple of run-ins myself.

'Spot your rig out back in the motel parking lot. Takes ten seconds to figure out the girl is more interested in you than a thousand bucks. By now it's pretty obvious what you intend, so I check all the spots I cleared and sure enough, cameras. Which means you intend to take your shot from below, and as we both know, there's only one place with cover.

'I knew what was coming, so I kept the dogs hungry. Didn't roll for the gas station that morning, but I wasn't going to wait. I was almost feeling sorry for you by the time you took your shot. I could have carried on down to the highway and cut you off, but you could have bailed on foot instead of taking the vehicle, and I didn't want to chance it.

'You realise I would have killed you in the logging yard if it hadn't been for the girl?'

I can't take this shit any longer.

'Why do you keep calling her that?'

'Who?'

'The girl. We both know who she is.'

'Enlighten me,' he says, but there is danger in his voice.

'Nineteen ninety-three,' I tell him. 'You're en route from Billings, Montana, to a hit in Milwaukee, only a snowstorm hits and you're forced to shack up in a hunter's motel. Where you meet a girl with, and I quote, "the craziest green eyes".'

He stares at me with his own watery blue marbles and I suddenly understand.

'You never got over her, did you?'

It takes him a while. Finally he just says:

'Some you don't.'

'Come on,' I say. 'Spill it. You meet her. You spend three nights and—?'

'You read the fucking book. You tell me.'

I shake my head. 'It stops. You never finish the story.'

'What makes you think I intend to now?'

'Because maybe I'm the one person on earth who could understand it.'

It's just a guess, but the hardness in his eyes dissipates by about a percentage point. He drums his fingers for a second, then he sits forward.

'What do you think? I drive away, and I know exactly one thing for certain: I can't ever see her again without putting a target on her back. So I let my work fill the holes. Twenty years pass, and you get to thinking "what if?". I mean, there were nights I went to sleep without seeing her face. But not enough. So one day I drive past. I tell myself, that's all I'm going to do, just drive past in the full and certain knowledge that she's moved on, married, found someone, started a new life. Put the fucking ghost to rest. Only she hasn't. She's still there. Same goddamn motel. She hasn't even changed the fucking curtains.'

'So, what? You drop in?'

'No. I see the house. It's not perfect, but it has possibilities. And I get this idea. I'm just gonna retire. Disappear. Nobody will ever know where I went. Understand, I'm not assuming anything. I don't know what she thinks about me, whether she even thinks about me at all.'

He stops for a moment as some mile-long fully loaded freight train of emotion thunders past.

'Anyway, I set it all up. It takes me two years to get the house ready, to make all the arrangements. And finally I pull the switch. Lights out on Sixteen. And that's the day I walk into the motel. She looks up and she sees me, those same green eyes. And you know what she says?'

'What?'

'She says, "You're too late."'

'Meaning?'

'Meaning I was too late. In every possible sense. Too late, because she had Stage 4 lymphoma. The hospital gave her a year. She lasted eighteen months. Too late, because she'd been through every stage of grief there was. At first she stayed at the motel because she hoped I'd come back. Then she stayed so that if I came back she could tell me to fuck off. Eventually she just stayed because she stayed, not because of me, just because.'

'What about Kat?'

'Holy shit. Talk about a mindfuck.'

230

'She like her? I mean, past the green eyes,' I ask.

'Sure,' he says. 'Only, different, too.'

'Different how?'

'Her mother let people use her,' says Kondracky. 'Kat, let's just say she's a survivor.'

A survivor. That's what Junebug used to call her and me. Until she wasn't.

'You had eighteen months. What were they like?'

Kondracky shrugs. 'One night we got drunk and fooled around, I guess. But it didn't lead anywhere. We weren't the people we'd once been. She was right. I was too late. I fucked up.'

He pushes his coffee cup away.

'Now you tell me something. If you knew who Kat was, if you knew I wasn't going to kill her, if you already knew who she was, why bother with all this crap? Exchanging prisoners. What was the point? Just to hear me tell some bullshit sob-story?'

'No,' I say. 'I was just hoping you'd tell me the truth.'

Kondracky stares at me, cold and hostile.

'Kat's mother,' I say, 'she's not why you quit. Okay, so you never got over her. Probably it chewed you up. I don't doubt it. But it's not enough, not on its own. You keep away for twenty years, then suddenly decide it's time to rekindle the old flame, and by doing so, you put not just her in the line of fire, but your new-found daughter as well? I get it, you treated Kat like shit, because if anyone ever suspected who she really was to you, she'd become a target. But you'd never have come back in the first place unless you had no option.'

The marbles that substitute for his eyes have become granite.

'You know the funny part?' I tell him. 'Kat saw through you better than I did. You didn't quit because you got all

231

misty-eyed about some chick you hooked up with back in the day. You quit because something spooked you. Because you got the fear. We all get it now and then, but yours got hold of you and it wouldn't let you go. And you weren't just scared of whatever it was that had you by the tail. You were even more scared word would get out that you had the yips. Not just scared, but terrified. And you know what? I think you still are.'

It takes a moment, but then his face cracks into a grin.

'You'd love to believe that, wouldn't you? "Oh, Kondracky's got the *fear*, he's *scared*." Because when you tell yourself the story that way you're not the one who dies. Only you *are* the one who dies, Jones, because you've somehow managed to stick your head so far up your own ass that it's never occurred to you to ask the only question that matters.'

'And what's that?'

'Who your real target is.'

88

'I know who my target is,' I tell him, looking him straight in the eye. 'My orders weren't exactly ambiguous.'

'Uh huh,' says Kondracky. 'And why'd they say they wanted me dead?'

'You're telling me you know why you killed everyone you killed?'

'Sure,' he says. 'I made it my business. You kill a man for no reason, pretty soon things start to get out of hand. You have to keep the bastards upstairs honest, or people end up getting killed for no reason at all. If they didn't tell me, I found out. I wasn't always sure. But most of the time I had a pretty good idea.'

He sits back, picking at his teeth with a wooden toothpick from a jar on the table.

'If you had to guess,' he says.

I shrug. 'I figured they were cleaning house. You knew too much shit about too much shit.'

'Sure, sure,' says Kondracky with a dismissive wave. 'Sooner or later everyone goes from asset to unmitigated liability, and gets mitigated. Or they just get tired of your face. But why now?'

'They didn't give me a reason.'

'What if the reason they didn't give you a reason is that there is no reason?'

I can feel my patience running out. 'What the fuck are you talking about, old man?'

Kondracky sighs like I'm five years old and I've got my shoes on the wrong feet.

'Jesus Christ, do I have to spell it out for you? You, Jones, are Number Seventeen, the ultimate badass, at least according to your own publicity. Nobody can come against you and prevail. There's exactly one guy on earth who isn't scared of you. One asshole who could get the job done, no questions. Only he's not for hire, because he retired. And nobody knows where he is.'

He pulls something out of his teeth and inspects it.

'You see where I'm going with this? The only way to kill you is to get me out of retirement. The only way to do that is to send you to kill me, knowing you'll fail. And knowing when you do, I'll hunt you down and kill you.

'You see?' he says. 'You think I'm your target. But I'm not your real target. I never was.

'The real target,' he says, pointing the toothpick at me, 'is *you*.'

PART FOUR

89

After I killed David, I knew what I was capable of and what I wanted to be, but there was unfinished business to look after first.

I needed to find out who had killed my mother.

The days following Junebug's death aren't a blur to me. They're not there at all. There's a name for it – traumatic amnesia. It's why kids sometimes recover memories of abuse years later, triggered by some sense memory. A smell, a colour, or finding yourself back in the room where it happened.

The first detail I can remember clearly is from maybe a week after. I'm sitting in some anonymous room. Like a classroom, except it was probably in a CPS facility. You know the drill, stuffed toys and posters to make it look homey, but there's no disguising the institutional carpet, the grey paint, the hard plastic tables and chairs, the sickly smell, and the faint air of despair pervading everything.

I'm at one of the tables, my legs too short for my feet to reach the floor. On my left is a woman from CPS. A social worker or psychologist probably. They call them the Designated Adult. She had short curly hair and thick arms and flowers on her blouse is all I can remember. Opposite me is a policeman. Plain clothes, in his fifties, with a red face and a walrus moustache. He asked me everything about the night my mother died, and I told him. Everything. The closet, the flashlight, the Spider-Man comic, the grinning skull tattoo on the man's leg.

It wasn't much, but it told me there had been some kind of investigation and, with the help of a lawyer, and despite the fact that Stockton PD fought me tooth and nail, I finally got my hands on the cold case file. But my statement was missing.

By then the bushy-moustached detective, Giller – his name was there in the file – was dead, killed when he drove his Mustang into a bridge support late one night after a messy divorce and a long night at the local strip club. It turned out he was Vice, not Homicide, which was odd, nor was he lead on the investigation, which was even odder given I was the only witness, but I couldn't see the significance.

Most of the girls who worked alongside Junebug had either straightened out or died. It took me four days of cruising the butt end of Walker Way before I found one who remembered her. Under the same flickering neon light where I'd sat with Junebug sucking green slush out of a jumbo cup a decade earlier, she told me two things that made everything click into place.

First, the Vice cops took a cut from the girls to turn a blind eye. They took it in a combination of cash and kind. It was protection, and if a pimp got too rough with a girl, meaning a broken bone or ambulance trip, they would come down heavy. Sometimes a cop would take a particular interest in a particular girl and come to regard her as his property, a kind of pimp-in-uniform. Junebug had one of those, she said, which made it even odder her death had been so egregiously overlooked. I wondered if her cop/pimp was maybe Giller, but she said no, the one with the big moustache took his cut in hard currency, not soft.

But then she told me the other thing. The tattoo I described on the leg of the man who killed my mother was a cop tattoo. A gang signal, a brotherhood of dirty cops who would protect each other.

The killer was a cop, or ex-cop.

And that was when I knew who had killed my mother.

90

Kondracky studies me, chewing on the toothpick, watching for my reaction. I stare back, as blank as I can manage, trying to give nothing away.

But he's right, because of course he is. It's not him they're trying to kill. It's me. Somebody wants me dead, very, very badly. And if I'm going to survive, I need to find out who, and why.

But first I need to kill the man in front of me.

Sure, I could persuade myself that if Sixteen's not the target, we don't have to do this. But it's a fool's logic. Nothing has changed: if I don't complete the job, it tells the world I'm afraid, and it's open season. Same goes for Kondracky: I tried to kill him, and if he doesn't respond in kind, it will never end for him either.

We could agree to walk away, but we would both be lying. And we both know it.

So I simply shrug. 'Maybe you're right. I'm not sure it changes anything.'

'My feelings exactly,' says Kondracky. 'Shall we get on with it, then?'

The deal was no weapons, but I'm not gullible enough to believe he obeyed that. I certainly didn't. I have a Brügger & Thomet MP9 tucked into my belt in the small of my back and a couple of Nammo grenades, cute little things you can clip

239

together like Lego. Our Bridge of Spies is a demilitarised zone, so we need to agree a grace period to allow us both to get clear.

'How long do you want?' I ask him.

'How long do *you* want?'

'I was thinking twenty-four hours,' I say, though I have no intention of waiting that long.

'I was thinking ten minutes,' says Kondracky, with exactly the same thought.

'How about we split the difference?' I say. 'Five.'

91

Lead on the investigation into Junebug's murder was a cop called DeAngelo. He was the first on the scene after the beat cops, according to the case file. He should have been the one who interviewed me. But instead he sent Giller, who wasn't even Homicide. But the lawyer who got me the file, who had dealt with them both, told me DeAngelo had been promoted from Vice, where he'd been Giller's partner.

DeAngelo was still alive, but had transferred down to LA. That's where I found him, retired on a fat pension, running a private security and executive protection business from an office in the City of Industry. I called him up and told him I was flying in from New York, working A&R for a label looking to sign some rap acts away from their current joints, that it could get edgy, and that I needed a driver and security for a week. If it worked out maybe there'd be a contract in it.

He jumped at the chance. I drove to LAX, where he met me and drove me to Hollywood so I could check into my hotel. In the hotel he made a big show of looking round like he was Secret Fucking Service, and insisted on checking out the room first. When he opened the door to assure me it was clear and I could come in, I pistol-whipped him into unconsciousness, dragged him into the room, zip-tied him to the bed and duct-taped his mouth shut.

I knew what I'd find when I pulled his pants leg up.

I'm not proud of what I did that day. But he earned it, every piece of it. Before he died, DeAngelo told me the truth: he was afraid my mother was serious about leaving this time, that she'd straighten out, maybe even get religion like the girls sometimes did, and that because he'd treated her and the other girls badly, there was a chance she could implicate him. He also wanted to send a message to the other girls he ran that there was no exit ramp from the life, not while they were his.

DeAngelo called in the disturbance himself. He had no idea there'd been a witness to the killing until he talked to the beat cops who responded. I'm guessing if he'd known I was there he would have killed me as well. When he learned of my existence, he couldn't interview me himself because I'd recognise him, so he sent his buddy instead. Giller never even bothered to write up the interview.

I've thought over what DeAngelo told me many times, the reasons he gave for killing my mother, but somehow they've never seemed enough. Maybe I'm fooling myself, trying to give her life and death a weight it's not capable of bearing, but what I believe to this day he didn't tell me is that he was in love with her. That he was furious with Junebug not just for leaving, but for not loving him back, for having the gall to have some vision for her life that rose beyond simply being his whore.

I say this because, for all of her desperate faults, my mother was a loveable person.

After DeAngelo finally stopped breathing, I walked to La Brea. It was one of those staggeringly bright and clear LA days when the smog lifts and it seems like the sharpness and clarity has been turned up a notch. I don't know if I expected to feel different, but I did. At the corner of La Brea there was a 7-Eleven, so I stopped in to buy a Slurpee, with which I drank a toast to Junebug.

It wasn't until later that I realised DeAngelo and I have the same colour eyes.

92

We exit the diner together, then split in different directions, backing away, hands lifted to show they're empty, until Kondracky disappears around one corner of the dying mall and I another.

Overnight, while Barb dozed in the back seat of the Grand Am, I'd pulled the mall floor plan and studied it, along with the geography of Rapid City. I assume he's done the same. The mall is single-storey – in the seventies, land prices meant it was cheaper to build out than up. The little diner is in the central atrium, all that remains of what was once a food court – close to access stairwells, but a fair distance from the entrances and the parking lot, where both of us have vehicles, and weapons.

I'd parked close to the entrance for speed of access, but maybe this was a mistake. The Grand Am's now a sitting duck for a shot from the roof. There was a silver Trooper that looked a lot like the one by the motel a hundred yards further out. I can't be sure it's Kat's but if it is, a ten-second sprint will take Kondracky out of my accurate range, leaving me stranded and outgunned.

The roof is my strongest choice – the mall is single-storey, so it's a matter of seconds to get up there – but what if Kondracky has the same idea and gets there first? Maybe I could head to the basement, to the delivery area and loading docks, bide my time in safety, then work my way round to the vehicle that way. But how long will Kondracky wait on the roof? And if he goes instead for the Trooper, I lose him completely.

As if all that wasn't enough, the mall has a tiny police substation attached. I'm not afraid of small-town cops, but the moment they hear gunfire they'll call for backup, at which point things get complicated and they are complicated enough already.

Time for a decision. There's a cargo elevator at the end of the passageway to the restrooms; near it is a fire door to a staircase, which I take up to where an access door opens out on to the roof. There's no alarm and the lock is flimsy. I shoulder-barge it open, weapon ready for Kondracky in case he got there by the service door at the other end of the mall, but there's no sign of him.

Using the rooftop AC units as cover, I work my way round to the north-east corner. The Trooper's still there. I keep moving, head on a swivel. Where the fuck is he? The mall roof is not that high – fifteen, twenty feet. If I drop down, I can make it to the Grand Am and load up. But if he's waiting at one of the exits, I'm fucked.

I'm almost at the other end of the roof when I see it. The second access door from the mall below, and it's open, the lock busted.

He got here before me.

A tenth of a second later, Kondracky opens fire from behind the stairwell cover. I reflexively kick the half-open door, slamming it into his face, and hurl myself down the stairs, rolling against the wall at the bottom and aiming at the door. But no Kondracky. Maybe he took the other set of stairs, or dropped off the roof, or is waiting for me to break cover and run for the Grand Am. But the cops in the substation must have heard the shots. Soon they'll be on their way up, so he has to be heading down.

244

I clatter down the stairs to the doors of what used to be a JCPenney and is now a flea market with a sign that says OPEN FRIDAYS 1–4PM. I smash the glass with the butt of my MP9. The entire door shatters and I simply step through. I cover the entrance as I scan for another way out: the door I came through is a choke point so I need an exit strategy. The windows have been boarded to make room for vendor displays of cheap antiques and off-brand consumables. The exterior doors have panic bars but they're chained shut.

The only option is a cargo elevator. As I hit the call button something rolls through the smashed door. I spin to see what it is, and am hit with the shockingly intense flash and concussion of a stun grenade. Blinded, my ears singing, I huddle behind a display of knock-off Tupperware, trying to stay invisible until my senses can recover.

As my eyes clear, I see movement. Kondracky shoulders in through the door, raking fire across the flea market to cover himself. Glass baubles, reindeer and angels on a discount year-round Christmas display explode. I'm still half blind and in no shape to duel him, so instead I spray fire towards the door, stumble into the cargo elevator and hammer the button for the basement.

Kondracky's rounds tear holes in the doors as they close.

As the elevator jolts down, I hear sirens. Backup for the mall cops. Kondracky and I need to take this fight elsewhere if we're going to avoid a massacre.

At the bottom, the doors rattle open and I roll out, covering the arc of the door. There are emergency stairs to the left that Kondracky could have taken from the central atrium, but he'd be here by now. That means he heard the sirens too and with me out of the way, he's headed for the Trooper.

To the right there's a loading dock. I throw up the metal shutter door and hug the wall as I run up the ramp to the parking lot. I pause at the mouth, ready for a dash for the Grand Am.

Too late. The Trooper's already roaring towards me from the far end of the parking lot. In the other direction a pair of PD cruisers squeal up to the mall entrance, lights blazing. Cops drop out, pulling tactical armour and weapons from the trunks, heading for the mall entrance. I could just make it to one of the cruisers – cops always leave the keys in the ignition – but boosting a marked vehicle is going to bring far too much heat.

I'm about to retreat back into the basement when I see a scrawny kid in store clothes, nineteen max, pulling on a helmet as he mounts a dirt bike. He has earbuds in, which is why he hasn't heard the cops. Helmet on, he kicks the bike into life and pulls away from the kerb.

I sprint towards him, but he accelerates and turns down between two lines of parked cars, forcing me to change direction. I leap on to the open bed of a rusted-out Ford Ranger, then the cab roof, and use it as a springboard. I sail through the air and slam into the rider, sending him sprawling to the ground. I pull the bike up and mount it. The kid picks himself up, dazed and angry, but backs off when he sees the gun. Behind him, the Trooper two-wheels into the parking aisle, almost rolling as Kondracky catches the kerb.

I twist the throttle. The rear wheel smokes and fishtails forward, then the bike snaps into a wheelie, almost bucking me off. The kid, who has had better days, plunges out of the way of the Trooper as I braaap out of the parking lot.

When I glance back, Kondracky is yards behind me, and gaining.

93

There's no way I can outrun him on the dirt bike, so I bunny-hop the median of the mall access road into oncoming traffic, but Kondracky sticks to my tail, rust cascading off the chassis as he bounces over the divider.

I mount the sidewalk, weaving and bobbing through lamp-posts and parking meters to deny Kondracky a shot. As the traffic clears in front of him, he raises his Glock, so I fake right, then deke left up a side street between an auto body shop and a hot tub dealer.

Kondracky misses the turn. I open up the throttle and roar past a storage lot to where a dirt road snakes up a scrubby hill. To my left, Kondracky vectors in from a cross street, but he's a hundred yards back now.

There's a bump as the blacktop transitions into dirt, the road steepening as it twists up the hill. The Yamaha's on home turf now, knobby lugs biting hard, while the Trooper lurches and bounces, shocks spent and tyres bald. It's all Kondracky can do to keep it on the road, and he's falling behind. Finally, I think, maybe I've got the upper hand.

Ahead, the road hairpins left. But there's a rocky hiking trail, a shortcut that goes almost straight up through the bush. I skid to a halt, then plunge off-road, following the trail up the fall line, handlebars dodging between trees, spitting out a rooster tail of rocks, dirt and exhaust behind me.

Below, Kondracky's forced to stay on the dirt road, drifting the loose corners as he tries to keep me in view, but steadily falling back.

The trail crests in a steep washout. I take it flat out, soar over the lip, and land among dinosaurs.

94

The Brontosaurus is the biggest, life-sized, and sitting at the top of the hill alongside a flagpole fluttering the stars and stripes. Steps lead down to a Tyrannosaurus and Stegosaurus. Beyond them is a Triceratops with a missing horn. They're freshly painted in a minty green, but the New Deal-era concrete bodies are old and flaking.

Rapid City is spread out below me. The road switchbacks down to a six-lane divided highway, the main crosstown thoroughfare. Beyond that, railroad tracks and the green ribbon of parkland along the river that splits the city in half.

And just like that, I know how I'm going to kill him.

The Trooper appears from the dirt road, which doubles as maintenance access. I wait until I'm sure Kondracky's seen me, then drop the clutch. A party of visiting Cub Scouts scatter as I rattle down a flight of concrete stairs to the park entrance.

Kondracky powerslides into the parking lot behind me. I could outpace him by heading off-road, but I'm not trying to lose him any more, so take the road, knobby tyres skittering on the unforgiving blacktop. Kondracky sticks with me, always a corner behind.

Towards the bottom of the hill I pull off-road, hurtling down through sparse trees with a clear path to the interstate. Kondracky takes the next best thing, a dirt road that drops down into the storage yard of a building supply. As I burst out on to the highway he tears through the chicken-wire fence, taking half of it with him, still wrapped around the Trooper.

I've timed my descent, and blast straight across all six lanes of the highway. A Silverado almost nails me, but he brakes hard enough to jackknife his trailer and sheds a houseboat which disintegrates into a fractal of plywood and fibreglass.

Chicken wire sparking on asphalt, Kondracky skids out of the storage yard behind me, explodes through the debris of the houseboat, and weaves across the remaining three lanes of horn-blaring traffic.

Ahead of me is the single railroad track, raised up slightly. I use the rise as a ramp to catapult myself over, landing the other side. Kondracky settles in on the other side of the tracks to parallel me. He's about to fire when he sees what I see: a bright orange double-header diesel electric pulling six thousand feet of mixed freight directly towards us.

He pulls right to avoid a head-on collision as the behemoth slams past, a wall between us, the slipstream almost pulling me off the bike. As each car flashes past in a drumbeat – *bentonite, ethanol, ethanol, bentonite, grain* – I glimpse Kondracky keeping pace. Frame by frame the wrap of chicken wire detaches and finally falls away.

It takes almost a minute for the entire train to pass. The moment the caboose recedes, Kondracky lines up a shot, but I peel left, towards the river and the ribbon of parkland that steepens into a ravine to the west.

Kondracky hauls the Trooper across the tracks to follow me.

Good. We're on the final lap now and he's doing exactly what I wanted.

I turn off-road into the strip of shallow, grassy, treed ravine that borders Rapid Creek. Kondracky follows, the Trooper skidding on to a path through the parkland, paralleling me, sandwiching me between him and the river.

He pulls the Glock again, but I use the margin of trees that line the river as a screen, dodging between them, accelerating and braking, as I make my final preparations. His driver-side window is open, but that's no good to me, so I brake, cutting behind him, then accelerate hard to pull level with him on the passenger side.

Kondracky thinks he finally has a shot, and fires through the side window, but I brake, and a second shot goes wide through the rear passenger window.

Perfect. He's doing the work for me.

I pull the Nammo grenades from my belt, clipped together. I yank out the pin, accelerate forward, lob it through the shattered rear window, then arc uphill and out of range.

The grenade bounces off the rear of the passenger seat and down into the footwell under Kondracky's seat. He frantically fumbles for it, almost losing control, but it's no good. The fuse is four seconds and he's used three. He wrenches open the door and bails from the Trooper, rolling and tumbling down the slope in a tuck.

A moment later the grenade detonates, blowing out the windows and doors. The wrecked Trooper lurches driverless down the slope to the river, taking air as it gathers speed, until it slams head on into a tree. The gas tank ruptures and the Trooper eviscerates itself in a ball of orange flame.

Kondracky rolls to a halt and scrambles to his feet, pressing himself against a tree for cover as he tries to reacquire me. But I'm already racing downhill towards him. I open fire, my shells thudding into the trunk, trapping him. He's dead if he doesn't move, so he sprints downhill, trying to keep the barrier of tree trunks between us to block my shot.

He'll be at the river soon, where he'll be trapped, and that's where I'll finish him. I can see him gasping for air. Yes, he's fit, but he's old, and he's already running out of gas.

But then he suddenly darts right, to where the ravine steepens.

I'm going so fast I overshoot, and lose sight of him for a second.

I skid to a halt.

Shit.

If I follow him into the ravine, I'm wide open for an ambush. But I can't let him get away. So I crank the throttle and head up to the edge of the slope, trying to locate him from above. But there's no sign of him. Ahead the river passes under a cross street which blocks my way, so I huck the Yamaha off the edge, sail through the air and land on the steep slope. The bike loses traction, I slide out of control for thirty feet, then manage to get it upright again. I roar down to the path that runs along the river and under the bridge, half expecting him to ambush me from behind a concrete support. But there's no sign of him. He's gone.

I skid round and head back a hundred yards in the other direction.

Nothing.

And I realise what he did.

When I went down, he came up behind me.

He could be anywhere now.

I've lost him.

95

I sit under the Brontosaurus, where there's a three-sixty view of Rapid City and no possible way for Kondracky to ambush me, and watch the sun sink over the horizon.

Kondracky's not about to give up. But Kondracky's not the problem. If somebody wants me dead, then killing him's at best a temporary fix. They'll just send another, and another, and another.

Sure, I can kill most of them. But I have to kill all of them. And they only have to be lucky once.

Without Handler's infrastructure behind me, I am no longer Seventeen.

I am a trophy animal.

It all goes back to Berlin. To the memory card containing the encryption key. It's now clear to me the real Berlin job was the brush pass. The hit earlier on the old man served a double purpose: it got me into the right place at the right time, and distracted me enough that they could spring the Tiergarten job on me with zero notice, giving me no time to think or ask questions.

The moment the memory card had been intercepted, I became not just disposable, but dangerous.

The only way Kovacs could have known where I'd be and what I'd be carrying was if Handler was in on it from the beginning. He sacrificed me, for what quid pro quo I can only imagine. Perhaps a monopoly on deniable covert actions for an agency like DIA. It would have to be something on that scale to make it worth it for him. But he always was ambitious.

And when Kovacs failed to kill me, he sent me after Sixteen.

But why is it so vital that I die?

Brutal as it was, the Berlin operation was nothing out of the ordinary. People like Moe get killed by people like me all the time. Death is an occupational hazard.

There has to be something I'm missing.

Something I haven't yet factored in.

The shadow of the Triceratops lengthens towards me, becoming infinite as the sun extinguishes itself behind the silhouette of Rapid City.

I run over the events of that day again and again.

And I realise, they all make sense. I understand them all.

Except one thing.

What Moe said to me as he backed away down the tracks, his eyes filled with fear.

Parachute. Parachute. Parachute.

He was trying to tell me something of desperate importance.

Important enough to send Kovacs to kill me, and me to kill Sixteen.

Parachute. Parachute. Parachute.

I need to know what it means. And there's exactly one man on earth who might tell me.

PART FIVE

96

By my twenty-first birthday I had killed two people.

I knew what I wanted to be, but I was still a rank amateur.

You can only teach yourself so much sitting in the Grande Bibliothèque. What I needed were teachers. I found them easily enough – skills training is a lucrative gig for ex-Special Forces and ex-spooks – but the really good ones cost. I paid for them with money I stole or earned.

Over the course of three years I learned to drive, shoot, fly, parachute, fight, and climb. Thanks to Montreal's cosmopolitan immigrant community I acquired seven languages I could make myself understood in, and became fluent in four. Night classes taught me how to read a spreadsheet and interrogate a database. I needed no training in withstanding pain: David taught me that. I went to security conferences where I discovered how to enter a locked building without leaving a trace, how to socially engineer my way into almost any corporation or institution, how to disguise myself, how to fool biometrics, and how to forge a passport. My tutors were ex-Mossad, ex-CIA, ex-KGB, ex-South African intelligence, and a man from the Estonian intelligence service who eclipsed all of them. I bought a round-the-world plane ticket and familiarised myself with every European capital, most of the Middle East, Moscow, St Petersburg, Beijing, Tokyo and a chunk of South America.

I made no attempt to conceal what I was doing. On the contrary, I made sure my mentors knew I was ambitious. I began to find men with tired faces sitting themselves next to me in bars, drinking too much but not getting drunk, gently sounding me out to see if I was interested in some government work.

I turned them all down, because I still wasn't ready.

The teachers I'd used were all ex. Sure, they retained contacts – no-one ever really retires from intelligence – but they were careful about what they said to a young prick like me. They offered to make introductions, but it wasn't introductions I wanted. It was knowledge.

I needed to know what I didn't know.

I needed to know what these people would never teach me.

I didn't need any more teachers.

What I needed was a mentor.

I found him on YouTube.

Tommy Humboldt was fifty-four years old, drunk as a skunk, and the video he'd posted had just gone viral. He had a big red drinker's face that leered into the camera, and greasy grey hair that spilled over a crumpled collar. He was sitting in an empty apartment with no furniture except a mattress and a flatscreen TV, and bitching about his treatment by the CIA, so brimful of self-pity he broke down in tears several times as he told his sob-story.

He was coming apart at the seams.

I liked him immediately.

Tommy was CIA, and not just serving, but senior. He was still, officially at least, Chief of Station in Beirut, Lebanon. Before that he'd been an instructor at Camp Peary, otherwise known as The Farm, the CIA's 9,000-acre training facility near Williamsburg where he trained assholes like me for a decade. He was nothing if not old school: he'd come up in the Agency at the tail end of the Cold War, when it was still

258

considered cool to fuck around and spend the afternoon stinking of whatever it was you'd drunk at lunchtime, then go back for more after, or more likely instead of, dinner.

Times had changed, but not for Tommy. He habitually drove drunk but his diplomatic plates essentially conferred him immunity, and the Beirut cops left him alone or even, in a few cases, escorted him safely home. I imagine they were paid handsomely for their services out of CIA funds, which Tommy was not above misappropriating. He also misappropriated CIA safe houses, which he used to fuck a long string of mistresses who included subordinates, contacts, and his opposite number in a rival intelligence agency.

Tommy was a walking time bomb of a security risk, but he had proved extremely hard to get rid of. First, his training, and years of professional deception, allowed him to sail through polygraphs with flying colours. Second, he was extremely good at his job. His methods, unorthodox as they were, worked like a charm. Third, he was immensely likeable. Weeks after I first saw his video, when we walked into a hotel in Milan together, his first question to the desk clerk was *'dov'è la fornicazione?'*, which he said in as loud and booming a voice as possible. Which was inspired, because no-one undercover, which we were, would ever behave like that.

It was Tommy who taught me the value of security by being totally-fucking-out-there.

97

The Greyhound stinks. Someone has vomited in a nearby seat and the attempt to clean it up was only partially successful, so now the entire bus smells faintly of a combination of puke and disinfectant, plus whatever individual prizes the other passengers are offering. A guy with oil-stained jeans and greasy hair is passed out on the rear two seats by the restroom, forcing passengers to step over him on their way to relieve themselves.

Barb and Kat sit together, the bus full enough that they keep their voices low.

'This is bullshit,' says Kat, still angry. 'Fucking men.'

'Some of them are women,' says Barb.

'What?'

'Some of the people who do that job, they're women. Young, some of them. Girls, even. I'm saying, it's not just a man thing.'

'You ever kill someone?' says Kat, a sudden suspicion growing.

'Lord, no,' says Barb. 'Not for want of provocation.'

Kat's silent for a while, staring at the pattern on the back of the seat in front of her, worn to a shine where former passengers have rested foreheads to sleep.

'I tried to kill someone,' she says eventually.

Barb stares at her.

'Mack. Yesterday. I had a shotgun. He didn't think I'd pull the trigger. But I did. That's why his ear—' She gestures up at her own, making a little explosion with her fingers. 'Only I wasn't aiming at his ear.'

She sees something in the other woman's face.

'I figured it was him or me.'

'You don't have to justify yourself to me,' says Barb. 'But he wouldn't have pulled the trigger.'

'Because?'

'Because of whose daughter you are.'

Kat laughs. 'You think he wouldn't have killed me because he was sweet on my mom? Come on.'

'That's not what I'm saying,' says Barb. 'He wasn't just sweet on her. I guess she never told you, but they went back. *Way* back. To before you were born. Right before you were born.'

Kate stares at her.

'I'm just saying,' says Barb gently, 'that maybe there's a reason you were able to pull the trigger.'

Kat sits back in speechless astonishment.

She's quiet for about fifteen miles after that, turning over rocks in her mind, things she'd forgotten, moments, desires, things she felt and did or almost did that seemed to come from a place in her that she didn't recognise or understand. And all of it fits.

'You okay, hon?' asks Barb.

'I guess,' says Kat. 'It's just . . . it's a lot.'

'Yes,' says Barb. 'That it is.'

98

Sun safely over the horizon, I buzz the dirt bike, lights off, down through scrub towards the lowest-rent apartment building I could see from my vantage among the sauropods.

By now law enforcement will have descriptions from the kid whose bike I stole, the waitress with the retainers, the schmuck whose houseboat is now scattered across six lanes, plus a high-resolution still from the mall CCTV. Moreover, the Grand Am is now behind a police cordon and a forensic team are already suiting up in Tyvek to take fingerprints, with State, Feds and ATF on the way. All of which means I am currently South Dakota's premier law enforcement target, and I need to take evasive action.

The apartment block is public housing, one of those places where no-one has much to steal and nobody asks too many questions in case they get asked back. It's a simple matter to slip inside holding the door for an old guy in a greasy fedora, bent crooked over his walker and oxygen tank as he shuffles out for a smoke.

Inside, I head down to the laundry area in the basement where, as always, there's an abandoned load someone has dumped out of a washer in irritation. I pick it up, apologising to a woman with multiple piercings and a 100% THAT BITCH tank top, and ferry it to a stairwell. I swap my clothes for a damp Nike tracksuit from a dude with a waist four inches bigger than mine.

It's a knock-off but I'll take it.

I head out to the rear parking lot. I need something that nobody's going to miss, for a while at least. Most of the vehicles look like they've been recently driven, but to one side there's an Oldsmobile whose hood and windshield are strewn with leaves and debris from a ragged maple that overhangs it. It clearly hasn't been driven in months, but it looks in decent shape. From the vintage my guess is it belongs to the old guy who's huffing nicotine out front, and is obviously in no condition to drive it any more.

Five minutes later I'm at the wheel of a blood-red '94 Cutlass Supreme with a plush interior, a full ashtray, an Aerosmith CD, and a HONK IF YOU'RE HORNY sticker.

The old guy knew how to live, I'll give him that.

99

Six weeks before Tommy made the YouTube video, the shit
had hit the fan. Tommy had wrapped his Merc wagon with
the D-plates around a Beirut lamppost and almost killed a
Lebanese student who turned out to be a nephew of the
Minister of Justice. A diplomatic scandal exploded and
Tommy was summoned home, it being made clear to him that
his career was over and he would be quietly put out to pasture,
in return for not being prosecuted for embezzlement of CIA
funds.

But Tommy was not the kind to go quietly.

He missed the plane home, and the next anybody knew,
there he was on YouTube in an anonymous apartment, rant-
ing drunkenly into the camera about the failings of the CIA,
the unfairness of his treatment, the brilliance of his operational skills, the size of his penis, and the personal defects of
his bosses.

Once or twice he got up to refill his glass with the extremely
expensive whisky that was evidently now his main squeeze,
and it became clear he was not wearing pants.

I was warming to him more and more.

Tommy might have been drunk, but he wasn't stupid. He
knew exactly what he was doing. The video was a very public
ransom note which he concluded with both a demand, and a
threat. The demand was simple: he wanted to keep his job, or
at least *a* job. He figured, probably rightly, that he'd given his

life to the CIA. For Tommy, retirement was the equivalent of being euthanised, and he wasn't having any of it.

The threat was brutal. If the CIA didn't take him back, he would go and work for someone else. Hezbollah, perhaps. Or the Russians. Or the Chinese. Or whoever. And he would share with them everything he knew, including the identities of the hundreds of CIA case officers and illegals he'd trained over the years, along with the details of every operation he'd ever been read in on.

He gave the CIA two weeks to make a credible public counter-offer. In the meantime he made it clear he was open to approaches from other parties.

Tommy Humboldt was gold. The CIA are squeamish about assassination, at least of their own, but Tommy had crossed a line. There had to be a price on his head, and a substantial one at that – a so-called open contract. Whoever gets there first and carries out the hit gets paid.

He was everything I could have hoped for.

I had two weeks to find him, and I would be up against the best.

The only clues I had were in the video. He was almost certainly still in Lebanon because the CIA had supplied all his alternate passport identities. He couldn't pass a border without being flagged, nor could he risk working with a smuggler who would sell him out to the highest bidder. Most likely he was still in Beirut, since he knew the city and no doubt retained good local contacts.

There was no time code embedded in the video, but three minutes in I could hear the sound of a plane throttling down. When I zoomed in on the blank flatscreen TV behind him, I could see the reflection of a plane with its landing gear down, clearly on final approach. It was a twin turboprop, which I narrowed down from the unique profile to a Swearingen SA-227. That meant it was short-haul and most likely a charter flight.

My guess was that Tommy, drunk and furious, had uploaded the video shortly after making it, so I used the upload date to scour through flights into Beirut on a flight-tracker website. There was only one SA-227 coming in that day, from Erbil. That gave me the landing time. I downloaded the KML file of its approach, loaded it into Google Earth, and spooled forward until I had the approximate altitude I could see in the video, twelve hundred feet or so. I moved my position around until the perspective was the same as the one I could see reflected in Tommy's flatscreen.

That gave me a bearing, a line stretching across Beirut, but I needed the distance. I took a screenshot, loaded it into Photoshop, zoomed in all the way and used the ruler tool to count pixels, measuring the width of the plane, the width of the window and the width of the TV. From there, high-school geometry put the location of the building between 2,500 and 4,500 metres from the flight path.

Two kilometres was still a needle in a haystack. But in the reflection, below the plane, there was the top of a cedar tree, and a fragment of skyline. That put Tommy at least three floors up, but no more than four. That narrowed it down to five apartment buildings, but the fragment of skyline in the reflection was only visible from one.

The plane was on the west side of the building, which meant it had to be one of eight apartments.

All of this took me less than four hours, and I never left my chair.

Later that evening I was on a plane to Beirut.

100

I'm not finished with Rapid City just yet.

The first store I hit is no good – all discount liquor, menthol cigarettes and domestic beer. But inside I can see a TV behind the counter. It's showing news footage of the day's events, a montage of flashing lights and Tyvek suits, plus an interview with the dirt-bike kid, during which they flash up a CCTV still of me. The skirmish between Kondracky and me is evidently the biggest news to hit this town in years. Even with a change of clothes, if I go inside this or any other store in Rapid City, I'll be made in seconds.

There's a guy outside panhandling, head bowed with a cardboard sign in his hands that says HUNGRY – VETERAN. Dude is probably no more than forty years old but he looks twice that. I guess the streets take a toll. I hit the horn, and it beeps feebly. He looks up. I roll down the window and gesture at him. He heads over, I make him an offer he's in no state to refuse, and he climbs in. His name is Fred and his stink is eye-watering, but he's friendly and sharper than he looks – he was a horse trader, he tells me, after the army, then launches into a diatribe about some big-time Nashville producer who stole a country song he wrote. More importantly, if there's one thing he knows, it's liquor stores.

Minutes later we're parked outside The Liquor Boutique, its windows piled high with ritzy booze.

The old guy stares in wonder at the bundle of cash I pull out. He listens intently, then nods and heads inside. Inside, a scene plays out in dumbshow as the clerk attempts to throw him out, but he literally waves the cash in her face, and her attitude reverses on a dime.

Deal done, he heads back to the Olds with two brown paper bags, and hands mine through the window. I check the contents.

'We good?' he asks.

'We're good,' I say.

'So you're that kid, huh?' he says.

'What kid?'

'The one who shot up the mall and blew up a truck down by the river. Saw your mug on the TV where you picked me up.'

'I don't know what you're talking about.'

Fred grins a toothless grin. 'Neither do I, kid. But I'll keep a seat warm in hell, just in case.'

He taps his nose, salutes, and wanders over to the door of the liquor store, where he settles against the wall, props his sign up against his knees, and cracks open the first of his liquid loot.

IOI

Lebanon is a country where children's exam results are celebrated by firing AK-47s into the air, and a really good result calls for an RPG. Arming myself was a short morning's work and an unnerving trip to the volatile southern suburbs.

I found Tommy's building and worked my way through the third and fourth floors. I narrowed it down to four apartments, since the light only came from one direction and the other four candidates had windows on two sides. On the third floor there was no answer at the first. The second was a young woman with a toddler, who told me her friend lived in the first apartment, and had been complaining about the sound of Led Zep being played loudly day and night in the apartment above, at least until it stopped five days earlier.

The day Tommy's video was posted to YouTube.

The apartment was empty, which didn't surprise me. Tommy was an old hand and knew the score. If I could track him down from a reflection in a flatscreen TV so could the worker bees back in Langley. The only reason I got there first was I didn't have to escalate my mission plan through an intelligence community kill chain full of grey men and women whose chief interest in life was covering their asses.

But Tommy was still a drunk, and drunks get sloppy. The apartment was filthy, full of take-out and delivery cartons, but there was something missing. On the video Tommy had been knocking back whisky like it was water, and at one point there

269

was a clink as he tossed an empty across the room to what was evidently a pile. But for some reason he had removed them all before ghosting. That told me they were important. I couldn't see Tommy carting a suitcase of them away, so I chose to look in the most obvious place. Each floor was serviced by a chute which dumped out into the basement. From there the garbage found its way to a dumpster out back. There, up to my waist in old diapers and rotting lamb shawarma, I hit pay dirt, and the moment I saw the bottles I understood why he'd not wanted anyone to find them.

The whisky was a Hakushu twelve-year-old single malt running around $250 a bottle, but it wasn't the price that made it important. It was the fact that it was ludicrously hard to get hold of, especially in a place like Beirut, and that Tommy was obviously and hopelessly addicted to the stuff.

I left most of the bottles there in the dumpster, but I took one, carefully cleaned it off and put it back in the apartment where Tommy had recorded the video for the next person to find.

102

Kat watches the cartoon landscape loop by for an hour, chewing over Barb's revelation. Then a thought strikes her.

'So. You and Mack. What's that about?'

Barb blinks.

'Come on,' says Kat. 'Maybe you didn't know exactly who he was, but you knew he was a killer. Maybe not at first, but at some point, you had to have realised. But you stuck with him. How come?'

Barb's turn to stare out of the window for a while.

'You don't think I asked myself the same thing?'

'Sure,' says Kat. 'Ever come up with an answer?'

Silence.

'Look at it this way,' says Kat. 'You're practically my step-mom. You don't think you owe me?'

Barb sighs. 'I was a skinny little kid,' she says. 'Tomboy. But last couple of years of high school I filled out and suddenly the boys came after me. Only I didn't want them. I wanted something different, some grand romance like the ones you read about in books. After high school I lit out, moved to St Louis, got a job in a bar. Got so I ran the place, baseball bat under the bar, you know the score. And one day my grand romance walked in through the door. He had cheekbones and snake hips and he'd read every book under the sun and he'd met famous people and he could talk for hours about any subject you'd care to mention and you'd pay money to listen to him. Well, I fell about as hard as you can fall. For about six months it was magic, all flowers and rainbows. But then it started to sink in. He was a bullshitter. He'd never met any of these people. He didn't know anything about philosophy or poetry. He just strung words together until they sounded good. Took me another two years to shake myself free of him. Meantime he took my money, got me started on shit that I should never have put in my veins. Beat me. Knocked me up twice. But none of that was a dealbreaker, because I just couldn't let go of my grand romance.'

'So what was the dealbreaker?'

'He wanted to whore me out so he could score.'

'Holy shit.'

'I walked out that night,' says Barb. 'He was passed out on the couch. And all I could think was how easy it would be to kill him. Smother him with a cushion. Or put another needle in his arm and push him over the edge.'

'What stopped you?'

'However shit it was to be around him, it had to be worse to *be* him. Why put the bastard out of his misery? Let him suffer.'

Kat snorts. There is far more to Barb than meets the eye.

'So Mack . . . ?'

'He never lied to me. He never swore at me. He never hit me. He never promised me anything he wasn't able to give me. He cleans up good when I come around. He cooks dinner. He never once told me what I should or shouldn't do, how I should dress or what I should think. Maybe I set too low a bar these days, but I'll take it over snake hips and bullshit any day of the week.'

'And it doesn't bother you, what he does?'

'What he did, hon.'

'He's doing it now.'

'Only because your fellow came along and wouldn't let a sleeping dog lie.'

'He's not my fellow. Just because I – just because we—'

'Sure he is. Why else you defending him?'

'I'm not—' But she stops, because she knows she is.

103

There was no way Tommy Humboldt was risking buying the whisky himself. Nor would he be stupid enough to have it delivered, which would have exposed his location. No, he was sending someone, and whoever was slinging Tommy's hooch had to be someone he trusted.

That meant someone outside the world of intelligence, since the basis of intelligence work is betrayal. There was only one realistic possibility: a lover, and not one of the paid kind who might be lured away by a higher bidder.

Tommy was in his fifties and hard living had aged him, so it seemed unlikely to be anyone under thirty-five. But he was of that generation who trade in for a younger model when the current squeeze ages out, so that put her in her forties at most.

The only store that sold Hakushu was on Saoud Street. There was a cafe opposite, where the taxi drivers would sit and gossip between fares. So I took a seat there, cracked open a travel guide, ordered endless cups of sweet, gritty coffee, and waited.

Three days later I saw her. She was older than I expected, but slim, well dressed, and wearing flawless make-up under a headscarf. As she turned into the doorway of the store, she looked both ways, as if to check if anyone was following her. That marked her out as both worried and an amateur, since a professional never looks back.

The Hakushu and other high-end Japanese single malts were up high on a shelf to the left of the counter, and it was easy enough to see when the clerk reached for one, then another, then another.

She left with the bottles in one of those boutiquey paper bags, gave the same nervous look as she exited, hailed a cab, and commenced a surprisingly professional dry-cleaning run – a circuitous route intended to shake any surveillance – involving two more cabs, a bus in the other direction, and an Uber which dropped her at the gates of the Sioufi Garden, where she continued on foot.

I dumped the rented moped I'd been tailing her on, and followed her through the park to a bougie villa near the Palais de Justice, where she let herself in with another double-glance behind her.

The rear of the building was surrounded by a high wall, but I could see a room on the upper floor whose shutters were closed, although it faced north and never got direct sun.

There was a black plastic garbage bin at the back. As I wheeled it to the wall, it clanked and I didn't need to look inside to know what it contained. I used it to scale the wall, dropped into an elegant little courtyard at the rear of the house, and let myself in through French doors which had been left unlocked.

Inside, I headed upstairs to the room with the closed shutters. The door was ajar, and I could hear voices. One was Tommy's, the other hers. They were speaking French, and she was pleading with him to give himself up. Tommy wasn't interested. She started crying, then there was some shouting.

I stepped into a bathroom opposite Tommy's door as she exited the room. But she didn't go downstairs. Instead she came into the bathroom. I held my breath behind the door as she cried into the basin, then splashed water on her face and dried it with a towel, straightened herself in the mirror, and finally headed out.

274

I waited until I could hear the clanking of pans in the kitchen, then pulled the Beretta I'd bought four days earlier, and kicked open the door.

Tommy was sitting on the bed, pouring himself a tumblerful of twelve-year-old Hakushu. He spun round as I entered, sending the tumbler flying as he reached for the pistol which he had stowed under a pillow. But he was slow, and drunk, and I had taken him by surprise.

It would have been an easy shot, and the bounty on his head would have made me a rich man, and my name into the bargain.

But I wasn't there to kill him.

I was there to save him.

104

Tommy was the ticket I'd been searching for into the world I wanted to inhabit.

But first I had to convince him to play ball.

That was the point of the bottle I left in Humboldt's abandoned apartment. I had gotten there first, but I wouldn't be the last. The next to arrive would find the bottle, and follow it to the liquor store just as I had. They would follow the woman in the headscarf – her name was Hayat and she was one of the lawyers who arranged visas for American diplomats, which was how Humboldt knew her – back to her bougie villa. He or she would see the room with the shutters and scale the wall and let themselves in through the French doors and hide in the bathroom and then when Tommy was asleep or drunk or taking a shit, they would put a bullet in his brain.

But if he decided to co-operate with me, I would protect him.

Tommy wasn't happy about being strong-armed. He was the opposite of happy. He ranted and raged but he only had three bottles of Hakushu and at the rate he was going through them he would need more by the weekend, and thanks to the bottle in his apartment there was now no way he could get them without leading an assassin straight to his bedroom door.

He decided to play ball.

★   ★   ★

276

Over the course of three days and the remaining bottles of Hakushu, Tommy told me how it worked. He told me how the CIA and every other major agency kept their hands clean by farming out the dirtiest work to freelancers who earned far more than they ever could in-house and were free to ignore the usual bureaucratic, legal and ethical constraints so long as they delivered results, shouldered all the risk, and maintained complete and utter silence.

He told me about the network of handlers, brokers of death and betrayal, each with their stable of day-players and stars, about the ranking system and how you might claw your way up the greasy pole by dispatching those above you. He told me how the open assignments were flagged, how jobs were bid on, and who decided who got them. He told me about Handler, Osterman and all the others, about their rivalries and their competition for jobs and operatives. And then he told me about Sixteen, his reputation, and that if there was one unbreakable rule I should follow it was this: I should never, ever, under any circumstances whatever, go up against him.

On the afternoon of the third day, we sent Hayat out for more Hakushu, with instructions to follow the exact same route she had previously. We told her she would be followed, but that she would never see who it was. We made sure the garbage bin was in the same position by the wall, full of empty whisky bottles. A couple of hours later we heard Hayat enter through the front door. She came up to the bedroom with the fancy bag full of overpriced booze. She and Tommy argued, she started crying, she straightened herself out in the bathroom, and then she went downstairs and started banging pans.

When the door burst open, I emptied the Beretta into the man who stood in the doorway.

I don't think I have ever seen anyone look more surprised.

105

From Rapid City I head south into Wyoming, where a massive thunderstorm lights up the blackness of the sky and the endless prairie.

Once I'm across the state line I relax a little. But not much: nothing would surprise me less than Kondracky hurtling out of the darkness towards me like some avenging banshee. I check my six constantly, but there's no sign of him.

I can't tell if this should worry me or not. I suspect it should.

I make Denver just after midnight, hit the lockup for a change of ID and clothes, then dump the Olds in long-stay parking where no-one will notice it for weeks. Transit takes me to the twenty-four-hour rental, where I present an almost entirely genuine New Mexico driver's licence and tell the Sikh girl behind the counter I'm in on the late flight from Albuquerque.

She looks at me for what seems a second too long, which makes me wonder if she's recognised me from a mugshot, or if some biometric or facial recognition software has triggered, but the TV in the waiting area is tuned to CNN and still obsessing about Iran and something tells me they aren't going to interrupt for a few firecrackers going off in South Dakota.

'On business?' she says, and I realise she's sizing up the generosity of my expense account.

I nod and smile. 'Commercial real estate. A few sites to check out.'

She tries to upsell me to an S-Class convertible but tempting as it is to travel in at least some kind of style, I need something with a little more flexibility. I tell her the sites are under construction, and plump for a Jeep Gladiator with 4WD, a V8 that could pull stumps, and room to spare for the remainder of my loadout. She looks disappointed, so I sign up for the Collision Damage Waiver and all the extras because it will goose her performance metrics, I stiffed her on the Merc, she has a nice smile, and, let's be honest, I'm probably going to need it.

106

Tommy recognised the dead man immediately, and I could see that he was shaken. The killer's name was Zhuk, he'd been trained by Russian military intelligence before going rogue, he was Handler's star client, and he was the closest thing Sixteen had ever had to a rival.

The fact the price on his head was enough to attract a man of Zhuk's calibre meant the CIA were very, very serious about wanting Tommy dead. I think that was actually the first time it hit him that without me he was a dead man walking. But there was something else too.

'You know what this means?' he asked me, prodding Zhuk's body with his foot as blood continued to seep out through the neat cluster of bullet holes in his chest.

'No.'

'It means,' said Tommy, 'you just sailed past all the shit.'

Tommy's brush with death, in the shape of Zhuk, was enough to convince him to negotiate. Through Hayat we brokered a deal with the CIA. Tommy would repatriate to the US and retire on a full pension with a medical discharge, the YouTube incident painted as a temporary psychotic breakdown brought on by occupational stress, which was closer to the truth than anyone cared to admit.

During the three months it took White House counsel to sign off on the deal, we moved from safe house to hotel, country to country, under assumed names and fake passports. In the process, he crammed the entire contents of the course he taught at The Farm in to marathon, sometimes twenty-four-hour-long, sessions facilitated by seemingly bottomless bottles of Japanese whisky.

Before we left Lebanon we dumped Zhuk's body in a back alley on the south side of Beirut, near the airport. I left a card on it with the number of a burner phone, which I didn't turn on until I got confirmation from Hayat that Humboldt was safely back in the US, and still a free man.

When I turned it on, there was a message from Handler.

A week later I had taken Zhuk's place.

107

The Greyhound is quiet now. Just the rumble of the tyres, the snore of the guy in the oily jeans at the back, the tizz of a pair of headphones, the rustle of fast-food bags, the back and forth of a simmering quarrel between a young couple two seats down. But then there's another noise, a noise that makes half the people in the bus suddenly sit a little more upright. The pair of oily jeans snaps out of his coma, peers backwards, and sees a cruiser with bullbars and South Dakota Highway Patrol markings in full-pursuit mode flat-footing it up the outside lane.

If he's hoping it's going to sail past, he's disappointed, because the prowler tucks in behind, lights strobing.

The Greyhound slows and pulls over.

'Don't sweat it, hon,' says Barb. 'We've done nothing wrong. Half the people in here got more reason to be worried than you and me.'

Kat cranes past the seat in front to see a state trooper squaring his hat as he climbs into the Greyhound. His weapon is holstered but there's something off about him she can't quite put her finger on. He exchanges a few inaudible words with the driver, who nods and gestures back.

The Trooper turns to the bus, standing in the aisle, and cracks a friendly smile.

'Routine stop, folks, nothing to worry about. Just need to check a few IDs.'

He begins to move down the bus, polite as you like. 'Thank you, sir. Much obliged, ma'am. You have a nice day.'

Oily Jeans squirms around, trying to figure out if he can get the rear escape door open without being seen, like a barfly who disappears out the back door when a cop walks in the front. But the cop pays no attention to him. Kat notices he's checking the ID of the women more carefully, comparing the photograph to the face for a second, but barely glancing at that of the men.

He reaches Barb and Kat's row halfway down the bus. And Kat realises what's off about him. His hair's a half-inch past his collar, he's wearing stubble, his pants are a size too big, and they're crumpled around combat boots which don't match his uniform. Kat glances over to Barb, and sees she's got the same vibe. Out the window, Kat sees a second person has exited the prowler. It's a woman, in civilian clothes, with cropped hair, black combat pants and a tactical jacket without law enforcement blazes. Over her shoulder, but half concealed by the jacket, she has a compact snub-nosed automatic. She scans the highway, a sentry on point.

'Ladies?' says the Trooper, smiling and holding out a thick-fingered hand.

'We don't have to show you shit,' says Kat, meeting his eye.

The Trooper's hand goes to his sidearm. Other passengers crane past headrests. Oily Jeans leans forward, taking a professional interest.

'Show me your fucking ID,' says the Trooper.

'I'll show you mine if you show me yours,' says Kat.

'What do you think this is?' says the Trooper, pointing at his badge, which proclaims UNDER GOD THE PEOPLE RULE.

'Picture ID,' says Barb. 'Otherwise who's to say you're not just some asshole who borrowed a uniform and a car.'

'I don't need to show you that, ma'am,' says the Trooper.

'Then we don't need to show you ours,' says Kat.

Somebody claps. The clap becomes a ripple of applause that runs through the bus. Oily Jeans grins and joins in, stamping his foot to keep it going.

The Trooper glances out the window to the buzzcut, who gives him a look as if to say *hurry the fuck up.*

'Okay,' says the Trooper. 'Off the bus, both of you, and keep your hands where I can see them.' He fumbles his holster backstrap off with his thumb.

'See,' says Kat, 'I don't think you're actually a cop. Ten to one whatever ID you have doesn't have any picture that looks like you. You can barely operate your own thumbstrap, and your friend out there looks hinky as shit. I'm thinking some of our fellow travellers here might like to dial 911 just in case. Or you could call for backup yourself, if you are who you say you are.'

A few passengers are now filming on their phones. A heavy-set black woman a couple of rows back thumbs a three-digit number.

'Ma'am, there's no need—'

She holds up the phone, on speaker.

'911, what is your emergency?' says the phone.

The Trooper strides over, snatches the phone. 'No emergency. Officer Nyquist SDHP on scene. We're dealing.' He hangs up, then pulls his weapon and shoots the woman in the head. Her blood and brains splatter against the window of the Greyhound.

The bus fills with screams as passengers dive behind seats. Oily Jeans pulls the escape lever at the back, but the Trooper kills him with a second shot before he's halfway out. The driver jumps out of his seat, but is slammed back into it by the buzzcut as she jumps on board.

'These two,' yells Trooper. He grabs Kat by her hair and shoves her to Buzzcut, who jams the Uzi in her ribs and frog-marches her off the bus. Trooper turns to Barb, who raises her hands and lets Trooper walk her out, not giving him the satisfaction of using force on her.

Buzzcut shoves Kat into the rear cage of the prowler. Trooper follows suit with Barb. The last thing Kat sees of the Greyhound is the body of Oily Jeans, hanging out of the emergency door. Then she and Barb are pressed back against the hard bench seat as Buzzcut hits the siren and pulls back out on to the highway, tyres smoking, lights flashing.

108

I head west through the night, mainlining truck-stop coffee and stale chocolate muffins to stay awake. There are uppers in a bag in the rear, but the last thing I need is the paranoia and jitters they sometimes give me. The Gladiator handles like a panel van but it's a relief to be driving something designed this century.

I almost miss the Veyron.

Almost.

I'm hardly in the mood for music, and curious about what I just glimpsed on CNN, so I bounce between AM talk radio stations, one fading into static as it's replaced by another.

The news is uniformly bad. Shit is getting real, with the Sixth Fleet en route to the Gulf of Oman. A US-backed resolution in the UN has been acrimoniously vetoed by China and Russia. In response the US says it has 'no option' but to issue a unilateral ultimatum to Iran to cease all nuclear operations, something they will never do with Israel fully tooled up on their doorstep. Khameini has issued bellicose statements describing the approaching carrier group as a provocation and vowing to defend Iran's sovereignty to the last drop of blood. The American ultimatum expires in two days' time, after which POTUS is promising a rain of fire which will make 2003's shock and awe on Baghdad look like a Walmart firework display.

It's past 3 a.m. now, the highway deserted, my hands on the wheel glowing in the light of a low full moon kissing the horizon. Moe's blood is long gone, or it should be, given the number of times I've scrubbed it away. But the truth is they haven't felt clean since that day in Berlin, and I'm beginning to wonder if they ever will.

It's not your problem, I tell myself.

You can't fix stupid.

They'd probably have gone to war anyway.

You weren't to know.

Nobody could blame you.

I repeat the phrases like a mantra.

And yet, and yet, and yet.

The world is tipping towards a potentially global, possibly nuclear, war. Nobody seems to have the slightest fucking idea how to stop it, not even Canada. It's 1914 all over again. On the streets of Sarajevo Archduke Franz Ferdinand has just been hit in the jugular by a bullet from a Fabrique Nationale pistol. Only this time it wasn't Gavrilo Princip who pulled the trigger.

It was me, in Berlin.

109

In the weeks and months after I took Zhuk's place, I made my bones.

I spent a week on my belly in the Congolese rainforest, crawling a mile a day through snakes and soldier ants to pull off a thousand-metre sniper shot on a Rwandan-backed Mai-Mai warlord who enslaved child soldiers. In Reykjavik, posing as a douchebag on his gap year, I took out an entire Belorussian hit team, hurling the last surviving member into a volcanic geyser. And in Syria, which I entered as a Turkish flight attendant, I penetrated and sabotaged a Russian-run chemical weapons facility whose existence the Syrians denied and which the West could not risk bombing because of the threat to the civilian population, or being accused of an act of war by Moscow.

Meanwhile, I was forced to fend off a barrage of attacks from challengers who assumed Zhuk's death at the hands of an unknown was a fluke and that I was a soft target who would allow *them* to sail past all the shit.

In the old days they'd put the heads of traitors on pikes by the city gates, or hang the bodies of pirates in cages at the entry to the harbour as a warning. I took a similar approach. The message got through eventually, because the attacks tailed off.

And then one day Handler gave me the astonishing news.

Sixteen was gone. Simply gone.

Since I had killed Zhuk, his closest rival, I was the Young Pretender. I could either crawl into his abandoned shell, or leave it vacant for some other slimy thing to inhabit.

'It's up to you,' said Handler. We were standing on the observation deck of the Rockefeller Center, with Manhattan laid out below us like a tablecloth and the Empire State Building glinting in the late afternoon sunlight. It wouldn't surprise me if Handler thought of himself as Satan, offering Christ all the kingdoms of the world, and their glory. Which, in a way, he was.

'It's a big decision,' he said. 'Give it some thought.'

I left Handler and took the elevator down with a bunch of tourists from Kansas who had tickets to Saturday Night Live. Behind them there was the famous photograph of iron-workers sitting on a steel bar during the construction of 30 Rock. Eleven men in a row, sixty-nine storeys above Manhattan, with nothing between them and the cruel earth but air.

One in every fifty of these men would be killed each year, and another permanently crippled. Their union motto summed it up bluntly: 'We do not die. We are killed.'

They did it because they had no choice. The fall of 1932 was the very lowest point of the Great Depression, and if they fell to their death there were a hundred others eager to take their place. Fate, or circumstance, had funnelled each of them to a point where risking their lives high above the surface of the earth was not just a logical choice, it was the *only* choice.

I had no family to feed, nor was I caught in the savage jaws of economic collapse. But every single event of my life had funnelled me towards this moment.

Yes, there would be money, fast cars, sex, and parkour. I'm not proud.

But more importantly, becoming Seventeen would be the ultimate fuck-you to everyone who had ever regarded me or Junebug as a victim. Nobody would ever be able to force me to do something against my will again. There would be no more Davids. No more DeAngelos.

I would be Lee Marvin.

I called Handler. Then I strolled over to Tiffany's, where I bought a plain silver band and had it engraved on the inside with the words:

We do not die. We are killed.

110

Tommy Humboldt was out of the CIA, but he wasn't finished with the world.

As part of his medical discharge, he was offered the addiction counselling of his choice. Like most boomers, Tommy was a hippy at heart. In his second year as station chief in Beirut he'd had a dune buggy freighted from California which at weekends he would roar up and down the beaches north of the city blasting Jefferson Airplane to confused locals.

Accordingly, he chose a weird version of the twelve-step programme run in the Arizona desert by a man who claimed to be, but almost certainly wasn't, a Navajo shaman. During the programme Humboldt found himself on a side quest that involved fasting for a week, climbing a mountain and imbibing a semi-lethal concoction of herbs and peyote that, the bogus shaman claimed, would connect him with God.

Humboldt connected with God. Boy, did he connect with God.

When he finally came down off the mountain, he cashed out his CIA pension, bought an old school bus, painted it with rainbows, got ordained by mail order and drove out to Utah where he set up a ministry dedicated to rescuing young girls from the clutches of the polygamist sects who marry them off to older men at the age of twelve or so.

Which, as you have surely figured out by now, is where I am currently headed.

III

I catch a couple of hours' sleep in the shadow of Factory Butte, the squared-off sandstone peak that soars out of Utah's desert floor. The sun wakes me as it lifts over the horizon, painting Capitol Reef and the Badlands beyond a vivid tangerine.

All I know about Humboldt's church is that it's off Route 24 somewhere near Caineville, but it isn't hard to find courtesy of the rainbow-coloured bus parked out in front of the ramshackle adobe building, one wheel supported on blocks.

I drop out of the Jeep, a gun in the small of my back and brown paper bag in hand. The desert is flat a couple of miles in every direction, there are no other vehicles in sight, and there's nowhere here for Sixteen to hide. He knows my history with Humboldt, I'm sure – Zhuk was his rival, and the circumstances in which I killed the Russian can't have escaped him. But there's no way he knows I'm here, and even if he somehow figured it out there's no way he got here before me.

As I head towards the entrance of the church, I see her. It's a girl with blonde hair, about fifteen, sweeping the entrance with an old-fashioned broom. She's wearing white, almost a bridal white, and she looks up with fear as I approach.

'It's okay,' I tell her. 'I'm not one of them. The polygamists. That's where you're from, right?'

She nods. 'They call themselves the Brethren.'

'Is he here?'

'You mean Father Thomas?'

'That's what he goes by now?'

She nods and indicates I should head inside. But as I pass she says:

'Wait. No guns.'

'What makes you think I have one?'

'I don't. Those are just the rules. Sometimes the elders, from the Brethren, they come here. They bring guns. But they respect the church as a sacred place. That's why we're safe inside, me and the other girls. But Father Thomas says if we make an exception for one, we have to make an exception for all. And then we're not safe any more.'

She smiles at me, and it's a perfectly bright, innocent smile. God only knows what she went through with the polygamists, or what Humboldt's actual motives are for setting up a ministry in the desert and rescuing teenage girls, but maybe it doesn't matter because out here in the morning sun under the blue of a Utah sky it's obviously working for her.

'Who is it, Dinah?' says a man's voice.

I turn to see Humboldt. He looks both different and the same. He's slimmer, tanned, clean-shaven. His hair is still long, but now completely white, matching the white robe he wears which matches Dinah's and I now realise must be some kind of uniform for his little cult.

His face falls as he sees me.

'You're not welcome here.'

'It's a church,' I say. 'You're not supposed to turn anyone away.'

'What would you know about the sacred?'

'About as much as you, I'm guessing,' I say. 'Besides, I brought an offering.' From the bag I slip not Hakushu, but Makoto, and not twelve years old but twenty-three. Just south

293

of 600 bucks a bottle, courtesy of Fred and Rapid City's burgeoning taste for bougie hooch.

'I don't drink any more,' he says, but with a glance at Dinah that tells me his protest is more performative than sincere.

'That's okay,' I say. 'You can watch me.'

He shakes his head. 'The only reason you would be here is because you're in trouble,' he says. 'And I don't want any part of it.'

'Quicker you help me, the quicker I'm gone. Quicker you can get back to . . .' I glance at Dinah, perfect in the sunlight. 'Whatever the hell it is you do here.'

'All right,' he says. 'But it's like she said. No weapons. This is a place of sanctuary.'

'So we do it out here.'

Humboldt just looks at me and steps back inside into the shadows of the adobe building. I step towards him, but Dinah puts herself solidly between me and him. She holds out her hand.

I will freely admit I am a major-league asshole. One of the greats. But even I baulk at getting into a beef with a fifteen-year-old polygamy victim with perfect skin.

'Okay, Dinah,' I tell her, pulling the pistol out of my back with my free hand and holding it out by the muzzle. 'You hang on to this until I'm done, okay?'

I can tell by the way she almost drops it as she takes it that she's not used to the weight of a weapon. So that's one less thing to worry about.

I step into the cool of the building. Humboldt nods at Dinah who heads out of the door into the sunlight with my gun. I lose her to the glare.

The moment she's gone Humboldt snatches the bottle out of my hand.

112

'Parachute,' I say. 'What does it mean?'

We're sitting in his office at the back of the building. The main body of the church is set up with neat cots for the girls. Apparently they stay here for a few weeks until Humboldt can relocate them. There are two other girls in addition to Dinah but they're at some kind of deprogramming session. Humboldt puts a glass up to his nose, swilling the amber liquid around.

'Context,' he says, and slooshes some into his mouth.

'The context is that Sixteen is trying to kill me.'

Humboldt swallows and stares at me. 'Well, fuck.'

'My thoughts exactly.'

'I thought he retired.'

'Well, now he's un-retired.'

'Why?'

'Because I tried to kill him.'

'Why would you do something as stupid as that?'

'Because I was given the job, and it was made clear to me I didn't have a choice.'

'We always have choices,' says Humboldt, sticking his nose back in his glass.

'Only it turns out he wasn't the target. Someone wanted me dead, and he was the only person they could think of who could do it. And the only way they could think of to get him out of retirement was to send me to kill him.'

Humboldt smiles. 'It's an elegant solution, you have to admit.'

'It's not been that elegant so far.'

'So who are "they" and why do "they" want you dead?'

'That's what I'm hoping you can tell me.'

Humboldt nods, pours himself more.

'And ... "Parachute". What does that have to do with anything?'

'Someone I killed. Before I killed him, that's what he said. Over and over again. Like it meant something. *Parachute. Parachute. Parachute.* You know what it means?'

Humboldt hesitates, then he tilts his head. 'First I need to know something else.'

'What's that?'

'Why the fuck you think I should help you?'

'Because if it wasn't for me, Zhuk would have put a bullet between your eyes and you wouldn't be sitting here in your Jesus robes playing St Francis of Assisi while you jerk off to teenage polygamy victims.'

'Christ,' he says, genuinely pained. 'You haven't changed, have you?'

'I saved your life,' I repeat.

'I repaid the debt in full,' he says. 'And now you're here, because you tried to kill a man, and now he wants to kill you. And if I help you, you'll probably kill him. And then you'll go on to kill other people. And we can add that to all the people you've killed since Zhuk. You can sneer at what I do here all you like. But I am giving these girls life. And you, you are taking it away. You're a net negative in the karmic balance sheet. The last few years I've been putting myself in the black. If I help you I'll be putting myself back in the red. You see the problem?'

'What if I told you after this I'm done?'

296

'People like you are never done.'

'All right,' I say. 'How about this? I tell you the whole story. You tot up the karmic bullshit. If there's a way to turn it black, you help me. If not, fuck, I'm done. I walk out. No obligation. Plus, if you listen, you get to finish that bottle.'

Humboldt sniffs his empty glass, glances at the Makoto, still a good three-quarters full.

'Okay,' he says. 'Shoot.'

113

I tell him about Berlin.

The hit.

The brush pass.

The memory card.

The guy with the Moe haircut.

Kovacs.

The pitcher being killed.

The Sixteen commission.

Vilmos.

The crypto keys.

When I get to the part about Iran, he leans forward in surprise.

'They're going to do what?'

'You hadn't heard?'

'I don't have TV,' he says. 'Or internet. I don't read newspapers. I don't even listen to the radio. All of that shit, I'm done with it. I don't need the noise. Nor do the girls.'

I deliver the bad news.

'What a gong show,' says Humboldt. 'They been busting a nut to fuck up Iran for decades. Remember McCain singing "Bomb, bomb Iran"? We sat in when the Joint Chiefs wargamed it. The only thing that stopped them was the threat of nukes getting tossed around. Because that shit has a habit of escalating fast. What's the *casus belli*?'

'Iran is supposed to have been sponsoring some kind of nuclear terror plot.'

'And they know this how?'

'Comms intercepts. Encrypted.'

'And that's what the crypto keys on the card were for?'

'Right,' I say.

Humboldt thinks for a moment. Then suddenly he sits back. He pours himself two fingers and downs them without any of the respect that a twenty-three-year-old Japanese single malt deserves, then pushes the lank white hair away from his face. His normally florid complexion is oddly pale.

'Holy Christ,' he says. 'No wonder they want you dead.'

'You know what it means? "Parachute"?'

Humboldt nods.

'And are you going to tell me?'

Humboldt sits there. And I can see he's doing the karmic calculus.

Finally he nods.

'It's a safe word.'

'What kind of a safe word?'

'CIA. Only disclosed to officers on covert assignment, and only authorised for use in extremely specific circumstances, namely an imminent threat to life.'

'And what does it mean?'

'It means,' says Humboldt, '"I'm an undercover CIA officer. Don't shoot."'

'You're saying—'

'The man you killed wasn't Hezbollah, or Iranian intelligence. He was CIA. He couldn't just come out and say so, because he couldn't be sure who you were. If you weren't CIA, he could burn the entire operation. That was the point of the safe word. If you weren't Agency, it wouldn't mean anything. But if you were, you'd know you were about to kill one of your own.'

My brain is still playing catch-up.

'Let me get this clear. You're saying the guy I killed – the guy whose stomach I ripped open – was CIA? A double agent?'

Humboldt nods. 'He was hoping you were on the team, and pleading for his life.'

I feel suddenly sick.

'But why would the Americans want me to kill one of their own? He already *had* the crypto keys. All he had to do was deliver them. It makes no sense unless—'

I stop.

'Fuck.'

114

A year before she died, Junebug bought me a Rubik's cube. I set about solving it, whiling away the hours spent by the ice machine. The first layer was trivial. The second layer was harder, but I soon discovered how to bring the squares into alignment. That bottom layer, though. For days, even weeks, it defeated me. Sometimes I would manage to complete it, only to discover I'd fucked up one or both of the other layers. I sometimes wondered if the cube was broken, if I'd scrambled it in some magical way that made it impossible to solve.

And then one day it happened. The last coloured square snapped into place.

I was so proud of myself. I showed it to Junebug. I remember her holding it up to the light, turning it in her slender fingers as if it was some kind of jewel.

'It's beautiful,' she said, and it was.

And now this puzzle cube is done too.

Berlin was a false flag, an operation which appeared to be carried out by one side, but was actually carried out by another.

The White House wanted to go to war. Maybe there was a good reason, a genuine fear that Iran would attack Israel or detonate a nuclear device on home turf. Maybe there was real intelligence that they couldn't share without burning sources they weren't willing to sacrifice, or would embarrass them. Or, what the fuck, maybe POTUS was looking down the road to election year and needed a ten-point goose in the polls.

But whatever the reasons, they didn't have proof. And without proof of Iran's intentions, there was no way of pulling together the international coalition they would need. After the WMD debacle in Iraq, catalysed by Colin Powell's absurd and debunked show-and-tell at the UN in 2003, the USA's word alone was no longer good enough.

The answer was straightforward: *manufacture* the necessary proof, along with a convincing provenance for it that even the most suspicious allies will not question.

Here's how it goes.

The US claims to have intercepted an encrypted comms stream between Iran and its agents in the West. The comms stream is entirely fake, but once decrypted will provide the justification for war. They could simply claim to have cracked the encryption, courtesy of NSA, but that would look a little too convenient. So, they stage a vicious little soap opera. They run a false flag operation in Berlin using two of their own assets – the Moe haircut and the BEBE T-shirt – who are instructed to brush-pass a memory card in the Tiergarten. Then, via Handler, they send me to intercept the brush pass and obtain the card.

The only people who know that Moe and the BEBE shirt are CIA are the CIA. To the rest of the world, they're legit Iranian intelligence assets, which means the crypto keys are real, which means when they decrypt the comms stream, the comms stream must be real also.

Hey presto, the provenance is confirmed, and the comms stream provides all the smoking guns the US, and more importantly its allies, require.

Only the whole thing is Kabuki. The catcher and pitcher undoubtedly had no more idea of the part they were playing

302

in the dramatics than I did, or of each other's true allegiance. The whole operation would have been highly compart-mented within the CIA, with only a tiny handful of senior figures read in. It may even have bypassed the seventh floor entirely.

There's just one problem. If it ever gets out that the keys, and by extension the comms stream, are fake, the shit hits the fan in every possible way you can imagine and some you can't. And there are exactly three loose ends who could under-mine their provenance: Moe, the BEBE T-shirt, and me.

It's beautiful. And evil. And beautiful. And evil.

'Fuck,' I say again.

'Exactly,' says Humboldt.

And then I hear something.

It's the burble of a V8 through a tuned pipe, pulling up outside.

Humboldt's eyes meet mine. We both know who it is.

The one thing I don't see is surprise.

'You warned him?' I say.

'How could I warn him? I didn't know you were coming.'

'So he warned you. Called you. Told you to string me along. Make sure I was unarmed.'

'I told you, I don't even have a telephone.'

'So how did you know he was coming?'

'Because he was always coming,' says Humboldt. 'Because you didn't follow the one single fucking essential piece of advice I gave you years ago, which is not to ever, ever, fuck with Sixteen. And now you have. And now you've brought him down on me.'

'Is it enough?' I ask him.

'What?'

'This. For you to help me.'

303

Humboldt's eyes swim. It's been a while since he touched alcohol. But he knows what I'm asking. His hand plays nervously with a set of keys on the big mission-style desk.

'These girls you save,' I tell him. 'It's never going to be enough to put you in the black with the universe. But . . . if what you say is true? A hundred thousand lives. Maybe more. Maybe a lot more. It could be enough.'

As I hear the words spill out of my mouth they sound unfamiliar, like the words of someone who gave a shit. Which, I have to remind myself, I don't. My job is to survive, not to save the world, or Humboldt's soul. It's just that occasionally, in order to survive, it is necessary to do the right thing.

Jingle, jingle, go the keys.

'You think you can stop it?'

'I have no idea,' I say, which is true.

'But you'll try?'

I nod, and I am shocked to discover that I mean it.

The jingling stops.

'Take whatever you need,' he says.

He stands up and strides towards the entrance. And just for a second I get a glimpse of the man Tommy Humboldt must have been once, before the booze and the women and the betrayal ruined him.

Maybe the shaman was a Navajo after all.

115

Humboldt goes to the doorway. From the office, I can see him silhouetted against the light. Beyond him, in the glare of the sun, stands Kondracky. Behind him there's a red F150 with lifts and superchunk tyres, an SVT Lightning, one of the fastest ever made. Too old to be a rental, probably picked it up with cash from Craigslist before we met. Which would be why the Trooper was riding light, since he'd already transferred the loadout.

Dinah appears from one side. She looks worried. My gun is still in her hand. She looks at Tommy with a question in her eyes, but he shakes his head. He nods towards my Jeep.

She runs to the rental, climbs in, starts up, and drives away.

I'm stranded now, trapped, unarmed.

All that stands between me and death is a crazy old alcoholic ex-spook in a white robe, standing in the doorway with his hands held out, touching each side of the doorway, forming a crucifix.

Something tells me the symbolism is not accidental.

'Go away,' he says.

'I can't do that,' says Kondracky.

'He claims sanctuary.'

'No such thing.'

'I'm a man of peace now,' says Humboldt, all puffed up with his own Godhead. 'But I will not let you pass. You want him, you go through me.'

'Fine,' says Kondracky. He heads back to the truck, drops the tailgate open, pulls something out.

When he turns back I see what it is: a loaded RPG-7 launcher.

He shoulders it, and points it directly at Humboldt.

'This how you want it to go, Jones?' he says, over Humboldt's shoulder. 'Hiding behind an old man's skirts? Thought you had more in you.'

'It's the finger on the trigger whose hand is covered with blood,' says Humboldt. And for some reason this seems to hit Kondracky. A darkness in his face I've seen before. Maybe somewhere in him there's still some flicker of conscience.

Just not when it comes to me.

Humboldt must know Kondracky's not about to back off. He's playing for time. *Take what you need.* He was trying to tell me something without actually telling me. I scan around for anything that could help. The whisky, half empty. A shelf of books – all hippy shit, Carlos Castaneda and Erich von Däniken, plus a couple of books on Scientology.

Maybe Tommy is trying to start a new religion. Maybe I should pray to him.

And then I see them.

The keys he was jingling. Big, rusty, old-fashioned. But in among them a glint of silver.

An automobile key, an old one, the fob marked VW with the silver worn off.

And it hits me: Humboldt still has to eat, which means he has to get groceries, which means there has to be another vehicle here somewhere. But where? There's no garage, and nothing parked in the driveway except the old bus on blocks.

I'm still trying to figure it out when Kondracky fires the RPG.

116

The grenade screams past Humboldt's right ear, down the hallway and into the study. It hits the back wall and explodes, punching a hole in the mud brick, blowing me off my feet and filling the room with dust, debris and smoke.

I stagger to my feet, ears singing Wagnerian arias, and through the murk and the hole punched in the rear wall, shining metallic purple in the sun, I finally see what the key belongs to.

It's Humboldt's beach buggy which, digging deep into his limitless supply of chutzpah, he must have persuaded the CIA to ship back from Beirut as part of his deal. Evidently, Humboldt was not big on maintenance because the thing is forty years old if it's a day and shot to hell.

But, fuck it, it's a vehicle.

I turn to the desk for the keys, but they're gone, blown off in the explosion.

I drop to my knees, tearing my nails as I scrabble frantically in the debris for them. Meanwhile, Humboldt launches himself out of the doorway towards Sixteen, who is still holding the smoking RPG-7. Tommy might have lost a few but he's still pretty well upholstered, and I guess he takes Kondracky by surprise, because he slams into him, lifts him clean off his feet and linebacks him to the ground.

In the rubble, something metallic! I grab the keys and run for the hole blasted in the wall. Behind me, Kondracky throws

Humboldt off and struggles up. He pulls a pistol, thinks about putting a bullet in Tommy's head, but instead blows out his kneecap and sprints into the building, firing after me.

I have maybe a hundred yards on him. For ninety-nine of them my luck holds out. But just as I make the buggy, something tears into my right side. My hand comes up wet with blood. Kondracky emerges from the darkness of the church through the jagged hole. The sunlight blinds him long enough for me to throw myself behind the wheel, start the buggy, and floor the gas, powersliding the buggy round to put the rear-mounted aircool between us, his rounds chinking off the engine block.

The buggy skitters and bounces across the desert floor. It's not until I glance back to see Sixteen running for his vehicle that the pain of the wound hits me. I clamp one hand to my side, trying to hold it closed while steering and crashing up through the gears with the other. The last thing I need right now is to faint from blood loss.

The gas gauge shows about a third full. Three gallons if I'm lucky. That'll get me sixty, eighty miles, assuming I can somehow keep ahead of Kondracky.

Behind me, I hear the whine of the SVT and a squeal of rubber as he skids out of the church's parking lot and accelerates up the highway to my left.

I can't tell if he just hit muscle and flesh or something worse, but my teeth are starting to chatter, which means I'm in danger of going into shock. *Fuck.*

I angle away from him, heading deeper into the desert. Kondracky hauls off the highway on to a track rutted out by 4x4s, paralleling me. He tries to pull off into the rough of the desert to cut me off, but even with its lifts it's too much for the Ford and he's forced back on to the track to avoid breaking an axle.

The pain in my side is getting worse; I'm shivering and sweating. If that wasn't enough, the gas gauge is down to a quarter and dropping. One of Kondracky's bullets must have hit the fuel tank. My range just went down to ten, twenty miles if I'm lucky.

I steer away from Kondracky and floor the gas, the buggy taking air as it flies over rocks and scrub, impacts jackhammering into my wound. Ahead, sandstone cliffs and hoodoos carved by weather into alien shapes rise out of the desert floor.

Behind me Kondracky has no choice but to follow me off-road. I'm starting to pull away now, but I need to lose him completely before my gas gives out.

Up ahead, an old mule track, rutted out and boulder-strewn, winds up into the moonscape before me. If I'm lucky, it will lead somewhere. And if not . . . I try not to think about it.

117

The Badlands are eerily beautiful, the track twisting up through geological strata heaved into crazy angles and laid bare like a slice through a layer cake.

At the top of the first rise, where the track hairpins out of sight of the desert floor, I look back to see the red Ford stopping. Kondracky gets out, taking in the road ahead, and the chances the SVT will make it. For a second I think he'll turn back. But then he squats down and picks something up in his fingers, rolling it around, then smelling it.

And I understand: it's either my blood or my gasoline.

Either way, he knows I'm finished.

The buggy coughs to a fuel-starved halt five miles later, where the mule trail flattens out to a dusty plain ringed by jagged peaks on three sides, the fourth edging a canyon.

The plateau is featureless with one exception: a ruined cabin, roof caved in a desolate V, door hanging open. At first it makes no sense. A cabin here? Then I realise what it is: a hermit's retreat. I've heard about them, some of them shacks like this, others literally built into the rock, others nothing more than a hole in the ground. All of them isolated, lonely, built as far as possible from human company by men who had variously gotten religion, lost their minds, been disappointed in love or life, or simply fallen foul of the law.

I peer over the edge of the cliff. The first pitch is precipitous, and even if I make it, once Kondracky gets here it'll be a turkey shoot. I consider the orange-red sandstone walls that surround me, but I'm in no shape to climb.

Which leaves the cabin.

I push the door open, and it falls off its hinges.

Inside is covered with a thick layer of dust, a few bits of lame graffiti and some broken-down furniture. There's a rat-eaten carpet on the floor, a fireplace with a few charred chair legs and a poker where somebody made a fire. By the door, there's a nail where a couple of decaying fan belts and some thick rubber tarp straps hang.

I turn to the doorway. The sun is going down, sinking inexorably.

The pain in my side is relentless.

I'm exhausted, weak from loss of blood, and completely unarmed.

I am literally at the end of the road.

And he's going to be here in fifteen, thirty minutes. Maybe less.

I sink into what's left of a chair to wait.

118

Sometimes I try to remember what it was like never to have killed someone. I think of the night it all changed, of that terrified kid, and all the shit that followed.

Who would that kid have become, if none of this had ever happened? Who would he be now? What would his life be like?

I wish I could meet him. No, not meet him, because I wouldn't want him to meet someone like me. But watch him, maybe, from a car, say, as he pushes his kid on a swing or pushes a grocery cart through a store, checking items off a shopping list. *Milk, Cheerios, toothpaste, cat litter.* Or climbs out of a three-year-old Corolla that just pulled into the driveway of a tract home, shoulders sloped with fatigue and ready to throw a frozen pizza in the oven, crack open a beer, and binge an entire season of *America's Next Top Model.*

And imagine how glorious, how utterly off-the-charts fucking *wonderful* it would be to be boring.

The sun sinks below the horizon, the final bead of fire burning itself out.

I think of Kat, of her body beside me in the darkness of the motel room.

I think of knocking on the office door in the half-light. What would I have done if she had answered? What would I have even said?

What if I hadn't abandoned her at the gas station? What then?

What if, what if, what if.

I push the thoughts away. Wherever she is now, wherever she's headed, she's better off without me. The fact she's Kondracky's daughter is enough of a burden for her to bear.

Maybe I should just sit here until Kondracky arrives. Let him have his kill.

Barb was right: the world would be a better place for it.

And yet, if I give up now they win. Not just Kondracky, all of them. Handler, and the ghouls who decided it was worth sacrificing two of their own, along with me and a hundred thousand or more innocent souls, just so they could get their war on in the Middle East.

Tommy Humboldt might be crazy but he put himself in the path of an RPG for me, not because he owed me anything, or gave a shit about my wellbeing, but because I promised him I would try to stop it.

And I realise: I'm not ready to die. Not yet. Not if I can help it.

119

I feel his truck before I hear it, at first a light tremor, then a vibration, then the familiar chug of the V8. I can picture the rooster tail of dust rising behind him, catching the last rays of the sun as he sees the abandoned dune buggy, pulls up, and kills the engine.

The sound dies away. A moment of silence as he sits there, thinking. By now he knows I'm no longer a threat. I'm a bug to be squashed, a rat to be trapped, a stray dog to be put down.

His truck door opens and his feet hit the ground. Footsteps as he circles the abandoned buggy. They stop as he squats to find the blood trail. Recede, as he follows it to the edge of the canyon, then get louder as he returns. A moment of silence as he stops, seeing where they lead.

Sound of the tailgate dropping. A metal container opening. Soft clunk of the cartridge being inserted, the click of the breech being locked, the schick of the missile being loaded. A momentary pause as he squares the launcher up against his shoulder, sights his target, unhurried.

And then it comes, the detonation of the rocket charge and a fraction of a second later, the explosion of the grenade itself. The blast wave is brutal, an earthquake. Dirt cascades down on to my face, then there's the clatter of debris as the remnants of the building rain down, littering the ground for hundreds of yards around with wood, metal and brick.

The noise fades and echoes away. I hold my breath. He stows the RPG back in the truck, then I track his footsteps over to what's left of the building, kicking aside rubble and foundations, looking for me, or what's left of me.

Eventually, the noise stops.

I can practically hear him thinking.

Then he says, loud enough for anyone within a quarter-mile to hear:

'You fucked up, Jones. No body parts. There should have been body parts.'

120

He walks. He walks and walks, his footsteps growing louder, then quieter, then louder, then quieter. Eventually it hits me what he's up to. He's walking a grid. Literally searching every square yard of the area around the homestead. Sometimes he sings tunelessly to himself, Johnny Cash. Sometimes he mutters words I can't quite catch, as if he was talking to someone who wasn't there. Eventually he stops. I hear the tailgate of his truck drop down again, the strike of a match, and I can picture him there, perfectly, sitting on the tailgate, just smoking and thinking and smoking and figuring it out.

It takes him five minutes to finish the cigarette. Then I hear him slide off the tailgate, and in that same loudhailer voice he says:

'Hey, Jones, I figured it out. You were clever, but I figured it out.'

His footsteps approach. Sound of rubble being cleared, shards of wood and glass kicked out of the way. Through an inch-wide knothole in the boards above me, I briefly see the stars appear. And then a million-candlepower flashlight blasts down through the hole into my hiding place.

'Well, well,' says Kondracky. 'What do we have here?'

The crawl space below the cabin was eighteen inches deep, built to store root vegetables, probably the only thing that kept the hermit alive over the winter months. I found a crude trapdoor hidden underneath the rotted-out rug. When the RPG hit, it blew the building apart. Hours later, my ears are still ringing, my head fuzzy from the concussion. But the joists above me are old-growth fir, hand-hewn and thick as an elephant's leg. They took the blast like they took everything else for the last hundred years or so, and as a result I am still alive, simultaneously trapped and hidden until now by the debris that rained back down on the trapdoor after the explosion.

The monstrous flashlight flicks off. My retinas burn. Then I hear another sound. It's a zipper being undone. There's a splash, and a stream of warm liquid splatters into my face through the knothole.

The motherfucker is pissing on my face and there is not a thing I can do about it.

Eventually it stops.

'Did you like that, Jones? I was saving it up for you this whole time.'

He chuckles to himself.

'I was thinking,' he says, 'we could have a little campfire.'

121

He builds the fire in what remains of the homestead's hearth. I hear him flip open a lawn chair, which he sits in heavily, like old men do when they take the weight off their feet. There's the sound of a bottle opening. He offers me some, and a trickle of Jack Daniel's pours into my hole. It's good, even mixed with his piss. I hear the clunk of his gun being laid at his feet, the snick of the safety being turned off in the slim chance I might try something.

In the distance, the same country station Barb listens to is playing on his truck radio.

'So,' he says. 'Jones, you figure it out yet? Why they wanted you dead?'

I stay silent.

He stamps on the floor with his heel. Yet more dirt tumbles into my face.

'What the fuck do you care?'

'It's like I told you,' says Kondracky. 'If I'm going to kill a man I like to know why. That's why you went running to Tommy, right? Because you figured he could throw some light on the proceedings. Did he?'

'Yeah.'

'And?'

I tell him the whole goddamn story. And he listens in silence, just grunting at certain points to express surprise or disgust. And at the end he says:

'Motherfuckers. They sold you out. Because they always do.'

There's a guttural darkness to his tone, an anger, that speaks to an old, unhealed wound, and a story to be told.

At this point every minute is a bonus. So I spit out the dirt that's fallen into my mouth.

'Want to tell me about it?'

He hesitates. And maybe it's the Jack, or maybe it's just the fact that it's been burning him up for years, but he dribbles some more whiskey through my breathing hole and begins a tale of betrayal and revenge, with himself as hero, that puts *Point Blank* to shame.

Maybe I'll tell it to you one day.

But that's not the point. The point is, as he rambles on, toasty by the fire, rocking back in his lawn chair under the stars, sipping Jack and occasionally permitting me a slug, I realise that I have finally discovered his weakness.

These old guys, they *love* to talk.

122

So I let him. And when his yarn finally comes to an end I say:

'Hey, Kondracky. How about this? I got a proposal.'

He chuckles. 'It better be a hell of a deal, Jones, because you're not in the strongest negotiating position I've ever seen.'

'How you gonna know unless you hear me out?'

He sighs. 'Okay. Let's hear it.'

I take a deep breath. 'How about we team up?'

'Do what now?'

'Strike out on our own. You and me against the world. You know how good I am. Everybody knows how good you are. Together we'd be unstoppable. The A-team of all A-teams.'

'You forgot the part where I retired.'

'If you'd actually retired you wouldn't be sitting here now. You know as well as I do you're bored out of your mind up on that hill of yours. That's why you write those shitty novels, because you miss the life and the closest you can get is reliving the glory days. Face it, Mack, I'm the best thing that's happened to you in years. Last three days, you've felt alive again in ways you'd forgotten. I know you have because so have I. Come on, what do you say?'

'What do I say? Well now . . .'

He tails off. I hear his lawn chair creak as he rocks back. Another glug of the Jack.

He's actually considering this.

His chair creaks again as he leans forward.

'What I say,' he says, 'is this. Number one, I'm too old for this shit. Number two, I'm *way* too old to be taken in by loquacious bullshit from some yap of a pup whose idea of a winning endgame is to hide his ass in a hole. Number three, who's to say you and me running around wouldn't be looking to stab one another in the back first chance we get. Sure, maybe we'd have a little honeymoon period, but eventually one of us sees the other looking at them funny and before you know it the knife's buried up to the handle. Number four, maybe you were right. Maybe I didn't tell you everything. Maybe I had reasons for quitting the game you couldn't even begin to understand. And number five—'

At this point he pauses. I hear him stand up. He stumps off and his footsteps recede. There's the sound of the truck tailgate dropping once more, and a metallic scraping. He heads back, and this time from the rhythm and fall of his steps it sounds like he's carrying something heavy. A loud clunk as he deposits whatever it is on the floorboards, then the sound of some kind of metal cap being unscrewed.

'Fifth—' he says, his voice becoming dark and edged with vitriol. '*Fifth*, my novels are not shitty.'

And with that he pours something into my knothole. Not piss this time, nor Jack Daniel's, but gasoline. It pours over my face, the fumes choking me as it spills around, soaking into my clothes, the ground, even down my throat. I screw my eyes shut, coughing and choking.

Above me, I hear the click of a Zippo being flipped open.

'This is it, Jones. Come out and die like a man, or I barbecue your ass down there.'

'All right, you old fucker,' I splutter. 'I'm coming out.'

I kick the heavy beams to dislodge them. Kondracky clears them out of the way, and the space above me reveals him standing astride the hole like a redneck Colossus, Zippo aloft.

His eyes widen as he sees what I'm holding.

123

There wasn't much in the cabin, but it was enough.

The tarp straps by the door were heavy rubber, eighteen inches long, with steel S-hooks at each end. The poker in the fireplace was cast iron, with a sturdy handle and a pointed end. Heavy enough to do a satisfying amount of damage at the right velocity. I took them both down into my makeshift coffin under the floorboards. I fumbled around in the dark and found a flat stone, which I used to roughly sharpen the poker as Kondracky talked and talked, relying on his old man ears, hearing dulled by gunfire, to deaden the sound.

What Kondracky sees by the light of the moon and the stars is me lying there, one strap hooked around my left foot like a stirrup, one around my right, and the third strung between them. I'm pulling back the poker like an arrow, using every atom of strength I still have, ignoring the tearing sensation in my wound, aiming it at his heart, a human crossbow.

I loose the poker. It rips through the air with astonishing speed and force. My aim's good, but Kondracky's already lunging for his weapon so instead of hitting him in the chest, it impales in his left shoulder, an inch or two shy of the armpit, and sticks there. The force knocks him clear off his feet, hand still straining for his weapon, and sends him sprawling on to a pile of rubble.

The pain is incandescent as I leap out of the crawlspace. I lunge for his Glock, but Kondracky's not beaten yet. He levers himself upright, the poker sticking right through him, lights the Zippo, and hurls it at me.

The gasoline fumes ignite, a fuel-air bomb that blows me backwards. I'm still soaked in gas, and I ignite too, a human fireball. I crash down in the dirt and roll to put myself out. I'm an H-bomb of pain – it feels like the landing has broken a couple of ribs – but the gasoline burns off quickly and I manage to extinguish my clothes. I scramble up to see Kondracky, still impaled, stumbling towards his gun.

We reach it at the same moment.

Kondracky gets his left hand on the grip. I grab his wrist with my right hand and the barrel with my left. His left side is weakened from the poker, and I've almost got it out of his grasp when I remember.

Kondracky is right-handed.

There's a disgusting sucking sound as he uses his good hand to pull the poker from his shoulder, then swings it at me. I can't protect myself without letting go of the gun, so it hits me square across the face. Blinded by blood, I stagger backwards. Kondracky gets back to his feet, his wound pouring blood, and tries to level the pistol, but I shoulder-charge him and quarterback him into the air. As we hit the ground together, I knee him as hard as I can in the balls.

Which are made of steel, apparently, because he doesn't let go of the gun.

We wrestle for it, desperate, slick with each other's blood. I can smell his old man breath, but his muscles are pure wire. Face to face, we strain for the automatic, each blocking out the pain, both of us knowing this is where it ends for one of us.

And Kondracky is Kondracky. He's Sixteen, and in his prime he would have been unbeatable. But the wound from the poker is bad, and I have, if nothing else, youth on my side. He refuses to give up the gun but slowly, fraction of an inch

323

by fraction of an inch, I manage to twist it around until, though he's still holding it, it's pointed at his face.

At which point his eyes suddenly open wide.

For a second I think he's having a stroke, or a heart attack, or some other cataclysmic age-related medical event, but what he says is:

'SHIT.'

His eyes are fixed on something behind me.

I mean, *really*?

'Come on, Mack,' I gasp out, still struggling to keep the gun pointed at him. 'You can do better than that.'

I wrap my fingers over his and start to squeeze the trigger.

But then I hear them.

Helicopter blades.

124

It's a light attack helicopter, a Boeing AH-6 with markings, scudding down from the ridge behind which it was hiding. Hydra rockets blaze towards us from the lateral pods. It's still a quarter-mile away, which gives me just enough time to haul Kondracky down into the crawlspace with me. The rockets slam into the ground beside us, sending gouts of earth, rock and flame over our heads, but our foxhole protects us.

Kondracky rolls on to his back and opens up with the Glock as the chopper flashes overhead and banks hard, ready for another pass.

Kondracky turns to me. 'Truck,' he says, and I know exactly what he has in mind.

We pull ourselves up and sprint towards the SVT as the helo comes at us again, this time with the minigun slung between the skids. Bullets rip a trail towards us, kicking up gouts of dirt like a deadly sandworm torpedoing under the desert floor. We split into two directions, a divided target. Kondracky hurls me the gun and I put enough shells in the cockpit window to momentarily blind the pilot, then dodge sideways as fangs of the sandworm rip past me and crawl over Kondracky's truck, tearing a stripe of closely packed shell holes into the red steel.

The AH-6 clatters overhead and begins another hard turn, still with another full pod of rockets. Kondracky throws me a booster and a grenade, then grabs the launcher from the bed

325

of the truck. I screw the booster on to the grenade and pull off the safety, then snick it into place for him, lining up the key. Kondracky retreats behind the truck, using the hood to steady his aim, while I break sideways to draw the helicopter's fire, zigzagging crazily as it closes.

'Fire, you motherfucker!' I yell at Kondracky as the AH-6 lets loose a volley of rockets. I zag towards the oncoming chopper. The rockets sail overhead and slam into a rock outcrop behind me. The blast blows me twenty feet through the air, and I roll to a stop, ears singing and all the breath knocked out of me.

I struggle to my knees, but I'm almost done, gasping for breath. The chopper's heading straight for me now, and opens up with the minigun, unzipping the desert, shells ripping towards me. I have nothing left, no way to avoid certain death.

Finally, Kondracky fires.

His aim is perfect. The rocket streaks into the chopper and explodes. It tumbles towards me like a massive shuriken, shedding blades as it twists and cavorts, slams into the ground and rolls past me. It augers into the rocks like a fastball thudding into a catcher's glove, and detonates into a fireball.

I lie there, face down in the dirt, gasping for air, trying to recover, feeling the heat from the wreck of the Boeing as it burns. It takes a good minute for my pulse to subside to anything I've recorded before. Then I hear something. I roll over to see Kondracky standing over me, filthy with blood and dirt, still toting the smoking rocket launcher over his shoulder.

'Well,' he says. 'That was fun.'

He holds out his hand to pull me up.

PART SIX

125

The container is dark, just the tiniest glow of light from vents high in the metal walls. Handcuffed to opposite walls at floor level, neither Barb nor Kat can even stand, let alone reach the doors, which have no interior handles. All they've been given is a bottle of water, which shuttles between them to allow each to take a sip.

They've been driving for hours now, the cop car abandoned and torched on a piece of waste ground where the blue shipping container, loaded on a flatbed, was waiting.

It's day once more by the time they finally arrive at their destination. The container doors open and light floods in. Before their eyes can properly adjust, Trooper, now dressed in work pants, a denim shirt and a beat-up cowboy hat, climbs in and hoods both of them. Then he and Buzzcut uncuff them and pull them out.

There's soil under their feet, and the air smells different, fresh, and almost fragrant. The light Kat glimpses from under the hood is simultaneously warmer and harder than she's used to.

'Where are we?' she asks, but all she gets in reply is a shove. Hands cuffed behind backs, guns jammed in their sides, she and Barb are frogmarched down a dirt track, sun hot on their skin. In the distance are men's voices speaking what sounds like Spanish.

Eventually there's the sound of a door being opened, and they transition from the heat of the day to a cool, dark interior that smells of wood, concrete and metal. The door closes behind them, then there's the click of a button, the whirr of an electric motor, and the rattle of a shutter door rising. They're pushed into a second space, much colder than the first. There's the sound of the door being closed, and then suddenly the hoods are removed.

The room is vast and almost empty, a dimly lit, smooth-walled cube with sixty-foot ceilings, featureless apart from three giant fans set high on a back wall and a set of pressurised pipes running from the floor to the metal trusses that support a metal ceiling.

The only other item is a pile of pallets in one dark corner.

Kat's instantly chilled, breath misting in front of her. Buzzcut uncuffs her, and she wants to hug herself warm, but Buzzcut drags her to one of the pipes, where with Trooper's help she handcuffs the two women together, anchoring the cuffs behind the metal pipe so they can barely move.

Trooper skids a new bottle of water over to them, which Kat catches with her free hand. He raises the shutter door again, and from outside finds a folding chair, which he places inside the door, along with a Canada Goose parka, which he throws to Buzzcut. Then he exits, closing the shutter door behind him.

Buzzcut settles into the folding chair, Uzi at her side. She pulls out her phone and starts playing something. Kat recognises the sound effects of *Bejeweled*.

'We're cold,' says Kat. 'Please, can we at least have something to keep warm?' She's shaking, but the truth is she can't tell if it's from fear or cold.

No answer.

'What do you want with us?'

Still nothing.

'Don't give them the satisfaction, hon,' says Barb, quietly. 'Let them think we're beaten. We'll show them.'

Buzzcut looks up. *'Pas de bavardage!'*

She goes back to her game.

330

126

It's dawn now; Kondracky's wound and mine are both more or less patched up from a medkit in the truck. He coughs every now and then, which worries me some, but he hasn't said anything.

We spent the night up in the hills, watching in case reinforcements arrived, but they never did. The wreckage of the whirlybird yielded no clues, the body of the pilot charred beyond recognition. Despite the girdle of bullet holes round its midsection, Kondracky's truck still drove, so we hit Salt Lake City mid-morning to resupply from another of my emergency caches. Now we're headed west, for no particular reason except to keep moving.

I can't tell if we're allies yet, or just a joint target, because Kondracky is still stewing about something, his bony hands gripping the steering wheel way harder than they need to.

'You know you can just say it,' I tell him. 'Whatever it is, just say it. Use your words.'

He makes a sour face. 'My novels,' he says, 'do not suck.'

'If it hurts,' I tell him, 'it's because it's true.'

By way of response, he punches the radio. Something blasts out, music from another geological era. I think it might be AC/DC or Scorpion. I reach for the dial but get the barrel of his gun in my face.

'My truck, Jones. My rules.'

I sit back. 'Seems to me the least you could do is admit you were wrong.'

'About what?'

'The real target. It wasn't me they wanted to kill. Or you. It was both of us.'

He stares at me, those watery blue eyes.

'Send me against you, and watch the fun,' I say. 'Two birds, one stone. Whichever man wins, he's shown himself. He's distracted, vulnerable. Let Ali go twelve against Frazier, then Sonny Liston comes in with fresh legs and it's a TKO.'

He chews on this for a while, but his face says he knows it's true. Eventually he chuckles.

'Can't blame them. You have any idea how much bad shit we know between us?'

He drums along for a moment on the steering wheel, thinking, then turns to me.

'Your offer still stand?'

We shake on it, because I guess that's what old farts like him do, but his grip is strong and I sense he means it. And I feel oddly moved. It takes me a while to figure out why but it's this: the fundamental building block of all operational intelligence work is betrayal. You gain confidence in order to betray it. You pretend to be one thing but actually you're another. All allegiances are not just temporary, but either transactional or performative or both. You either want something from the other party, or you're trying to convince them of something that isn't true. There is no such thing as trust. We live and die alone.

And yet there's something about the handshake that makes me trust Kondracky.

Maybe Handler was right. Maybe I'm losing my edge. Maybe Kat was right, and I'm a romantic. And maybe

Kondracky's right, and he'll do exactly what he said and, when my back's turned, bury a dagger. But I have an odd faith that he won't. Maybe it's because we're the only two people on earth who can understand what it's like to be the other. To be marked for death every moment of every day, targeted by an armada of wannabes roving your attack surface for a vulnerability, like wasps on a too-ripe plum.

And I'm moved, because not since the day I watched Junebug vanish from my life from a cupboard in a motel in Stockton, California have I ever felt I have had an actual ally.

127

'So, what's our next move?' says Kondracky.

I'm still gnawing on the promise I made to Humboldt, but Kondracky's no part of that, so instead I say:

'Maybe the better question is what's their next move?'

Kondracky's face gets a darkness to it.

'Maybe they already made it.'

'What do you mean?'

'Phones are how they tracked us, right?'

'I think so.' Which is why my iPhone is now switched off and rattling around in the bottom of an all-metal ammo case impervious to radio frequencies.

'So maybe it wasn't just *our* phones they were tracking. Call the girls.'

'The moment I call we're back on their radar.'

'Use a burner from the loadout,' says Kondracky. 'They can't be tracking that.'

The Salt Lake City payload included two unused burners. You can never have too many.

'What if they're monitoring *their* phones? The moment we call, they have the SIM, and it's the same deal.'

'Sacrifice one of them. That way all they get is a single ping. Just *do it.*'

I check the back of my hand. Kat's number is written there. I took it off my phone before it went in the ammo case. I wasn't sure why at the time. I guess now I know.

I dial. It goes straight to voicemail.

'Fuck,' says Kondracky.

'It doesn't mean anything,' I tell him. 'Maybe her battery died. Maybe—'

I don't finish, because the burner phone rings. UNKNOWN CALLER.

I show it to Kondracky. He nods. *Answer it.*

I put it up on the dash, as Kondracky pulls over to listen. We're surrounded by flat prairie, the road stretching straight to the horizon in both directions. At least we're not about to be ambushed.

'Hey, champ,' says a voice.

It's Handler.

'What do you want?'

'Just checking in,' says Handler. 'Seeing how things are going.'

'How did you get this number?'

'How do you think?'

So it's true.

'Fuck you, Handler,' I say. 'I know what you did. Berlin, the whole deal. You sold me out.'

'Wrong, kid,' says Handler. 'You sold yourself out. Started getting a conscience. I've seen it before, and it always ends the same way.'

'What's your point, asshole?' growls Kondracky.

Handler laughs. 'Is that who I think it is? What is this, some daddy-figure shit? Or are you guys married now?'

'Cut the shit, Handler,' snaps Kondracky. 'What do you want?'

'It's more a question of what you want. Dykstra and Bernier pulled two women off a Greyhound yesterday, two hours east of Rapid City. One looks like a dime store Dolly Parton, the other has green eyes and attitude. They're okay, for the moment. But that situation is subject to rapid change.'

I swap a glance with Kondracky. 'You really think we're going to sacrifice ourselves for them?'

'No,' says Handler. 'You're going to die whatever happens. And, personally, I don't give a shit about the girls. They're just a way to expedite the process. What did you call Dykstra? A butcher? I'm not going to argue. And Bernier's worse. So factor that in.'

Kondracky takes the phone.

'What exactly do you want us to do?'

'I'm going to give you a set of GPS coordinates,' says Handler. 'Write them down.'

The deal is brutally simple: at 6 p.m. tomorrow we go to the location Handler has given us, an address in the industrial part of Detroit, likely brownfield wasteland surrounded by the decaying hulks of factories and meat processing plants. And then we get out of the vehicle with our hands visible. Handler isn't specific about what happens next but once we're 'off the board' as he puts it, Barb and Kat go free. If we don't make the rendezvous, or attempt to free or even locate the hostages, their captors have explicit, irrevocable orders to liquidate them.

'We'll be there,' says Kondracky and hangs up.

128

I take the phone and jab the button to power it off.

'What aren't you telling me?'

'He's right,' says Kondracky. 'We can't win this.'

'What the fuck are you talking about? Sixteen, Seventeen. The A-team. That's the whole point.'

'Some A-team,' says Kondracky. 'You've got a hole ripped in your side. And your goddamn poker didn't just take out my shoulder. I think it clipped my lung.'

So that's why he's been coughing.

'I don't care. We can take them, Kondracky. You know we can.'

'Think about it, Jones. They sent an AH-6, unmarked, which means it had FAA clearances. They tracked our phones. When you called the girls, they had the burner in seconds. Handler isn't freelancing this. He has the backing of an agency, maybe more than one. You know what that means.'

And he's right, I do.

It's just like I said. If you, an individual, go up against the security service of a nation state, be it Mossad, or MI6, or the CIA, or GRU, or whoever, you will lose. Because they have billions of dollars at their disposal, effectively infinite resources, the best minds of their generation, and technology which is ten years beyond anything available to you commercially. It also means they are no longer concerned about deniability. Which means they will continue pouring resources into the situation until it is resolved.

It's not that it isn't a fair fight, it isn't even a fight.

I stare at the GPS coordinates I've scribbled down on a gas station receipt.

'So, what? We're really doing this?'

Kondracky starts the truck again.

'Of course we aren't.'

He pulls back on to the highway.

I stare at him. 'What? I thought you just said—'

'He's bluffing about the women,' says Kondracky, cutting me off as he moves up through the gears.

'He doesn't have them?'

'Of course he has them. But he's not going to kill them, because if he did we'd have nothing to lose, and the prospect of that scares him shitless. Which it should.'

'Okay, he doesn't kill them. But Dykstra, the guy's a psychopath. And Bernier, I've heard stories.'

The thought gives him pause. 'Look,' he says finally. 'You've met them. They're survivors.'

That word again.

'That's it?' I say. 'They're survivors, so they can take it?'

'Listen, kid,' he says. 'You think if we turn ourselves in he's going to let them walk? The moment we're dead, so are they. So, yeah, they can take it. Besides, I figure we have until six tomorrow.'

'So, you have a plan?'

He thinks for a second, then holds out his hand for the second phone. I hand it over. He dials a number from memory, holds it up to his ear. A voice answers. I can't hear what it says, but I get the sense that it's a woman.

'It's me,' says Kondracky. 'I figured you'd keep the number.'

The woman's voice says something harsh.

'Yeah, whatever,' says Kondracky. 'You still using SANDCASTLE?'

338

129

SANDCASTLE turns out to be a disused airstrip ten miles off the highway near Wamsutter, Wyoming. The office buildings are overgrown, and the runway potholed and sprouting grass, used by kids for impromptu drag-racing from the tyre marks. It's late in the day when Kondracky pulls up near one of the rusted-out hangars, where a cracked concrete apron has been turned into an epically shitty skateboard park. He checks his watch, and scans the sky.

'You sure this is a good idea?'

'Nope,' he says.

Thirty minutes later we hear helo blades. I tense up, but it's just a regular commuter bird, an Airbus with private markings. It settles on to the crumbling cement apron, sending cans and chip bags left by the skaters flying. The blades whirr down, and the door flips open to a set of stairs. A private security drone in black, carrying a submachine gun, steps out. Kondracky opens his jacket to show he's not armed, and I do the same. The guard nods into the cabin and a white woman in her seventies steps out. He helps her down the stairs, and she heads towards us. She walks with a stick, one leg much weaker than the other, giving her an odd, semi-circular gait that looks painful but probably isn't. Her hair is ash-grey and precision-bobbed, and she's dressed beautifully in what looks like French couture, with impenetrable sunglasses. She has the air of a much older Marianne

339

Faithfull. Despite the lines of age in her face, she's undeniably beautiful.

'Are you going to tell me who the fuck she is?' I hiss to Kondracky.

Kondracky looks at me, amused. 'You really don't know?'

As he does, the woman reaches us.

'Nicole,' says Kondracky.

She takes off her sunglasses. Her eyes are a piercing blue, sharp as razors. She stares at him.

'Well?' she says. 'Do I at least get an explanation?'

Kondracky smiles. I get the sense of a long, complicated history between these two. Sexual, maybe. Romantic, who knows. Business, certainly.

'After this, I promise.'

'Could someone please tell me what the fuck is going on here?' I say.

She turns those eyes on me.

'Nicole, this is—'

'I know who it is,' she says, and holds out her hand for me to shake.

It's cold, and a little limp.

'Nicole Osterman,' she says. 'You killed my best girl.'

130

Osterman is a woman. She must have been born just after the war, into a world where women were still regarded as the weaker sex, despite the fact that many of the most deadly spies of WWII were women. Britain's SOE had thirty-nine female agents. Odette Sansom, for example, left three daughters at home in Somerset to mobilise the Resistance in occupied France. She was captured by the Gestapo, starved, beaten, her back broken, toenails pulled out and her body burned. She not only gave nothing up, but survived to testify against Ravensbrück's camp commandant, who was subsequently hanged.

Osterman's disability – a childhood infection destroyed the muscle, Kondracky tells me later – meant she was never going to be an effective operational agent, but that didn't stop her. Instead she became an earlier version of Handler. Sixteen was her protégé just as I was Handler's. Which, I learn as they talk, is why she is still monumentally angry at him for disappearing when he did.

'You betrayed me,' she spits, one manicured finger jabbing a pointed nail at him from the rear of the chopper, to which we've decamped to parley.

'I had my reasons,' is all Kondracky says, defensive.

'Which were?'

'You know damn well what they were,' he says, then corrects himself. 'Are.'

'You could have beaten them. I told you. If you'd just—'

'Just what?' says Kondracky.

She sighs. 'I don't know.'

I have not the faintest idea what they are talking about, but Kondracky's eyes are haunted. And I realise, I was right. He's afraid. Not of her, not of me, not of Handler, not of anything I know about, but something else. Something nameless and dark and odd.

'But to disappear without a word of explanation. Without giving me any way to contact you. Do you know what that did to me? It fucked me. Fucked me completely.' Her anger is rising again. 'Handler, that – Christ, I don't even have a word for him. You're his, aren't you?' She turns to me, accusing.

'Used to be.'

'Yes, and now he's betrayed you. Because that's who he is. Did you know he's the one who suggested I send Kovacs?'

So it was Handler. All along. From the very beginning.

'Maybe that's the kind of man we all are, deep down,' I say.

'No,' she says. 'He was never like that.' She means Kondracky. 'Which is why what he did to me was so . . . brutal.'

'Come on,' says Kondracky. 'Let's face it. If you'd known where I was you'd have sent someone to kill me. That way you could have your Seventeen, instead of Handler.'

Nicole beams. 'Well, of course, darling. All's fair in love and war.'

She lights a cigarette, taps out of the open door of the chopper. 'Now, tell me why I'm here.'

'How would you like to take down Handler?' says Kondracky.

'Don't you think I would have already, if I could?'

'You couldn't, because he had Jones here. Seventeen. And nobody would move against him. But now he doesn't. You could have us both, temporarily. Help us take out Handler, and it leaves you back on top. Where you should have been all along. Think of it as my way of repaying a debt.'

'It's not that simple. The boy, he's good, of course.' She blows smoke. I guess she means me. 'But he's not the reason no-one will move against Handler.'

'Why, then?' says Kondracky.

'The word is,' says Nicole, stubbing out the cigarette on the sill of the Airbus, 'he has a Dead Man's Switch.'

131

The UK has a fleet of four Vanguard-class nuclear-powered ballistic missile submarines, each carrying sixteen Trident II nuclear missiles. This is Britain's entire nuclear deterrent. There are a set of complex release procedures in the case of nuclear war, which cascade down the chain of command from the Prime Minister to the poor bastards who have to actually fire the things.

But what if the entire British government is destroyed in a pre-emptive nuclear strike? The only people with statutory authority to order a nuclear strike are the Prime Minister and the so-called 'second person', usually his or her deputy. If they're both dead, the chain of command decapitated, what happens then?

The answer: each submarine carries aboard it a handwritten letter from the Prime Minister – the so-called 'letter of last resort', which gives the submarine commander orders as to how to proceed. The orders are secret, and the letters are destroyed unread the moment the Prime Minister leaves office. They are only opened in the event of an obvious nuclear attack, or if no UK naval broadcasts are received for four hours.

There are said to be four possible options: put yourself under the command of the US; head for Australia; retaliate; or use your own judgement.

The letters form a Dead Man's Switch.

132

'It's digital,' says Nicole. 'He has records of every operation he's ever been part of. Who commissioned it, who the target was, how it was conducted, the result, how much he was paid, the source of the funds, everything. Video recordings, audio, spread-sheets, photographs, you name it. The whole thing is fifty-something gigabytes. He encrypted it, then uploaded the whole goddamn thing to the Dark Web. Everybody's got it. Not just intelligence services, but journalists, WikiLeaks, Anonymous, private citizens, you name it. Most of them don't know it's his, or what it is, or what's in it, but they know it's something.'

'And if he dies, the encryption key is released,' I say.

'Exactly. At which point every major intelligence service in the world, and most of the minor ones, suddenly find them-selves covered in shit. But not just them, the politicians who ordered the actions. The things you did. But not just you. Every one of Handler's operatives. The point being—'

'—it's in everybody's interest to keep him alive,' says Kondracky.

'Right. The Russians would love to know all the shit the Chinese have been up to, but not if it means their own dirty ops being exposed.'

'So if someone comes against Handler, he can call in support from . . . everyone.'

Nicole nods. 'I mean you two, together, you're good. But no-one's *that* good.'

I let this all sink in. 'I don't get it. Who releases the key? How do they know he's dead? What if someone gets to them first? What if they decide to release it on their own? I don't care how good his operational security is, that's a point of vulnerability, and every spook on earth is going to be looking for it.'

'I don't know the details,' says Nicole. 'But it's biometric. The whole thing's automated.'

'Is that even possible?' asks Kondracky.

I have to think. 'He'd have to have some implant. Every so often it pings a server somewhere with his biometrics, and if the server doesn't see what it expects, which is Handler alive and well, the encryption key is released and the shit hits the fan. I mean . . . it sounds crazy, but this is Handler. Anything's possible.'

Kondracky shakes his head. 'Sounds like bullshit to me.'

'Maybe,' I say. 'But I'm not sure it matters.'

Nicole leans forward, engaged. 'What do you mean?'

'All that matters is people believe it's possible. It's irrelevant whether he actually did it or not. He *might* have, and that's a risk they can't take. The encrypted file could be garbage. There could be no implant, no biometrics, no server. Nothing. But so long as there's a possibility there might be, everyone who's potentially implicated will send the cavalry to save him.'

We sit there in defeat for a while, then suddenly Kondracky looks up.

'I know how we do it.'

133

In a world where people live their lives looking over their shoulder, Handler never did. It was always your shoulder he was looking over. But now I know why: he thought he was untouchable.

That went for his living situation, too. He never told me exactly where it was, but he described it in such loving, lurid detail I could picture it perfectly: the seven bedrooms and fourteen bathrooms, the twin lagoons with rock features and waterfalls, behind one of which was a wet bar, the art deco pastiche colour scheme, the mirrored corridors, the neon-lit faux-movie-theatre front entrance with fieldstone walls guarded by two antique Chinese dragons, the entertainment pavilion, the yoni sculpture, the twenty-car garage full of exotics, the twelve-foot walls and armoured-steel gates. Possibly the most enormously satisfying moment of his life came when a billionaire arms dealer name-dropped the A-list architect he'd used for his own mansion.

'Oh,' said Handler casually, at least the way he told it, 'I had him do my pool house.'

Osterman's Airbus clatters away. Kondracky changes the dressing on his wound, his coughing becoming more frequent. I can hear a rattle now, which suggests there's blood in his lungs. I try to put it out of my mind and use the second burner phone to Google the pool house architect. His name takes me to a list of other high-end domestic architects in the *New York*

Times Magazine ('Who Are Today's Frank Lloyd Wrights?'). An image search on each of the names finally throws up pay dirt. There, in all its glory, is what is unmistakably Handler's abode, in all its garish, ironic glory. It resembles nothing more than an eighties-era Miami shopping mall. All that's missing is a Sunglass Hut. The pictures are from a spread on post-post-modernism in *Architectural Digest* which refers to Handler as a 'reclusive art dealer', which I suppose is true in a way, if you consider death an art.

Handler's ghastly palazzo is in Indian Wells, California, an off-the-hook desert enclave at the foot of the mountains, with two championship golf courses and an airstrip. His neighbours include Bill Gates and Charles Koch. Security for the 700-acre site is run by a former head of the Secret Service, but Handler has his own team as well.

There's enough detail in the pictures to sketch a rough floor plan. Kondracky works on it as I drive. The pictures don't show everything, but Google Maps gives us the outline of the building and together we piece together the geography. But there's something the pictures don't show, something that Handler clearly didn't want plastered over the pages of the magazine. It's a void between the master bedroom – I was right about the mirror on the ceiling – and the study, which features a wall painted with fake books.

The void is what worries us. It could be a closet, or a bathroom. But given its location it could also be a safe room, a metal-walled panic room with comms equipment and enough supplies for Handler to last for days, and certainly long enough for the cavalry to arrive.

Together, Kondracky and I formulate a battle plan. It's strange to be doing this with someone else, but also strangely comforting. The odds are so stacked against us it's almost funny. Once we break cover, we'll be facing not just Handler's

348

security, or the enclave security, or Handler's extended family of elite motherfuckers like me, but the combined forces of every intelligence agency who has a presence on the western seaboard. If we're going to prevail, we need to execute everything perfectly, and we'll still need luck on our side.

But I think we have a chance.

134

We drive in silence for hours. My side aches and I can tell by the way Kondracky spools the wheel on left turns that his shoulder wound is killing him. His cough is getting worse, though he tries to hide it.

Night falls. In the green glow of the dash he looks suddenly old, vulnerable even.

For some reason he keeps glancing in the rear-view. I check back a couple of times, but there's nothing there, and no reason anyone would be following us. I would put it down to that ingrained situational awareness of his, but there's something in the way his pupils flick to the mirror that suggests it's something else. Something to do with the darkness I glimpsed before.

I figure if I don't ask him now, I'm never going to find out. 'Hey, Kondracky,' I say.

He turns, surprised to have the silence punctuated, or maybe relieved.

'Want to tell me why you quit? I mean, why you *really* quit.'

He stares ahead. It's a good minute, maybe two, before he finally answers.

'I did a deal,' he says quietly.

'Who with? The Devil?'

It's a joke, but he turns and looks at me dead on, and I swear I get the chills.

'The ghosts.'

'Ghosts? Like, how? You mean, what, your conscience—?'

'Ghosts,' he snaps. 'Actual fucking ghosts.'

He checks the rear-view. 'It started slow. At first, there'd just be little details I couldn't get out of my mind. A face, a smell, a sound. You ever get that?'

The face of a woman, contorted in rage.

A man's stomach ripped open on a subway track.

A chipped fingernail, hanging over the edge of a bathroom tub.

'Sure.' I nod. 'I think everybody does.'

'That's what I told myself,' says Kondracky. 'Then, once in a while I'd get the fear. I'd get convinced I was being followed. Like there was always someone behind me, only whichever way I turned, they were still behind me. Then I started to see them. Just glimpses at first. I'd catch them in the mirror or the corner of my eye. Then they started to get bold. I'd be in the middle of a job, and suddenly there'd be one of them in the room with me and whoever it was I was supposed to kill. Then two. Then three.'

He has to stop, his mouth dry.

'The worst was when I killed someone. Any time I did a job, when I was driving away, there'd be one sitting next to me, like you, and the latest one in the back. Still bleeding. Guts hanging out, everything. And that night they'd come in battalions. Crowding around. It got so I thought about blowing my own head off, just to make it stop.'

'Why didn't you?'

'Because that's what they wanted. They were waiting for me. Watching me, because they knew one day I'd fuck up, make a mistake, or just end it all. And then I'd be theirs.'

I feel suddenly cold, pull my jacket around me. He's full of shit but here in the dark with the prospect of what lies ahead, the crazy old fucker is getting to me.

'But you knew they weren't real, right?'

He turns to me, eyes burning. 'Of course they were real.'

He goes back to the road.

'You still see them?'

He shakes his head. 'That was the deal. Last job I ever did was Ankara, Turkey.'

'The torturer, right?' I know this shit backwards. 'Did a lot of work for Bashar al-Assad's people.'

'Right,' says Kondracky. 'Big fat guy. Cornered him in an elevator but he put up a hell of a fight. That night they came for me in the hotel room. All of them. And I couldn't take it any more. I told them, you leave me alone, and I'll quit. I'll never pull a trigger again. Once I'm dead, you can have me. Do the fuck what you want. But until then . . .'

'And that's why you had to disappear, because if you didn't . . .'

'Some fucker like you would come along, and I'd have to break the deal.'

I think back. 'That's why you missed Tommy with the RPG, and shot him in the knee not the head.'

Kondracky nods, but his eyes are haunted. He glances in the rear-view mirror. And then it hits me.

'Christ. You broke the deal, didn't you? The guy in the helicopter.'

Kondracky nods. He glances in the mirror again.

'Who do you think's back there in the jump seat?'

135

Indian Wells is an obscene, bloated jigsaw of golf courses and country clubs crawling with private security, CCTV and overpaid cops. From the satellite view in Google Maps, Handler's particular gated community, the most exclusive and salubrious of all, is walled and protected along three sides. The fourth side butts up against Eisenhower Mountain, an odd, low, nub of a peak where the San Jacinto Mountains meet the Santa Rosa Range, so that's our target.

We arrive around three in the morning. From the highway we find a fire road which winds up Eisenhower's backside. From there we find something that looks like a trail. Our only asset is surprise, so flashlights are out of the question, but I have IR goggles in our loadout, which impressed Kondracky, so I let him wear them. I follow him up to the ridge, where he pulls them off to see the Milky Way glittering above us, and Indian Wells glittering below.

From my backpack, I unload a miniature drone and VR set-up. Google's satellite imagery gives out at exactly the level of detail that would actually be useful, and the dataset is three years old, so we need to be absolutely certain what we're getting into.

Kondracky rests on a boulder as I don the goggles. Our battle has taken a lot out of him. The rattle in his breathing is louder now, and something in the angle of his shoulders as he sits there on a rock, elbows on his knees, tells me he's only got so much left in him.

353

I hope to God it's enough, because we both know I cannot do this on my own.

I power up the tiny black drone and the goggles flick into life. The brushless motors are almost silent, the props razor-sharp and engineered to cut through the air with as little turbulence as possible. The goggles are HD, with an encrypted, frequency-hopping, high-powered video feed from the low-light camera. But all this comes at a price: I have maybe ten minutes' flight time, and Handler's palazzo is easily two miles away.

The drone soars up and away. Suddenly I am a bird, an eagle, swooping over the rocks and brush and creek beds and wash-outs, over the perimeter road with its high wire fence, past the maintenance buildings, over the southern end of the golf course, to where Handler's palazzo sits at the end of a cul-de-sac.

'What can you see?' asks Kondracky.

'Twelve-foot walls, all round. Cameras every twenty to thirty feet, wall-mounted. Metal gates at the front, another service entrance round the back.'

'Security?'

'One foot patrol, looks like an MP5. No, wait, two. Just came out of a cabana. I'm guessing that's the guard station. Probably at least two more inside the house.'

'Can you zoom in?'

'Camera's fixed.'

'So get closer.'

'If they spot the drone, we're fucked,' I tell him.

'We need to know what's in that void.'

I circle round to the rear of the house, by the service entrance, and crawl around the pink stucco walls to the corner of the palazzo between the master and the study.

'I'm at the north-east corner,' I tell him.

'What do you see?'

'Nothing. No windows on either side.'

354

'What about the roof?'

'Not a thing.'

'Fuck,' says Kondracky. 'It's a safe room. He's installed a rebreather. No way of smoking him out. Our only chance is to get to him before he gets to it.'

'It's got direct access from the bedroom and study. If we fight our way in he'll easily have enough time.'

'Give me the goggles,' says Kondracky.

'There's only a minute or so of battery left.'

'So hurry the fuck up.'

I leave the drone hovering, pull off the goggles, and put them on Kondracky's balding head.

'Holy shit,' he says, suddenly transported into mid-air. 'This is wild.'

'One minute,' I remind him.

'Okay, go left. Left more. Up. No, too much. Now left again. Keep going. And stop.'

'Thirty seconds.'

'It's glitching.'

'The battery's dying.'

'Show me three-sixty.'

'I need to get the bird out of there before it drops out of the sky.'

'THREE-SIXTY.'

I rotate.

'One more.'

'Too late.' I pull back on the right stick and forward on the left, sending the drone shooting back towards us and skywards, sucking the last of the juice out of the battery. Moments later it drops out of the sky into thick brush on the other side of the perimeter fence, dead.

Kondracky pulls off the goggles.

'How much C4 do you have?'

136

The sun is still fifteen degrees below the horizon but the stars are beginning to fade. We need to be there before dawn. We change into black clothes, cover our hands and faces with black face paint, and load up backpacks. C4, lightweight rope ladders, grappling hooks, automatics, and as much ammunition as we can carry. We hike back up over the ridge and down towards the valley. It's slow going – there's no trail, and twice we find ourselves on ledges, forced to backtrack to find another way down. An hour later we're at the valley floor, but Kondracky's slow and getting slower.

'You want to rest?'

'He's got my fucking daughter. No, I don't want to rest.'

We use wirecutters to penetrate the perimeter fence, using thick brush to disguise the spot where we cut through. We're barely through when headlights appear out of the blue pre-dawn light. It's a security truck.

'Vibration sensors on the fence,' says Kondracky.

We lie absolutely still, heads down. The voices of the armed guards reach us as they step out of the truck and scan the fence line with tactical flashlights.

'Don't see anything, do you?'

'Probably coyotes again. They dug under twice already.'

They scan around for a few more seconds, a flashlight beam settling on us for a moment.

'You got something?'

We hold our breath. Then the beam moves on.

'Nah. Mark the spot and let's check back in an hour when it's light.'

One of the guards heads past us to the fence, so close I could grab his ankle. He uses an orange spray can to mark a spot twelve feet from where we actually cut the fence. Then they head back to the truck, shit-talking a co-worker they'd both secretly like to fuck, and drive away.

We breathe again.

From the perimeter fence we skirt the maintenance depot, transfer station and water treatment plant to the edge of the eleventh hole, then work our way up the side of the fairway, where trees provide a modicum of cover from the lightening sky. A sudden noise sends us sprawling to the ground, but it's just an automated sprinkler system firing. From the green on the ninth we hack through a thin strip of woodland, to where a steep artificial rocky escarpment rises to the wall of Handler's villa.

It's fifteen minutes before dawn. Kondracky's bagged, the exposed skin around his eyes pale and his face drawn with pain. I'm not in much better shape, but I hide it as much as I can. I let him rest against the wall as I pull the C4 from my backpack, shape it into a rough cylinder with a divot at one end, then insert a detonator with a remote trigger.

'Three minutes, okay?'

He nods, and I wonder whether he's actually capable of it. But there's only one way to find out. We set timers on our watches. 'And . . . go.'

Three minutes. I leave him there and work my way around to the front entrance. A single security camera covers the front of the gate, but the fat convex lens tells me it's wide, so I can't get closer than the corner of the wall. A second covers the approach, but the field of view is narrower. At thirty yards with a rifle, it would be a simple shot. Maybe even with the

MP9 if I switched it to single fire, but we are still in stealth mode, so it's down to my old faithful, the Welrod.

Two minutes. I take aim, drop my pulse, squeeze . . . and then stop myself, feeling my palm is damp. My nerves are getting to me. I wipe the sweat off on my pants and aim again. This time I fire, the Welrod making no more sound than a hand clap. The globe lens shatters, and the camera slumps on its mount.

Game on.

Ninety seconds. I run along the wall to the metal gate, keeping out of view of the second camera, clamp the C4 to where the two halves meet, then continue round the wall until I'm opposite where I left Kondracky.

One minute. I throw up a grappling hook with a featherweight rope ladder attached. Two tries, then it snags firmly. As I climb up, teeth gritted against the pain from my broken ribs, the wound on the other side opens up yet again. I feel the muscle tear. But there's no going back now and Kondracky's in worse shape than me.

Thirty seconds. I pull myself to the top of the wall. Below me, a guard exits the cabana, motioning to the foot patrols as he bitches into a radio. 'Just lost Camera 4. No, no sign of entry. Nothing on Camera 5, but we're checking it out. I told you we should have got the German system.'

Fifteen seconds. The two sentries flank their boss, covering their arcs as he heads to the main gate. I glance over to the other wall. Where the fuck is Kondracky? And then I see him, clawing his way over the top.

He raises his hand, counting off silently on his fingers like a TV studio floor manager.

Three.

The head guard puts his ear to the gate.

Two.

'I don't hear anything,' he says, and turns away.

One.

137

The thunder of the shaped charge splits the dawn in half, birds squawking into the air from the trees where they were roosting. The metal gates rip apart. I don't want to tell you what happens to the boss guard because I would like you to sleep tonight. The other two pick themselves up, concussed and bloody, taking up positions against what they assume will be a frontal attack. Another guard comes running from the house, and a fourth from the cabana.

Their attention is so fixed on the smoking hole in the gate that they completely miss us, using the thick wall as a catwalk, paralleling each other as we skirt past the front entrance of the house and around to the back, where the lighted lagoons and entertainment pavilion glitter in the dawn's half-light.

I leap from the wall into the closest lagoon, which is about three feet deep, while Kondracky makes it to the water feature, sluicing down the slick artificial rock as if it were a water slide. He lands heavily, and I see him stumble and grab his shoulder for a second, but then he's back on his feet. We sprint past fairy-lit palm tree trunks and the six-foot-high yoni sculpture, past the wet bar and outside kitchen, and into the house proper, taking turns to cover each other as we round each corner. Inside the house an alarm is sounding, shrilling hard, lights strobing.

We duck behind a corner as yet another guard runs past towards the front, then move on, using the floor plan

Kondracky worked out in the truck. It takes us to the north-east corner, where the bedroom and study are squared against what must be the safe room. But then as we sprint down a shocking-pink corridor with art deco mirrors and gold accents, our luck runs out.

I glimpse Handler, wearing only a bathrobe, staring at us in astonishment, an open door behind him, then a good-looking guard whose uniform apparently includes shorts appears from the side of the doorway and opens fire. Evidently he's more decorative than practical because his aim is poor, firing from the hip and scared shitless, but it gives Handler time to turn and run for the door.

Kondracky fires, dropping the guard in shorts with a single burst. Handler looks back and trips over the dangling belt of his terry bathrobe. I dive for him, and get a hand on the bathrobe, but Handler slips out of it and, completely naked, into a windowless room. I glimpse a bed, a desk, a toilet and a flatscreen TV before an armoured metal door slams shut.

And suddenly we're the meat in the sandwich because by now Handler's security are responding to the gunfire, streaming back into the house, yelling into radios. Kondracky and I turn and open fire, bullets ripping through walls, windows, furnishings, artwork, carpets, and woodwork, until they finally retreat, dragging two casualties with them.

Kondracky and I catch our breath, the ground littered with shells, air filled with smoke and the stink of cordite in our mouths, the room completely wrecked. Kondracky's face is grey and drawn, and he's gulping down breaths as though he's having trouble getting enough air.

'We have to get in there,' he says, when he finally can, meaning the safe room.

'How? We can't smoke him out if he's got a rebreather. The

360

entire Seventh Cavalry's going to be here inside of an hour, never mind cops and estate security.'

'C4,' says Kondracky, trying not to cough.

Is he losing it? 'I used it all on the gate.'

'You know that, and I know that,' says Kondracky. 'But *he* doesn't know that.'

138

Kondracky looses off the occasional round to keep Handler's goons at bay. I head back to the safe room. There's a CCTV camera above the safe room doorway, but it points away and I'm gambling on it not showing the door itself. I hammer on the thick steel with my fist.

'Handler,' I say. 'Listen to me. I have five hundred grams of C4 here. I'm shaping it into a charge. I'm going to attach it to the door.'

I listen. Nothing. I hammer again.

'I know you can hear me,' I say. 'So listen. I don't know if it'll breach the steel or not. If it does, it'll kill you. If it doesn't, it's worse. First you'll get the pressure wave. That's going to rupture your eardrums and your lungs and compress all the little gas bubbles in your blood. Then the decompression wave hits you, and all those little bubbles explode inside you. Remember that scene in *Total Recall?*'

I hear a crackle. Handler's voice comes over an intercom.

'Nice try, kid. But you're making this shit up.'

From the doorway there's a crackle of gunfire as Kondracky exchanges fire with the guards, who are making another foray. He's not going to be able to hold them off forever.

'I'm attaching the detonator now.'

'You do this, the girls are going to die, and so are you.'

'Taking cover now, Handler. Detonation in five, four . . .' I back away, raising my voice. 'Three, two . . .' If this doesn't work, Handler's right, we're all dead, all four of us.

But as I'm about to say 'one', the door opens. It takes Handler a moment to realise he's been duped, but it's long enough for me to arm-bar him in the face then shoulder-charge him, stark naked, back into the room.

'Go, go,' I yell. Kondracky falls back, spraying the corridor with fire one last time as Handler's guards attempt to push forward again, and ducks inside. I slam the door behind him. Moments later, shells hammer into the hardened steel of the door, but it's too late. Handler's trapped with us in the safe room.

Kondracky pulls open a drawer. There are T-shirts and underwear in there. He throws them to Handler, cowering on a bench, covering his dick with one hand while he wipes blood away from his nose with the other. 'Put these on, for Christ's sake.'

Handler pulls them on. Outside there are shouts, guards hammering on the door. A CCTV camera shows the room, the guards confused and uncertain what to do.

'How do you think this ends?' says Handler, pulling under-shorts over his skinny white legs. 'You have no idea the amount of shit you stirred up.'

'That's what we're counting on,' I say. 'Now tell us where the women are.'

Handler guffaws. 'That's what this is about? Sir Lancelot and Sir Galahad riding in on white horses rescuing the damsels? Give me a break.'

Kondracky slugs him with the butt of his Glock. Handler slams hard against the wall, then slumps back down on to the bench, his cheek broken, vision blurring.

Outside, on CCTV, one of the remaining guards approaches the door, cautious, scared.

'Boss,' he says. 'What's going on? Talk to us.'

'Tell them you're okay,' says Kondracky. 'To back off and wait for instructions. Somebody's going to leave soon, and they're going to let them. And if anybody fires, or does anything we don't expect, tell them we'll kill you.'

Handler pulls on a T-shirt, wiping blood from his face with it as he does. He's shaking, his bluster gone. Like Tyson said, everybody has a plan until they get punched in the face. He repeats Kondracky's instructions, word for word.

On CCTV, the guards retreat.

'Good,' says Kondracky. 'Now, the girls.'

Handler stays silent.

'Okay, listen,' I say. 'Let me tell you what we know. We know about the Dead Man's Switch. We know about the biometrics. We know you think the Seventh Cavalry's coming to save you, and if you can just hold out long enough you'll survive. But here's the problem: The Dead Man's Switch makes you the perfect hostage. The only thing your supposed rescuers care about is keeping you alive and their secrets safe. Which means that Kondracky here can do whatever he wants to you. So long as your heart keeps beating, they don't care what else he does.'

Handler's eyes get a haunted look.

'So you can tell us now, or you can tell us later. But you are going to tell us, believe me.'

I hand Kondracky the first of the burner phones, the one that they tracked. 'Number's programmed in.'

'Good luck,' he says, his eyes meeting mine.

'Yeah.' I pause for a second. We've gamed this out all the way to the end, but there's no guarantee it plays the way we intend. 'See you on the other side.'

Kondracky grins. 'One way or the other.'

I point the gun at Handler. 'Open the door.'

He reaches for a button, hand shaking. The lock snaps open and I step outside. Kondracky closes the door again.

I head down to the parking garage. Halfway down I hear the screams begin.

139

For once the Bugatti Veyron is not overkill.

It's crimson red, one of Handler's stable of exotics in the cavern of his parking garage. There was a canary yellow 1964 Porsche 901 parked next to it but I didn't have the heart to risk fucking it up or have it shit the bed on the freeway by throwing a connecting rod.

I don't yet know where I'm going except away from Handler's palazzo. Kondracky's idea was inspired: hold Handler hostage, tying up whatever reinforcements might arrive, and use the threat of triggering the Dead Man's Switch to hold them at bay, and distract them from our actual intentions.

I have no idea where Barb and Kat are being held or how long it will take me to get there. But Handler's safe room is set up for long-term occupancy, with food, medical supplies, water, and a rebreather replenished from an internal oxygen tank. In principle Kondracky could last for a week or more, and nobody's going to try an assault, because if Kondracky kills Handler the sky falls on all of them.

I have to go somewhere, so I head north on I-395, the old gold prospector's highway through the Sierras where Stephen Spielberg filmed *Duel*. Given the timeline there's no way Dykstra and Bernier got further south than Palm Desert, and it gives me the option to head east or west once I finally know where the women are.

Half an hour later the second burner finally rings. It's Kondracky.

'Did he talk?'

'Eventually.'

'What did you do to him?'

'You don't want to know.' He sounds tired.

'But he's still breathing?'

'Listen for yourself.'

I hear a moaning which must be Kondracky holding up the phone to Handler.

'Any sign of reinforcements?'

'Shit ton of sirens. I'm guessing they set up a perimeter and the infantry are standing around while the brass have their heads up their asses trying to figure out what the fuck to do.'

There's a sound that sounds like an old car trying to start. I realise it's Kondracky chuckling. It sounds like his lungs are congested. Whatever he did to Handler must have taken it out of him.

'Kondracky, you okay? You don't sound good. Mack?'

'Never better.'

'I need you to hang in there. Only way they stay back is if they know you're still a threat.'

'When was I ever not a threat?' he says.

'So where are they?' I ask.

'Sonoma.'

Of course they are.

Sonoma, where Handler has his goddamned thousand-acre organic vineyard.

Kondracky gives me the address. It's a controlled-atmosphere grape storage facility, one of hundreds such in wine country, another sliver of Handler's empire. The facilities are divided into numbered bays. I ask which bay, but I know what it will be before the answer comes back.

Seventeen.

'What about Dykstra and Bernier? Did he stand them down?'

'That's the bad news,' says Kondracky. 'He can't.'

'What do you mean, he can't?'

'The girls don't get released until they have visual confirmation you and I are dead *and* Handler's say-so. The order can't be countermanded. I guess he figured we might try to change his mind.'

'So I take them both out.'

'That wasn't their only order.'

'Go on.'

'If they come under attack, first order of battle is liquidate the hostages.'

140

Barb and Kat are cold.

A white dial thermometer up on the far wall reads just above the frost point. But they're not dressed for it, forced to hug and rub each other's arms with their one still-free hand to keep from shaking uncontrollably. They've tried yelling at Bernier, who sits by the door, Uzi by her side, playing *Bejeweled* on her phone, but she simply put her earbuds in and ignored them.

Neither has slept. Bernier swapped with Dykstra around eleven for the midnight shift, then swapped back at dawn as the metal building made sharp cracking noises in the first rays of sun. They caught whispered conversation as the watch changed, glances thrown their way that made Kat feel like she was being sized up as a piece of meat, a carcass on a marble slab.

Their captors took everything from them: watches, phones, rings. Barb wears a plain gold band that was her mother's, that she hasn't taken off for more than a decade. When she objected to Bernier painfully pulling it off, she got a punch in the face which left her left eye and lip swollen.

Kat worries about Barb: she acts so tough, but there's a vulnerability to her too, the softness of the kid younger than her who fled to St Louis to tend bar, fell in love with a manipulative junkie and stayed with him far longer than she should have. She gets the odd, strong sense that in some unspoken way Barb still misses him and that it's not Mack's dependability that has attracted her to him, but his danger.

They're hungry and thirsty, but all they've been given is yet another bottle of water. It's another sign to Kat that they are being kept alive temporarily, like the lobsters in the tank of a grocery store, claws rubber-banded shut, waiting to be plucked out and dropped in a pot bubbling on a stove and boiled alive.

Kat has no intention of being boiled alive. Her wrists are slim and for hours she's been trying to slip her hand through the cuffs shackling them to the pipes, closing her eyes and trying to dislocate the bones of her hand and thumb. Her skin is red-raw from the effort and her hand has begun to swell. Barb can feel every movement and her eyes meet Kat's as she subtly twists and pulls. It feels like Barb is trying to tell her something, but it's impossible to talk while Bernier or Dykstra are in the room.

They've each been allowed to use the bathroom once. Kat gets the sense that, left to their own devices, Dykstra and Bernier would just let them soil themselves, but instead Bernier grudgingly takes them individually out of the big door, hooded, to a space beyond where there's a bathroom. There she uncuffs them, watches them relieve and clean themselves at gunpoint, then cuffs them again and takes them back, while Dykstra guards the other, also at gunpoint. Dykstra and Bernier are clearly professionals, and as the hours ebb away, Kat senses the pan of water into which she and Barb will be dropped coming to a boil.

141

The Veyron climbs steadily in the Sierras.

Am I really doing this?

If there's a chance that by sacrificing ourselves, Kondracky and I could win the release of the women, shouldn't we do that? It's not their fault they got wrapped up in this. If Kondracky and I had never separately set foot in Milton, none of this would have happened.

Men like Kondracky and me are chaos agents. We leave toxic wreckage in our wake wherever we go, and then we run away, trusting to fate that we will never see it again. We're cowards, when it comes right down to it. And then, when by some quirk of that same fate, we are brought face to face with what we've done, what's our reaction? To clean it up, which right now we could, very simply, by handing ourselves over?

No, we create more wreckage, more chaos, in some quixotic attempt to make everything right, to redeem ourselves, pretending we're heroes when the truth is we are long beyond redemption.

I think about calling Kondracky up and telling him all of this.

But then I remember that Handler is a lying, conniving, self-serving piece of shit who almost certainly has no intention of releasing Barb and Kat even if Kondracky and I offer up our own heads up on a platter. Surrendering now will achieve exactly nothing. We're way beyond that.

It's four, maybe five hours to Sonoma. I wish I felt more confident that Kondracky will last that long. Up ahead I see a sign for Deadman Summit. I hit the gas.

The Bugatti's sixteen cylinders slam me back in the seat.

142

Kondracky sits back on the bench. Handler fought back harder than he'd expected, buoyed by the knowledge Kondracky couldn't kill him. All the fingers on Handler's right hand are broken now, and he has three teeth less than he started with this morning. His left kneecap is gone, a bullet in it. It wasn't until Kondracky pulled a knife and threatened to cut chunks out of his face that Handler finally relented.

Truth is, he's exhausted. Being old sucks at the best of times, but when you have an open, infected lung wound, and the lung has collapsed into the bargain, it sucks particularly badly. He coughs, and bright red frothy blood comes up. He knows that's bad, and so does Handler, who sees it through the one eye that remains open.

Vanity of vanities, says the Preacher,
Vanity of vanities! All is vanity.
There is no remembrance of former things,
nor will there be any remembrance
of later things yet to be
among those who come after.

Kondracky realises too late that he's saying the lines from Ecclesiastes out loud, head nodding as he slips into a semi-delirium, the gun dangerously close to slipping from his grasp. If Handler wasn't so badly injured he'd have taken him there and then, but as it is he just watches him through that one good eye, and Kondracky knows that he's biding his time.

There's a hammering on the door. Kondracky checks the CCTV. A bunch of figures in black commando gear, full body armour, no markings of any kind. CIA special ops, by the looks of it.

He hits the comms button. 'Go away or I kill him.'

'We need proof of life.'

Kondracky kicks Handler's shattered knee. Handler screams. 'That do?'

'What are your demands?' asks the figure in black.

'My demands are that you go away,' says Kondracky. 'First sense I get you're trying anything, I blow his head off. There will be no warnings. Am I clear? You'll be the first to know if and when anything changes.'

He has to mute the comms button to cough halfway through. No point in them knowing what kind of shape he's in.

Handler levers himself a little more upright on the bed, grimacing with pain. The sheets are soaked with blood.

'What's your endgame here?'

'Once Jones gives me the all clear,' says Kondracky, 'you go your way, I go mine.'

Handler manages something like a laugh.

'You think they're just going to let you go?'

Kondracky shifts, trying to get comfortable. 'That's between me and them.'

'You realise he screwed you, right?' says Handler.

'How'd you figure that?'

'Left you here holding the baby, while he gets away. Maybe he gets the women, maybe he doesn't. Either way, you're left to find your own way out.'

Kondracky coughs, bringing up more of the red foam.

'Truth is,' says Handler, sensing traction, 'you don't owe him a damn thing.'

'Sounds like you're trying to make me a proposal.'

'Maybe I am.'

He takes Kondracky's silence as permission to forge ahead.

'Come on, Kondracky. You know the score. He stepped into your shoes. He never earned them. You walked away – you had your reasons. But you're back now. You're as good as ever. What I'm saying is, fuck him. Fuck Seventeen. Pick up the reins again, take back what's yours. Come and work for me. Face it, Kondracky. You're hurt bad. You're not going to make it like this. But you open that door, we'll put you back together. You'll be the six-million-dollar fucking man. Better, stronger, faster. How about it, Kondracky? What do you think?'

Kondracky spits crimson on to the floor. His breaths are coming shallow now, head getting lighter by the minute.

'I think,' he says, resting his head back against the metal wall again, 'you should stop talking before I hurt you some more.'

143

The vineyard is at the end of a long, quaint road that winds through the hills between Napa and Sonoma. It's patched together from old family farms that have been bought up and agglomerated into Handler's viniferous empire. The main entrance has big brick pillars and security cameras, but I'm trusting the satellite vineyards that form the composite are not so well secured.

I dump the Veyron at the side of the road without regrets. I still hate those goddamn cars. I pull on my backpack, now full of ammunition for the MP9, hop a fence, and head through a field of vines, staying low to keep out of view of Mexican pickers two fields over, and towards where Google Maps shows me the main complex is.

The storage units are out of sight of the road to preserve the image of quaintness that makes wine country a tourist trap, but there's nothing quaint here. They're grey industrial metal bunkers, three storeys high and together the size of a city block. A couple of flatbed trucks are parked on the concrete apron in front of them along with a forklift and a few piles of pallets. Vertical tanks of compressed nitrogen soar out of the earth at one end, with feeder lines to all the storage units. The flat roof is covered with squat refrigeration units, fans whirring and compressors thrumming.

I work my way down the line of doors, past fuel and water tanks used to fill the vineyard tractors and sprayer. There's no sign of any security. Maybe the plan was to keep a low profile.

Or maybe Handler lied.

There are twenty units total. Seventeen is towards the far end. There's another flatbed here, but this one carries a steel shipping container. I check the plates: the other two are California, but this one says 10,000 Lakes. Minnesota, close enough to South Dakota. The doors are open, but the container's empty, apart from a discarded water bottle.

Handler wasn't lying.

I could call Kondracky right now, talk tactics. But if there was anything I needed to know he would have called me, and both of us know better than to distract the other. This is on me. Kondracky has enough to deal with.

I run, keeping low. The main door is massive, twenty feet high, but there's an access door beside, and a window. Inside, it's well lit, but I can't see anything except a second, interior shutter door that must open into the climate-controlled storage. It's closed, and there's no sign of occupation.

I hesitate. The girls are here – the shipping container is evidence of that. But still my guts are telling me something's wrong. If Barb and Kat are inside, one of Bernier or Dykstra will be guarding them. But where's the other? They should be standing sentry, but there's no sign.

Where are they? Bathroom break? Coffee run? Whatever their reputations, they're professionals.

It doesn't make sense.

I listen for voices, but the noise from the refrigeration units above is too loud.

Nothing for it. Finger on trigger, round chambered and magazine full, I silently open the man door and slip inside. I stalk, silent as a cat, towards the big door to the interior compartment.

There's a red button to open it.

I listen again for any sound from inside. Nothing.

Relax shoulders. Deep breath. Back up against the jamb of the door, ready to roll in and take fire.

I hit the red button. Everything goes to shit.

144

The explosion jolts Barb awake and makes Kat jump so much it hurts her wrist. The metal walls rattle and shake, reverberating after the boom dies away. Bernier leaps up, knocking the folding chair over backwards, snatching up her Uzi, snapping off the safety and switching it to full automatic in a single fluid movement. She hammers on the door, yelling for Dykstra and it slams open. Dykstra has his Steyr at the ready too. He yells 'Go, go, go!' at Bernier, but she hesitates, glancing back at the women.

'You know what to do,' says Dykstra. Kat notices that he puts his hand on Bernier's shoulder: an oddly intimate gesture, a hint at something more than a professional relationship. Bernier nods. They both exit, the door slams shut, and there's the clank of a lock being thrown. Moments later, the cavernous space is thrown into darkness, followed by a loud whooshing from above them which Kat realises is the sound of ventilator fans being turned to maximum. The pipe they're attached to grows suddenly much colder.

With the only light now from a red emergency EXIT sign over the unreachable door, Kat turns to Barb. 'What was that? What's happening?'

'They're trying to kill us,' says Barb.

145

I'm a doll in the fat hand of a giant child, hurled with infant fury against the wall behind me. The back of my head slams against a metal stanchion as the tantrum of an explosion rips the metal door to pieces, ruptures my eardrums, burns my face and hands, blows out the entire front of the unit, then brutally dumps me head first on to the concrete floor.

When I come round, the world has changed. The unit is devastated, flaming debris all around. The roof sags. I spit out a tooth. My nose is broken, maybe my cheek too, and there's a brutal pain in my abdomen and my leg where foot-long shards of sheet metal, ripped apart by the blast, are impaled in my stomach and thigh. I can barely crawl, but I drag myself to what's left of an exterior wall, where some kind of chemical hopper now lies on its side, offers some kind of cover.

I take a chance and, closing my eyes, pull out the piece of metal in my stomach. The pain is astonishing but I don't think it's caused any internal injuries. I toss it to one side, where it clatters to a halt, and press down with my left hand to try to stop the bleeding.

The shard in my leg is another matter. It could have severed, or at least nicked, my femoral artery. I'm not spurting blood, so for the moment I've a chance of staying alive. But if I pull it out, or move the wrong way, all that might change, and I could bleed out in a matter of three or four minutes.

I shuffle off my backpack. In there is the thing I need: a tactical tourniquet, with a strap to go around a limb and a plastic handle to tighten it and cut off the blood supply. Once I've done that, maybe I can pull out the shard and if I'm lucky, gain some mobility. But I'm just rolling the strap around the top of my thigh when I see something.

It's Dykstra, appearing from a unit at the far end, and I realise with dismay that Handler, slippery to the end, had all this prepared, booby-trapped in case he was forced to give up the location. A hundred yards behind Dykstra is Bernier, both of them sprinting towards the ragged hole the explosion has ripped in the facade. I can't let either of them see the state I'm in, so – still half blinded from the flash and seeing double from the concussion – I lever the muzzle of the MP9 over the top of the hopper and fire.

Dykstra ducks behind the container truck, while Bernier runs to the wall of the storage units, where she's hidden from my view. I poke the automatic out as far as I can and fire blind to keep her back, but Dykstra takes the opportunity to make a run from the container to one of the water tanks.

I can't pin one down without letting the other get closer.

I'm not dead yet, but I will be.

146

'This place, it's cold storage,' says Barb. 'My cousin has an orchard. They store the apples in places like this. They can flush out the air and pump in something else. Nitrogen, maybe? It keeps the apples fresh. Only once they do that, you can't breathe.'

From outside there is the sound of gunfire. 'Maybe that's them,' says Kat. 'Mack and Jones.'

Kat can feel her breathing getting faster. She furiously twists her wrist, trying yet again to slip it through the noose of the cuff.

'Stop,' says Barb.

'It's almost free. If I can just get my thumb under . . .'

She tugs and twists, the metal biting into her skin, now drawing blood.

'I mean it,' says Barb. 'STOP.'

Her voice is sharp, but hoarse and breathy. She's having problems breathing too.

'You okay?'

Barb ignores the question. 'Relax. Let the cuff go loose.'

Something tells her Barb knows exactly what she's doing. She lets the cuff fall loose.

'Now hold still. Don't move.'

Outside, the gunfire is relentless. Kat tries to block it out. She supports her wrist with the other hand as Barb pulls something out of her hair.

'That bitch missed this because I wound her up about the ring,' says Barb.

A bobby pin. Barb straightens it out, then strips the plastic off the end with her teeth. She bends the end into a squared-off S-shape, and inserts it not into the keyhole of the cuffs, but into a small round hole on the other side.

'That asshole in St Louis, about the only favour he ever did me was teach me to pick handcuffs.' She has to stop for a moment. Her lips have changed colour, becoming darker. Kat figures in the red light that means they're turning blue.

'It's a double lock, see. Everyone thinks you just mess with the keyhole, but first you have to do this, then that frees up the other side. This one's the hardest, because there's a spring. Shit.'

The bobby pin folds under her pressure. She has to straighten it out again.

'Head's getting a little light.'

Barb's breaths are coming fast and shallow. Kat, too, can feel a heaviness creeping over her that she knows is danger-ous. Barb's bobby pin folds again. 'Goddamn it!'

'Come on,' says Kat, steadying her wrist. 'You've got this. You can do it.'

'I can't get my breath,' says Barb. 'I can't even see straight.'

She takes a couple of deep breaths, blinks her eyes clear, then goes back to the pin.

Kat hears a tiny click.

'That's it,' says Barb. 'That's the first part. Now turn your hand over the other way.'

Outside the gunfire starts up again.

Kat turns her hand over and Barb inserts the bobby pin into the keyhole. Her lips are definitely darker now, her face ashen. Kat's head aches. She remembers reading about climb-ers on Mount Everest, the altitude sickness that made them want to simply lie down and go to sleep in the snow. That must have felt like this.

At that moment the bobby pin slips out of Barb's hand and drops to the floor.

Barb sags. 'I can't do it, hon. My head ... I can't see ... I can't breathe ... I'm sorry.'

'Let me try,' says Kat. She stretches down, hand anchored to the pipe, trying to feel for the bobby pin on the floor, invisible in the darkness. Her fingers grope around on the cement, finding something ... but it's just a sliver of wood from the construction. She keeps going, and eventually, tucked behind the pipe, she locates the bobby pin.

'Barb,' she says. Barb opens her eyes, her head back to resting on the pipe, barely conscious. 'Barb, tell me what to do.'

'It's no good,' says Barb. 'You have to practise. Took me a week the first time.'

'Just tell me.'

'You push it in and press, like you're the key. But you have to find the right direction.'

'What do you mean, the right direction?' asks Kat, but Barb doesn't answer. Her head slumps.

147

Dykstra and Bernier are in no hurry: they know they've got the upper hand. We've been exchanging fire sporadically for what seems like an hour, but is probably more like twelve minutes. They've evolved a routine: Dykstra gives covering fire from his position behind the water tank while Bernier ratchets closer, pressed against the wall, out of my line of sight and my line of fire.

The disused unit they booby-trapped is now fully aflame, the tinder-dry wooden pallets stored inside a roaring pile of fire whose heat I can feel on my face. But what worries me most is the roof above me, whose metal is starting to buckle under the weight of refrigeration units and fans.

I have to get clear. But I'm pinned down by gunfire and though I now have the strap of the tourniquet around my leg, each time I try to tighten it, Bernier ratchets towards me.

And if I move without the tourniquet, a severed artery is a death sentence.

Then I remember: I still have one of those cute little Nammo grenades in my backpack. One on its own isn't going to do anything. But craning over the hopper to see where Dykstra is hunkered down, there's a potential force multiplier.

The fuel tanks. One has a yellow handle, meaning diesel, which burns so slowly it might as well be vegetable oil. But if the other is gasoline, I'm in with a chance.

I click in a fresh magazine. It's my last, and I'm going to need most of it. I loose a couple of rounds down the wall towards Bernier to keep her honest, then track over to Dykstra. To his left is the diesel tank. I put a couple of holes in that, then another four in the tank beside it, praying that it's full. Thank Christ, it is. Something gushes out, but who knows what?

Dykstra glances at the fuel tank. I think he knows what it means.

Good. I'm counting on it. Pulling the pin on the Nammo almost breaks my teeth. I keep it clamped shut, blocking out the pain and the creeping lightness in my head. Above me the roof sags and shudders. Behind me the fire edges steadily towards me.

Dykstra swaps a look with Bernier, still out of my line of sight. He nods and I see his lips mouthing silently to her. Three, two . . .

On one, I release the handle of the grenade.

Dykstra makes a break, running towards Bernier.

Bernier steps out from the wall, slamming covering fire into the chemical hopper.

And I lob the grenade.

148

Kat pokes the bobby pin into the keyhole, feeling for the lock mechanism. She thinks she feels something move, but she can't make the lock turn. Barb's unconscious now and there's no waking her. What did she say? 'You have to find the right direction.' She takes some deep breaths, trying to clear her head, then inserts the bobby pin the other way. The mechanism feels different: there's a groove of some kind that the pin locks into. But it still won't move. Then she notices her wrist's hard against the metal of the cuff, pulling it tight. She slacks off the cuff, and feels the lock turn.

The shackle opens. Her wrist is free.

She stumbles over towards the door. There's a red emergency exit button. She hits it, and electric motors whirr into life. The door shifts a fraction of an inch, then stops. The motors strain, then cut out. She tries the emergency button again, but she must have tripped the breaker.

Light trickles in through a tiny gap that has opened up at the bottom of the door. Kat gets her fingers under the door and strains to lift it, but it won't budge.

She scans the room. *There has to be something I could use.* The folding chair, flat on its back. A few crates on pallets in the corner. She looks up to the ventilation fans. Maybe if she could get up there? But they don't lead outside. Then she notices something glinting at the bottom of one of the pallets, reflecting light from the gap under the door.

She works her way around the pile of pallets, supporting herself with one hand because her head is spinning. And at the back she finds it. An electric ride-on pallet truck, like a mini forklift.

The key is still in it. She turns it and the dash lights up, the battery indicator showing less than an eighth full. Maybe it's enough? It takes a moment to figure out the controls, but it's a simple yoke. She pulls it towards her, and the truck whirrs backwards, forks sliding out from under the pallets.

Outside, more gunfire. A migraine jackhammers her temples. She aims the truck at the door and pushes forward on the yoke, slamming the forks into the metal. It buckles, but doesn't give.

She backs away and does it again. Same thing.

Third time she keeps the yoke pressed forward, rubber wheels spinning on the smooth concrete floor for a moment, but then the thin sheet metal splits and the forks punch through.

She hits the lift lever. The forks rise, crumpling the door and opening a bigger gap at the bottom, maybe ten inches at its highest. She backs up to try again, but the truck makes a mournful sound and stops, battery exhausted.

Kat jumps down and runs over to Barb. There's a tight pain in her chest from the exertion, but she grabs Barb under the arm and drags her over to the door. Gently laying Barb down, Kat slides under and out.

The brightness of daylight hurts her eyes, but she takes an enormous lungful of warm air that clears her head. Clambering to her feet, she sees that the door has been jammed shut with a pry bar. She pulls it out and hits the open button. But the circuit breakers are still tripped. She reaches down, thinking to drag Barb through, but Kat's skinny and only just made it through herself. So she grabs the bottom of the door and, with every remaining ounce of her strength, lifts.

The door slides up another foot or so. It's enough. She drags Barb into the light and air.

'Barb, Barb, come on, wake up,' says Kat, rubbing Barb's freezing hands, the fingertips as blue as her lips. 'Come ON.'

Barb stirs, her eyes flicking open as the oxygen hits her.

'It's okay,' says Kat. 'Just breathe. Big breaths.'

149

The throw is blind, and takes all my remaining strength. But as the grenade leaves my hand, a lightning bolt strikes me. I hear an animal cry out in agony, only it's me. I don't know what just happened, only that it's bad.

The grenade sails in a high arc, hits the ground, bounces a couple of feet, and explodes right by the fuel tank. It's gasoline. The spill flares, then the half-full tank explodes and engulfs Dykstra in the fireball. He staggers a few feet forward, ablaze. He's an easy target, and I take him down with a quick burst. He drops to the ground, still burning.

Then I see what the lightning bolt was.

The effort of the throw has severed my femoral artery. Crimson blood pumps out. In thirty seconds I'm going to be unconscious. In three minutes I'll be dead. I already feel faint. I drop my weapon and grab the handle of the tourniquet with both hands and start twisting it.

As I do, there's a cracking sound. The main support beam in the roof, weakened by fire, buckles under the weight of a refrigeration unit. It plunges down fifteen feet towards me, then by some miracle stops, snagged. But it's going to collapse completely at any moment.

And that's not the worst.

Bernier kneels by the still-burning corpse of Dykstra. As I watch, she rises, and in her face I see the face of the woman with the telephone, the same hatred and fury, and I understand: I just killed the man she loved.

She raises her Uzi and strides towards me, no longer caring if she lives or dies.

I let go of the tourniquet, which spins loose. The blood gushes out again. I fumble for my weapon, hands now slippery with my own blood, and fire.

But the magazine is empty. I'm out of bullets.

Bernier manages some kind of smile.

She stops six feet away and aims her Uzi at my head.

150

Kat looks up at the sharp crack of another explosion. It's followed almost instantly by a second WHUMP, and a feral bellow of pain.

The voice belongs to a man, and something in the quality of it tells her who it is.

She feels something stir in her, something she's only felt once before.

The big doors are open to the delivery yard. Racked up against the wall is equipment used to prune the vines and carry out repairs, along with orange hard hats with visors and ear protectors, and orange Kevlar chaps.

Orange hard hats. Kevlar chaps.

She knows what they're used for and what else must be here.

151

Bernier hears the stammering burble of a small-bore two-stroke rise to a scream behind her. She pivots round to see Kat, running towards her with a Stihl chainsaw lofted high.

She tries to fire, but Kat is too close and moving too fast. She brings the chainsaw down with all her strength on Bernier's shoulder. It arcs down, driven as much by its own weight as Kat's heft, gnawing through twelve inches of cloth, skin, muscle and bone. Kat jettisons the chainsaw as if it were white-hot and recoils backwards in horror, Jackson Pollocked with blood.

Bernier drops to her knees, then falls forward, Uzi chattering, bullets skittering harmlessly across the loading apron until the mag is empty.

Kat stands immobilised by shock, the chainsaw still coughing on the ground by Bernier's body. Then there's a grinding, metallic sound from above me as the roof finally collapses. I scramble towards her, vision fogging as my artery empties. She runs towards me and drags me the last few feet. A second later, the refrigeration unit comes crashing to the ground where I had been, haloed by the raging funeral pyre of the cold store.

I roll on to my back, and open my mouth to tell her about the tourniquet, but before I can get a word out the world turns black.

152

Once in a while, a figure appears on the CCTV and offers to negotiate, but Kondracky tells them the same thing each time. Go away, or I kill him – and each time his voice is a little weaker, but the fear of Handler's encrypted blackmail file being released to the world keeps them at bay.

Kondracky's hardly a digital ingénue. His choice to stay analogue was just that, a choice. He knows they must be preparing a Plan B. Contingency protocols via elite hacking squads at NSA, Mossad and GRU. Long-dormant, single-use interception malware in routers and switches at network hubs, DNS poisoning, emergency backdoors built into every mobile device and commercial operating system on the planet. If necessary they'll bring the entire network infrastructure, the internet itself, crashing down, regardless of the consequences.

But all of that takes time.

And so for now they sit unmolested. Handler's cot is now covered in congealed blood from wounds that have clotted. Kondracky leans back, skin pale, no longer the relentless, unstoppable force, but a fragile old man with a collapsed lung, edging into sepsis.

Once or twice Handler thinks he's caught him nodding off, and starts a move towards the gun. But each time he does, Kondracky's eyes snap open. Handler knows Kondracky can't kill him without sacrificing himself, but he still has both Botoxed cheeks intact and he intends to keep them that way.

And so they sit there in silence, kings in an endgame as a single pawn advances up the board.

The burner phone rings.

Kondracky jerks into full wakefulness. Eyes on Handler and finger on the trigger, he answers. 'Jones?'

'It's done,' I say.

I'm in a truck. Kat knew to tighten the tourniquet without being told because apparently limbs being severed by agricultural machinery is enough of a thing in a place like Milton that stopping arterial bleeding is basic country shit. She found the keys to the truck in Bernier's pocket and is now driving. I'm laid out on the back seat with Barb beside me keeping the tourniquet tight. I've given Kat directions to SANDCASTLE. Osterman's number is in my phone.

'They're safe?' asks Kondracky. 'The girls?'

'No thanks to Handler,' I tell him.

'What happened?'

'Booby trap. Nearly killed me. If it hadn't been for Kat . . .'

'What'd she do exactly?'

'Let's just say she takes after her old man.'

Kondracky's face cracks into what's left of a smile.

'What about you?' I ask.

'We're good,' says Kondracky.

'You're going to do what we planned, right? Use Handler to get away?'

Kondracky is quiet.

'Mack,' I say. 'We had a deal.'

'That's right, kid,' he says. 'You had your deal, and I had mine.'

153

Kondracky puts a bullet in Handler's head.

Handler slumps, dead.

Kondracky sits there for a moment. Then he checks his magazine, reinserts it, and does an odd thing. He fires a single shot into the mattress.

Then he raps on the door and tells the special ops team, who have been positioned just out of sight the whole time, that he's coming out. He opens the door, calm as you like, and strolls out with his hands in the air, his weapon held high in one hand, pointed at the ceiling.

The team – I'm assuming CIA though they bear no insignia – appear at the door, two either side, two on their knees, all body armour and yelling in command voice at him to get down, to drop the weapon, to keep his hands where they can see them.

But Kondracky doesn't. He lowers his gun, and the entire unit opens up on him.

154

I've seen a lot of people killed, but I still can't watch that part.

The rest I have, all of it, everything from the moment I left, over and over. The footage is from the internal camera in Handler's safe room, which was recording the whole time. It was all on the iPad Nicole delivered, after the surgeon she dispatched on her helicopter to SANDCASTLE patched me up and sent me on my way.

I didn't ask how she got it but a woman like Nicole Osterman has resources.

The bullet into the mattress confused me at first, but I figured it out afterwards. When he checked the magazine he saw there was still a round in the chamber, so he shot the mattress to get rid of it.

He was making sure his weapon was empty.

It was his way of saying that this time he really was done with killing, that Handler would be his last victim. That it was, for him at least, finally over, and he was ready to face the ghosts.

PART SEVEN

155

Every morning, after coffee, I roll the die.

If it comes up one, I make eggs.

If it comes up two, I take the dogs for a hike in the woods. I know where the mama bear lives now and she's used to me and the dogs: we keep a respectful distance.

If it comes up three, I check all the vantage points on the road that snakes down into town for cameras, traces of human presence, and make sure the brush is cleared on the first three.

If it comes up four, I clean my weapons.

If it comes up five, I run an extra ten miles on the treadmill.

And if it comes up six, I pile the dogs in the back of the truck, stow a rifle in the rack, and head down to the gas station to grab a paper.

Vern has retired, but I pay him to keep his ear to the ground. His network of bored old retirees and their wives – mom fixes your hair and dad fixes your lawn tractor – is second-to-none: nothing and no-one escapes their notice. Barb runs the motel now: she's made some changes, no longer hostage to Kat's mother's ghost. She calls me up on the landline with details of every guest she doesn't know personally, and I have a master key to the rooms. She's given up smoking, for the most part.

Barb uses the landline to call me because I no longer have a cellphone or internet. I don't miss it. I'm slowly working my way through Kondracky's surprisingly extensive vinyl collection and may have begun to develop a taste for Nilsson and Cheap Trick. I still find Steely Dan unlistenable but I'm working on it and these things can change. Under the couch I discovered a treasure trove of VHS tapes and DVDs. I'm enjoying the early work of Alan Pakula, and the original animated Spider-Man.

Today I roll a six, so the dogs leap into the truck bed, the electric gate slides open, and I worm my way down to the gas station. As I pass the fourth bend, where I have let the vegetation grow to provide cover, I duck.

Vern still owns the gas station, but Kat runs it now. In between customers she works on some kind of graphic novel inspired by her relationship with her mother and growing up as a fatherless kid in a motel. The illustrations are pure Kat – spiky, eccentric and by turns venomous and sentimental. I'm not sure yet where it ends, or if I will make an appearance, but if I do I'm not expecting it to be flattering.

When she gets bored with that she goes out back to where she has built a makeshift range. The clusters of shots get tighter every day. She is truly Kondracky's daughter. It's like I said: when you kill someone for the first time, you also kill the person you used to be. It was true for me with David and it was true for Kat with Bernier. But she has one advantage over both him and me: she isn't sentimental, tied to some notion of what could have been or might have been. She might be the single least romantic person I've ever met, and perhaps the most fearless. She's an arrow in flight, aimed for some target as yet unknown. I have an idea what it might be, but I keep it to myself.

Sometimes in the evenings she comes up to the house. Those mornings I don't roll the die: I diligently scrub away every trace of her existence, including unscrewing the drain in the shower and removing any hair that has found its way in there.

We've talked about moving away. About disappearing, and reappearing someplace else with new names and new faces. A beach in Mexico or Bali, go the full Bourne. But I fucking hate beaches and so does Kat. Besides, it's a myth to think you can disappear. Maybe twenty years ago, or even ten, but not any more. Wherever we go, there we are, and there they will find us. So we stay.

She told me everything that happened between her and Sixteen, and her and Dykstra and Bernier. I have a feeling she left some parts out of the latter, but I'm not going to press her. She'll tell me one day if she wants to. Not everything has to become part of a story.

I don't know if Kat loves me. I doubt it. I'm not sure she even likes me. What I feel for her doesn't have a name, at least in any language that I'm familiar with. But we are two bodies who strapped ourselves together in order to go over Niagara in a barrel. We made it over the falls, the barrel broke apart, and now we cling together, circling in the backwash, still breathing.

I pull into the gas station. The dogs jump up on to the side of the bed, always happy to see her. She gives them dog treats she keeps in a jar by the register, then puts the nozzle in the tank to fill. It will only take a few bucks: I hardly go anywhere.

Through the window I hand her a thick package in a bubble mailer.

'This is it?' she asks.

I nod. She checks the address.

Henry Chu, Friedman & Franklin, NY, NY 10020

'Where should I send it from?'

I hand her a die. 'Six neighbouring states. First roll gets you the state. Second roll: one is the biggest city. Two is second biggest. You get the idea.'

'You're sure about this?'

'I figure it's what he would have wanted.'

'What about the title?'

We talked about this the other night. *The Sixteenth Man* always seemed like a mouthful.

'I changed it.'

'What to?'

'*Sixteen.*'

She considers this, blowing a strand of hair out of her eyes.

'Better. Not much. But it's better.'

I changed some other things too, just to throw sand in the gears of anyone who might try to use it to find him, or me.

156

Handler, it turns out, was not a bullshitter. The digital dossier was as real as the Dead Man's Switch. His death triggered the release of the encryption key, which unlocked the archive, which became public. Governments tried to shut it down, threatening journalists and anyone who downloaded it, published it, commented on it or repeated any of the 'allegations' it contained – I say 'allegations' in quotes because as far as I can tell everything in it is completely true – with everything from prosecution to death, and in some cases, worse.

It didn't work. Information wants to be free, and now every detail of it is out there.

Some innocent souls thought it would change everything. That the great game of espionage, assassination and betrayal would be forever altered for the better. Well, that didn't happen. Heads rolled, a few politicians resigned in disgrace, one or two of the unlucky or unpopular ones ended up at the Hague or committed suicide. A lot of journalists wrote books, all of which were extremely bad. Everybody involved in the black arts of intelligence work pretended to be Extremely Outraged then went back to doing the same thing they'd always done.

Nicole included the whole thing on the iPad along with the video of Kondracky. Like everyone else in the business I went straight to the index – Handler had even indexed the damn thing – to look for my own name. I was there under all my aliases – aka SEVENTEEN – and all my jobs were detailed.

But I realised as I skimmed through how much the bare telling of them misses: the roar of a Bugatti Veyron, the expression on the face of a woman swinging the speakerphone at me, the feel of a man's guts as my fingers search for a memory card in his still-warm innards in the dark near an U-Bahn stop in an unfashionable part of Berlin.

When I tell this to Kat, she laughs and tells me 'maybe you should write a book'.

Well, maybe I should.

There was one extra ghost waiting for Kondracky on the other side. When Kondracky shot Tommy Humboldt in the knee to spare his life, the pain triggered a massive heart attack. A deputation of Brethren searching for the luminous Dinah found him unresponsive, lips and fingertips blue, amidst the wreckage of the church. CPR failed, and he was pronounced on the way to the hospital. I guess Tommy really was on the side of the angels, though, because by all accounts the funeral in his Utah church was packed with girls he'd rescued, some now with families of their own.

Tommy, however, got his wish: the invasion of Iran never happened. The Berlin job, the fake brush pass intended to authenticate the false information that would justify the attack, was the penultimate entry in Handler's dossier. It was one of the less lurid details, so nobody paid much attention to it. But with the *casus belli* completely undermined, the Sixth Fleet turned around, and the US ultimatum was allowed to quietly expire without a single shot, or nuke, fired.

Kondracky killed a lot of people, but when he put that final bullet into Handler he may have inadvertently ended up saving orders of magnitude more lives than he ever took.

Maybe the ghosts will cut him some slack because of that.

I like to think so.

157

With the truck full of gas, copies of the *New York Times* and *USA Today*, and a bag containing milk, eggs and beer, I head back up the hill.

I still don't know if the big windows are bulletproof or not. Part of me doesn't want to know. The same goes for the forest that overlooks the house. When I first saw it, way back when I first drove into town, it made no sense, what Handler would have called an unmitigated risk.

Later, when I realised Kondracky had deliberately manu-factured a choke point at the fourth corner, it made more sense, but it was still a strategic weakness.

Later still, when I found out about Kat's mother and why Kondracky had ended up in Milton in the first place, it made even more sense: his choice had been restricted by wanting to be as close to her as he could. I assumed he'd been unable to buy the parcel of land containing the forest, and had been forced to make the best of it.

Only I was wrong. I found the deeds in the safe after I spent a miserable three hours cracking it, along with the documents I needed to effectively assume Kondracky's identity. The survey shows the property includes about ten acres of forest the other side of the road.

He could have cleared it any time he wanted.

Kondracky made a conscious decision to expose himself. Sitting in his chair, listening to *Countdown to Ecstasy* for the ninth time, I begin to understand why. When you live years of your life at a certain level of heightened awareness, it becomes habitual. Maintaining a window of vulnerability prevents you from falling into complacency, which turns out to be the single biggest danger you face.

In one of the drawers I found an almost full pack of Marlboro cigarettes. Just one had been smoked. I knew instantly what it meant. He must have given up smoking at some point, bought his last pack of cigarettes, smoked his very last one, then left the remaining nineteen in the drawer, simply to prove that he didn't need them.

In the same drawer I found a pistol, a piece-of-shit service revolver from between the wars that looked like it hadn't been cleaned in years. For a moment I was confused: why would a man like Kondracky, who took such enormous care with his arsenal, keep something like this lying around the house? When I saw the magazine was empty it made even less sense. But then I saw there was a single round chambered, and the hammer cocked. It didn't take a genius to figure out who or what it was for.

I left it there. It seemed like a wise precaution.

158

The dogs are asleep, snoring gently in the kitchen, paws twitching, emitting little muffled woofs as they pursue imaginary rabbits in their dreams. But I have work to do.

I take a seat at the typewriter. The chair is hard-backed, unforgiving. *Good.*

I slip a fresh sheet of paper into the Remington.

I already know the title, so I type it, underline it, and sit back.

On the horizon thunderheads are rising: there will be an epic storm later, curtains of rain charging up the hill towards me and hurling themselves futilely against the glass.

One day someone else will come too.

Someone like me.

And I will be ready for them.

ACKNOWLEDGEMENTS

Just as the possessory credit ('A Film By') for the director obscures the labour and skills of the rest of the cast and crew who work on a movie, the author's name on a the jacket of a book elides the work and contributions of a multitude of others. Many people play a part in its creation, some without ever realising it, not just through direct help but through encouragement, belief, knowledge, advice, example, editing, facilitation, emotional support, or simply taking a chance on an aspiring writer when they have yet to prove themselves.

This list is far from complete, but *Seventeen* would not exist in its current form and perhaps not at all, were it not for the following people: Roswell Angier, the late Rev. Ivon Baker, Giles Blunt, Robert Chandler, Jo Dickinson, Eve Hall, Sarah Lotz, Philippa Lowthorpe, Claudia Milne, Oli Munson, Jessica Sykes, the late Prof. Stephen Wall, and Caroline Wood.

Above all, however, I would like to thank my family: my mother Pat Young who supplemented her income for decades by writing articles and short stories, never asking anyone's permission for anything, and if permission was denied, doing it anyway; my sons Ted, Sam and Heath who endured many different versions of this story as it evolved; and above all my lovely wife Heather Cole Brownlow who has supported me unconditionally for more than twenty years while simultaneously allowing me the all the elbow room writers greedily demand when they're deep in the weeds of a draft.